You First

Also by Caitlin Moss:
TO THE GRAVE

SIXTEEN SUMMERS

THE CRACKS BETWEEN US
NOT MINE TO LOVE
YOURS TO LOVE

You First

A NOVEL

CAITLIN MOSS

Cover design by Custom by Erika Plum
ISBN: 9798387358500

AUTHOR'S NOTE

First of all, I am so thankful you have chosen to read *You First*. Unlike some of my other novels, this one is a light, feel-good romance. Even so, it does contain some heavier topics readers may want to be aware of, including the death of a parent. While this occurs off the pages, readers will find the main character's mother still plays a pivotal role in her life now.

Further information or content warnings are available on my website.

Now, without further ado, get ready to laugh out loud and fall in love with Leo and Genevieve.

Happy reading!

XO,
Caitlin

*For the people that jump head-first into love
after having their hearts broken,
the believers in second chances,
and the lovers that no longer have to wonder,* what if it was us?

1

SUNDAY

Bridal showers are crazy.

People just give you a bunch of expensive shit for being in love.

They sit in their circle of chairs like a modern séance and oooh and aaah over the wrapping paper, holding a delicate hand to their chest and gasping at the sight of a brand new set of dishes or bedsheets.

In a way, I get it. I get pretty stoked about new bedsheets too, but I don't care what anyone else is sleeping on.

Taking a swig of whiskey out of my teacup, I lean against the cased opening to Nora's mother's living room, and suppress a yawn as I watch my soon-to-be sister-in-law, Nora, open her second set of water glasses. But honestly, it could be the third or fourth. This is her third shower after all. *It was necessary*, she said. A work one, a friend one, and now, a family one. She wanted it to be intimate. Special. And she wanted me to be in charge of it.

I took the reins with great pleasure and coined this one, Whiskey in a Teacup. Because that's Nora. Pretty, perfect, and polished. But once you get close and get a good sip of her personality, you'll soon discover she's just a damn good time. Plus, we love Reese Witherspoon.

Nora looks stunning today, as always. Her long dark hair is curled in meticulous waves cascading over her shoulder, contrasted against her off-the-shoulder white sundress with a slit on the right side, revealing her perfectly tanned and waxed legs. Her smile is perfect and polite, and she says all the right things to let all of her guests know she's grateful for their gifts and so, so, so, so, *so* excited to be Mrs. Michaels.

Nora is good for my brother. William adores her. He has for five years. He went from being the brooding, playboy athlete in college to a love-drunk puppy that would bend the universe for the woman he loves.

I never would have thought I'd see him like this, but I'm happy for him.

Though, I'm not necessarily thrilled to be sitting at Nora's third bridal shower even though I'm putting it on. We have a week of wedding events mapped out and strategically scheduled for the next five days and I'm already exhausted and all weddinged-out.

"Could be you one day," my cousin, Abigail, comments in a hushed whisper while nodding at the elaborate gift opening séance before us.

I snort into my tea cup. "I could never."

"Really? I always thought you were keen on tying the knot," she says, eyeing me.

"Well, maybe. But I certainly won't be having any showers."

Abigail raises her eyebrows, waiting for me to elaborate.

"I mean, I can't. I am medically allergic to opening gifts in front of people," I explain, still whispering.

"Really?" She's skeptical.

I swallow the whiskey I just sipped from my teacup. "Really. I break out in hives."

"Mmm, pretty sure that's social anxiety."

"Doronophobia," I correct and Abigail squints. "On my third birthday, Gamma got me a Jack In The Box that malfunctioned and shot out when I opened it. It gave me a bloody nose and everything."

Abigail laughs. I shoot her a glare, and she straightens.

"Anyway," I emphasize. "Mom—God rest her soul—said I was never the same after it."

A smile is buried under my cousin's pink lips, and I do my best to restrain mine. We will always be the two cousins goofing off together no matter how old we get.

"It's a mild case," I say, and Abigail unleashes her full smile. "Fine. It's probably just social anxiety and a large dose of disdain for bridal showers."

"That's more like it," she whispers, then adds, "Who the hell thought we should have another shower five days before the wedding anyway?" Her tone is gruff and unapologetic.

I snort into the teacup, pressing the porcelain against my lips and drowning my laugh in whiskey.

"We had to," I whisper. "Her aunts from Philly weren't able to come to the ones earlier this spring."

"So send a gift. Who cares if you miss a shower?" she continues to whisper, our eyes both staying fixed on Nora delicately pulling back the cream iridescent wrapping paper from a toaster oven.

"Apparently Bernadette and Wilma," I answer, nodding at the two women to Nora's left, flanked in floral dresses that could have been sewn from my mother's curtains in the nineties.

"How old are her aunts?" Abigail asks.

I shrug, my lips pressing into a smile. "Bernie and Wilma are her great aunts, I think."

"Aah," Abigail says, clicking her tongue against her teeth. "There aren't going to be any more games, are there? Because I'm seriously tired of Honeymoon Bingo and answering questions about whether or not Nora or your brother made the first move."

"Hey, that game was fun," I argue. I at least tried to make the shower games somewhat entertaining. The look on Nora's pretentious mother's face when she realized it was, in fact, her perfect daughter who made the first move will live in infamy as one of my favorite memories. Nora isn't the goody-two-shoes Mrs. Lorraine Wellington thinks she is.

Hence… the whiskey in the teacups.

3

"Okay, fine. It wasn't half bad," Abigail admits.

"At least I didn't force everyone to make wedding gowns out of toilet paper."

Abigail jerks her head back and we make eye contact. "That's a thing?"

"Yes, a stupid thing."

"What's the point of that game? You don't get any inside information and you waste good toilet paper."

"Ah, but you may win some hand lotion for creating the most beautifully hideous monstrosity."

Abigail snorts a laugh and it's far less subtle than mine, making the heads of each guest turn in our direction.

She clears her throat. "Sorry. That's an amazing toaster oven, Nora. Excited for you. So many great bagels in your future."

Abigail plasters a smile on her face and my cheeks grow hot with laughter. I press my lips in a straight line and make eye contact with Nora with an expression that says, *I'm sorry we're bored but I love you.*

She flashes me a perfectly witty and wry smile.

I know what her family's expectations of this soiree are, and I happily executed the event. Fresh flowers from the farmer's market adorn each table covered in white linens and tealight candles. I hunted high and low for unique and delicate teacups from every antique shop in the Seattle area. The playlist is the perfect mix of Patrick Droney, Adele, Taylor Swift, and Leon Bridges. The charcuterie boards only offer specialty cheeses, gluten-free crackers, and salami roses. The silver towers of tea sandwiches, fruit platters with strawberries and melon cut into flowers, and an assortment of French pastries all make this shower look like it was cut from one of those bridal magazines I used to look at when I was a little girl.

Except I filled glass carafes with every kind of whiskey instead of juice for mimosas. Honey. Cinnamon. Apple. Rye.

I smile despite myself as I throw back the rest of my whiskey in the kitchen while the polite chatter and ostentatious laughter echo in the other room. My phone buzzes in the pocket of my blush-colored maxi dress as I set my cup on the counter.

I pull it out to check the message.

Staring at the phone in my hand makes the world evaporate until I feel like the moon in the middle of a Van Gogh painting with everything else swirling around me.

For a moment, I forget what I was just feeling. Excitement. Happiness. Joy. It all disappears at the sight of his name until I'm just lost and sad and angry.

Damien: Genevieve, I miss you. It doesn't feel right I'm not going to be at Nora and William's wedding. I said I wouldn't go out of respect for you but I'm afraid I will regret not going. Please reconsider. People only get married once.

The backs of my eyes begin to swell with emotion as I read his words, unable to determine what to say until a second text rolls in.

Damien: Well, some people only get married once.

I smile. For all the ways we were different, we were both cynics about marriage, except when it came to William and Nora. William, my big brother. Nora, Damien's childhood friend.

They set us up. We'd be perfect for each other, they said. And we were. For three years. In so many ways, Damien was my dream guy. Tall, handsome, kind—the perfect gentleman from the first martini we shared. He's a successful artist, frequenting galleries in Seattle, San Francisco, and New York City. It's rare for someone to make a living out of being an artist but that's the thing about Damien: he's rare. He'd take me dancing and home to meet his mom. I'd go shopping with his little sister and have lunch every other Thursday with his grandma. All signs pointed to Happily Ever After.

But even when you have everything on paper, it can still fall apart. We didn't have time for each other. With his constant travel between Seattle and New York, we missed each other, and

5

we fought all the time. I couldn't travel with him, so he asked me to quit my job.

It's just a desk job at Boeing, he told me. *It's not like you actually fly the airplanes.*

But it was a job I had dreamed of. I always wanted to be a technical engineer. I'm successful in a field dominated by men, and I am so proud. But Damien was just irritated. I could do that anywhere, he told me. For a different company even. But I didn't want to. I love standing on my own feet. I have a great job and an apartment in Seattle overlooking Pike Place Market. I don't ask anyone for anything—money, favors, nothing. Except for him. I just asked for his time, and we could never agree on a compromise. Especially because he wanted me to compromise for him. Not him for me. And I refused.

So we split. It hurt to say no. At times, it still does.

It's been a strange six months since we broke up. With Nora and William getting engaged and preparing to get married, I realized there is nothing like a wedding to highlight my singleness.

Sometimes I wonder if that's the only reason I miss Damien at all. Maybe the upcoming nuptials are shining a spotlight on my alone-ness and when it's all over I'll remember how much I despise him. Even still, I don't want that. I don't want the three years we spent together to be labeled a waste. Every person in my life has been there for a reason, even if the reason has made me cry and question my love life choices. I force myself to believe that because this was a piece of wisdom my mom told me before she died. And at twenty-five years old, I still believe it.

I draw in a long breath and let it go slowly, still staring at my phone. I have never wanted to tell anyone yes and no at the same time.

Just as my thumb goes to type a response, he texts again.

Damien: Please answer, Genny.
Please.
Then I'll leave you alone.

For good.

My heart sinks.

No, more than that.

My heart falls out of my chest and lands on the floor, then everyone here in their Louboutins and silk stomp on it as they pass by.

"What the fuck did he say?" Nora mutters, grabbing my arm and standing just a few inches from me.

I register her penetrating stare and play dumb. "Who?"

"Stop," she says, soft and low. "You only make that face after a fight with Damien. What did he say?"

I sigh. "Nora, it's nothing—"

"It's not nothing. I love him but I know how he can be. Charmingly manipulative. Especially when he feels left out."

I swallow. "That's what it's about then, huh? He's just feeling left out."

"He wants to come?"

I nod.

She rolls her eyes. "Well…"

"Well what?"

"That's up to you."

I swallow hard. "It's not though. Nora, he was your friend first."

She tucks my loose blonde hair behind my ear. "I know. But you are going to be my sister. I don't know everything, but I know how to be loyal."

She smiles sweet and kind as she looks down at me. She's my age but she feels like a big sister.

"So you want him there?" I ask timidly, not knowing if I even want him there or not. I don't want him back and I don't want to see him. But I also don't want to be the crazy ex-girlfriend that forbid a lifelong friend from going to Nora Wellington's wedding.

She shrugs and draws in a breath like she's going to explain, but her attention gets drawn away as Aunt Wilma grabs her arm. "Nora, darling, can I steal you a moment? I just need…"

Wilma's voice trails, and Nora offers an apologetic smile as she follows her aunts to circulate the room. I don't know how she's not exhausted. She's been up to her eyeballs in mingling and wedding arrangements for nearly a year, and I have never seen her yawn.

My brother is marrying a unicorn.

A few guests thank me for the beautiful event, and I offer them their party favor of French macarons with a note that says, *Thank you for celebrating the sweet couple!*

Abigail is probably cringing at the pun.

As the crowd finally trickles out of Nora's mother's home, I find myself at the picked-over charcuterie table, sighing and pulling out my phone again.

Me: I don't even know what to say.

It doesn't take long for him to respond.

Damien: Say it's okay. Say I can come. Say you forgive me.

But I don't forgive him. Not yet. He said some horrible things when we broke up. Things that still wake me up in the middle of the night and cause my mind to spin. When he doesn't get his way, he lashes out in just the right way that I would feel the sting from him then wonder if I caused the lingering burn. When Damien and I were good, it was fantastic. But there's something about him that always left me hanging. Maybe I loved the chase more than I loved him.

I draw in a breath.

Damien: Say we can be friends.

A pause and then…

Come on, Genny. Don't be stupid.

My face falls. I knew this was coming. Assholes can only hide behind their groveling before they say something that reveals their true identity.

> *Me: I'm not going to tell you what to do, Damien. I wish you well. But I'm not being stupid and I don't want to be friends.*

My breath rumbles out of my lips as I hit send. It's open-ended and ambiguous. He'll hate it. Good. His life and his choices are not a reflection of me nor are they my responsibility.

"Phew!" Nora exclaims as she wraps her arm around my shoulders. "Now that that's over, I could use some whiskey."

"You didn't have any?"

"I had one but I couldn't have more," she says as she taps her forehead against mine. "What would Aunt Bernadette have told Bunco club?"

I laugh and immediately pour her some honey whiskey, her favorite. Then a splash more for myself.

"Von's tonight?" she asks after tipping back the brown liquid. "William reserved a front table."

I groan. "I am going to be so tired at work tomorrow."

"Who cares? You'll drink more coffee and survive. I only plan on marrying your brother once."

I laugh with a shake of my head and take a sip of whiskey.

"Abigail is coming. Plus, Taite, Cora, and April," she says, naming off all her bridesmaids. "And all of William's groomsmen will be there too."

I cough, the whiskey tickling my throat in a way that makes me feel like I'm inhaling it. "All of them?"

She rolls her eyes and smiles a perfectly suggestive smile. "Yes, all of them. Even Terrence."

I withhold a laugh. Nora has been letting me know Terrence is amazing and single for months. Though, he's been living in Japan so I can't confirm any of that. But I couldn't care less about seeing Terrence. There is only one person I'm not ready to see...

"Leo?" I manage, though even saying his name sends prickles of irritation up my spine until the hairs on the back of my neck stands straight up.

"Yeah, of course. Why wouldn't he?" Nora answers with a click of her tongue as if the notion that Leo not attending tonight is ridiculous. He's William's best friend. Of course he'll be there.

"I just thought he wasn't coming into town until Wednesday," I muse, crossing my fingers that Nora is mistaken.

"Yeah, right! You know William had him get to town as soon as he could. I guess Leo's been crazy busy with work, but those two are inseparable." She shakes her head, smiling.

I'm not smiling though—not even trying to. Just when I thought dealing with Damien was going to be my biggest issue this week, Nora hits me with the knowledge that Leo will be in town a whole three days earlier than I anticipated.

Tonight. Leo will be there tonight.

I stare at my whiskey, wishing it was an antacid.

"Look, I know you and Leo can't stand each other, but all William wants is for you two to play nice this week," Nora says, placing a delicate hand on my arm.

I bark out a laugh.

"Please," she adds.

"*I* will not be a problem," I say. Leo always starts it. He always has. Ever since we were kids.

I throw back my shoulders and shake off the nerves and hesitation bubbling in my chest. I've grown up a lot since then, but I still dread seeing him. It wasn't always this way. He used to be the one I wanted to see. The one I cared most about. But I haven't cared about him since high school. At least, I've tried with all my broken heart not to.

2

SUNDAY

"Tequila shots all around!" William swirls his finger in the air as our server stands at the head of the pub-height table in the front room of Von's 1,000 Spirits. From the outside, Von's looks like a dive. A dirty, gritty bar in the heart of downtown Seattle with sticky floors and grungy customers.

It's not though.

It's a narrow slot just a few blocks from Pike Place Market with polished hardwood floors, comfortable bar seating in the front and middle, and dining tables in the back. The bar stretches along the majority of the restaurant, framing glass shelves filled with liquor from floor to ceiling, lit up against the dim lighting of the bar. Dozens of countries' flags swoop and sashay along the ceiling, warming up the space with their bright colors while also giving it some character. The music is loud but not nearly as loud as my brother.

"I'm not drinking tequila, thanks," I say to the server, and she pauses.

"Yes, you are, Gen," William argues with inebriated enthusiasm. "It's the week of my wedding and you are my little

11

sister and we're going to celebrate how I want." He lets out an obnoxious hoot of excitement, and if he weren't my brother, I'd probably think he's a douchebag.

I roll my eyes and turn to the server. "Whiskey, please."

"Tequila," William argues, pointing at the server.

She flashes a small smile and winks at me.

I win. She'll bring me whiskey.

"I will never understand your aversion to tequila," William laughs.

"Because I still have not quite recovered from overindulging in it," I answer, pressing my lips together.

His demeanor freezes as his mind replays the memory. "Junior year in college, right?"

I raise my eyebrows and flash a sardonic smile, refusing to make eye contact.

"That was four years ago."

"And like I said, still recovering."

"I could have sworn you've had tequila since," Abigail chimes in, leaning into me.

I shake my head with a sigh. "It's really a shame. I used to love a spicy margarita."

"That's Leo's favorite drink."

My heart slams against my ribcage at the mention of his name. I press my lips tightly together; I'm sure the skin surrounding my mouth is turning white.

"Hey, man, where is he by the way?" Terrence asks down the bar table. We're quite the group tonight but I blame that on Nora's ability to have three best friends that she had to have in the wedding, plus the sister and favorite cousin: me and Abigail.

Maybe having five bridesmaids isn't ridiculous, but I don't think I'd ever do it that way. I don't think I'd do any of it the traditional way if I ever decide to marry someone. I want to be in the woods or at a vineyard, miles away from people and cell phone reception. I want a photographer and an officiant and a couple of witnesses for legal reasons. But that's it. No showers. No reception. No luncheons. No wedding parties. No obligations for my friends.

Not everyone sees this as an obligation, I'm sure. Nora and

William both have magnetic personalities. They're the inviters. The party starters. The go-getters. The charismatic, welcoming leaders of their friend group.

Nora is the trailblazer. Taite is the wild one. April is the brains. Cora is the sugar on top. She's also eight months pregnant, and her husband, John, is a groomsmen with Terrence, Marcus, Jake, and—much to my chagrin—Leo.

"Well, I don't know but he better get here soon because I am not going to last too long with you hooligans," Cora laughs and sips her sparkling water.

Nora smiles at her friend and taps her forehead against hers.

"Leo had a meeting today, so his flight is getting in later than he thought. He'll be here any minute though," William answers as the server arrives with twelve shots of tequila rimmed with Tajin and one shot of whiskey.

"Oh, I think you brought one extra," I say, holding my whiskey shot and raising the extra tequila shot to the server. "One of our friends is expecting."

The server opens her mouth to either protest or apologize, but is quickly silenced by the man that just entered the room in a gray suit and white-collared shirt unbuttoned at the top.

He wraps his warm, long fingers around the shot glass, inadvertently intertwining his fingers in mine. "I believe that one is mine," he says, his voice deep and his smile sharp.

He looks older since I last saw him, even though it's only been three years. The good kind of older. The stubble on his face creates shadows and dimension on his perfectly chiseled face. The crow's feet surrounding his rich, chocolate-colored eyes remind me he's always laughing and smiling. His dark brown hair is grown out enough to reveal the thick curls I used to love, and the way his collar is undone is making him look perfectly disheveled in that just-hopped-off-my-yacht way.

Obnoxious, I tell myself.

"Leonardo," I say, nodding and releasing the shot of tequila.

He licks the Tajin and smiles, not even having the decency to break eye contact as he throws the clear tequila back.

I roll my eyes.

He's the same as always. Irritatingly beautiful.

Overcompensatingly confident. He forgets I knew him when he was the gangly twelve-year-old boy that couldn't beat me in HORSE. A stupid game where the first player has to shoot the basketball into the hoop from anywhere on the court—or in our case, the driveway—and the second player has to make that exact shot. If they don't, they get a letter. The goal of the game: don't spell out HORSE.

Leo was always a starter on every basketball team he played on, all the way until college. But he could never beat me; it drove him mad and made me cackle with giddy laughter. *Witchcraft,* he'd always exclaim. Never *congratulations.* Never *good game.*

Such a sore loser this one is, standing in front of me throwing back tequila before even saying hello.

"Shot for shot tonight?" he asks, sucking the remaining Tajin off his bottom lip.

A loud and sharp laugh escapes me. "You're on, pretty boy."

He nods at me with the shot glass in my hand, and I throw back my whiskey in one burning gulp.

"Evie Genevievie." He smiles down at me, an expression of pride on his features. I scrunch my nose at the stupid nickname he created for me years ago. Absolutely zero people call me Evie, and I'm someone with an obnoxious amount of nicknames. Gen. Genny. G. Genny Bear. Genevieve. But never Evie. "How you been, kid?"

I try not to flare my nostrils at his use of the word 'kid.' "Well, and you?"

He nods, his gaze bouncing off the floor and landing back on mine. "Good."

"Leo!" Nora exclaims, empty shot glass still in hand as she wraps her arms around the Best Man.

"How many drinks have you had?" he asks, returning her hug with a laugh.

"Two. I promise." She winks and I swear she's the only human that can wink and not look like a complete flirt. "I have to pace myself this week."

Leo lets out a low rumble of a laugh. "I got your email.

Looks like I'm going to be busy," he says, looking at me because I'm standing here listening when I should just find my seat next to Abigail.

The server returns with our food orders and more drinks, breaking me from my awkward stance next to the table.

I turn to Abigail who's engrossed in a conversation with Taite about New York City and how happy she is since she crossed the bridge and started living in Brooklyn.

"I love Brooklyn," I add, a wistful insertion to a conversation I'm not a part of.

"But not enough to move there," William argues—the big brother that has to be right. Always.

I glare at him for inadvertently bringing up Damien.

"Doesn't mean she can't love it," Abigail defends me.

"Plus, Brooklyn is a place you don't forget. It creates memories just by breathing in the air," Taite says. "You all really need to give the East Coast a shot."

"Not for a man," I mutter, plopping a fry in my mouth.

"Absolutely not," Nora says at the same time, falling elegantly into her stool next to William and shoving her fingers in his thick blonde hair. He gives her a lazy grin in response.

"Really? Why not?" Terrence asks, dipping his buffalo chicken wing in ranch dressing.

William looks to Nora for the answer, and she tilts her head with a sympathetic look.

"Well, for one, my mother would kill me," Nora says.

I nod. It's true. Lorraine will be holding onto the reins of this marriage as long as she can. William doesn't think it will matter, but he's completely forgetting that when you marry someone, you marry their entire family. At least partially. And I'll admit, there are going to be some stressful Christmases in his future.

I laugh and then swallow the lump in my throat. I miss my mom. What I would give to spend one last stressful Christmas with her. To have her call and nag me about what time I can be there. To watch her fuss around the kitchen and yell at my dad about burning the biscuits for the country gravy she made from scratch on Christmas morning. To give her one last gift and tell her I love her so damn much.

But cancer is an asshole and we don't get any more last times. Tears sting my eyes and I look up from my pork confit fries and meet William's eyes. He offers an empathetic smile and blinks his own tears away. No one knows it just happened. No one saw the tears. No one even thought that the mention of Lorraine set off a thousand memories and what-could-have-beens in our minds.

"Gotta stay on Mrs. Wellington's good side, huh?" Leo adds, breaking the exchange between William and me.

I look over at him, straight across from me to William's left. Leaned back, his elbow catching the back of the pub chair where his jacket now rests. He rotates his full tequila glass in his hand, a slow rotation between his thumb and middle finger, and I just watch in a daze until he freezes.

My gaze shoots up to his.

"Shot for shot?" he asks.

I don't normally take two shots in a row, but I also don't like to back down from a challenge this early in the game. I size him up with my eyes.

"I dare you," he adds.

"Well, I've never said no to a dare." I smile, raise my glass, and throw back my whiskey.

Leo and I stare at each other a beat too long and I'm suddenly self-conscious about every memory we share. Simpler times back then. But complicated ones too.

I clear my throat, ready to change the subject and my line of sight. "So, Terrence, I hear you're all over the world these days. Where's your office now?"

"Been working out of Japan the last eight months," he answers, his smile cutting into his mostly manicured beard that needs a trim.

"Wow! That's amazing! How lucky for William that you decided to fly across the globe to be here," I say, my phrasing and overt enthusiasm even makes me cringe.

"I've always wanted to visit Japan," Cora says, rubbing her belly.

"Me too. Do you speak Japanese?" Taite asks, leaning her

chin on her hand and batting her eyelash extensions at Terrence like she's Jessica Rabbit.

I smile to myself. She likes him.

"*Watashi wa sukoshi shitsu te iru,*" he answers and shrugs. "I know a little."

Our eyes all bulge and we nod impressively.

"That's so cool. They say the best way to learn is to live there," Taite says, her fingers delicately holding her blueberry lavender cocktail.

"I always wish I spoke a different language," I say, dipping a French fry in cheese sauce and then forking some pulled pork on top.

"Me too. One of my biggest regrets was not double majoring in Spanish," April adds.

"Now, that's not true," Leo pipes in.

The table turns to him, no doubt thinking he's responding to April, but he's looking at me.

"You are fluent in Pig Latin."

The table erupts in laughter.

"*Es-yay. Ow-hay ould-cay I ver-ey orget-fay?*" I say then pop a French fry loaded with pork, carmelized onions, and cheese sauce in my mouth. *Yes. How could I ever forget?*

"*It as-way most-allay y-may avorite-fay ality-quay of ours-yay,*" he replies, grinning wide and leaning on his elbows. *It was almost my favorite quality of yours.*

"You mispronounced almost," I argue.

"Did not."

"Did so. It's *lmost-ay,*" I counter.

"Sounds French," Abigail says with a huff and downs the rest of her cocktail, holding it in the air until she makes eye contact with our server.

Leo and I stare at each other, our eyes shifting, brows furrowing. Both of us sizing up the other. Both of us probably remembering how we left things. I didn't expect him to be a feeling. What happened between us was stupid. I was young. Naïve. It was a mistake. An embarrassing mistake.

But it still hurt.

And I can't tell if he's sorry for what he said back then or

17

embarrassed because it's been eight years since he said it and we haven't talked about it.

Abigail rattles the ice cubes in her drink over my head, snapping my attention away from Leo.

Our server approaches our table. "Another round?" she asks, making eye contact with everyone.

Everyone nods, except for Cora who's still sipping her sparkling water. I hold up a finger. "Could I get a beer instead please?"

"Hey, shot for shot?" Leo says.

The waitress pauses, her eyes darting between us. I stare at him, not wanting to lose but not wanting to get wasted on a Sunday night. I do have a job to get to on Monday morning.

"A beer, please," I say to the server and turn to Leo. "Guess that means I get an H."

He grins, his dark eyes sparkling in the dim lighting.

"Wait. What?" Nora asks.

"You know the game HORSE?" William says to Nora's puzzled expression. She shakes her head. "The basketball game."

"Oh!" Recollection washes over her face. "Yes."

"These two fools used to play constantly when we were kids because my man, Leo, here could never beat her."

Nora's mouth drops in one of those shocking smiles. "You beat the starting point guard from U-Dub in basketball."

"Well, HORSE." I shrug.

"She was always an excellent shot," Leo says, and his words vibrate over my skin. "But she could never beat me in Mercy."

Mercy? The game where we laced fingers, palm-to-palm, each of us trying to bend the other person's wrists until they hollered, *Mercy*.

I cackle.

"What? Not so tough without a basketball in your hand, are you, kid?" he taunts.

"You are twice my size. Don't look so smug," I retort.

He rolls his eyes and bites his lower lip.

I draw in a breath, ignoring the chill running through my body and pretending I don't remember this feeling as even more drinks arrive at the table.

"These two couldn't stand each other growing up," William says with a laugh and nod in our direction.

"Thankfully we've learned to tolerate each other," I say.

"Aw, you're so nice to me," Leo mocks, flashing me a closed-lip smile. I glance at him for half a second.

We both know tolerate isn't the right word.

When I was eleven, my mom heard us bickering and asked if I liked him. I let out a hock of disgust because I was still at the age where boys had cooties and Leo made my skin crawl. Mom unleashed a coy smile and said, "Just remember: when boys are mean to you, it doesn't mean they like you. It just means they're mean." I nodded, processing. "But the same goes for you. If you like someone, don't be mean to them."

It was great advice, but I didn't listen to it.

"You played basketball in college, right?" Taite asks me.

"Just one year at Gonzaga," I answer, dipping a fry in cheese sauce.

"Why only one?" she presses.

I shrug. "I wasn't all that good."

"That's bullshit. You were a baller," Abigail defends me, then turns to Taite and April. "She busted her knee."

They groan with sympathy as I nod in agreement. "Left me with an old lady knee and an obligation to focus on my studies."

"Good for you," April raises her glass, then scrunches her nose. "But I'm also sorry. That's really disappointing to endure an injury like that from something you love."

"It is. Thank you." I smile, resting my chin against my hand. "It all worked out though. I like my job. Plus, I'm only 5'7". It's not like I would have made it to the WNBA or anything."

"You would have, and you still could," Leo says, and I scoff in response. "Seriously, that was your dream."

"Guess it's not my dream anymore," I say, swallowing hard. I wave a hand, knocking his comment out of the air. "Dreams are stupid without a plan anyway."

"Genevieve," Leo says, his words direct and his eyes zeroed in on me. "You averaged eighteen points and seven assists per game. You had two triple-doubles during your first season at

Gonzaga before you got hurt."

I shrug, sipping my beer and avoiding his eyes. I hate that he knows my stats from a time in my life that no longer exists. I hate that he paid attention. But the knowledge that he knows and even remembers settles deep in my gut, fluttering and aching until I will myself to ignore it.

"I have no doubt you could still hit those stats. You would have one hundred percent made it in the WNBA," he continues, sitting back and rotating an empty glass between his fingers to punctuate his statement.

I lean my elbows on the table, feeling the heat of anger spark in my gut. "What? Like you? You hit those stats too and rode the bench when you played for Portland."

Leo stares at me, anger flashing in his eyes because I know I hit a wound. But there's a hint of satisfaction there too, because I just revealed I paid attention to him too.

Leo played for the NBA for one season. I saw him once, cheering on his team from the bench, enthusiasm and excitement plastered on his face. But I knew better. I knew he was struggling not being able to play. He was a starter since third grade. I knew he felt like he wasn't good enough anymore. That's not true, of course. But when every majorly talented basketball player in the world is trickled down to a group of 547, the chances of starting are slim. He disappeared from the roster after that season, and William told me he decided to pull out after he was offered a job in the athletic department at UCSF.

"Hey, but at least I made it," he says, his jaw clicking.

"Right," I agree, letting my bitterness fall away and remembering what an accomplishment that is on its own. "Congratulations."

"Thank you." Leo's words sound almost forced and he hesitates a moment before returning the subject to me. "It could have been you. You're short, but you're quick."

I scoff out a laugh. "Not with this knee."

"You underestimate yourself," he says, and my chest tightens.

I have a million things I could say back but I don't want to continue this conversation. This conversation reminds me of when I didn't hate him. It reminds me of when we'd stay up until midnight, shooting hoops in my driveway. Or go over stats after the games on Friday nights. It reminds me of a time that no longer is, so I remain quiet, clamping my mouth down and shutting off the memories.

There's a beat of eye contact between Leo and me that feels too much like empathy to be comfortable, so I look away.

"The coolest little sister there ever was," William says, raising his glass to mine.

I pout and give him embellished puppy-dog eyes, letting him know he's the sweetest big brother as we clink glasses.

"Only she's not so little anymore," Leo adds and throws back his shot.

William shoots a sharp look in Leo's direction before getting pulled back into the conversation with Nora and Terrence.

I freeze—my beer just inches from my lips. "Did you just imply that I'm large now?"

"What? Wait, no. I just—" His eyes widen and his cheeks flush. Good riddance. Sound the alarm. Leo is actually blushing on my account.

"Are you embarrassed? Not so sure of yourself now, are you?" I tease.

Abigail laughs and rolls her eyes to the other end of the table. Cora is holding something up on her phone for Taite and April to examine. Abigail is saying something to Nora and William, and Terrence escapes to the bar with the rest of the groomsmen.

All at once, I feel like I'm alone with Leo and I hope he gets up to join his friends across the room.

"That's not what I meant," he says instead.

I swat a hand in the air. "Don't worry about it. I didn't take offense."

"You never do." His eyes narrow on me until I'm pinned by his gaze, my entire body paralyzed by his expression.

My shoulders drop in exhaustion. "What's that supposed to mean?"

"I think you know."

I shake my head. "Why are you like this? Why can't just say

21

what you mean, *Leonardo*?"

"You can call me Leo. Like you used to."

I roll my eyes. "I want to call you a lot of things. Your name is not exactly at the top of the list."

He lets out a grumble of a laugh, and I can tell it's because he doesn't know if he should continue to badger me. "Someone's in a bad mood tonight," he mutters.

"I was annoyed the second I saw you," I respond, avoiding his eye contact.

"You're still mad at me, aren't you?" he asks, leaning over the table.

"Nope," I answer, frowning and feigning disinterest.

"Okay."

"Okay." I blow air out from between my lips. "Another shot?"

"You've hardly touched your beer."

"Is this just how it's going to be? You making constant observations?" I bite back as my phone buzzes on the table.

I swallow seeing the name light up my screen.

Damien: That isn't an answer, Genny. Let's talk. In person. No distractions.

I stare at the phone, my face drooping.

"Is that him?" Nora says, her tone light yet accusatory.

My head snaps in her direction. I open my mouth to say, *No*, but I nod my head, groaning at my own response.

"For fuck's sake. Give me that!" Nora holds her hand across the table.

"Who's him?" Leo questions, looking at everyone but me.

"Damien, I'm guessing," Abigail huffs, slurping the last of her margarita.

Leo shoots his gaze in my direction, tilting his head ever so slightly. His jaw is set and there's a look in his eyes I can only describe as disappointment. "That fucking guy?" He clicks his tongue across his teeth, leaning back.

I draw back. "Why is that so strange? We were together three years."

"Three years too long," Abigail says.

"Hey—" I turn to her, my gaze scorching her face.

She shrugs. "Look, Damien's great but terrible for you."

I stay quiet, remembering all the ways we were good while feeling the sting of disapproval from my cousin.

"They weren't terrible together," Nora says, offering me a sincere smile.

"No, they were just too much alike," William adds.

"No, they aren't," Leo says, his tone definitive and his face washed with irritation and disgust.

I lean my elbow on the table, squaring off with Leo. "That's an awfully strong opinion to have about a couple you never knew."

"I know both of you." He speaks with such arrogant directness that if I didn't know better, I'd think he was an expert on my relationship with Damien.

I flash him a petulant look. "But not together."

"I didn't have to," Leo declares, placing his forearms on the table and leaning forward. Sometimes I forget how tall he is. Or maybe this pub table is just small because he's so close now. "You wasted your time with him."

"Wasted time is not a wasted life."

"I didn't say that."

"Then quit badgering me."

We hold our stare for too long. Heat travels up my neck. The flush hits me like a wave and I snap myself out of it.

"Whatever," I say, snatching my phone off the table and putting it in my clutch. "I'll respond later. Tonight isn't about that. It is about having fun with all of you."

Nora leans over my brother. "I'm going to set you up with someone that will be at the wedding."

William groans.

"No, no, stop. Listen." Nora flails her hands in the air, demanding attention. "There are going to be so many single friends from college there. Might find the man of your dreams." She wiggles her shoulders and I roll my eyes.

"No, thank you," I say. "I just want to be single for a while."

"Well, maybe just a hookup." Nora waggles her eyebrows at me and I laugh.

"Nora—" William groans.

"No, I'm good," I say.

"What a responsible choice," Leo interjects, flicking invisible lint off his shoulder like he's superior. Like he's the responsible one. It's laughable really, and fury lights up my gut.

"Dude, you are the most single person in this room—" I begin.

"Besides Terrence," William interjects. My eyes cut to my brother.

"Besides Terrence," I agree.

Terrence overhears, raising his glass and hollering, "Aye!"

My gaze zeroes back on Leo. "You wouldn't know commitment if it bit you on the neck, and yet you think you're the king of being responsible with other people's hearts."

Leo's stare sears into me like white-hot fire burning my face and a flush creeps up his neck.

We stare at each other for a long moment. My heart hammers. His nostrils flare. It has become perfectly clear we have a lot of unsaid words bottled inside of us, and if I look at him a moment longer, all of mine are going to spill out.

I blink away and look for the server, begging her to be close. "I could use another damn shot."

"Easy there, kid. I thought you didn't want to get wasted." Leo chuckles.

"Stop calling me kid. I knew you before you even hit puberty."

He laughs—a real one this time—and drags a hand down his face. "I knew you when you first shaved your legs."

We're going tit-for-tat then, are we?

"I knew you when your feet were longer than your legs. You walked around looking like a damn clown," I say, glaring, and William howls with laughter.

"I knew you when you had braces," he deadpans, not at all reacting to William's heckling.

"I knew you the first time you smoked weed and thought you were going to die." I raise my eyebrows and press my lips into a straight, triumphant line.

William pounds his fist on the table, laughing so hard he can barely breathe, no doubt remembering Leo's blatant pot-induced panic attack. I'm pretty sure that weed was laced with something because it only inflicted sheer chaos on Leo's precious, straight-edge brain.

Leo glares at William then fixes his gaze on me, his posture unmoving. "I knew you when you stuffed your bra."

Abigail giggles. "Me too."

I scoff. *Where is her loyalty?* My ears heat but I don't back down. "I knew you when you stole jewelry from your mother to give to your seventh-grade girlfriend. Ariel, was it?"

Leo starts to shake his head but still doesn't give a full reaction. "I knew you when you hit the parked car in the Target parking lot and drove away without leaving a note."

"Criminal!" Nora gasps, a playfully shocked hand to her chest. My nostrils flare.

"I knew you when you had acne and stole my mom's face cream because you were so embarrassed to go to the eighth-grade dance with Allison with a zit-face."

"Burn!" William shouts.

I cross my arms. Was the insult juvenile? Absolutely, but someone has to knock this guy off his high horse he's been riding too long.

"I knew you—" he begins but is interrupted by our next round of drinks arriving at the table. I don't know what he was going to say, but it doesn't matter because it feels like a complete sentence.

I knew you.

And I knew him.

3

SUNDAY

I don't know how to be around Leo. I don't know how to shake each and every memory embedded in my skin no matter how many years pass. I thought time would move forward, and so would I. Instead, I just feel stuck in a memory that happened eight years ago, and time has only amplified the hurt.

I shake the thought and raise my shot of whiskey to the sky. "To Nora and William," I toast. "William, my favorite brother, you are the luckiest bastard in the world to get Nora to agree to marry you. And Nora, good luck!" I wink. We clink glasses, and I throw back the brown liquid.

The whiskey warms in my belly and sends a wave of dizziness to my brain. Between the three shots and half a beer I've had tonight, in addition to the teacup whiskey I drank earlier, I really need to slow down.

Or eat more, at the very least.

I pick at my pork confit fries as the chatter and discussion about the week ahead continues. My mind and eyes keep wandering to my clutch. It's as if the messages from Damien on my phone are burning a hole in the cream leather, sending smoke signals to get my attention. It doesn't matter how many times I laugh or how much fun I'm having or how many times I push Damien to the back of my mind, Damien always pushes himself to the forefront. Even after six months of being broken up.

"All right, you youngins. I need to get my swollen feet home," Cora says, standing and rubbing a hand over her belly and turning to the other groomsmen congregated at the bar to watch the TV screen. "Now, if I can convince my husband it's time to go. John! Time's up!"

The guys turn, slapping hands and backs and saying, *see you tomorrow*.

"You staying out, Genevieve?" Taite directs the question at me.

"Maybe just a little longer," I answer.

"All night," Nora says, dancing around the table and giving me a drunken embrace, our cheeks squishing against each other.

"I thought you said you were pacing yourself for the week," I say, peeling her off me.

"Sorry, Von's does it to me," she says, then her body wiggles with a drunk shimmy.

"Don't blame the bar," Abigail says.

"Right. Blame your husband," I say, playfully glaring at my brother.

He offers a drunk, happy smile and holds up his hands. "Hey, I haven't hung out with Leo in a minute."

"You two are children," I say as they each take a swig of beer.

"I feel like they're forever eighteen in my mind," Abigail says.

I laugh then bite my lip hard. *Leo will always be eighteen to me too.*

We ignore their brooding antics and get immersed in conversation, and I casually switch my drink for water. After another hour of mindless chatter, Taite and April Uber to their hotel. Nora stands to say goodbye and wobbles on her heels.

"Oh no," she groans. "I accidentally got drunk."

I snort out a laugh.

"Those impending nuptials driving you to the bottle, Ms. Nora?" Abigail says, then mouths to me *I'll get her home.*

I nod as Abigail grabs both her and Nora's clutch. They say goodbye to me, William, and Leo.

"Aw, I'm not ready to go home," Nora groans, an exaggerated lip just inches from William's mouth. He smiles and then kisses her. It's drunk and sloppy and makes the rest of us cringe.

"All right, Bridezilla, let's get you home," Abigail says, taking Nora by the shoulder.

"I am *not* a Bridezilla," Nora slurs then holds a hand to her mouth. "Oh shit! Am I?"

"No, you are just Drunkzilla," I say, then scrunch my nose. So stupid.

"Good one," Leo whispers and I shoot daggers at him with my eyes. He rolls his eyes and says, "I'm going to go break the seal. I'll be right back."

After they leave and with Leo in the restroom, I turn to my brother and ask, "You ready to get married?"

He rubs his lips together and stares at the table like he's caught in a daydream. "Absolutely. I love her so much."

"I'm happy for you, brother," I say, reaching across the table and giving his arm a squeeze.

Moments after the ladies exit Von's, Abigail runs back in. "William, I know you want to have a playdate with your friend and sister, but Nora just puked on the sidewalk. And I could use some help getting her home. The driver is going to be so pissed."

My eyes fall closed. Poor Nora.

"Oh, shit. Sorry, sis," William says and jumps to the rescue, giving me a quick hug before rescuing his bride-to-be with Abigail.

I wave them off as the server returns with the check.

Oh. Shit.

I forgot nobody paid.

"Thank you," I say, then open the black leather case and scan the digits of the total. "Fuck."

Weddings are freaking expensive. I slide in my credit card

and hand the case back to her as Leo reappears.

"You kick everyone out?"

"Yep," I answer, watching the server go run my credit card.

Leo's gaze follows mine. "Your brother is such a cheapskate."

I wave him off. "It's his wedding week. Plus, Nora was puking on the sidewalk, so I think he just forgot."

He reaches into his back pocket and pulls out his wallet.

"No, really. I insist. It's fine—my treat." I give him a small, forced smile.

"You don't have to play polite right now. We can split it. Fair's fair."

"Since when do you like to play fair?" I query with a surly smirk.

His lips slide into a slow smile as he holds his credit card up between his index finger and thumb, rubbing it gently like he's unsure of what to say next.

"Even when I cheated, I still lost," he says finally.

"HA!" I bark out. "You sure did." I encase his hand holding his credit card in mine and shove it toward him. "Put it away, Leonardo. Like you said, I'm a big girl now."

He picks at his teeth with his tongue and shakes his head. "That bill was at least eight hundred dollars, Evie."

"Nine seventy-five."

"Jesus…" He laughs, returning the card to his pocket and pulling out four one-hundred-dollar bills.

"Put it away, fancy pants."

"Evie," he counters.

"Don't call me Evie. I hate it."

I don't really. It's just something about the way it falls out of his mouth that unsteadies me.

"Fine. Gen…" he pleads with just my name.

"You must hate that I'm successful."

"No, I hate that everyone stuck you with a thousand-dollar bill on a Sunday night." He steps closer. His scent absorbs my senses—the perfect mix of good body lotion and expensive cologne. A smell delectable all on its own but radiating off his skin, it's way too familiar. So I take a step back.

29

Our patient, adorable, and loyal server brings back the leather case and hands it to me. I jot down a twenty percent tip and sign it, slamming the case shut with the pen on top, punctuating the end of an enjoyable and expensive evening. It'll be a blow to my credit card but it's fine. I love my brother.

"I hate that you're paying," Leo says.

"I hate that you don't think I can," I retort, spinning on my heel and heading for the front of the restaurant. Leo follows closely behind. I wave to our server who hollers, *have a good night*, and open the door to the crisp June air in the heart of downtown with the distinct smell of industrial pollution and saltwater.

As I step on the concrete, Leo grabs me by the elbow spinning me around to face him.

"I know you can pay, I just don't think you should."

"How chivalrous." I roll my eyes.

"Since when is being decent chivalrous?"

I shrug, opening my mouth to say goodnight.

"Let me walk you home."

"Again with the chivalry."

"Please."

"It's fine. I only live three blocks away. I walk this route all the time."

"Not at eleven-thirty at night," he scolds.

"You don't know me anymore," I argue as I start walking and he steps with me. I notice his jaw pulse out of the corner of my eye.

"There's going to be a heat wave this week."

I stop, not hiding my confusion. "Changing the subject now?"

"No, but violent crimes are more likely to get committed when it's warm out."

I blink at him like I'm bored.

"There was an actual study, Genevieve—" he begins to argue but I hold up my hand.

"Spare me, please." I roll my head in the direction I need to walk, pulling my arms tighter against my body. We stand under the red and yellow neon sign of the restaurant for a moment as he waits for me to grant him permission to accompany me home and I, on the other hand, search for a reason to say no. The streets are mostly empty, which means less people will give me trouble, but also less people will witness any trouble that may arise.

I let out a deep sigh and look at Leo standing before me, one hand in his pocket with his Rolex shining in the streetlights and the other holding his suit jacket. He looks like a GQ model and it irritates me.

"You're so annoying."

He squints and jerks back like I spit lemon juice in his face. "I'm sorry, what?"

I stare at him a beat. "Nothing," I sigh.

"I'm walking you home," he reiterates, ignoring my pleas for independence.

"If you must," I relent.

"I must," he says, draping his suit jacket over my shoulders.

"Oh, I don't need your jacket." I let out a nervous laugh, feeling stupid. It's just Leo. We've known each other since we were kids.

"You're cold."

"I'm n—"

"Shh. You are," he silences me, refusing to let me win.

"Take it. I'm fine." I pull the jacket off and hold it out to him.

"No."

"Take it," I repeat with more force.

He slowly shakes his head staring down at me, jaw pulsing again.

"Leo." I shove the jacket at him, and he grabs my arms.

"Just take the jacket, Evie."

"I don't need it," I argue, pushing against his arms. I stumble forward into his chest and he catches me to right me up, but I fight off his touch for the sake of fighting and throw the jacket at him. His nostrils flare and I restrain a smile. He notices, only fueling his irritation more.

"Why can't you just let me be nice to you?" he asks, holding out the jacket again.

Because I hate you. Because I'm still mad. Because I don't know how to let you be nice to me anymore, I think but instead I say, "I'm not cold."

"You have goosebumps, Evie. You're being childish," he says as we continue our tussle over the jacket.

"You're being bossy," I say, pushing him because I've resorted to my twelve-year-old coping mechanisms, but he grabs me, and I twist in his arms. Then I yelp as his teeth sink into my shoulder. We separate and my jaw drops as I stare at him. "Did you just bite me?"

I see he's resorted to his twelve-year-old coping mechanisms as well.

"You pushed me." He shrugs.

My jaw is on the sidewalk—I'm so astounded I almost laugh. He didn't bite me hard. It didn't hurt and it won't leave a mark, but he…bit…me. I almost laugh.

For a moment, we just stare at each other—a mixture of shock, humor, and annoyance on our faces. Leo's jaw pulses and then he speaks.

"Are we done now?"

I glare at him as he holds out the jacket one last time.

"For real, Evie. I'm done fighting with you," he adds, unmoving.

"And you say I'm childish," I scoff and reluctantly shrug into the jacket, wrapping the collar tight around my shoulders. His overwhelming scent consumes me and makes my stomach do a weird flip-flop thing. I close my eyes, pretending he doesn't have an effect on me. "Guess that means I'm H-O now." I smile as I give him a sidelong glance.

"Didn't realize we were still playing," he says, stepping casually in stride next to me, his anger evaporating into the pavement.

"The game we started earlier just never finished I guess." I shrug, fixing my eyes on the crosswalk as we make our way across First Avenue, down Union.

A pregnant pause fills the air between us until finally, he speaks.

"No. We never finished."

Something about the way he says it, makes me feel like I'm living in a dream. Maybe it's the whiskey I drank or the scent of him wrapped around my shoulders like a hug I haven't felt in eight years. Or maybe it's the emotions of the wedding and the texts I got from Damien earlier, but my eyes water, and I hold them open, praying the wind of the city dries up my tears.

Leo clears his throat, disrupting the peaceful cadence of our steps. "I'm sorry about how we left things."

I feign misunderstanding. "We were fine the last time we saw each other at William's college graduation party—"

"No, I mean before that."

I search my memory for the previous time I saw him. "At my mother's funeral? Honestly, Leo, I didn't pay much attention to anything that day. It's really all a blur—"

"Before that." He stops abruptly, making my steps cease as well.

The buzz of the city is the closest thing to silence I know and the quiet between us feels so loud. I stare longingly at the glass doors of my apartment building. We're only half a block away. We almost made it. So close. So far.

"Evie," he says, his voice low, soft, pleading with me to look at him.

I don't correct him. I close my eyes and draw in a breath, letting the air escape my lungs with the weight of this conversation. Then I let out a small laugh to release the tension.

"It's all good, Leo. Really."

"I don't feel like it is—"

"And I feel like you're holding on to something that is no longer there." I ignore the quake in my voice.

"It's not?" he asks, but I know it's a challenge.

I swallow hard. There are too many memories trying to swim to the surface.

"It's not," I confirm, and he deflates.

"You might as well talk to me, Evie. You can't avoid me all week," he says.

"Yeah, well, I can try," I say as I watch his gaze fall to the sidewalk and my gut churns with remorse.

We never meant to hurt each other—we just...*did*. And

maybe the teenage girl in me still doesn't want reconciliation, but I'm realizing that maybe the woman I am now has been waiting eight years for it, so I add, "I don't want to talk about it tonight."

He opens his mouth and then closes it. For once, he's at a loss for words.

"We were wrong. Stupid." I shrug. "Just kids. You can let it go."

"I just feel like since then we've barely seen each other. I mean, we have but we don't—it's just things aren't the same." His words are a jumble of explanations and statements that don't quite make sense, all while making perfect sense.

I stare at him. This isn't my fault and he knows it, and I don't need to overexplain it. We just need to let it go.

"We're good, Leo."

His eyes fill with skepticism as he narrows his gaze on me.

"You sure?"

"Positive."

"All right." And we resume walking the short way to my apartment building.

"Just be careful with Damien."

"Oh my god," I grumble. "You don't have to do this big protector act, Leo. He's my ex of three years."

"I know. But maybe in those three years, there was a side of him you never saw."

No, I saw it, I think but instead I pout my lips and step closer, saying, "Oh God, was he an ax murderer? A secret sex worker? Drank the blood of virgins? Made breast milk cheese illegally and sold it on Craigslist?"

"Breast milk cheese? What the hell? No." He lets out an exasperated sigh and scrubs a hand down his face. "He just wasn't good enough for you."

I swallow his words in one emotional gulp. In my mind, Damien was good for me, even if he wasn't right for me. Mostly because I refuse to villainize my exes and declare our time together a waste.

"That's not true," I whisper. "He was good."

Leo presses his lips together, refusing to acknowledge my

confession. He rocks back on his heels, his angry hands in the pocket of his slacks.

"Goodnight, Evie," he says with a nod.

"Goodnight, Leonardo," I whisper.

I watch him as he turns to walk to his Uber that just pulled up to the curb and slips inside. I keep watching as the black sedan continues through three green lights and turns right, the taillights disappearing around the corner.

Finally, I close the glass door to my apartment building, nodding at the doorman as I enter the elevator. I tilt my head back on the wall as I ride up all eighteen floors, still feeling like Leo is right next to me. I jump as I realize I'm still wearing his jacket.

I shoot him a text, wondering if it's still his number.

Text me when you get to your Mom's.
I forgot to give you back your jacket.

It is still his number.

Leo: Good thing you'll be seeing me all week.

I smile at the thought then wipe the smile off my face. My heart pounds over a simple text and every memory we've shared replays in my mind like my favorite home video. I pull his jacket tighter around my shoulders. Because it does, in fact, feel like a warm hug I haven't felt from him in too long. My arms physically ache as I realize how much I need it.

4

MONDAY

"How was Nora last night? She hasn't answered any of my texts," I ask Abigail, phone to my ear. I grab my latte off the counter at Café Ladro and mouth *thank you* to the barista.

"I bet she's still asleep. The poor thing. We fed her cheese crackers and Gatorade but I don't think it was helping," Abigail answers. I can hear the wind in the background. "William thinks she got food poisoning."

"Von's would never," I playfully exclaim, pushing out of the café.

Abigail barks out a laugh. "That's what I said. I had to remind William that his perfect fiancée had a solid eight drinks and only ate half of her chicken, apple, and walnut salad. The poor thing knows better than to mix tequila with lettuce and nothing else."

I laugh. "She's just nervous she'll overindulge and not fit into her dress."

"Yeah, well, her body would have appreciated if she didn't overindulge in tequila, and chose the lobster macaroni and cheese to eat instead."

"True," I say, walking down the sidewalk toward my apartment building. "Well, I'll probably drop off some hydration tablets and green juice after I stop at home to change."

"Such a good sister," Abigail coos. "Did you feel okay today?"

"Mostly." I hesitate, wanting to tell her how much my mind was spinning after Leo walked me home. "But I am on my fifth coffee."

Abigail laughs. "Thank God, I don't have to work today."

"You're taking the week off?"

"No, I'm working Tuesday and then I'm free through Sunday, so you get to enjoy me all week."

"With pleasure."

"Also," Abigail adds like she just remembered something very important.

"Hmm?"

"What was the deal with you and Leo all night?"

The back of my neck breaks out in a cold sweat as my heels click against the sidewalk. "What do you mean?"

"You talked the whole night. Well, teased. Did you end up leaving together?"

"No," I say quickly.

"Really?"

"Well, I mean yes. He walked me home. But that's it."

Abigail scoffs. "Well, I didn't mean like, did you sleep with him, just that... okay fine. Leo is super cute these days and I think he's got the hots for you."

"Great," I mutter.

"Don't you? The way he looks at you is like he can't stop. No matter where the conversation goes or whatever is happening, every time I looked at him, he was somehow always looking at you."

"Sounds like a stalker," I say with a laugh as I pull the glass door to my apartment open. "It also sounds like you were paying very close attention to him, Abigail."

"I don't like boys," she responds, laughing. She starts to say something else but I don't hear her because Leo is standing in the lobby of my apartment building next to the security desk.

"Abigail, I'll call you back." I don't wait for her to respond and I end the call. "Hey," I say, stepping toward him.

He's dressed in tan shorts, crisp, white Nikes, and a baby blue t-shirt. The summery color palette of his attire is making his light brown skin look two shades darker. Again, straight out of a magazine, only this issue pertains to enjoying a crisp glass of chardonnay at a bistro in Italy as opposed to last night's attire of how to dress for success in the boardroom.

He grins, his gaze sweeping over me from my heels, the two coffees in my hands, and then my face.

"What are you up to?" I ask when he meets my eye.

"I had a late lunch with my mom and thought I'd swing by and grab my jacket so you don't have to bring it to the luncheon on Thursday." Then he leans in, and says, "Turns out your scary security guard won't let me up to knock on your door."

"Thanks, Ronnie," I say to my favorite security guard. He's seventy-five with white hair, a dark sense of humor, and an aversion to utter bullshit. I turn back to Leo. "You'd be surprised how many strange men try to visit my apartment."

"Well, thank God for security, otherwise your neighbors might think you have a side hustle as an escort."

"No, I only have an OnlyFans."

He makes a quick noise of surprise—a mix between a cough and a laugh. A cough-laugh. A caugh. I smirk, loving that I made him uncomfortable.

"All right, Leonardo, let's go get your jacket, so you don't catch a cold."

"For you, Ronnie. Extra foam." I wink, handing him the coffee.

"Thank you, Ms. Michaels."

"My pleasure. I'll see you in a bit."

My heels clack against the marble floors until we reach the elevators. I sip my Americano to distract myself from being alone in the elevator with Leo. Our backs rest on the mirrored wall in the back and we stand a good two feet apart.

"Do you remember what you used to say about elevators?" he asks, staring at the doors.

I roll my eyes in his direction. "Why do you do this?"

"It's just a question." He smirks, staring down at me.

"Yes, a question with an insinuation. Just stop. Yes, I think elevators are for kissing." I turn to face him. "Is that what you want? To kiss me? Or just make fun of me?"

He opens his mouth but doesn't speak. It's infuriating. I just want to scream, *say what the fuck is on your mind!*

I don't though, I just stare him down. Well, up. He's very tall. Even with my three-inch heels I only reach his shoulder. My thoughts trace back to when I shut him down last night and asked him to leave. His vague hesitancy is because of me.

The doors ding on the eighteenth floor, disrupting our stare. I walk out without speaking, letting him trail behind me until we're inside my apartment.

"Nice place," he says, admiring the view of Pike Place and the Great Wheel next to the water from the front door. The sun is still high and burning despite it being so late in the day; it won't set for another four hours. Daylight lasts forever during the summer in Washington.

"Thanks. I pay for it myself," I say as I kick off my heels, leaving them in the middle of the entryway, and mindlessly flip through my mail.

Absolutely nothing of importance. I toss the stack on the countertop and it scatters across the white quartz.

"Of course you do," he says, picking up my heels and lining them neatly against the wall near the door.

I suppress a smile and open my mostly empty refrigerator. "Want a drink?"

"I'm good. Thanks."

"All right," I say, closing the refrigerator and turning to see him gather my junk mail and tap it into a pile.

I shake my head and unleash the smile I was restraining. "I forgot how anal you are."

"I'm not anal. I'm organized."

"I feel like you're about to look in my cupboards and get mad my glasses don't match."

"What?" He scowls, and I laugh.

"See? I can see the aneurysm happening in your brain at just the idea of it."

He huffs and crosses his arms. "Doesn't matter."

"Really?" I ask. "Even if half of them are plastic and neon green and the other half are an eclectic mix of depression glass and mason jars."

"I don't care." He shrugs.

"Even if I have twenty-seven coffee cups with stupid sayings I got off Etsy?"

He forces a frown and shakes his head.

"My plates are plastic. The toddler kind with ridges so my food doesn't touch." I lean against the counter.

"Whatever makes you happy. I know you hate when salad touches your mashed potatoes."

"Understandable."

"It is," he agrees and grins, not breaking his gaze from mine.

"It's driving you crazy that you don't know if I'm lying or not."

He laughs. "I don't care what you eat your food on, kid."

"Don't call me kid."

"If you eat on toddler plates, you're a kid."

"Good thing I don't." My lips slide into a smile and for a moment we just stare at each other. He twists his lips and squints.

"I don't believe you."

"You should." I shrug, tilting my head back toward the cupboard behind me. "Check."

"No," he says.

"Suit yourself." I lift my body away from the counter and start walking out of the kitchen. "Let me grab your jacket so you can get going."

He nods and checks his watch. "Yeah, I told your brother I'd be over soon."

I spin around—avoiding him is continuing to be impossible. "I'm going over there."

Leo looks around the room, his forehead creased with confusion. "Are we not allowed to go over at the same time?"

I shake my head. "No, we are. If you give me a sec to change we can go together."

He nods, his eyes floating to the cupboards.

"If you check, you lose!" I holler, closing my bedroom door. I hear his laugh muffled on the other side.

Leo is the nosiest person I've ever known. I used to get home from practice in high school and find him in my bedroom, wading through my dirty laundry on the floor and my Beanie Baby collection in the corner, searching for ammunition so he could shit talk during HORSE. He even read my diary... twice. The motherfucker.

He'll check. I know he will. It's in his nature.

I unzip the back of my black slacks, letting them fall off my legs as I slip my gray blouse over my head and onto my floor.

"Put your clothes in the hamper!" he yells through the door.

I scrunch my nose and smile at the door. "Mind your business, Leonardo!" I yell as I grab a sundress and sandals from my closet. I stare at my clothes on the floor, placing them in the hamper with a reluctant toss. I equally hate and love how well he knows me.

People are funny that way. Leo doesn't really know me. Not anymore. And yet, there are some things that are inherently me and he's never forgotten.

I stand and look at myself in the mirror in the ensuite, throwing on some deodorant and a little dry shampoo to the roots of my hair. I stare at my perfume bottle and hesitate. I wear it most days, but I don't want Leo to think I put it on for him.

"You're ridiculous," I mutter to myself, adding a spray to the pulse points on my wrists and neck.

I escape my bedroom and see Leo snap up from behind the counter, a guilty expression on his face.

I twist my lips and glare at him. "You lose."

He laughs. "Guess I get an H."

"I'm about to give you an H-O for invasion of privacy," I laugh.

"I am slightly disappointed you lied so well. Well, except for the coffee mugs. You really need to minimize."

"Absolutely not. And I guess you missed the princess plate I held on to since I was a kid."

He turns to check, and I laugh.

41

"A princess plate would suit you."

"Aww, what a compliment." I throw his jacket at him, and he catches it, his grin spreading wider as I step next to him and fish out a tube of hydration tablets from the cupboard. Nora will be forever grateful. "Let's go."

We exit my apartment and step onto the warm pavement scorched by the evening sun. Normally, June is rather gloomy and not quite warm, but a heat wave is striking the West Coast this week, and today isn't even the hottest day. This is entirely unusual for the Pacific Northwest. Heat warnings are all over the news. The shelves at Walmart are bare from everyone buying portable AC units because most people don't have central air—even kiddie pools are sold out.

It gets hot in western Washington, but not like this.

"William said it's supposed to get up to one-oh-five Wednesday," Leo says, walking next to me. Hands in his pockets, his shoulders relaxed, and his eyes hiding behind his sunglasses.

"Rehearsal is going to suck balls," I say, already feeling the trickles of sweat beading on the back of my neck. "How hot is it right now?"

He checks his phone. "Only eighty-five."

"Oof. My blood is still thick from this winter."

A laugh tumbles out of his chest. "Washington weather is insane. It's cold, wet, and rainy until it's like, absolutely not."

"For real," I say as my phone starts ringing. I see Nora's name as I pull it out of my crossbody bag. "Hello, my dear. I am on my wa—"

"Genevieve, I'm freaking out."

"Okay," I say, slowing my steps. "What's wrong?"

"I could absolutely kill your brother."

I make a full stop, glancing at Leo with wide eyes. His brows are drawn together in confusion and he steps closer. I mouth, *Nora.*

"What'd he do?" I ask, knowing it's probably not a big deal. I love Nora but she can be a little high-strung. She can't help it, I know—I've met her mother. And on top of that William isn't irresponsible. He is kind and thoughtful and rarely forgetful.

"It's what he didn't do!" she shrieks. I wince and pull the phone away from my ear.

What's wrong? Leo mouths and I shake my head with a shrug and mouth, *I don't know.* I curl my index finger, beckoning him closer to eavesdrop.

Leo leans down so his ear is near the phone on my ear. The scent of his cologne hits me and flutters in my gut. He'll always smell like a memory. A memory I've buried, but when he stands this close, it all plays back in my mind.

I ignore it and try to focus on Nora on my phone.

"Okay. What didn't he do?" I try to glance at Leo, but my gaze hits his jaw and travels down his neck until his warm, honey skin disappears under his baby blue collar.

"He didn't pick up our rings!"

Leo's throat makes a noise like he's just swallowed a laugh. I smack his arm and scold him with my eyes.

"Well, I'm sure it's not that big of a deal. He can get them tomorrow, I'm sure—"

"NO!" she cuts me off. "Brilliant Stone is closed on Tuesdays."

"Why?"

"Does it matter?" She lets out a groan of irritation. "Wednesday is spa day while the guys golf, then the rehearsal and Thursday is the luncheon. Honestly, we would be cutting it way too close anyway—the wedding is Friday!"

I nod at each event this week, knowing it requires my attendance and partly wishing I could go golfing with the guys instead of having some stranger tickle my feet in a small bathtub.

"Okay, so go now. It's only six-thirty. I'm sure they're still open."

"We have to be at dinner with my parents at seven and I swear, my mother will hang me up to dry if we're late."

I want to say screw your mother, but I also know her parents are paying for this very elaborate wedding and one of their most prominent personality traits is unattainable expectations. Leo grins down at me like he can read my thoughts.

"I thought you weren't feeling well. I was on my way with hydration tablets and condolences," I quip.

"What? I'm fine. I got it out of my system and slept it off most of today only for William to come home and say he didn't do the *one thing* I asked him to and that Leo is supposed to be coming over."

I forgot nerves and adrenaline are strong combatants for a hangover.

"Yeah, I thought Leo was supposed to come over too," I say, looking at Leo. He shrugs and half-smiles—the innocent bystander. "He's actually right here."

"Why?"

"I stole his jacket last night and he was picking it up and then we decided to head over together," I answer plainly, my mind hanging on the last word.

"Well, that's not helpful now."

I clear my throat. "Okay," I say as calmly as I can. "Are you calling to vent or for a solution?"

"Solution!" she yells and Leo presses his lips together, turning away so he doesn't laugh.

"I can go get them. If you call and let them know I'm allowed to. It won't be a problem," I offer.

"Really?"

"Really," I say, while also wondering why she didn't just ask straight up.

"You are the best. Oh my god, I swear, I'm marrying William so I can have you forever."

I laugh. "At your service. Call them. I'll head over now."

We hang up, and I let out a sharp breath. "Well… change of plans."

Leo breathes out, letting the air rumble his lips. "She is intense."

"She's nervous. Weddings are stressful. I get it." I wave a hand in the air. "So, as I'm sure you heard, I have to pick up their rings from the jeweler and you are off the hook for hanging out with my brother while he's in the doghouse." I flash a mischievous grin.

"Want company?" he offers then looks down and scratches

the back of his neck. I can't tell if he's unsure if he wants to, or unsure he should have offered.

"You don't have to. I'm sure you have other things you could be doing…" I say, feeling him out.

"I don't have anything going on." He shrugs. "And I'd hate for you to walk alone."

"It's not the middle of the night."

"Doesn't matter." He smiles, small and uncertain yet completely genuine. "The world is a dangerous place these days. Carjackings… murderrrr."

He draws out the "r" sound, making me laugh.

"Well, I wouldn't mind it," I say finally.

We resume walking down the street, bustling with people. Seattle is so eclectic. There are the business people in their suits and slacks. The artists with their ink-smudged fingers and eye for beauty. The musicians with their cased instruments, lighting up one last smoke before sound checks. The hipsters in their black v-necks and beanies. The sports fans dressed in Seahawks, Mariners, or Kraken gear and athletic war paint. The downtrodden tourists wearing flip flops and binoculars while taking pictures of the gum wall. All within several city blocks.

"Where are we going exactly?" Leo asks.

"Brilliant Stone. It's just around the corner actually."

"Sounds like a pot shop."

I laugh long and loud. "It does," I agree, then nudge his elbow with my shoulder. "Specialty rings."

"With a side of specialty weed?"

"You wish." I roll my eyes.

"I mean, I kind of do. I need a redemption story."

I laugh again, remembering his pot-induced panic attack in high school.

"You don't get a redo. I don't want to corrupt one of my favorite memories," I emphasize.

Leo grows quiet, chewing on the side of his bottom lip.

I subconsciously note his hesitancy but consciously ignore it as I open the doors to Brilliant Stone.

We have to wait several minutes for a jeweler to see us. Then the said jeweler has to double check with her manager or whomever it was that spoke to a frantic Nora Jean Wellington on the phone that we are indeed allowed to pick up the rings.

After that, there are no issues.

The jeweler asks for us to wait a moment, then returns with three cream-colored boxes lined with velvet and containing thousands of dollars worth of metal and diamonds—his wedding band, her wedding band, and her newly cleaned and polished engagement ring.

I smile as I look at them. Leo isn't paying much attention, mostly just perusing the glass cases filled with diamonds, sapphires, and promises.

"Is there anything the two of you would like to look at?" the jeweler asks, eyebrows raised and a presumptuous smile on her face as she looks between us.

"Oh, no thank you," I say, placing the rings in my purse. "Have a good night," I add and hurry toward the front door, not bothering to see if Leo is following me.

We burst out of the air conditioning and into the perfect heat of a summer evening. The air hits my skin like a warm blanket, and I can't help but smile.

"Who said I didn't want to look at anything?" Leo asks, following me out onto the streets of the city.

"Ah, is there a lady friend you failed to mention?" I ask, eyebrows raised as I slip on my sunglasses.

"Maybe," he says.

"Oh." My face falls unintentionally, and I swallow hard. I wish I was more prepared for that answer, and now I'm embarrassed that I'm blushing.

Leo smiles wide and brushes his knuckles on my scarlet cheeks. "I was just joking. Don't look so disappointed."

I slap his hand away and scoff. "I'm not disappointed. I was just... surprised."

"Really?" he asks, and his mouth twitches with disbelief.

"Yeah, I mean, I'd pity the woman who had to handle someone like you," I tease. Another failed attempt at recovery.

He presses his lips into a small smile, studying my face then gives one solemn nod. "You hungry?" he asks, changing the subject.

"Oh, Leonardo, have you forgotten? I am always hungry." I grin, and his returning smile mimics mine.

My phone dings in my purse and I ignore it. Then I remember, I could ignore the entire universe when I'm in Leo's presence. I don't know if that should excite me or terrify me, but I'm bracing to find out.

5

MONDAY

We sit on a bench near the Great Wheel, looking out at the glistening water of the Puget Sound, sipping mango lemonade, and stuffing our faces with gyros. My mom loved it here. She loved gyros and had an almost disgusting obsession with tzatziki sauce. She is probably the only person who could buy a bulk container of tzatziki sauce from Costco and finish it before it expired.

I smile to myself, taking a bite and letting myself be mesmerized by the water.

"You thinking of your mom?" Leo asks.

Tears spring to my eyes, and I laugh them away. "What gave you that idea?"

"Your expression is different when you think of her."

I scoff lightly, both confused and intrigued by the observation.

Leo and I really don't see each other often anymore and when we do, we both purposely keep our distance. Both of us side-stepping around conversations and interactions with each other. But I do remember when he hugged me at my mom's funeral. I was twenty-one and he was twenty-two. He was going down the line of my family, hugging my dad, my Gamma and Gampa, my Aunt May, my Uncle Jerry, then he landed on me. Most of that day is a blur but those moments are still crystal clear. Leo hesitated—his arms jerking up then down quickly before wrapping around me. My arms stayed at my sides until they wrapped around him on impulse. I loved everything about that hug—the weight of his arms, the smell of his suit, the feel of my heart beating. "I don't know what to say," he said. I pulled back and smiled. "Me either."

And that was it. We both didn't know how to say more. I always thought he didn't want to.

"Yes, I was thinking of her." I pull in a deep breath. "I'm almost always thinking of her."

Leo keeps his gaze intently on me as he nods. The right side of his mouth twitches up slightly. "She loved gyros."

"And tzatziki sauce," I add.

A laugh rumbles out of his chest coating my heart, like velvet on sore skin. I smile at him then take another bite.

"How have you been since she died?"

"Fine mostly." I shrug, my mouth half-full. "At least because I feel like I'm supposed to be. I'm twenty-five. Self-sufficient. I should be fine. But then other times I'm terrible. I feel like I'm so lost without her, you know? Like she was the one I was supposed to call after my breakup. She's the one that should have helped me plan the bridal shower, and she should be toasting to William and Nora on Friday." I pause, chin shaking, the memories bubbling in my chest. "But she's not. And I still haven't figured out how to stop missing her."

He's quiet for a moment, dragging a thumb over his mouth as he searches for words that I know don't exist. "Because you aren't supposed to stop," he says finally. "You're supposed to remember her in everything you do, in all the places you see, and in all the people you love. Because a little bit of her is always going to be inside you."

I smile, tenderness quaking in my throat. He holds my gaze a moment, his expression serious. Then he unleashes a smile.

"And it's a good thing because your mom was the bomb."

A laugh bursts out of me. "You hang out with too many millenials."

"Ooh, the hate is strong with this one," he says with a smile that tells me he's very pleased with himself.

I laugh harder, and it feels so good to release the heaviness of the conversation.

"It wasn't that funny," he says, his tone dry as he takes a drink of lemonade.

I let out a long, bubbly sigh to calm my laughter. "True. You really aren't very funny."

"Hey, you laugh at my jokes," he says and then furrows his brow. "I'm funny. Ish."

"I'm just easily influenced," I reply. "How's your mom by the way? I miss her."

He nods. "Good. She's coming Friday."

"I can't wait to see her." I smile, then tilt my head thoughtfully. "Is your dad coming?"

Leo shakes his head. "He can't make it up but he sent a gift."

I nod in response. "How is he?"

He shrugs. "Same as usual."

He doesn't elaborate, and I don't really expect him to.

"I'm sorry."

"It's okay. I guess I actually have learned to be okay with them not together."

I press my lips together, nodding. The divorce wrecked Leo. His parents split when he was eighteen, and then his mom had Leo live with his grandparents the summer before college while they sorted out the house. It was terrible. Looking back now, I know it must have been the moment Leo realized children only get to know parts of their parents, but never them entirely. And sometimes the people you rely on the most can disappoint you. Even so, I can tell he's made enough peace with it that it doesn't need to be discussed.

Leo leans forward, crumbling his wrapper in his hand and shoving it in the brown paper bag on the ground next to us.

"I got a question for you," he asks, wiping tzatziki sauce from his lips with a napkin.

"Shoot," I say, plopping the last of my gyro in my mouth.

"Are you surprised your brother is getting married?"

I inhale my bite which makes me cough. Leo slaps my upper back with his hand as I continue to cough and attempt to swallow. It wasn't the question, even though it did surprise me. This is just another reminder that I forget to do basic things like swallow when Leo is in my presence.

"You all right there?" Leo asks, his hand staying on my back.

I cough again and Leo hands me his mango lemonade. I take a long slurp, letting it coat my throat so I can speak. "What's the context?"

"Of the question?" His forehead crumples.

"Yeah, like, am I surprised in general or surprised it's this week already?"

His eyebrows draw together, his dark eyes still curious, his hand still resting on my upper back. My skin burning underneath. "I guess in general. Because, honestly, between the two of us, I never thought he'd be the first to get married."

"Really?" I draw back, and his hand falls. "Because he's been with Nora for five years and in that time I think you've had two-and-a-half serious girlfriends."

"You've kept tabs?"

I flush but swat a hand in the air. "You're deflecting."

"So are you."

"Am not."

"Answer my question."

I sigh, staring out at the sun setting over the water sending a golden hue across the water and spilling into the city like fireflies in a jar. I can feel Leo's eyes on me—my hands as they fidget, my chest as it moves up and down with each breath, my face as I contemplate.

"I think, in theory, it's surprising because we both know how William was growing up and through most of college." I give Leo a knowing glance and he lets out a small laugh. "But after he met Nora, he kind of changed. And I think that tells me it's real. Because love—real love—transforms people."

He nods, letting my words soak in, as he turns to face the

51

water.

"Have you ever been in love?" he asks.

My head snaps in his direction, surprised. His mouth turns down and he shrugs as if saying, *it's just a question.*

"Kind of." I swallow, turning back to the sunset. "I mostly think I was in love with the feeling. And the longer I'm without it, the more I want it back. But that's all Damien and I were: chasing feelings hoping they'd last. But we burned out." I shrug, letting the pause linger. "So, to answer your question: maybe. And I hate that that's my answer because I'm twenty-five and you'd think I'd know what real love feels like."

I turn back to Leo, he's sitting back on the bench, his long legs sprawled out, his arm outstretched behind me on the bench. Again, looking like he stepped out of a magazine. His expression is one of quiet desperation, as if there are a million thoughts and words he wants to say but he can't decide how or where to start. I stare back. No doubt mimicking his expression.

A boat's foghorn sounds off in the distance, snapping us out of our eye contact.

"What about you?"

"What?" he asks, leaning forward.

"Have you ever been in love?"

He nods. "Once."

My heart hurts a little when he says it, and I don't know why. But I'm thankful when my phone rings into my thoughts.

"Nora, hi," I answer.

"Did you get them?" is all she says as a greeting. The murmurs of the crowded restaurant nearly drown out her voice.

"Of course," I say, pulling the rings out to look at them and make sure they didn't vanish out of my purse.

She squeals. "You are a lifesaver. Look, I know Taite is my Maid of Honor but if I could change it, it'd be you."

I snort a laugh. "I don't need an honorary title to do my future sister favors."

"Ah, you're the best. Can you bring them tonight? Is that too much trouble?"

"No, not at all. Leo and I just finished eating."

"You went out with Leo?" she asks. I can't tell if she's

intrigued or shocked. I keep my eyes fixed on the water even though I know Leo is listening.

"Kind of. We only got gyros from Pike Place."

"Ahh, well then both of you should meet at our apartment if you can. Thirty minutes? We're about to leave the restaurant."

"Sure," I agree. Then we say goodbye and hang up.

"She'll love you forever," Leo teases.

I laugh. "She better."

"Can I see them?" he asks.

"What? The rings?"

He nods and holds out a hand.

I pull the boxes out of my purse and hand them over one by one. He inspects each in the barely visible sunlight. A thin rose gold band lined with dainty diamonds for her wedding band. William's ring is a solid tungsten band, the metal so dark, it's almost black. Her familiar engagement ring is an emerald-cut diamond on a rose gold band. The two-and-a-half-carat diamond ring looks tiny pinched between his large thumb and index finger.

"They're pretty, huh?" I say as I wistfully look at the diamonds in the sunset light.

"They are," he agrees. "Try hers on."

I laugh. "Why?"

"Because I dare you." There's a challenge in his eyes as he holds out the ring to me. The same expression he gave me when he dared me to dingdong ditch Mrs. Clyde, the angry old woman across the street. Or when he dared me to stand in the middle of the grocery store singing "We Belong Together" by Mariah Carey at the top of my lungs. Or when he dared me to jump in the Sound, fully clothed, in the middle of March. My mom was pissed about that. She was worried I would get hypothermia from swimming in the frigid salt water.

This dare has nothing on dares past.

I cock an eyebrow. "It's not going to get stuck. I have smaller hands than Nora."

"You sure?" A challenge mixed with amusement is written in his eyes. His mouth twitches as he leans back, waiting, wanting to prove me wrong.

I hold up my left hand and wiggle my fingers. "Hobbit hands."

He laughs. "I double-dog dare you."

"Oof. I'm trembling with fear," I taunt, holding his stare. His eyes are unshifting, dark portals of affection sucking me back in slowly. Nerves explode in my stomach, so I blink away. "Okay, fine." I slip the rings out of the box and onto my finger.

I hold up my hand in the rapidly disappearing sunlight. They're beautiful. They glisten and shine, sending reflective lights across Leo's face. He takes my hand in his, examining my hand and running his fingers over mine and sending jolts of heat to the depth of my belly. "It suits you."

"Really? I feel like it looks a little gaudy on me." I intentionally pull my hand out of his and wiggle my fingers.

"You can pull off anything," he says, his voice low, his message apparent.

"Thank you," I say, offering a smile and wondering when we're going to say it. He tried to last night and I cut him off. I closed the door, and I shouldn't have. I clear my throat and say, "Well, now you have to try on William's."

"Why?"

"Because I dare you." My lips curl into a sly smile.

"Fine," he says, shoving the ring on his hand quickly and holding up his hand. "You like?"

"It doesn't suit you."

"The ring doesn't?"

"Marriage."

He laughs. "Why not?"

"You've half-assed every relationship you've ever had."

"You don't know that," he argues.

"Um, hello, my brother tells me everything and you always had one foot out the door. Even I could see it from three degrees of separation." I cross my arms and lean back.

He shrugs. "I'd only be all in for the right person."

I smile fondly. Beneath the good looks, the charm, and the mildly tormenting nature, he's a softy. "Well, I hope you find her, and I hope she's incredibly patient because you are guarded."

"Layered."

"Did your therapist tell you that to make you feel better?"

"Yes," he answers, seriously.

I laugh. "You're ridiculous."

We stare at each other for a few moments, until I'm crossing and uncrossing my legs and fidgeting with my hair. "We should take these off," I say, slipping the too-big rings off my finger and placing them in their respective boxes and in my bag.

I reach out a hand to take Leo's, but his face is washed in panic. Much like the night he thought weed was going to kill him—eyes wide, jaw slack, brow glistening.

"No..." I breathe.

He pulls hard on his fingers. "It's stuck. Fuck, Evie. It's stuck." He's in full panic mode. Face pale. Brow sweating. "What do I—how do I? Fuck."

I hush him. "Here let me see," I say, taking his hand in mine, quickly noting the ring is stuck-stuck. His ring finger is already beginning to swell as I attempt to twist the ring off his finger. "Hang on, I have lotion."

Dropping a small amount on his finger. I rub along the length of it, small, gentle strokes that feel like the perfect setup for a well-timed sex joke.

When the joke doesn't come—no pun intended—I sneak a glance at him, hoping he's looking at his finger but he's looking at me. I stare back, continuing to lubricate his finger. In an instant, I know it isn't all in my head. He's been reliving the same memory since last night and we're both pretending we're not. I swallow, pushing my thoughts away then begin twisting the ring slowly, but it won't get over the knuckle.

"I thought it fit," he says. My eyes fall closed and I laugh—some of the twisted and complicated emotions releasing from my chest. "If we have to get this cut off Nora is going to kill me."

"Obviously," I say. "But don't worry. It'll come off. This happened to me in high school. Your hand just needs to start sweating."

I wrap my fingers around his fingers and squeeze creating heat between our skin. After a few moments, I bend down, create a small opening with my hand, and breathe into it as if I'm trying to fog up the glass of a window. My lips brush against his skin, and the rest of my body tingles with awareness.

I try to think of anything else.

Baseball.

Lambchops.

Climate change.

Voter registration.

Taxes.

Absolutely anything else that will calm my heartbeat pounding in my ears. Anything that will set the butterflies in my stomach free. Anything that will make the chill on my spine disappear. Anything that will get me to ignore the goosebumps that have risen on Leo's flesh.

I close my eyes and swallow, focusing on the task at hand and not what I become in Leo's presence. We've been able to side-step each other for years, ignore the past. We've let us be a memory—a faint recollection of feelings and impulses that ended poorly on a starry night in June.

Breathing into our hands again, I grab the ring, twisting and pulling simultaneously. Hard. Fast. And the ring is off. Relief and my weird headspace go with it.

"Ah-ha! See? I know what I'm doing!" I exclaim, with a triumphant grin and the ring slipped on my thumb.

His smile grows as he looks at the ring on my thumb and then at me. I stare back, unsure of what to say. What to do. How I even feel. My entire brain has instantly become a tapestry of confusion, longing, and regret.

Unsaid apologies, hardest-kept secrets, and unfulfilled promises dance between us.

He draws closer, not breaking eye contact. His movement is slow and deliberate—a magnetic pull until we're just six inches apart. I part my lips and his gaze drops, drinking my mouth in for a moment before staring back into my eyes.

A group of friends stumbling along the dock steals my focus, and I clear my throat.

"We should go," I say. "Nora and William will be home soon."

He nods, rubbing his hands on his knees, his shoulders slumped. His posture and facial expression are a glimpse of how he was when we first met—a gangly preteen hopped up on Mountain Dew and hormones with peach fuzz on his upper lip. Sometimes I miss that Leo. That Leo was safe and easy. That Leo didn't hurt me. He taunted and teased. But he never won. He never destroyed me. The Leo in front of me is the biggest heartbreak of my life. I'm grown enough to admit that to myself. I wonder if he realizes it.

Just as quickly as I see his boyish side, it disappears, and the man Leo has become emerges. Tall, strong, handsome, and always the gentleman. He stands, reaching out his hand to me.

"Shall we?" he asks. Him, pretending he didn't just almost kiss me, and me, wondering if that's actually what was about to happen.

I shovel everything he makes me feel away. "We shall."

I take his hand and we stand, turning to walk toward Nora and William's apartment.

"H-O, H-O," he says into the night.

"What?" I turn, confused.

"Getting the ring stuck. Pretty sure I deserve an O for that."

I bite my lip, restraining my smile. "I guess we're tied now, but you're going down, Leo."

"I might be going down." He reaches out with soft and strong fingers, tucking my hair behind my ear and making fireworks explode down my spine. "But I'm taking you with me."

6

MONDAY

"He did what?" Nora exclaims, one hand on her hip, eyes bulging, the vein in her neck ready to explode.

"Oh, relax. The rings are fine," William defends Leo about the ring debacle.

I told Leo not to say anything, but he did to William and Nora overheard with her Spidey-wife-sense.

"I swear to God, you are the most stressful human, Leo." Nora groans, and I laugh.

"I'm offended because I happen to know you just came from dinner with your mother," Leo retorts. William coughs hard enough for the beer to slosh over the lip of the bottle as he hands it to Leo over the kitchen peninsula.

Nora's eyes become slits of smoldering lava. "My mother is fine," she says, with a heavy emphasis on the 'fine.'

I press my lips together.

"I'm just her only child."

William nods quietly as he wipes the beer off the gray stone countertop. Leo smirks into his beer bottle, leaning against the counter. I remain as still as possible in the living room so as not to draw attention to me or my unhelpful opinions. But Nora whirls around from their kitchen to face me. "Right, Genevieve?"

"Right," I choke out, forcing a smile. When my gaze meets Leo's, I want to melt. The walk over here was relatively quiet. I even pretended to check important texts from Abigail and Taite to avoid speaking out loud to Leo. Not for lack of words, but because I have way too many. A million questions. A million why's. Starting with why he said what he did eight years ago and why it made me so angry.

Now, he's staring at me like he wants to explain. His fingertips are playing with the neck of his beer bottle and he keeps licking his bottom lip and holding it between his teeth. Over and over. A nervous habit he's done since he was twelve.

I hate that I know this.

I hate more that he's nervous because I know it has nothing to do with William and Nora.

"Beer, Gen?" William asks after guzzling a third of his.

"No, thank you," I answer and take a seat on the couch.

"Will, honey, please don't drink more than one," Nora says, patting his belly and kissing his cheek. "We need to look good for wedding pictures."

William smiles. "Don't worry. I'm photogenic."

Leo laughs. "Nora, if you are worried about your pictures turning out, you shouldn't have Will in them."

Nora giggles. "Stop it. William is the most handsome," she says, squeezing his cheeks with her hands and kissing his face. "Which, speaking of. Can you guys please convince Terrence to shave his beard? Or trim it?"

"I thought beards were in. You don't like it?" Leo asks, his tone teasing.

I laugh, propping an elbow on the back of the couch.

"You told me you like it, didn't you, Gen?" William asks.

Heat hits my cheeks as the intensity of Leo's gaze heightens.

Terrence is handsome, sure, but his beard is getting out of control. "Well, yeah, like, last month. But it's rather unruly. There's a fine line between sexy lumberjack and Gandalf."

William and Nora laugh. Leo doesn't. He smiles a quiet and

charming smile then licks his bottom lip and bites it.

Nora squeals and claps her hands together. "You're walking with Terrence down the aisle! I'm telling you, you two would be so cute together!" she exclaims, her moment of genius changing the subject.

I draw back, tired of the suggestion. "Oh, no. I'm not…"

I'm not what? I don't know. I have no words. I swallow and involuntarily meet eyes with Leo. He hasn't touched his beer and based on how warm my skin feels, he hasn't stopped looking at me.

"Hell, no," William says. "Terrence cannot date my sister."

"Oh, stop, they're adults," Nora smacks his shoulder.

"It doesn't matter. She's my little sister, and he's my friend that I know way too much shit about."

Leo is painfully quiet.

"I'm only planning on enjoying the wedding." I plaster a smile on my face and avoid Leo's soul-penetrating stare. "Plus, Damien and I just broke up six months ago. I'm not interested in anything serious."

"Well, not serious," Nora says, a flashy smile on her face. "Just for fun!"

"No." William leaves no room for misinterpretation or error when he speaks. "Leo knows. We love Terrence but that guy can't touch you with a ten-foot pole."

Leo jerks his gaze away from me and looks at William but doesn't say anything.

"Good thing it's not up to you!" Nora sings and then laughs.

I laugh. Or try to. It more or less comes out like a strangled cough.

I mindlessly check my phone so I can avoid the attention of the conversation and Leo's eyes. There are two unread texts. One from Abigail and the other from Damien. The blood falls from my head and hits my stomach. I check Abigail's first.

Abigail: Have you seen Nora? Is she alive? She won't text me back.

I let out a low breath.

Damien: Genny.

That's it. That's all he says and yet, I can hear it as if he's whispering my name in my ear. An ache in my chest pulses. I haven't thought about Damien since last night at Von's.

I've been distracted.

"Was that Damien again?" Nora asks, her eyes shifting from my phone to my eyes.

I shake my head like the liar I am then glance at Leo. He looks less nervous than he does sad. His mouth is turned down and his gaze is holding on to me.

For a moment, I almost tell him to let me go.

"Liar," Nora calls me out.

I open my mouth to tell the truth, then lie. It's not like the truth is interesting. Damien only texted my name and yet, it has enough power to knock my emotional center unsteady. "Abigail would like you to text her back. She's worried about you after last night." I flash an audacious smile.

Nora leans over the counter and buries her face in her hands. "I was hoping no one would talk about it."

"You puked on the sidewalk," William says, downing the last of his beer and pulling an arm around his fiancée.

"And the smell of your beer is going to make me puke on you," Nora says, leaning into William's arms, her brown hair falling over her face. She pushes it back and looks at me. "My mom said Damien is going to come to the wedding."

I shrug in response. I don't want to see him. But I don't feel like it's my choice.

"Is that okay?"

My eyes fall to the floor. "I mean, his parents are going to be there. You've known him your whole life, Nora." I shrug once again because apparently that is the only way to convey how I feel. Unsure. Confused. Helpless. Spineless. "I'll be fine."

William nods with a moment of solidarity eye contact, but doesn't say anything. He knows the breakup put us four in a weird position. Damien has known Nora forever—their families are practically intertwined, so of course, they should all be at the wedding. And of course, I'm dreading seeing the man I thought I was going to be with forever.

Nora dries her hands on a paper towel and throws it at Leo. "What's wrong with you? You're never this quiet."

Leo shrugs. I try not to laugh.

"Oh!" Nora squeaks and walks around the peninsula to Leo and grabs his arm. "Come here for a second."

"No," Leo teases, a half-smile splayed on his lips.

Nora hushes him and then glares at William. "No peeking."

William holds up his hands in mock surrender, his gaze following them down the narrow hallway to their bedroom. He turns to me.

"Why would she keep your wedding gift here? Everyone knows you're notorious for peeking," I say, chewing on my thumbnail.

William smiles. It's small, and to anyone else, it'd be typical, but I know there's thoughtfulness behind it. "Want to sit outside for a bit?"

"Sure."

I join him on the balcony. It isn't a huge space, just large enough for a small patio table, a grill, and two lounge chairs. But the view of the Space Needle in the distance makes it exquisite. I sink onto the white cushion on the lounge chair next to him and yawn.

"And it's only Monday," he says in response to my yawn.

I laugh through a second yawn. "It's past my bedtime. And I drank a lot of whiskey yesterday."

"That you did." He thinks for a moment. "Thanks for being so chill about hanging out with Leo tonight. I know how much you hated him growing up."

A huff of a laugh pushes out of me in one breath, then I recover. "Well, he was super annoying as a kid but he's not as bad anymore. You can consider it a wedding gift."

William laughs and I grin, praying my smile masks my feelings and disguises our history. It doesn't matter though, because William is staring out at the city lights, paying no attention to what secrets my expression is telling.

"You ready?"

"Yeah," he says thoughtfully, not looking at me. "I am."

"I'm glad you're marrying someone I like," I confess, crossing my ankles and lacing my fingers at my waist. The breeze is cool enough to forget the warmth of the day but warm enough to remember the heat wave is still heading toward us.

"Same. I don't think I could ever marry someone that didn't love you the way I do." He rolls his head to look at my surprised expression. "I know, I'm getting all mushy, but I love ya, Gen. I don't know what I'd do without you."

I pretend to gag even though I truly appreciate the sentiment—sometimes us siblings don't say I love you enough. Ignoring the emotion rising in my chest, I say, "Well, for starters you would have terrible taste in music."

He barks out a laugh. "You always did know the cool, new stuff before everyone else."

"Still do," I chide. "You also would have made Dino chicken nuggets the first time you invited Nora over for dinner."

"Dino chicken nuggets are delicious," he argues.

I shoot him a playful glare. "No argument there, but I'm sure Ms. Nora Wellington was far more impressed with Croque Monsieur and braised lamb chops than Dino chicken nuggets and store-brand ketchup."

"The ketchup was at least organic."

I grin and shake my head at my sweet and precious, young-minded older brother. He runs a hand through his thick, sandy blonde hair and laughs.

"I never did tell her you cooked that meal," he confesses.

"Stop it," I say, playfully aghast until a laugh bubbles out of me.

"No, I didn't." He grins at me.

"Starting your marriage off on the wrong foot."

"It is absolutely built on lies."

"You're doomed."

"Bound for disaster." He sighs, tipping his head back and looking out at the city.

The murmur of the city fills the air between us. I close my

eyes a moment, feeling like I could sleep for the rest of the week right here on this lounge chair.

"Do you think Mom would be proud of me?"

I shoot my eyes open and look at my brother. He turns to face me, waiting for my answer.

"Of course," I answer. "Mom would be so proud of you. I wish...I wish she were..." I struggle to get the words out as emotion floods my throat, "...here still."

He nods, slowly absorbing my words as he opens the door of grief that reminds us how much we miss her.

"Me too, Gen," he says. "Me too."

I press my lips together and swallow the desperation for my mom billowing in my chest before I tell him I'm so proud of him too.

"You know, Dad's worried about you," he says, making me forget what I want to say.

"Wha—why?"

"You don't go home anymore."

"That's ridiculous. Dad and I have lunch once a week—"

"Yeah, but not at the house."

My eyes frantically search the air for the right explanation: I live in the city now. I don't make it to West Seattle often. I'm busy working. They're all shitty little excuses though.

"He needs you, Gen. I know it's hard, but he needs you home too."

My eyes flood with tears, and emotion strangles my voice. "It's not home without Mom."

"Yeah, but for Dad, it's not home without you."

I blink. Tears fall, and my heart aches.

"I'll try to be better. I just..." I attempt to swallow my tears and pick at my cuticles. "I just miss her and it's easier to not be reminded of her, I guess. Everything in that house was touched by her." I shrug, letting the tears fall.

William reaches out wordlessly and takes my hand, squeezing once because he understands and twice because he loves me.

A throat clears behind us, and we look up from our lounge chairs to see Leo standing in the doorway. "Well, your fiancée fell asleep."

I wipe my cheeks and William sits up. "For real?"

"For real. She really is zero to one hundred and one hundred to zero. One minute she was up explaining your… thing that I can't tell you about and the next, she flops back on the bed and passes out."

I laugh then sniff away the remnants of my tears. "It's late. I should get home and you should go to bed too. You've got a busy week ahead of you." I stand and brush down my sundress.

"Yep," William says, wrapping his arms around my shoulders for a bear-like squeeze. "Love you," he murmurs in my ear.

I give a tight-lipped smile and a curt nod. "You too."

"I can walk you home," Leo offers.

Our eyes lock for a moment. I'm too tired to say I'm fine, so I simply nod.

"Y'all don't want to catch an Uber?"

"It's ten blocks," I say, and William stares at me like that's his point exactly. "It's only nine-thirty."

William rolls his eyes and slaps his hand against Leo's, pulling him in for a hug.

"Make sure she gets in her building?" William says like the protective brother he is.

"Of course," Leo answers without hesitation.

I keep my eyeballs fixed in place so they don't roll off my head. "You two are so macho. What would I ever do without you?"

William shoves me on the shoulder. "Shut up, squirt."

I let out an exhausted sigh and walk back inside, swiping my purse off the counter and meeting Leo at the door.

"Goodbye, brother, I will see you way too much this week." I wink then turn to Leo at the door. "Shall we?"

"Night, Will."

William nods and salutes from the kitchen.

I am painfully aware of the hand Leo places on my lower back as he opens the door, and even more aware that I don't want him to remove it. He keeps his hand in place until we reach the elevator doors, and he drops his hand to hit the button. My chest tightens at the absence of his hand, and my lower back burns and tingles where his palm once was, further reminding me this is a bad idea. One touch and I'm ready to come undone.

I turn to Leo when we're safely inside the elevator. "You don't have to walk me home."

"I know." His eyes stay fixed on the elevator doors, his jaw set and his hands gripping the handrail behind him.

I nod. "Okay." I fidget with the side of my dress, words climbing up my throat and my self-consciousness trying to shove them back down. But my self-consciousness loses the battle, and my word vomit tumbles out. "I promise I am a capable adult. I don't need a babysitter or a bodyguard. Though there are times when I think it would be nice to have one, but then it might also be annoying. Because if you have a bodyguard, you must need one and then they have to be around all the time and then you're never alone—"

"Evie," he cuts me off.

"Hmm?" I raise my eyebrows and press my lips in a line.

He stares down at me, his twisted mouth relaxing as he lets out a breath of a laugh. "I want to."

Three short and patient words hit me harder than I want them to. Because when Leo wants something, he knows just how to get it.

And I know I don't want to stop him—I never have.

7

MONDAY

"You were quiet in there," I say as the elevator dings, announcing its arrival on the bottom floor.

Leo licks his bottom lip and bites it softly, his brown eyes glancing at me and then drifting through the lobby to doors leading outside.

I smile, knowing he's nervous to give me an answer.

He clears his throat, rubbing his thumb along the width of my lower back as he guides me through the outside doors. "I guess I didn't have much to say."

"You always have a lot to say."

"Not this time," he says, dropping his hand from my back and stuffing it in his pocket.

"Why not? You talked my ear off down by the water."

He shrugs.

"What's wrong?"

"Nothing."

I tilt my head. "Are you mad at William for something?"

He cinches his eyebrows together and shakes his head. "No, I was just thinking."

"About what?"

He scoffs through a half-smile. "Evie, it was just... nothing. I'm tired. We were out late last night."

"Right," I say. I'm too gutless to ask him why he almost kissed me, and even more of a coward to ask him if he regrets it.

A chill runs down my arms as we turn the corner toward my apartment building, and the wind picks up pace, whipping through each skyscraper.

Leo freezes, his jaw drops and he holds out his empty hands. "I left my jacket at Will's."

I wave a hand in the air, withholding a laugh. "Not so organized anymore," I tease, then add, "Well, you certainly won't need it this week."

"No, but I was going to offer it to you," he says. I stare at him blankly and when I don't say anything he continues, "You're cold."

I smirk as I resume walking. Leo follows. "Guess that means you're H-O-R," I nudge his side. "But no worries. I don't mind freezing to death." I cross my arms, rubbing my upper arms against the summer evening's chill. "It's actually kind of nice. Tomorrow it's supposed to hit one-hundred degrees."

"One-hundred-and-ten on Friday."

"Yikes." Again, this is not western Washington weather.

"I am going to melt in my suit." He chuckles, a low rumble, his hands still in his pockets as he walks in stride with me. "I'm surprised Nora isn't freaking out more about the weather and the heatwave that's about to hit."

"Nora isn't as high-strung as she seems."

"You say that like I don't know her."

I laugh. "Okay, she's not as high-strung as her mother."

"No one is as high-strung as her mother," he adds. I elbow him playfully.

"I think she just loves William and wants to get married. She wants it to be beautiful and have all the pieces come together but I think if William is at the end of the aisle, nothing else matters."

"How poetic of you," he teases.

I give him a light shove with my shoulder. "Be quiet. The

weather is the least of her worries."

"You love her, don't you?"

"Of course. Nora's great." I pause, studying his unreadable expression. "What? You don't?"

"No. I do. I just…" He picks at his teeth with his tongue as he contemplates, staring at the crosswalk sign that just turned red in front of us. "I feel like she's always trying to set you up. You know?"

I shrug. "So? Doesn't she do the same to you?"

He rubs his brow. "Well, yeah, but I don't care."

"You just care when she does it with me." I point out this obnoxious fact with eyebrows raised.

He shrugs. "I don't like it."

I let out a breath of a laugh, easing the animosity from my chest. "Why?"

"Because I feel like she's always trying to make you feel like you need to be with someone."

I shake my head. "No, I think she just knows it's been hard since Damien and I broke up so she's overcompensating my heartbreak by setting me up with someone else. Someone to mend the wounds so I don't have to lick them myself, I suppose." I let out a soft, self-deprecating laugh as we stop at the crosswalk.

He steps closer and I swallow, his close proximity absorbing my senses and devouring my stability. "Is that what you need? Someone to lick your wounds?"

"Leo…" I laugh, shaking my head but my heart rotates in my chest.

"Is it?" he asks. Another step closer. More oxygen evaporating from my lungs.

"No?" It comes out like a question, then I reassure myself. "No, that's not what I need. I don't need anyone right now. Or maybe ever." I shrug. "But that doesn't mean I can't still be ruined for men since my breakup."

"All right. I'll just say it: Damien is a douchebag." Leo holds out his hands in front of him like he just scorched his fingers on a hot plate of food. The light turns green and he starts walking. I skip a step to catch up.

"He is not." Why I defend Damien to the bitter end, I'll never know. Because what I truly mean is: he wasn't a douchebag all the time.

"Yeah. He is," Leo argues, and I withhold a laugh. Leo selectively cares.

I cross my arms. "William likes him."

"William is a terrible judge of character."

"Ah, says the man he's chosen to be his best friend." I flash a quick smile and give Leo a sidelong glance.

He shakes his head. "William panicked about you being alone after your mom died and he jumped on the first person Nora suggested and then…I don't know how, but Damien convinced you he was worthy of your time."

I grab hold of Leo's arm, making him slow down both with his steps and his words. "Wait. Wait. Wait. What do you mean he panicked about me after my mom died?"

"I mean, he was worried." Leo shrugs.

I come to a full stop, eyebrows raised. Leo turns around and stares down at me as I speak. "Like what? I was depressed? Suicidal? Because, depressed, yes. Suicidal, no. Is that why he wants you walking me home all of a sudden? Because he saw me sad last night at Von's and now he thinks I'm going to jump in front of a moving car. Or maybe lay down on the tracks." My mind spirals to William's insistence to have Leo get me home.

My anger heats in my chest, fills my lungs, and travels to my neck and cheeks. "I have proven myself very capable since our mother died four years ago. I picked out the casket and helped Dad organize the bills my mother diligently took care of over the years. I made meals and hired a lawn service to take care of their yard because my dad is too sad—and quite frankly, getting too old to maintain it. I sent out thank you cards and executed my mother's will. And yet, William is worried about *me*."

The audacity.

Hearing me unleash the storm inside me, Leo grabs my wrist, sliding his hand down until he's holding my hand and making me walk next to him. "He just loves you."

My chin snaps back. "There are other ways to love someone than to set them up on dates and make sure they aren't single so they aren't *alone*." I say the last word with a hock of disgust. "I'm fine being alone. Honestly. Truly. One hundred percent fine. Happy." I rattle off the list and wonder if it sounds like I'm trying to convince Leo or myself. He nods along like he understands but doesn't necessarily agree. And I want to convince him I'm fine. As if he would somehow convincingly relay the information to William and Nora so they would let me be. I groan in irritation. "And you know what? Damien was a dick. He was the worst. His job was always the most important. His apartment. His traveling. His family. His life. All of it mattered more than me."

There is so much more I could say. And I want to. I want to remember every bad memory. Every harsh word. Every disagreement. Every time Damien made me feel small, unimportant, second-best, and incompetent so I can prove to Leo I am not the broken little sister of his best friend.

I can't get the words out though because Leo hushes me. Pulling me to a stop before we reach the doors to my apartment building. His hands take me by the shoulders, gently pressing me up against the stone wall of the building. He stares down at me, his eyes gleaming with intensity, affection, and confessions. He runs his knuckles over my cheek until his hands are cupping my face. I'm certain I've forgotten to breathe. "Nothing matters more than you, Evie. You deserve an entire universe. He didn't even try to give you the stars."

Leo's long and firm body is pressed against me, and I can feel the heat from his skin through our clothes, making my heart flutter. My gaze falls to his mouth. Thousands of memories are on his perfect lips and each one rushes to the forefront of my mind. The depth of my belly pinches as he breathes, low and unhurried, his lips moving closer at an achingly slow rate. I study his face, just inches from mine. I know every curve. Every expression. The freckle on his cheekbone. All three flecks of yellow in his eyes. The crease between his eyebrows that first appeared when he was seventeen. I know his face. His heart. But I've lost the last eight years of him, and it's like we're both trying to get it all back this week without talking about why we lost it.

But right now, with my face in his hands, his breath on my skin, and his lips so close to touching mine for the second time this evening, it all feels completely right. I know as soon as we separate, we'll panic and question everything.

Like we always do.

"Why don't you like it when Nora tries to set me up, Leo?" I ask, giving him a chance to say it out loud.

He licks his bottom lip and bites it as his eyes drop to the pavement.

"Why don't you like it, Leo?" I repeat. He draws in a deep breath. I place my hands on his chest. I can feel his heartbeat on my fingertips. Staring at his blue button-up in front of me, it hits me. "You'll never say it out loud, will you? Because you regret it."

"No—" he says, holding my face in his hands.

"You do." I nod, swallowing my hope.

"I just don't—"

"Genny?"

Both our heads snap in the direction of the voice.

The interruption feels like we've been dunked into an ice bath. Damien is standing at the open glass door to my apartment, jealousy in his eyes and his fist tightening around a bouquet of lilies.

8

MONDAY

"What's going on?" Damien marches forward, pink and white petals float to the sidewalk as he swings the bouquet at his side.

Leo drops his hands from my face, slowly sliding them down my side until one hand rests on my lower back.

"Damien." He nods.

Damien's eyes flit from Leo's to mine like a razor through tender flesh.

"Damien, what are you doing here?" I ask. A stupid question, really. He's at my apartment to see me. Why else would he be here?

"What is *he* doing here?" Damien's eyes burn into Leo, who is completely unfazed. Unbothered. I've always loved that about Leo.

"Walking me home. William suggested it," I say as if I need to answer to Damien.

I don't. I know that. Yet, here I am, in Damien's presence, and I've shrunk somehow.

Damien nods.

I step toward him and away from Leo. The warmth from his

73

hand leaves an imprint on my back as I take Damien in for a polite embrace that holds a million words.

"I didn't know you'd be here," I say, pulling back.

"You didn't answer your texts."

I glance at Leo. He's simply observing, hands in his pockets, a curious yet protective expression on his face.

"Um…" I clear my throat and tuck my hair behind my ear. "Thank you for walking me home, Leo. Text me when you get back to your mom's place?"

We hold eye contact for a moment. His eyes asking if he should stay. My eyes telling him to please go. Finally, he blinks and nods, grimacing even though I know he's trying to smile.

"Later, Damien."

Damien nods, watching Leo walk away until he disappears around the corner.

"Want to come up for a bit?" I ask.

He nods and follows me inside. Each click and clack of our shoes across the marble and every ding of the elevator fills the elaborate awkward silence. I shift uncomfortably on my feet, sneaking glances at Damien on the opposite corner of the elevator. He's pouty. His brown curly hair is slightly disheveled in that *I'm-an-artist* way, his green eyes droopy, and his lip is puckered and turned down like he's some sad, lost little puppy. Endearing and adorably handsome through rose-colored glasses. But I guess I've taken those off sometime in the last six months.

I don't feel bad for him. I'd much rather disappear from this moment and the conversation we are yet to have.

He wordlessly follows me down the hall to my apartment. I don't have to turn around to see his head is down and his hands are in his pockets. We enter silently. My once warm and happy abode feels twenty degrees colder than it did when Leo was here just hours ago, raiding my cupboards and making me laugh.

"Want to sit?" I ask, gesturing to the couch as I turn on the lamp on the side table.

The sky is inky outside my windows, except for the twinkling of the city lights.

Damien falls into the corner of the couch, staring out at the view outside. "I miss being here."

I nod. "You always liked this place."

"Why didn't we ever move in together?" he asks, elbows on his knees. A painful concern etched on his forehead like I was the one keeping him from committing to me.

I laugh. "Damien, you didn't want to."

"That's not true."

"Okay." My face straightens. "Is 'I don't want to live here' code for something else because those were your exact words to me."

"Well, yeah. Here. I didn't want to live here in this apartment specifically. But that doesn't mean I didn't want to live with you. Genny, I asked you to move to New York with me." He turns to me, taking my hands in his.

I squint at him, questioning his sanity. "Right, and uproot my life here."

"You're always so pessimistic, Genny."

"Am not." I shake my head adamantly.

"You are. You always look at the glass as half empty and I was always trying to make you see it as half full."

I nod slowly. "So, I would be seeing it as half full in New York?"

"Yes!" he answers then shakes his head. "No. Kind of. I mean, it's a big world, babe. I want you to experience it."

My back stiffens. "Number one, don't call me babe. Two, I can still experience the world and live in Seattle. My family is here. I'm not leaving my dad."

"You don't even visit your dad."

The verbal blow hits me in the sternum so hard I almost cough. I blink heavily, rage pulsing in my jaw.

He rubs his hands together, leaning forward, arrogance in his eyes. "Look, I had high hopes for us but in the end, it feels like that was all I was operating on: high hopes."

I laugh incredulously. "Hope always runs dry, doesn't it?"

"I guess it does." He stares at me. His eyes, his smile, his smell, and even his stare used to be the most familiar things to me. But right now, it's like I'm picking a fight with a stranger.

"Why are you even here?"

"I want to have this conversation with you."

75

I huff out a breath. "Which conversation is that?"

"The one where you give me your blessing to go to the wedding."

"You're really trying to drag this out, aren't you?" I say, ignoring the anger tickling my throat and rolling my eyes. "Look, Damien, I told you, I don't care if you go to the wedding."

"You don't?"

"Why should I?" I hold up a hand in the air, presenting my carelessness on a platter. "Your parents are going to be there. Last I heard, so will your sister. Nora was your friend growing up, you're practically cousins. I'm not going to be the kind of person that tells someone they can't go to the biggest celebration of another person's life. It's not fair to you. And it isn't fair to Nora."

"You really won't be mad?" He tilts his head and squints. I can't tell if he's surprised by my answer or my refusal to pick a fight.

He used to love it when I'd pick a fight. The sex was always better after. Hate sex was always our thing. It's fun for a while, but the whiplash between love and hate is exhausting when it lasts for three years.

"I won't be mad," I declare, pressing my palms against the cushions on the couch. "Now, if there isn't anything else you feel the need to discuss—"

"Will you be sucking face with Leo?" he cuts in.

"Sucking face? Jesus, what are you? Thirteen?" I ask, a helpless laugh bubbling out of me.

"Will you?" he reiterates.

"Maybe." I shrug. I'm being petty. Nothing has happened between Leo and me, but I want to torment Damien. Just a little bit.

"Maybe?" His posture doesn't change, and to the naked eye, it would seem he doesn't move at all. But there's a tiny splotch of red on his neck that arises only when Damien is angry and right now, it is damn near maroon.

"Who I do and don't 'suck face' with is not your concern." I run my fingers through my hair pulling it away from my face.

"You said that first, right? When Abigail told me she heard you were seeing Ilene a week after we broke up."

"We were broken up."

"For a week!" I press my fingers between my eyebrows. "Look, I'm not even upset anymore but you could have at least had some decency to not pick the one art dealer that tried to sleep with you on several occasions while we were together."

"You're blowing it out of proportion."

"Then don't worry about me and Leo." My breath hitches as I mention us together. An unnamed unit. An unclaimed love affair. We aren't either of those things but deep down, in the pit of my dreams and desires, we could be. I wouldn't have thought that last week but having him in town this week changes things for me.

"So, you two are a thing."

"None of it is your business."

There is an angry, frustrated pause. The two of us are so silent, the hum of the refrigerator sounds like a scream. My fingers play with the hem of my dress as I stare at Damien. He won't look at me. His forehead is crumbled, his mouth turned down. His eyes are full of sorrow. He is looking everywhere in this apartment for a sign or a reason for him to stay or be right or win. I know he is. That's what he does. It's all he does.

"I think you should go."

He nods, giving me a hopeless sidelong glance. That's when I see it. Damien is heartbroken. The breakup is just now hitting him even though it crashed into me six months ago. As he stands, he reaches for my hand and pulls me up to him.

"Of all the memories we forget as time goes by, please, don't forget that once upon a time, we were good together," he whispers, tucking my hair back from my face.

My eyes swell, because I want to remember that too and I'm starting to forget. I'm starting to wonder what I was doing all those years with him. I'm done crying over Damien. I've been done.

"I was never the one you should have worried about forgetting." I look up at him, my eyes holding his. A familiar embrace landing on my hips as he pulls me closer. I breathe him

77

in as he hugs me. "I'll see you at the wedding," I mutter into his shoulder.

He nods, a pained expression on his face as I walk him to the door.

After I close the door behind him, I flop back on the couch. My eyes are heavy. This was the longest evening after the longest day after a night of too much whiskey.

And it's only Monday.

Thank God I'm only working tomorrow and then taking the rest of the wedding week off.

I yawn, my eyes falling closed. I strip off my dress and throw on a pair of cotton shorts before returning to the kitchen and filling up a glass of ice water. I chug half of it and hear a soft knock on my door.

I stomp over to the door, ready to berate Damien for the extension of his pity party, but I'm at a complete loss for words when I see Leo through the peephole.

I look down at my bra and shorts. *Crap.* "Hang on, I don't have a shirt on!" I yell through the door and then open the coat closet, hoping there's a hoodie. There's not, only a peacoat and three winter jackets. I grab one and wrap it around my body, wanting to open the door to Leo as quickly as possible because I assume something is wrong.

"Everything okay?" I ask, swinging the door open.

He smiles, slow, hesitant. Completely disarming. "Nothing. I just…" his voice trails as his eyes drift over my puffy jacket. "Nice coat."

I look down at my overstuffed ensemble. It covers my shorts in their entirety, so my legs stick out of the bottom. I look ridiculous.

"It was the closest thing I could find," I counter, then exhale sharply. "How did you get up here?"

"I made friends with Ronnie."

I huff out a laugh. His likeability is infuriating. "Of course you did."

"I wanted to give you space to talk with Damien, but I…" he runs a hand through his hair, his eyes searching the ground for words. "I came up as soon as he left."

"Come in," I say, swinging the door wider and gesturing for him to enter. "Did he try to fight you?" I laugh.

He flashes a slow, half-smile. "He's on the verge of tears."

"Really?" I whirl around.

"Sobbing like a baby."

"You're joking."

"Does it matter?"

My heart twists. Point made. It doesn't matter. I don't care about Damien's reaction to our conversation because I'm not responsible for his emotions or his heart.

Leo strides over to the windows, his fingertips nervously rubbing against his legs.

"Are you going to tell me what this is about? Because I get it, Damien can be a douche, but like, he isn't a serial killer. I handled him for three years. There's nothing I can't handle from him now."

Leo cocks his head to the side with a sad smirk. "I'm just tired of us getting interrupted. I'm tired of us not talking. I'm tired of knowing exactly where you are and never seeing you."

"We see each other often enough." It sounds harsher than I intend for it to, and it shows on his expression.

"But we don't actually *see* each other anymore, you know?"

I cross my arms awkwardly over my puffy coat, keeping my distance. "Okay. But we're seeing each other enough this week to make you sick of me so…"

"So, that's just it. I'm not going to be sick of you. We used to be friends, Evie. Actual friends. And I get it if you're still pissed but I want us to be okay again." He steps closer.

I ignore the flutter in my stomach and slap my hand on his forehead to check his temperature. "You feeling okay? The heat getting to you?"

He laughs. "Jesus, let me talk, Evie."

I restrain a laugh in my throat, crossing my arms. He stares for a second, amused. I raise my eyebrows, urging him to get on with it but my heart is hammering. I don't want to do this. It's been eight years but no, I'm still not ready.

While "tolerate" was too harsh of a word, "friends" feels too weak. It feels like a completely watered-down version of what he meant to me. There's a reason my guard is up around him, and simply asking to be friends again isn't going to break it down.

He pauses, staring at me with desperate eyes and a twisted smile.

"We used to…" he begins then stops. His eyes search for the right words to say, and I know he doesn't have any.

The pause is excruciatingly long. I can't take it.

"But we don't anymore." I shrug. "And that's okay. I'm good. We're good."

He bites his lip and steps closer. "You are?"

"Do I not seem okay?" I ask, raising my eyebrows.

A small chuckle escapes him. He seems a little tortured and completely unsure of how to make the point he wants to. Frankly, I'm too tired and I know my exhaustion is going to make me burst into unnecessary tears.

"It's late, Leo. Just…" My eyes fall to the floor. "Let's talk tomorrow. Okay? I really want to go to bed."

He stares a moment, a small smile pulling at his lips.

"I just have some regrets."

I swallow and force a smile. "Well, I'm sure you'll still have them tomorrow."

He scrubs a hand down his face. A small laugh escapes his mouth, and he looks over at me. "You're infuriating."

We have that in common.

I draw back. "Way to convince me to let you stay."

He makes a fist and taps his forehead. I know he's holding back. Words. Emotions. Apologies. But right now, I'm the gatekeeper and I can't handle it.

When he meets my gaze, both our faces explode with unrestrained smiles. It's hard not to smile around each other.

He pulls me into his arms, the gigantic coat and I sink into him. His warmth and smell invade all of my senses, waking up too many suppressed memories. "Will you be at the rehearsal?"

I tilt my head back, still tangled in his arms. I realize this hug is about four and a half heartbeats too long, so I pout to distract myself from the expression on his face as he gazes down at me. "I have to be."

He laughs again and ruffles the top of my head, sending my blonde locks in my face. I rake my fingers through my hair so it's out of my face and ignore the somersault my stomach just did.

"So, I guess I'll see you Wednesday," I say, pulling away.

"Right." He bites his lip and turns to open the door, but he pauses and faces me. "Everything good with Damien?"

I want to laugh. "Um, good in that he didn't kill me."

"Is he going to the wedding?"

I nod slowly.

"Do you want me to fight him?" he asks, cocking a playful eyebrow.

"Stop." I laugh because I can't help it.

"Slit his tires?"

"He doesn't have a car."

"What a loser. Your brother hooked you up with this guy?"

I laugh again, placing my hands on Leo's chest to push him out of my apartment so I can sleep. "He's a city boy."

"Just Ubering his way through life?"

"Leo, I'm tired," I say, exhausted.

"Should we egg his house?" He grins and my mind flashes back on a million memories. Maybe not a million. But damn, we sure did egg houses back in the day. "Like old times?"

I smile, hopeless. Tired. And full of the warm fuzzy feeling I've only ever felt with my brother's best friend. The one person I thought I trusted until I didn't.

The thought shocks me out of the warmth and makes me shiver.

I don't know if it's because I'm tired, but tears fill my eyes. I don't blink, praying they'll dry but one escapes my lashes, crashing down my cheek and landing on my lip.

Leo reaches out and swipes it away with his thumb. The action is tender, thoughtful, and careful. Exactly the Leo I used to know. Until he wasn't tender or thoughtful or careful. He was reckless. He was harsh. He was cruel. I hate that I know that side of him too.

"I want to stay," he whispers. "Let's talk. Finally."

"I'm just so tired," I say, breathing out quickly and

composing myself. "William mentioned something about my dad tonight and then Damien coming over and I just...I just feel extra emotional with the wedding and everything. I really just need to sleep."

He waits. His mind clearly racing to find a way to make me let him stay.

But I don't want to have this conversation now. When I'm tired and overly emotional. When I've just had Damien on my couch. When I'm replaying the conversation I had with William on his balcony.

"Please, Leo," I nearly whisper. "I'm good, I swear."

He nods with so much hesitation I'm afraid he won't listen to me.

But he does and walks out of the apartment, so I can curl up in my bed and fall asleep.

Finally.

9

TUESDAY

I almost called in sick to work.

But everyone at work knows it's wedding week and I knew they wouldn't believe me. Plus, I really don't want to get any side-eye from Jonny in HR. So now, here I sit, staring at my tape dispenser wondering if I should tape my eyelids open.

"Why are you still here? It's nearly lunchtime," my team leader, Cassandra, says behind me. Even though she's technically my supervisor, we stick together like glue as the few token women in this industry.

I spin around in my office chair and look around my cubicle wondering why she thought I wouldn't be here.

She raises her eyebrows expectantly. "You said you'd come in Monday for team meetings and then Tuesday to tie up loose ends before you take the rest of the week off for your brother's wedding. Right? Or am I confusing the dates?"

"No, it's this week. I thought you just expected me to be here the full day," I answer, shaking my head.

She rolls her eyes and crosses her arms. "Okay, rule follower. There is really nothing I need from you today. Go enjoy a crazy week with your family." She turns to walk away then pauses, shifting on her black pumps and dragging her eyes up and down the length of me. "And go take a nap, you look exhausted."

I laugh, pressing my fingers to my eyes. "I am exhausted."

"Well, then get out of here. I mean it," she teases, walking away.

I stare down at my chipped nail polish, remembering the full week ahead. Nail salon tomorrow followed by the rehearsal dinner, luncheon Thursday, and the wedding Friday. And a hundred tasks tacked on in between, I'm sure.

The combination of exhaustion and the conversations of yesterday is sitting heavy on my chest, and work is not the best distraction. At least, I know it's not where I need to be right now. I click out of a few tabs and I sign off, grabbing my purse with a heavy sigh.

Cassandra's right. I need a nap. But first, there's one place I need to go.

I pull up to the old forest green craftsman house in West Seattle. Maple trees line the street, glowing bright green in the heat of the day. I glance at my dashboard. It's ninety-nine degrees, and I know Dad doesn't have air conditioning.

People don't need it in Washington, they say. They are wrong though because on the rare occasion that it's one hundred degrees, the air inside an old house like this feels like humid misery.

I step out of my car and onto the sweltering pavement. My heels click against the cobbled stone pathway lined with pale pink petunias leading to the bright yellow front door. Yellow was my mom's favorite color. The yard is in pristine condition and I make note to email the brothers who own the lawn company taking care of it. Even the rhododendron bushes have already been pruned since last month's bloom. I run my fingers over the rough white railing, dried and chipping in the sun, willing myself to step on the porch. But first, my eyes land on the old basketball hoop weighed down with cinder blocks at the end of the driveway that wraps around the side of the house to the detached garage.

It doesn't take long for a memory to surface.

"That's HORSE!" I exclaimed, just eleven years old.

"How is your sister this good?" Leo asked, brown eyes studying me like a scientific specimen. He was new to the neighborhood. He didn't know me all that well yet.

William laughed. "She learned everything she knows from me."

I shoved my brother on the shoulder. He retaliated by putting me in a headlock and messing up my hair. I slipped out of his hold, and ran straight into Leo. He stumbled backward, tripping on the neighbor's cat Tip-Toe and landing in the bushes.

"Sorry," I muttered, embarrassed I pushed him so hard. We were the same size at this age. He wouldn't hit a growth spurt until sophomore year of high school.

I held out a hand to help him out of the bushes and he laughed, taking my hand. But instead of letting me pull him out, he pulled me in. I was head over heels and covered in the sappy residue from the rhododendron flowers.

William keeled over in laughter.

"I want a rematch," Leo said, trudging out of the bush and picking up the basketball and dribbling to the end of the driveway.

"Famous last words," I taunted, brushing the dirt, leaves, and pollen off my red t-shirt.

Then we played again, and I won. Later Mom brought out Otter Pops and asked why I had so much dirt in my hair.

I can still see Leo's face. A splotchy burn of crimson traveled into his cheeks and he bit his bottom lip so hard I thought he was going to make himself bleed. He was clearly nervous I'd tattle on him and he'd have to go home, but I wasn't a snitch and I didn't want him to go home.

Plus, I beat him eighteen times in HORSE that day. That must have been humiliation enough.

I stare at the old basketball hoop and swallow, realizing I could replay so many days like that in my mind all the way until we were seventeen and eighteen. Just two wannabe grown-ups—mad at each other and mad at the world, burning each other down when no one knew.

Turning back to the front porch, I take each step with intention until I knock on the door. I knock only because I didn't tell Dad I was coming, mostly because I spent the entire twenty-minute drive convincing myself not to turn around.

"Genny Bear, it's you!" my dad exclaims, swinging the front door open. The smile on his face tells me he's just as surprised to see me as I am that I showed up. I haven't been here since just after mom's funeral, with the exception of Thanksgivings and Christmas Eves. Six whole visits in three years. The weight in my stomach sinks.

"Hey Dad," I say, stepping toward him with a small smile.

"I thought you were a Jehovah's Witness there for a second." He chuckles, patting my back.

"Well, I could still tell you about our Lord and Savior if you'd like," I offer and he laughs.

"You hungry? I was making soup."

"Dad, it's a hundred degrees outside," I counter, feeling the drip of sweat on my lower back.

"Not in here." He flashes a wry smile over his shoulder as I enter my childhood home, the cool, crisp air stinging my face.

"You got AC?"

He chuckles, sounding older than my dad used to. Back in high school, everyone thought he was the coolest, with his dark hair clean cut and his attire constantly consisting of tracksuits and basketball shorts. The boys wanted to be him—he was young, fun, and incredibly good at playing and coaching basketball. Now, I'm realizing he's only two out of those three things, marked by his salt and pepper hair and the deep grooves on his face.

"I had it installed last summer. Didn't I tell you? I am too old and worked too damn hard to sweat in my own house."

I smile wide. "Well, in that case, I'd love some soup. Is it tomato?"

"Of course. And grilled cheese made the right way."

My stomach growls. It is the worst meal to have during a heatwave but it's the only meal that tastes like home. Plus, I'm sure Dad sets his thermostat to sixty-two degrees. I shiver, the dampness of my blouse now feeling like an icy washcloth.

The aroma in the kitchen lodges a pit in my chest—tomatoes, fresh basil, and warm butter in a seasoned cast iron skillet. The scent of the meal travels through my brain chemistry straight to my memories, to a time when Mom was alive and life made sense.

Dad sprinkles parmesan on the golden-brown toasted bread and flips it once more, searing the parmesan to the crust. He repeats the action on the other side, then butters two more pieces of Texas toast.

"Pepperjack or sharp cheddar?" he asks.

"Both," I answer, grinning like a child. I don't know the last time he made me this meal, but it was always his go-to.

"Just like your mom."

I press my lips tight together; my entire body feels overwhelmed with emotion.

"You know my doc said it's time to cut back on this kind of stuff," he says.

"Really? You been feeling okay?"

"Ah, healthy as a horse." He shrugs. "Just can't change the year on my birth certificate so naturally, I'm being told to eat more 'heart-healthy' food—whatever that means."

I nod, carefully ignoring the worry in the back of my mind. I don't want to think about my dad getting older. I only have one parent left, and I need him for many more years.

"Well, maybe you should listen to him. Mom will kill you up in heaven if you head there before holding your first grandbaby," I say, masking my worry with a stupid joke that takes hold of my throat and squeezes.

He laughs, then stays quiet. I watch his hands diligently preparing my food. His hands are weathered and covered in age spots. His left hand still houses the gold ring telling the world he belonged to my mom for thirty years. I don't consider my dad old—he'll still hoop with me and William on occasion just like he did when he coached in high school—but the way his hands look at this moment and the mention of his doctor, remind me that he's getting there.

"Here you are. A perfect, artery-clogging sandwich," he says as he slides a bowl of soup and a grilled cheese sandwich in front of me at the kitchen table. "If you told me you were coming, I would have made something nicer." He doesn't mention that I never come here but he doesn't have to.

William was right: I never come home. Not since Mom died.

"This is perfect," I say, ripping the crust off my grilled cheese and dipping it into my soup.

We eat quietly, the sound of our spoons clinking against the ceramic echoing in the kitchen. I take it all in. Every bite of salty soup. Every slow breath my dad takes. The ten-year-old floral potholder hanging from the stove—my mom's favorite. The navy carpet on the cherrywood stairs. The markings etched into the molding of the doorway to the kitchen, reminding the bones of this house of how much we grew up here.

I let out a shaky breath.

"What made you stop by?" Dad asks finally, wiping his salt and pepper beard with a napkin.

I take another bite of my sandwich, delaying my answer.

There are so many reasons…

Because William tattled and said I didn't.

Because the wedding is making me emotional and miss Mom.

Because I'm feeling things for Leo, and I want to go back in time to when I slept in this house and Mom was alive and the world made more sense.

Instead, I give an honest and far too simple answer, "Because I love you."

Dad reaches over and places his hand on my arm. "Love you too, Genny Bear."

My chin quivers and I breathe out through my lips, making them rumble. "I'm sorry I don't come home often."

His eyes fall downcast, and he returns to eating his soup as he nods. "Life doesn't make sense without her, does it?"

I shake my head, tears brimming over my lashes. "I miss her every day."

"Me too, Bear."

"It's hard—" I choke on my sob. "It's hard because I avoid coming here because it hurts. But staying away hurts just as much." I shrug, wiping the tears from under my eyes. "I'm sorry."

"Honey, don't apologize. You lost your mom. It's okay to take some time to grieve. Hell, half of grieving is figuring out how to. Because no matter how many handbooks there are or what your therapist says, it's always going to feel different when you're in the middle of it."

I nod. "Right. I just…" I let out an emotional groan. "I just have a million things I want to ask her still."

Tears well in my dad's green eyes, and he smiles as they fall down his cheeks. "So ask her. Talk to her. Because as much as you have a million things you wanted to ask her, she had a million things she still wanted to tell you." He laughs. "You know your mother never stopped talking."

I laugh through my tears then let out an emotional sigh.

"Until she did," I whisper, offering a sad smile.

"Until she did," he agrees. "But if you pay attention, she'll find a way to answer you."

I nod.

"But you have to pay attention, Genny Bear. Don't get stuck in that head of yours." He smiles knowingly.

I tap my fingers against the old table as I contemplate my dad's words. There's a water ring from my emotional support ice water glass I always had as a kid. A red grape juice stain from when Mom made a 'fancy' dinner for Abigail and me, complete with juice in wine glasses. I tipped mine over. Twice. I smile as my eyes and memories drift over the table. My eyes land on the space next to William's usual spot at the table and land on the chip on the surface. A sharp chunk the size of a dime missing from the top.

Leo did that.

He was working on his science project with William, and I was making personalized hair bows for all the girls to wear on the basketball team. The robot they built malfunctioned, spinning in endless, violent circles, smearing every single name painted on the ribbons. Leo tried to save the rest of them by smacking the robot away in an awkward panic. He smacked it too hard though, and the shoulder of the robot dug into the wood and collapsed with a final mechanical hum.

89

We all stared at the table in shock. Springs, batteries, screws, and metal scraps littered the table and the surface was smeared with red and black paint.

Then we all looked at each other and burst out laughing. It wasn't until we realized Mom might be mad that we panicked and started cleaning frantically.

The paint came out fine.

The chip remained.

Sometimes memories are whispers of what once was. Other times they're scars permanently reminding us that life is messy. Sometimes we can clean it up and no one would ever know it happened. Other times, life leaves a sharp indentation in our mind and causes the memory to come alive at the sight of where it occurred.

We worried Mom would be livid. She wasn't. She rarely got mad at Leo.

In the end, William and Leo decided not to rebuild the psychotic robot and Leo stayed up all night with me and my mom remaking the ribbons. William was going to but he was fired from the task because his handwriting was awful.

"We had some good memories at this table, huh?" Dad asks, disrupting the memory playing in my mind.

I smile. "We did."

He knocks on the wood. "Never getting rid of this guy."

"I'd hope not."

He reaches over and squeezes my hand again. We hold each other's gaze for a moment, wordlessly reminiscing and holding on to the love woven into the walls of this home.

"You finished?" I ask, breaking the moment and standing to collect our dishes.

He nods, leaning back in his chair. "Busy week ahead, huh? Leo said you kids had fun Sunday night."

I huff out through my nose as I head to the sink to begin washing the dishes. "When did you talk to Leo?"

"This morning," he answers matter-of-factly as he stands to grab a dish towel to wipe the crumbs off the table.

"Oh really? What for?" I play nonchalantly, continuing to hand wash the dishes.

"He brings me coffee every time he's in town."

I cough. "Seriously?"

He nods, his mouth turned down. "Well, sometimes a few times, depending on how long he's in town. You know us. We're early risers and he stops in about six-thirty or so."

I watch him diligently wipe the table down, not looking at me, just focusing on his task.

"Oh. You never mentioned it."

He shrugs. "I've always had a soft spot for Leo, ever since he moved up the street and wound up on my team. And then after the divorce…"

I let out a low breath, remembering how destroyed Leo was. He was eighteen and a week away from graduation when his parents split up. His dad ended up moving to California the following year and eventually started a different life with his new wife in Santa Barbara. Last I heard from William, Leo has five and six-year-old half-brothers now. I'm not sure how much they see each other, but I know the transition wasn't easy.

Leo and his dad were incredibly close up until the divorce. It blindsided him even though his parents argued all the time. He probably thought that was just why everyone says marriage is hard. Leo didn't realize it was because his parents were headed to the end. He loved his dad, but he blamed him. And his dad broke his heart.

"That was really hard on him," I say.

My dad nods in agreement. "And you know that kid became family in middle and high school, and I promised Louisa I'd look out for him just as much."

I smile. "I love Louisa. Leo said she'll be at the wedding."

"She wouldn't miss it." Dad smiles.

I nod, pressing my lips together, wanting to ask my dad so many things. "What do you guys talk about?"

"Me and Leo?" My dad turns to the family room and collapses in his overstuffed recliner.

I nod, following him and taking a seat on the blue couch.

"Everything. Work, God, family, relationships." He shrugs. "Life in general."

I pick at a loose string on the sofa. "That's good."

Dad tilts his head down so I have to meet his eyes. "Then why do you look so depressed about it?"

I smile and shrug. "No reason. I'm just glad he has you."

Dad nods as the moment lingers.

"Oh! I almost forgot." He shoots a finger in the air and starts walking toward the staircase. "I was going through the attic and I found your memory box."

"I already went through my memory box," I say, confused.

"Nope, nope." He shakes his head, picking up his pace on the stairs, and I follow. "I found another. I'm trying to get through everything in the attic and, let me tell ya, thirty years in the same house has caused me to wonder if your mom and I were hoarders."

I laugh. "You're not that bad."

"My goal is to only have Christmas ornaments left up there by September."

My chest tightens at the thought of what memories lie up there, covered in dust and mothballs.

"I can help," I offer.

"Good," he says, as we reach the doorway to my childhood bedroom. "Start with taking that box with you."

I stare at it. A green file box sitting on my old striped bedspread. I have no idea what's in it. And I have no idea why it's green.

The doorbell rings. "Be right back," Dad says, turning back down the stairs.

My eyes dance around the room. A wooden shelf with all of my basketball and track trophies. My old vanity with Polaroids taped around the mirror. Mostly pictures of me and Abigail, but a few with my mom, Dad, and William. I pluck the picture of me and my mom and slip it into my pocket.

Stepping into my bedroom is like stepping back in time. I wish I could talk to the girl that used to live here. I wish I could tell her to hold on to every moment. I wish I could tell her life will not turn out how she expects, that people will hurt her when she least expects it. That people will be gone before she even knows it. That there is nothing more precious in life than loving every single person God places in front of her. But mostly, I want to tell her she's going to be okay. Hearts break, yes, but it only means it's because she loved.

I sigh as I get to the box and pop off the lid.

It's not much. Just a few random yearbooks that didn't make it in my last box. My graduation tassels. But then, my heart drops at the sight of the contents beneath the yearbooks. Dozens of movie ticket stubs. Gum wrappers with notes. A journal with one of those stupid, dingy locks on it. And three torn-up pictures of Leo and me.

God, I was so mad at him and no one knew.

When my heart broke in private, it almost hurt more. No one was checking on me. No one knew the details. No one knew the effort it took to not fall apart at the mention of his name.

For a brief moment, I remember the anger so tangibly, I'm there. Curled in bed, crying and staring at my phone, wondering if we'll ever go back to the way we were.

10

TUESDAY

"I'm sleeping at your place tonight," Abigail declares over the Bluetooth speaker in my car as I drive home.

"Why?"

"Don't offend me, child." She lets out a dramatic, evil cackle, then draws in a breath. "Because I want to. And you have AC. And we are headed to the nail salon in the morning anyway, right? I need you to keep me accountable."

"Feeling a little too forced into getting pampered?" I tease.

"Listen, I love having my nails done but getting them done is just..." her voice trails off.

"A waste of time?" I venture because I agree. I hate sitting there for forty-five minutes unable to read or type or scratch my nose.

Plus, my feet are ticklish.

"Yes," she groans. "Am I being a bitch for not wanting to go? I feel a bit like a bitch."

"No, you're just busy."

"Right. Oh! And I need help deciding which dress to wear to the rehearsal dinner. One is floral but I'm worried there's too much white in it for Nora's mother to not throw a tantrum."

I laugh because I know the tortured worry she's feeling. She almost bit off Abigail's head for getting pink highlights in her hair before the wedding. They're beautiful and suit her perfectly, but Mrs. Wellington's face went sour because this is not a "punk rock" wedding. She also nearly had a panic attack when she learned of my tattoo. It runs from my ribcage down my hip to the top of my thigh—a mixture of lilies and orchids. When she realized it isn't visible in my bridesmaid dress she hollered, "Praise Jesus!" and for some reason, I felt so relieved to please her.

She has that pretentious effect with a side of downright scary that causes even the likes of me and Abigail to panic for her approval. At one of Nora's bridal showers, a woman wore a pink dress with white flowers on it and Lorraine gave her side-eye the entire evening. I have overthought every outfit since.

"That reminds me. I need help zipping the dress I'm wearing so you'll have to just get ready here too."

"Well, duh," she responds. "Anyway, I will be at your place around six or so. I'll bring sushi."

I smile. "See you then."

Within minutes of being in my apartment, I pass out on the couch in a dead-to-the-world slumber.

I wake up to a knock on the door and drool on my cheek.

My eyes open before the sensation hits my fingertips and they land on the green box on the glass coffee table. I blink for a few moments, remembering the contents, before forcing myself into a standing position.

I shuffle to the door without checking my appearance in the gold-framed mirror in the living room.

"Bonjour!" Abigail sings, holding up two bags of takeout.

"Sushi is Japanese," I say.

"Consider me cultured," she responds as she glares at me. "And you look like a troll. What happened to you?" Her tone is unforgiving as she waltzes over to the kitchen and sets our sushi on the peninsula.

I reach an instinctive hand to my hair and find a bird's nest on the right side of my head. "I took a nap."

"Ah, must have been a good one since you have a road map on the side of your face." She laughs, tucking a loose blonde and pink lock behind her ear. "You feeling okay?"

I nod, then pull my hair on top of my head in a top knot. "Just a crazy couple of days."

Abigail opens up the takeout container and then pauses, bracing the counter and staring me down. "I talked to you twenty-four hours ago and saw you thirty-six hours ago. There was no mention of crazy. Spill."

I slide the container with the Buddha roll toward me and open my chopsticks as I take a seat on the barstool across from where she stands. "I don't even know where to start."

"Start at the part after we talked yesterday afternoon." She rubs her chopsticks together and raises her eyebrows. "I'm here all night."

I hate that I think of Leo first and dismiss the idea of talking about it with Abigail. She doesn't even know what happened in high school. None of it would make sense.

"Well, William mentioned to me I don't go home anymore," I admit.

"Which is true," she interjects, plopping a piece of nigiri in her mouth. She agrees with William so quickly, the guilt in my gut calcifies.

"Right. And because it's true, I started feeling guilty. Then when Leo walked me home, Damien was waiting outside." I twist my lips and wait for a response.

Abigail starts moving in slow motion—her chewing, her chopsticks diddling with the roll in front of her, her eyebrows as they pull together. All in slow motion.

"Yeah. So, he came up and we talked—"

"Hold on. Rewind." She waves a hand in the air. "Leo walked you home from where?"

"My brother's."

She raises her eyebrows, restraining a smile.

"What? William wanted him to."

"Mmhmm," she says, smug, fixing her eyes on the sushi in

front of us.

"He's staying with his mom fifteen minutes from here," I reason.

"He walked you home two nights in a row?" Abigail asks.

"Leo and I are friends," I reason, keeping my voice even.

She scoffs, her mouth full. "Honey, you and Leo haven't ever been friends. When was the last time you talked to him?"

"We see each other often enough. His best friend is my brother."

"But, like, when's the last time it was just you two?"

I stuff another piece of sushi in my mouth to hide any tells my answer will reveal and shrug. "Doesn't matter. We both went off to college, I moved back to Seattle to work for Boeing, he moved to San Francisco to work as marketing director for the athletic department at UCSF, and now we aren't as close."

Abigail blinks heavily. "I didn't ask for your resumes."

I shrug, suppressing a laugh.

Abigail stares at me a moment, picking at her teeth with her tongue and no doubt searching her brain for something to say. "Alrighty."

I nod as if that settles it. "Now, do you want to hear about my conversation with Damien?"

She leans over the counter. "With all due respect, no. Unless you've kissed and made up because, in that case, I will perform an exorcism tonight." She slaps the counter as punctuation.

I laugh, rubbing my face with my hands. She's right. Damien is old, repetitive news that is only resurfacing because it's wedding week.

"Isn't that your mom's handwriting?" Abigail asks, pointing at the green file box on the coffee table behind me.

I follow her gaze; I forgot I hadn't shoved it in my closet before I fell asleep. "Um, yeah. I went home today and Dad sent it with me."

"Aww, I want to reminisce!" She claps her hands and prances over to the living room.

I groan to disguise my trepidation. I know what's in there and I would prefer she didn't. "I'd rather not."

She purses her lips as she drums her fingers over the lid.

"What shall we do then?"

"Watch corny romantic comedies and snuggle with this sushi on the couch."

Abigail gestures a chef's kiss. "I really wish we weren't cousins so I could marry you."

I snort. "Yeah, it's also unfortunate I'm not gay."

Abigail flops on the couch, remote in hand. I take the box back to my bedroom before I mosey over to the couch to start our romantic comedy marathon armed with sushi and a desire to fall back asleep.

And I do. Forty-five minutes in.

I wake up sometime after the sun has gone down, so I know it's past ten.

Abigail is snoring on the opposite end of the couch. I grab a throw blanket and toss it over her, before discarding the take-out containers and heading to bed.

After washing my face and brushing my hair, I enter my bedroom and spot the box right away. I don't really want to go through it because these aren't "surprise" memories. They're specific. The beginning and the end of something. This isn't memorabilia I'll pull out of the box and think, *remember when?* It's the memorabilia I'll hold in my hands wondering why I could never forget.

But I want to look at one thing: the torn pictures. It's funny that there are only a few because we knew each other forever—ten years of first days of school, holidays, sleepovers, basketball games, and school dances. A decade of memories, but for some reason, these were the only ones I kept.

Just as I scoop them from the box, a fourth picture catches my eye. It isn't torn, and I know I didn't put it in there because it's from my junior year in college. I didn't know this picture from Thanksgiving that year existed. It's a candid shot. I'm holding my plate of apple and pumpkin pie in one hand while the other hand is midway from the plate to my mouth, each finger covered in whipped cream. My head is thrown back in laughter—one of the few moments I laughed that day. Leo is behind me, holding his plate and looking down at me, a restrained smile on his face. I tuned him out that day. I didn't make small talk or play HORSE like old times after dessert. I had my reasons. Reasons that still feel valid to this day.

I drop the photo back in the box and pick up the first torn one I see. Leo and I are back to back, my lips are puckered, and my arms are crossed in a faux tough stance. Leo is mid-eye roll. I almost smile but I know better. Because I remember what happened that night.

In the next torn photo we're on the Ferris wheel at the fair. I'm smiling my biggest, cheesiest smile with my hands propped under my chin as if I'm framing my face. Leo's arm is outstretched in front of us holding the camera. His lips are pouty and he's cocking one eyebrow. A stupid teenage picture. But one where I can still hear the laughter. I can still taste the cotton candy. I can still feel his hand as it brushed my thigh, and I can still hear him as he turned to me and apologized. I flip the torn pieces over and see Leo's faded handwriting: *Scones are better than elephant ears.*

I swallow hard at the memories of the rest of that night.

In the last picture, we're sitting around the bonfire in my parent's backyard. Abigail took this one. I'm smiling, holding up my s'mores. Leo's next to me in basketball shorts and a white t-shirt, biting his bottom lip like he does with a small smirk. He isn't looking at the camera. He's looking at me.

It used to be my favorite picture of us. Secretly, of course. I wouldn't have dared tell William. But now there's a tear right down the center, putting each of us on separate parts of the picture.

The watermark on Leo's shoulder reminds me of how hard I cried when I tore it up. God, I was a dramatic teenager.

My heart and my fingers ache to text him. I want to ask him if he remembers. I want to hear if he has regrets and if that was what he wanted to talk about last night.

I sigh, feeling every bit as dramatic as I did when I was seventeen. I put the pieces of the photographs back in the box and replace the lid.

This was all easier to think about when we didn't see each other. When we didn't speak. Now, my heart is racing knowing I'll see him tomorrow. And the day after that. And the day after that. A mixture of excitement, resentment, and nerves churns inside me until I can no longer identify what I'm actually feeling.

Maybe it's the heat. Maybe it's the wedding festivities. Or maybe it's Leo, and it always has been.

Back Then

PICTURE 1: S'MORES

"Again," Leo said, dribbling toward me.

"No," I laughed out the word.

"Why?" He palmed the basketball in his hand and towered over me. He was very tall at seventeen.

"You are so whiny!" I said, pulling out my hair tie to redo my messy bun. The chilly March air tickled the back of my neck. Our high school seasons were just ending, but HORSE on the driveway was a year-round commitment. Rain or shine—and there was a lot of rain.

"Am not. I want a rematch." He pouted and let his eyes turn into saucers. "Please."

I laughed. "You've wanted a rematch the last six games."

"Never give up, right? Your dad taught us that."

I rolled my eyes. "Oh, please. Dad's not out here, Leo. You don't have to kiss Coach Michaels's ass when he isn't even present."

William cackled. "Seriously, dude. Give it up. Gen has the cleanest shot. Every time."

Leo's mouth dropped and he stepped toward me to

continue the argument but was interrupted by Abigail rolling up in her black Jetta and honking her horn.

She popped out of the car holding a grocery bag. "S'more time!"

"What took so long?" William asked.

"You mean, 'thank you,'" Abigail shot back. "Come help me start the fire."

William grabbed his hoodie off the driveway and followed her through the house to the backyard.

"One more game." Leo stepped toward me, palming the ball. He had a smile on his face he only reserved for me.

"Why can't you let it go tonight? I want a s'more."

"And I want to beat you." He stepped closer, spinning the basketball between two fingers.

I watched him a moment with my arms crossed then finally relented. "Fine."

"Your shot." He tossed me the ball.

I dribbled once then threw it up right from where I was standing next to the front porch.

Swish.

"The fuck?"

"Language. My parents are home," I teased as I retrieved the ball and passed it to him.

He stood where I stood and shot. It hit the backboard then bounced off the rim and out.

"H."

He grunted in frustration as I paced to the top of the driveway to the detached garage, then took the shot. It rolled around the rim and eased its way into the basket.

He followed and made it.

I smiled as I went up again. I stood at the free-throw line marked with blue chalk. *Swish.*

He followed. *Swish.*

"You gave that one to me," he said.

"Just want to make sure you at least don't miss your free throws."

"I don't."

"Bellarmine," I deadpanned, not elaborating but I knew it

pissed him off. I didn't want to say he lost that game, but he missed three free throws in the second and third quarters. They lost the game by two.

He shook his head in irritation. "Never gonna let me live that down."

"Coach Michaels always says there's a reason—"

"They're called free throws. Yeah, yeah," he finished for me as I took another shot.

His turn. He missed.

"H-O."

I found another spot on the driveway.

"Brick!" he yelled.

I made it.

So did he.

Another shot.

He missed.

"H-O-R. Come on, Bishop. Play harder," I said, planting my feet for my next shot.

"You look pretty," he said just as the ball left my fingertips. Airball.

Flustered with warm cheeks, I glared at him. "Really?"

He grinned like he knew exactly what he was doing.

It's just a game. It's just a game, I repeated over and over in my mind. He didn't really think I was pretty. No way.

He took his next shot and made it. I followed with shaky fingers and missed.

"H-O-R. H," he said, then took his next shot. After he made it, I took my turn.

"I had a dream about you," he said just before the ball was released from my fingertips. He was standing close, and his voice vibrated over my skin, making my heart pound erratically. I had never understood when people said their hearts skipped a beat, but I was certain this was it.

It hit the rim. *What the hell, Michaels? Get him out of your head.*

"So, we're playing dirty?" I asked.

"Always."

I laughed. "H-O-R, H-O."

"You shouldn't call yourself names," he teased, and I rolled my eyes.

"You're the only ho I know," I heckled as he shot and missed. "Ha!"

He bounce-passed the ball to me rather aggressively. I turned around and shot backward. The sound of the ball hitting the net made me smile. Leo took his turn. He hated shooting backward and tried to ban this kind of shot last year because he said it was unrealistic. William laughed at him and we vetoed the rule change request.

He shot backward and made it.

"Oh, look at you, getting better and better," I teased, dribbling to the other end. I shot a jump shot from the corner and made it.

He missed.

"H-O-R-S, H-O."

He grunted in frustration.

"Tired?"

His jaw clenched. "Angry."

"Maybe that's your problem, Leo. You're too sensitive," I said, my tone teasing as I continued to dribble down the driveway.

"Oh really?"

"Really." I dribble out to the street. "You let your emotions dictate your game."

"That's called passion," he retorted.

"Not when it doesn't make you play better."

He grumbled an incoherent comeback.

"You fouled out at Bellarmine and Mercer Island."

"So?"

"So?" I dribbled twice. "It wasn't necessary. There was no need. You were pissed because Jaden Barrett kept driving past you because you weren't paying attention to his feet."

"Excuse me?" He cocked an eyebrow.

"Jaden is right-handed," I continued, dribbling again then demonstrated. "Watch. If you're right-handed and you pump fake, your right foot goes back."

"I don't pump fake like that," he said, crossing his arms.

"Well, because you're actually good at it," I responded. "But not all D1 high school players are—like Jaden. And you know nobody shoots like this."

Leo watches my feet. "Well, certainly not you."

I flashed a cocky grin. "Right, someone that actually gets buckets."

He clicked his tongue and waved his hand. "Get out of here…"

I let out a loud, evil cackle. "No, seriously. I heard Kobe talk about it. Come here," I said, pointing at the pavement in front of me.

He assumed the position in front of me, pretending to guard me. I pump faked and drove passed him. He knew what I was going to do and, even still, instinct told him I was shooting. "Quit falling for it. Watch my feet."

This time I went up for a real shot and he stood back and watched my feet, nodding as I made it.

Leo collected the ball from under the hoop, grinning wide. "I love hearing you talk about basketball," he commented then shrugged as he dribbled. "Well, I think I just love hearing you talk."

I swallowed at the praise but recovered with, "Are you complimenting me? Leo, I'm blushing."

"You should be. I'm paying attention to you," he said and shot the ball from the same position. I didn't watch it go in. I watched his lips spread into a slow smile as he looked at me.

I cleared my throat, glancing away. "Wow. If you take this coachability to the court, maybe you won't foul out as much," I taunted.

"You talk so much shit about me fouling out all the time, but didn't you get a technical against Bellarmine?" he asks, grabbing the ball.

I glared at him. "You know how the refs are at prep schools."

He grinned, passing me the ball. I caught it at my chest.

"That was passion," I added.

"Whatever, Evie."

"You, on the other hand," I emphasized, "Let your emotions affect your game and you know better. You just need to focus… and watch their feet."

I shot again. Leo's eyes followed the arc of my shot. I made it.

He collected the ball from under the hoop and then dribbled to my place on the driveway.

"I hear you," he said, making an identical shot.

"You are the most talented D1 player I know. I just want you to remember it when you make stupid mistakes."

"Are you complimenting me?" he asked with quizzical eyes.

"Yeah," I confessed. "I pay attention to you, too."

He smiled, and I turned, dribbling toward the street. I heard him half-scoff, half-laugh behind me.

"Where are you going?" he asked, a mixture of annoyance and amusement in his tone.

"I've been working on this shot. It's half-court range," I say, bouncing it twice and continuing my lecture. "Quit beating yourself up when you screw up. It makes you lose your focus."

"That's not why I lose my focus," he said as I released the ball from my fingertips from the middle of the street.

I made it, but I didn't celebrate because I was far too distracted by how he was looking at me. His gaze was intense— a serious expression covering his features. It was the way he said the words and the way his face changed as he said them. I knew he was talking about me.

I swallowed. "What do you mean?"

He buried his gaze in the concrete and shook his head. "Nothing."

"Okay," I said as the ball rolled down the driveway to where we stood in the street. I handed the ball to him and his fingers brushed mine. I didn't let go of the ball and he didn't take it. We just stared for a moment. "Am I… distracting?"

He reached out with his fingers and brushed a loose strand of hair out of my face. "Very."

I smiled, feeling thankful for the grayish darkness of the evening so he couldn't see me blush.

He broke our gaze and took the shot. He made it.

"From downtown? Are you freaking kidding me?" I shrieked. "I've been working on that for weeks."

He laughed. "I'm actually pretty good at basketball, Evie."

"I'm actually pretty good at basketball, Evie," I mimicked him as I retrieved the ball, scooping it off the driveway and tossing it up to basket—half-granny shot, half-dumb luck.

Swish.

"Aw, man, for real?" Leo threw up his hands.

"For real." I set the ball on the ground.

He imitated the shot and missed.

I laughed. "All right, loser, that's HORSE. Time to roast marshmallows."

"Rematch."

"No, I'm hungry."

"Please."

I kept walking but heard him begging behind me; I could practically see his hands pleading. "Evie…"

"No, you suck. Get over it."

"Hey!" he said, shoving me lightly in the shoulder. Well, lightly for him. Seventeen was the year he grew eight inches and gained twenty pounds of muscle. I stumbled up the steps, skinning my knee on the wood. "Oh, shoot, sorry, Evie. I didn't mean—"

He was crouching at my feet, hovering over me with this protectiveness he always had. Only this time, when he touched my leg, goosebumps rose on my skin.

"It's fine," I said. "I'm good."

"You sure?" he asked. He was more worried than necessary and a part of me wondered if he was coddling simply so he could touch my leg. And an even bigger part of me wanted to milk the moment so he would keep touching my leg. But I knew better. Abigail and William were inside, and so were my parents. If anyone started suspecting anything, all of this would change. Leo and I both knew that.

"Sure, it's fine. I'll just press charges for assault but it's fine," I said.

He peered at me and my tormenting nature. I glared back.

Then, because we could only hold it for a few seconds, I grinned a contagious grin that spread over his lips as well, and we burst out laughing.

"Hey, do me a favor?" he asked, catching my elbow as I turned to get up.

"Maybe..." I watched his facial expression trying to guess what his inquisition was.

"Tell Will I won."

I scoffed out a laugh and crossed my arms. "No way," I answered, shaking my head. Leo was making me feel things, but not enough to fake defeat.

"Please," he begged with praying hands and a pouty lip. "Just this once."

I pretended to think for a moment, but really, I just wanted to look at him. The sharpness of his jaw, the softness of his lips, the familiarity in his eyes. It was one of the first times I truly realized the attractiveness that everyone spoke of at school. Or rather, it was the first time I realized I was becoming attracted to him too. My heart fluttered, and I cleared my throat to stop it. "Fine," I relented.

"Really?"

"Really," I said plainly.

He held out his pinky. "Swear on it."

I wrapped my pinky around his, ignoring the electricity that sparked at our touch. So did he. I wondered if it was just static or if it was the spark people often spoke of when they had feelings for someone else.

"I swear," I said, and he grinned, victory covering his features. Then I held up my crossed fingers on my other hand from behind my back. "Sike!"

His jaw dropped. "You're a liar."

I cackled at the preposterousness. "Keep telling yourself that." Then I hopped up and opened the yellow front door, yelling, "William, your friend is a sore loser and pushed me down because he sucks at basketball!"

"What?" William asked, holding a can of soda as he was just about to make his way back outside to where my dad was starting the fire with Abigail.

Leo scoffed. "Will, your sister is a liar!"

"You two..." my mom said from the kitchen with a smirk and shake of her head.

"I'm bleeding, Leo!"

"You're a clutz!"

"Temper, temper!"

We continued to roast each other until we had warm marshmallows and chocolate in our mouths. At some point, I smiled at the camera, Leo smiled at me, and Abigail took the picture.

11

WEDNESDAY

"So, Genevieve, somebody texted me with the strangest question just now," Nora says, both her hands under the blue light next to her chair while her feet soak in the tub of water at her feet.

"Oh, really," I say, showing my nail tech what color I've chosen. Nude. It'll go perfectly with my dress. We're all wearing a mix of nude, champagne, and blush pink. Muted yet feminine. Mine is a one-shoulder chiffon gown fitted through the waist and flowy through the bottom.

"Leo wanted to know what your favorite flower is." She restrains a twisted smile.

My cheeks instantly burn and my heart pounds. "Why?" I stammer out the question.

She shrugs. "I thought maybe you'd know…"

I shake my head and meet Abigail's gaze.

"What'd you tell him?" Abigail asks.

"Orchids. Like your mom," Nora says with a sympathetic smile in my direction.

It's true. I love orchids, just like my mom. But that's not the only reason. They're beautiful, yes, but I love them because they're hard to keep alive. And like anything in this world worth cherishing, they need to be cared for, understood, and attended to. They can't be ignored or discarded. They need the right amount of sun and water, otherwise, they'll wither away one petal at a time.

"Which one is Leo again?" Taite asks, walking back from washing her hands in the sink.

"Tall, dark eyes, dark hair, well dressed," Cora answers, rubbing her belly.

Taite nods, her eyes searching her memory.

"Not the one that had eyes for you," April adds and Taite blushes.

"No one had eyes for me," she lies, and we all laugh.

"Terrence doesn't play it cool when he sees someone he wants," Nora says. "I love him, but don't expect anything beyond this weekend. He's a bachelor for life. Sorry, Gen."

I scrunch my nose, irritated. "I do not want Terrence. Have fun, Taite."

She laughs.

"Terrence is William's glow-up friend," I add.

Abigail snorts.

"What do you mean?" Taite asks.

Nora leans over to Taite's chair. "She means Terrence was kind of nerdy when he was William's roommate in college."

"I thought he roomed with Leo," April says.

"After freshman year, when they moved off campus."

"Ahh." April nods, then adjusts her massage chair with the remote so she's shimmying and her boobs are jiggling, making her laugh.

"Anyway, Terrence was so shy and quiet and about four inches shorter," Nora says.

Taite's jaw drops.

I laugh. "It's true. He went through his final stage of puberty at nineteen."

"Then he got Lasik that revealed his baby blues, and made all the ladies swoon," Abigail says.

"Really?" Taite twists her face. "I would have liked to see

him in glasses."

"It was very *She's All That*," Abigail jokes, rolling her eyes. "Like, wow, he's hot now that he's four inches taller and took off his glasses."

I laugh through my nose, then meet Taite's gaze. "But Terrence is cool. He's a good one. Even if he can't commit."

Taite grabs her phone and swipes something away. "Whatever. I live in Brooklyn. I don't need commitment, just a good time."

"Here, here," Abigail says, raising her champagne to toast. "Now, if you know any single women you'd like me to meet, let me know."

April studies her. "I might know someone." She smiles and looks away like she's dreaming up the whole setup. "I'll let you know."

Abigail leans forward, intrigue in her eyes. "Really?"

April gives a petite shrug. "Maybe."

"So, is my wedding just going to turn into this party where everyone pairs off by the end of the night?" Nora asks, downing the rest of her champagne.

"Isn't that what you want?" I tease, remembering her insinuations from two nights ago.

"Ugh, but you better not," Abigail groans. "I'm not letting Damien near you."

"We don't need to worry about Damien," I say, then immediately giggle as my nail tech scrubs my heel, and my involuntary kick nearly kicks her in the face. My jaw drops in mortification. "Sorry, I'm really ticklish."

My nail tech smiles and puts my half-scrubbed foot back in the hot tub.

"Thank you, by the way," Nora says in a more hushed tone, leaning toward me. "For being cool about Damien coming."

I bite my lip and smile. "Honestly. It's fine. We're grown-ups. We broke up six months ago."

"I just know how hard the breakup has been…"

"Right, but…" I think for a moment. "I think it's been hard because we were together for so long, not because we didn't see the end coming."

Nora tilts her head, pondering.

"I mean, we cared about each other but never enough to change anything about ourselves. We wouldn't even make adjustments. Isn't love about sacrifice?"

She flashes a small smile and squeezes my arm. "Someone is going to come along and change his whole world for you one day. I just know it."

I stare at her with playful despondence. "Don't count on it."

Abigail hobbles over to us, her nails done and her feet in bright pink flip-flops.

"I like that color," I comment on the blush pink shade she chose.

"Me too," she says, admiring her nails. "I think it'll match my dress perfectly. Thank you, by the way, for not making us wear ugly dresses." She winks at Nora.

"My wedding will be a lot of things but never ugly." Nora laughs, long and melodic.

As the techs all finish our nails and we finish our champagne, my mind keeps wandering back to what Nora said about a text from Leo asking what my favorite flower is.

I swear, if I get back to my apartment to change for the rehearsal and there's an orchid with a note saying, "Let's talk," I will cringe.

But still, there's this small part of myself that still feels seventeen, hoping it means something.

12

WEDNESDAY

It's funny that after centuries of the same ceremony, we still feel the need to practice it.

All of it is pretty standard, and even with an uptight bride's side of the family, Nora and William's rehearsal went off without a hitch. We practiced walking to the music. Nora held a false bouquet made from the bows from her Whiskey in a Teacup shower. They kissed. We cheered. We all got really sweaty.

The glass museum where the wedding is located has air conditioning, of course, but where the ceremony is located is made of glass. It's called the Glasshouse because that is exactly what it is. Glass walls that curve to a cathedral-like ceiling and orange, red, and yellow blown glass flowers hang from the ceiling. It's magnificent all on its own, but for a wedding it is magical.

During a heatwave, however, it is hotter than Satan's armpits no matter how hard the AC roars.

Afterward, we migrate to one of my favorite Italian spots in Seattle: The Pink Door.

"The funny thing about The Pink Door is the door isn't pink," Leo whispers as we enter the restaurant from the cobblestone alleyway. We make our way through the front of the restaurant, past the stage with a local band playing bluesy classics to the back where the windows open to a spectacular view of the Great Wheel and the crisp, sparkling water of the Puget Sound.

"Yes, it is," I argue, following the host to the back of the restaurant where they've set up four long tables for the wedding party and our closest relatives.

The tables are covered in white linen tablecloths with blush-colored peonies and other summer blooms. White long-stem candles and antique chandeliers wrapped in flowers give the room a warm glow, while the setting sun is shooting light against the brick walls of the place. It is charming and beautiful. Elegant and chic.

"No, it's not. It's salmon."

I snort. "You're such a guy." I look at his light pink button-up. "Your shirt is pink."

"Salmon," he retorts.

I roll my eyes. "You're an infant."

"It is." He examines his shirt like he's checking.

"You are colorblind."

"Am not."

"Sit down, Leonardo, and order some food. You get whiny when you're hungry."

He drags a hand down his face and laughs, taking his place across from me on the long stretch of white linen. The wedding party migrates to one side while the parents and relatives situate themselves on the other. Everyone is flushed from the heat of the day and relieved to be sitting inside an air-conditioned restaurant.

"I'm just thankful to be out of that oven," William says, sitting down next to Leo.

"Hopefully, it won't be as hot Friday," Nora says, crossing her fingers.

"It will be wonderful no matter the weather," I confirm with a smile.

The server comes with bottles of crisp white wine and fills glasses, taking each of our orders. Antipasti are eaten. Wine is refilled. Meals are delivered. Toasts are made, and the table hums with chatter and excitement.

"Now Ms. Genevieve, on behalf of Damien's mother and myself—" Mrs. Lorraine Wellington giggles, a gushing hand to her chest, "I just want to thank you for being the bigger person and telling Damien he can come to the wedding, despite, well… everything."

Mr. Wellington shoots her a look I couldn't quite read, but I ignore it.

I swallow my bite of *Penne al Fumo* and press a white napkin to my lips, nodding. "I wouldn't want to keep him from one of his childhood best friend's most important days."

She clutches the air and holds it to her chest, and I can tell she wants to touch me but she's too far away. Five people too far away and now, the entire wedding party is staring at me after oversharing. I focus on my pasta and eggplant and take another bite.

"Who's Damien again?" Taite asks. She may be Nora's best friend, but she never remembers anyone in her life.

"Genevieve's ex," April says, then mutters. "Bad breakup. Broke up with her right before Christmas."

Terrence winces and Leo shoots him a look. Clearly, everyone but Taite knows the rise and fall of Damien and Genevieve, and they all have their opinions.

"Then why is he coming?" Taite asks.

"Exactly my question," Leo says so quietly, I'm sure I'm the only one at the table that heard it. I lean closer to the table to say something to Leo across from me, but I'm cut off by Nora.

"He's the kid I grew up with. You must remember. He was short until he wasn't and annoying until he…well, wasn't."

Taite stares at Nora with blank eyes.

"Frogs," Nora adds, eyebrows raised.

Recollection flashes over Taite's face, and she laughs so loud she covers her face with her napkin until she can take a breath. She sighs and rakes her fingers through her long reddish-brown hair. "Ugh, I hated that kid."

Leo chirps out a laugh. "Me too."

I tilt my head and shoot him a look. He smirks, holding eye contact.

"He used to put frogs down our shirts!" Taite exclaims leaning into Leo, a hand on his arm. He laughs and so does she. Jealousy prickles at my neck, and I blink my eyes away.

"Terrible," he says.

Nora laughs. "But he wasn't as bad once he went through puberty."

"Exactly," Taite agrees, grabbing her glass of wine. "He had this short guy complex until he didn't."

Everyone within earshot laughs. The comment even elicits a smile out of me, but my eyes are drawn back to Leo. He's saying something to Taite and she's laughing, then she rolls her eyes and nods. My blood heats in my veins, and I want to ask what he just said, but instinct reminds me to pretend as if I don't care.

"Truly, Genevieve, I don't know if I would be as cool about it if I were you," Nora says, drawing my attention away from Leo.

I cinch my shoulders back, standing taller, then I shrug with one shoulder. "It really is fine," I say but I am so tired of it coming up in every discussion. I look up from my plate. Leo is no longer whispering with Taite but looking straight at me.

"Well, I for one, am proud of you," William adds, "considering how much moping around you've been doing."

Blood rushes to my ears and I'm thankful I wore my hair down in long blonde waves. "I have not."

"You have," William argues and Nora cringes, trying to disguise it with a bite of her risotto.

I wave my napkin like the white flag that it is. "Leave me alone. This has been a hard breakup and he happens to be an ex that won't go away because of...connections." I wave a hand at the table full of his family friends.

It's an honest admission, reminding me how thankful I am to actually be getting over him and seeing the light at the end of this long and torturous breakup tunnel.

"No," William says, holding up a finger. "There was that one guy in high school you said went to Seattle Lutheran or something, but you wouldn't tell me his name. Which is probably a good thing because you know Leo and I would have loved to roll up on him."

My eyes practically somersault off my face. "Tough guys," I mutter.

"Seriously," William continues. "You were so depressed for the whole summer, sitting in your room cranking Kelly Clarkson's *Since U Been Gone* and then following it with *All Too Well* by Taylor Swift." William grins wide and teasing.

I want to murder him. But instead, I laugh into my wine, and say, "I was just young," while Terrence, Jake, and Marcus start singing the bridge.

"The dude took your v-card and broke up with you," he says with a hint of disgust.

"Whoa!" Abigail laughs out.

Leo squints across the table, anger flashing briefly. I ignore him and glare at William. This isn't dinner conversation but clearly, everyone has had enough wine to think it's perfectly fine to embarrass me over fifty-dollar pasta.

"Everything is a big deal when you're seventeen," I reason, praying my cheeks aren't as deep scarlet as they feel.

"I think losing your virginity is a big deal," Nora chimes in.

I wave off Nora. "This isn't rehearsal dinner conversation. All's well that ends well," I say.

I look at Leo. I can't help it. He's zeroed in on this conversation even as everyone else returns to their own. His shoulders are pinched back. His grip is tightening around his fork. And my embarrassment continues to warm my cheeks.

We hold the stare for only a few moments without saying anything, but I hope my eyes relay the message: *I'm okay. Don't worry.*

I break the trance and reach for my wine, jumping slightly as I feel the toe of a shoe rub against my ankle.

"You all right?" Abigail leans over and asks.

"Hiccup," I answer quickly, "Excuse me." I attempt to make eye contact with Leo but he's saying something quickly to Nora. He gives me a sidelong glance and flashes an apologetic smile.

YOU *First* | CAITLIN MOSS

It could have been an accident. But the prolonged glide up my ankle to mid-calf tells me it wasn't. Goosebumps rise on my flesh and I hate that he still elicits this reaction out of me.

"How the hell are you cold?" Abigail asks with a laugh, staring at the goosebumps on my arm.

"My wine is cold," I lie, pretending to shiver.

Leo fully grins, clearly satisfied with himself. I want to wring his neck. He stops the server and asks for something. Moments later, the server hands him a pen. He pulls out a scrap of paper and writes something.

I ignore him. Or try to.

Instead, I turn to John sitting next to me. He's the quietest of them all and married to pregnant Cora. "Excited for the baby?" I ask.

"I am," he begins, but Cora jumps in.

"But I swear this heat is going to put me in labor early," she says, holding her glass of ice water up to her head.

John smiles and opens his mouth to speak again, but Nora does first. "I told you, Cora, if you feel sick at all during the ceremony, I want you to sit down, okay? We don't need that baby coming too early."

Cora laughs.

"When are you due?"

"Next month," she says with a breath.

I meet eyes with John. His eyes are full of fear and worry and love. I give his arm a quick squeeze, "It's going to be great," I say as Leo tosses the balled-up scrap of paper at me. It hits me on the nose.

"What the hell, Leonardo?" I grab the paper from my lap, realizing it's not a scrap of paper. It's a gum wrapper. I ignore my heart palpitations and open it.

I gave you goosebumps.
H-O-R, H-O-R

I scoff at the implication of his arrogance, leaning back in my chair and staring Leo down. But as hard as I'm trying not to smile, the feat is impossible. I bite my lip but my smile cuts

119

through, and Leo starts laughing.

"What just happened?" Cora asks, glancing between us. John shrugs, never one to comment.

"Nothing," I say. "Leonardo just thinks he's funny."

"I am funny," he says with mock offense.

"Ish," I reply, not hiding an ounce of sarcasm.

"That's a true statement, Leo," Abigail laughs, then turns back to April on the other side of her. She's been engrossed in conversation with her for most of dinner.

Leo flashes a small, taunting smile at me. I hate that he knows exactly what he's doing to me. Despite myself and my knowledge of being played like a violin, I laugh and roll my eyes but my gaze lands right back on him.

You think I'm funny, he mouths.

Ish, I mouth back.

Then I excuse myself to the other end of the table to check on my Dad and be polite to the Wellingtons. My mental reason is manners. My true reason is so I don't fall heart over heels in front of everyone.

After another thirty minutes of half-tipsy conversation, Dad signs the check and we file out of the restaurant.

"Genevieve, will you be helping with the luncheon tomorrow?" Lorraine asks, looping her arm in mine, her Chanel perfume wafts toward my nose.

I'm slightly taken aback. "Did I need to help?"

"Oh, dear, we need all the help we can get," Lorraine says then leans in more quietly. "I love Taite, but she is not fulfilling her duties as Maid of Honor. Honestly, Nora should have chosen you for the role."

"Oh, Lorraine, no need. I'm happy to help without the title." I squeeze her hand and offer a polite smile. "What time do you need me there?"

"Would eleven work?" she asks, though I know she's telling me. "The luncheon is at noon and should last until two, which gives all of us plenty of time for the wedding party to get to the hotel for the evening."

I nod, smile, and bid her adieu.

The air is thick and sweet as we step out of the restaurant

and into Post Alley. Aunt Bernie and Aunt Wilma walk with the Wellingtons, my dad, Cora, and John down the cobbled street to the lot near the market after I hug them goodbye. Everyone else shuffles into their respective Ubers that pulled up along Virginia Street. April and Abigail nonchalantly share an Uber, and I smile to myself.

"That would be a cute couple, yeah?" Nora nudges me. I raise my eyebrows.

"I make no comment on anyone's love life unless they tell me," I say, and Nora laughs.

"Love you," she says in my hair, squeezing me tight. "See you tomorrow."

"Of course," I say, then hug my brother.

"Where's your ride?" he asks.

I raise my brows. "So you're worried about how I'm getting home but not concerned about telling a table of friends about how I lost my virginity?"

William blanches. "Sorry," he breathes, clearly embarrassed. "It slipped?"

"That's a stupid question," I say.

He smiles apologetically. "I don't know why I said that. I'm sorry."

I nod, letting it go. "I forgive you." Because I do. My brother is and will always be some level of annoying but I do love him.

"So your ride is...?" he questions.

"Coming," I say, though I haven't pulled up the app yet. But honestly, I live four blocks away. I'm walking. "See you both tomorrow."

He grins with the excitement of Christmas morning. "Two days."

Nora squeals. "Two days!"

I laugh and wave as they drive away. My heels shift in the ridge of the cobbled street and I decide to pull up the app on my phone.

"Can I walk you home?" Leo asks, stepping toward me, hands in his pockets. His Rolex is poking out and his sleeves are rolled up revealing the bottom of his three-quarters sleeve tattoo.

I should call an Uber. I should get home, take a long bath, rest my feet, and drink lots of water. It was one-hundred-and-five degrees today. Instead, I say…

"Yes, please."

He smiles, holding out his arm to me and I take it, stepping alongside him. "Though I must warn you, my heels are very high." I gesture to my strappy nude heels.

"Will you be walking extra slow?" he asks.

"As molasses," I confirm. "You might even have to carry me."

He grins wider but doesn't say anything. He just chews on that damn bottom lip.

We continue to walk and a sharp pain shoots up the balls of my feet. I wobble and tug on his arm. He grabs hold of my waist and steadies me.

"Sorry," I mutter, and he stops walking.

"Saddle up, Evie," he says, crouching down in front of me so I can jump on his back.

I scoff out a laugh. "I'm wearing a dress."

"I won't look."

I cross my arms, peering at him with a smile on my face. I contemplate my short champagne-colored dress and the teeny tiny thong I'm wearing underneath.

He throws a smile over his shoulder. "Relax, Genevieve, and say thank you. You're walking like a baby deer."

I glare at him and jump on his back with a humph. "Thank you, *Leonardo*," I mutter in his ear. My lips brush against his ear and he tightens his grip on my thighs. I know it's all unintentional, but it all makes me want to come undone.

With my chest pressed against his back and his arms under my thighs holding my dress down, my feet feel immediate relief. But the scent of his cologne on his neck is making my heart flutter. I wonder if he can feel each beat with my chest pressed against his back.

"You bringing anyone to the wedding?" he asks.

"No, you?" I say softly in his ear.

He shakes his head.

"Really? No, cookie-cutter girlfriend this time?" I tease, trying to ease him out of his headspace.

"What's that mean?"

"It means you've dated the same type of girl over and over in all the years I've known you."

He tilts his head, shooting a look at me over his shoulder. "What? Like I have a type?"

"Kind of," I answer, thinking of all the girls I've known about.

He laughs, skeptical. "All right. Then tell me: what's my type?"

I stare at him, suddenly at a loss for what to say. I embellished. Leo doesn't really have a type. He's dated short girls, tall girls, girls of different races, and girls with different professions. There isn't a hair color or look that he's ever favored from what I recall. The only common denominator is that he's always been half-committed.

"Girls that deserve more than what you've given them," I breathe out the statement, immediately wanting to eat my words.

"Really?" he asks. His voice shows no emotion, but he's picked up his walking pace. I'm pretty sure I offended him and he's on a mission for clarity.

"You've always had one foot out the door." I shrug against his back. "At least, from what William told me."

He fixes his eyes in front of him and hikes me up on his back. The warmth between our bodies in the heat of the night grows to a scorching level. Sweat drips between my breasts and I'm certain when I pull away there will be a wet spot on Leo's back.

We're quiet for several painful minutes before the tension dissipates and the silence is comforting again. I curl my hand tighter around his bicep to get his attention before I speak.

"You can put me down. We're almost to my apartment."

He stops, and I slide down his back, careful to keep my dress down. There's a line of sweat down the back of his shirt, deepening the color of pink. He grabs the front of his button-up and shakes the fabric away from his chest.

I look down and laugh. "Oh my gosh, so much boob sweat."

He chuckles and chews on his lip, not commenting but his gaze slides down my body before we start walking again.

"Taylor Swift's *All Too Well*, huh?" he asks as we draw closer to my apartment building, and I laugh.

"Guilty as charged." I flash an unabashed smile.

"The fun-sized version?"

"Unfortunately, that's all we had back then." I laugh, tucking my hair behind my ear.

He nods, smiling, clearly thinking. "But Kelly Clarkson. That threw me a bit…"

"Why? I love Kelly Clarkson. Her breakup songs are classic."

He jerks his head to look down at me. "*Since U Been Gone,* though?"

"Hey, I had to get over you at some point," I laugh, pulling my windblown hair from my sweaty neck. It was a loaded thing to say. I know it was. I said it on purpose.

The pause lengthens until he speaks.

"*Half A Heart.*"

"What?" I turn up my gaze to meet his.

"*Half A Heart,*" he repeats. "That's the song I played on repeat after."

I laugh. "You hated One Direction."

He slows his steps until he comes to a full stop and looks at me with an expression tender enough to make me fear what he's about to say.

"But you didn't."

We freeze. The cars keep whizzing by, the streetlights change from yellow to red to green, the low hum of the city continues to buzz all around us, but Leo and I stay completely still. We just hold onto each other with our stare. Unbreakable eye contact that is tearing open memories like unexpected packages arriving on my doorstep.

I breathe out, an uncertain smile touching my lips. I have no response.

Leo's expression is a mix of far too many things.

Frustration. Anger. Regret. Admiration.

"I'm sorry I freaked out," he says finally.

I nod, pressing my lips together in a small smile. "It's okay. It was a long time ago."

He steps closer, taking my wrists and holding them against his chest. His skin is pure heat under his button-up. "It doesn't matter if it was a long time ago, I shouldn't have..." he loses his train of thought. "I wish it all played out differently. And I think about it all the time."

"And you're just now apologizing?" I deflect and laugh. His dark eyes fall to the pavement and I realize he's serious. "Look, Leo. Your parents had just split up."

"In the most unoriginal way," he adds.

"True. But life is usually pretty unoriginal," I say. "And you were only eighteen. Life is confusing."

"Right," he agrees. "But you... you made sense."

The tension in my shoulders releases with a laugh of disbelief. "I feel like I just confused you more than anything."

"No, you scared me," he confesses. "Still do."

I stay silent, trying to remain expressionless even though his words are reminding me of every bruise he inflicted on my heart.

"And back then the idea of you and me seemed impossible and now it seems..." He laces his fingers behind his head and steps away from me.

"More impossible?" I offer.

He drops his hands and laughs. "See? Just like that. Just one comment makes me want to apologize to you in a million more ways. I shouldn't have done what I did, Evie. I shouldn't have...we should have never had sex."

I jerk back, swallowing my humiliation. "You've already told me how much you regret it. No need to beat a dead horse," I breathe, the pit in my stomach sinking. My eyes look all around me. The light post. The crosswalk. The sidewalk. Then land on the door to my apartment building.

"No," he says, taking my shoulders so I have to face him. "No, no. That's not what I mean. But I took your virginity, Evie."

I scoff with an uncomfortable smile. "I'm aware."

His hands cup my face and he stares at me with tender eyes, his gaze carefully holding mine as if I might break. "I wish I could have given you a better first time."

I laugh, remembering the torn picture of us on the Ferris wheel in my apartment. A moment in time that turned into an unforgettable night. I tilt my head, making my cheek rest in the palm of his hand. "It's okay, Leo. It was a good first time."

"It was?" he questions with so much concern in his eyes that I laugh.

"It was," I confirm with a smile and my hands on his chest. "You were sweet and gentle. We may have had no business doing it but… I'm not worried about it, so you don't need to be."

"So…good?" he asks.

I laugh again. "Good."

"Really?" His stupid ego.

"Really."

He cocks an eyebrow. "I've gotten better."

I smack his chest but I can't withhold the laugh that bubbles out of me. I step away from him and then turn around with my arms crossed. I tilt my head and smile at the first boy to have my heart.

And the first one to truly break it.

"Well, the days and weeks and years that have followed, I've wanted to skin you alive but—"

"Oof. You are choosing violence today," he says, a smile pulling at the right side of his mouth.

I let out a breath of a laugh, contemplating. Against my better judgment and a hundred reasons why not, I let the words spill from my lips.

"Do you want to come inside?" I ask.

There's a flash of desire in his eyes before he answers. It terrifies me as much as it makes goosebumps rise on my skin.

"Yes," he says.

And I lead him through the glass doors.

Back Then

PICTURE 2: FERRIS WHEEL

It had been a year of gum wrapper notes and pretending to hate each other for the sake of my brother. I played the part well, rolling my eyes at him when he was at the house and groaning when William said he was joining us at the spring fair.

Leo tripped me as soon as we walked through the Blue Gate entrance to the state fair. I stumbled forward and Abigail grabbed the back of my sweatshirt to steady me.

"Whoa, too much tequila, Gen?" she asked, but I paid no attention.

"Leo, what the hell?" I stalked toward him, finger in the air, ready to berate him.

William stepped between us. "Stop, Gen. It was an accident."

My eyes shot like daggers from my brother to Leo. I narrowed in on him as he bit back a smile. "Leo's whole life is an accident. I bet your parents didn't even plan to have you," I muttered, turning back to the ticket booth stand. "And, no, I haven't had too much to drink. I had two drinks before we walked over from the lot."

We slipped some tequila from Dad's liquor cabinet and poured it into a plastic water bottle, stashing it under the backseat. Then when we got to the parking lot of the fair, we passed around the bottle. Through fits of giggles and coughing, we probably had the equivalent of two shots. But we were all seventeen or eighteen and felt like the coolest rebels as we bought our Dizzy Passes to ride endless fair rides as the sun set.

"What first?" William asked, adjusting his bracelet.

"Classic Coaster," Leo and I said in unison. We exchanged a look, but I crossed my arms and gave him my cold shoulder as if he irritated me.

"Nice choice, Michaels," Abigail said, grabbing my hand and leading us to the giant wooden roller coaster.

We waited in line for an hour before pairing off and entering the ride cars.

"Hey, it's McKenna and Rachel!" William hollered.

I didn't have to turn around to know he was waving at them in line. I quickly spotted the redhead and her best friend, both wearing skinny jeans and tank tops. McKenna had a thing for Leo for months now. Rumor had it, he took her to the movies the month prior. Not a rumor, really. I was in the room when Leo and William were talking about it. I slammed the fridge and plunked the jug of milk on the counter to let them know I was in earshot. Leo swallowed hard and said, *never mind.*

Abigail and I shot them a wave and they hopped and fluttered their fingers at us, but the rollercoaster jerked forward before we could say anything. The distinct *clink, clink, clink* let us know we were about to hit the peak before the drop. Butterflies erupted in my belly as we went flying. Hands in the air. Wind burning our cheeks. We screamed and laughed for two full minutes until we jerked to a stop and got off.

"Next stop?" Abigail asked, windblown and breathless.

"Ferris Wheel!" I shouted.

"No, we should wait for McKenna and Rachel to get off," William said, but my gaze found Leo.

He looked back at me with an expression in his eyes I could only interpret as an apology. Then he bit his lip and glanced away, saying, "Yeah, sure."

I nodded slowly, understanding he might actually have feelings for someone else, and that this quiet crush we had for each other was just that. Not that it surprised me. Leo was popular and I heard enough from the other girls in the locker room to know he had options.

"Are you losers going to ditch us?" Abigail stepped in. "Because your mom said you have to keep an eye out for us." She mocked the last part of the sentence because the truth was, we were very capable without them, but moms worry, and she felt like we were less likely to get trafficked if we were in a larger group.

"No—" Leo said.

"Yes—" William laughed out at the same time.

"It's fine," I reasoned. "McKenna's cool."

Abigail rolled her eyes as the two other girls clamored down the steps, giddy with just-off-a-rollercoaster laughter. McKenna jumped on Leo's back and said, "Boo!" like Leo couldn't hear her squealing from behind him fifteen seconds ago.

"Hey," he said, his voice low and smooth.

I forced my gaze away and saw Rachel smiling up at my brother and nervously picking at her nails, and that's when it hit me. *Ooooh, William is into Rachel. Got it.* I nodded as I let the information settle. She clearly had it bad for him.

"Next ride?" I asked then turned to McKenna and Rachel. "Do you guys want to join us?"

"Can we? I mean, I don't want to intrude…" McKenna said in response to me but looked at Leo.

"No, it's fine. Leo would love it. Wouldn't you, Leo?" I smiled at him, and his nostrils flared as he glanced at me. I couldn't tell if he was embarrassed of me or going to murder me.

"Cool! Let's ride the Cyclone!" McKenna clapped her hands once and bounced around in front of Leo. She wasn't being obnoxious. This is just her personality. But her suggestion was the last and probably only ride I refused to get on. It was a ride with three spinning arms, each arm sprouting off into another three arms where riders are strapped in. Each arm spins. And if that wasn't bad enough, the entire ride spins on its axis as well and each arm rotates until riders are upside down. Tequila or not, it made me sick.

"I can't ride that." I laughed uncomfortably.

"Really? Why?" Rachel asked as she reapplied her pink lip gloss.

"Motion sickness," William answered for me. I nodded once to confirm.

"What? It's my favorite!" McKenna said.

"Mine too," Abigail chipped in. "I usually ride it by myself because Genevieve can't hang."

I shrugged. True.

"But you guys go ahead. I'll meet you after," I offered.

"I'll stay with you," Leo said, his voice cutting through the crowds and lights like butter.

"You don't have to," I said at the same time William said, "Really?"

He answered William. "I'm not riding that. I saw on the news it got stuck and everyone was stuck upside for an hour." McKenna's face fell. "But go, I'll find you after."

She bit her lip and smiled like he promised her eternity.

"Hey, be nice," William murmured as he stepped closer to me.

"I am nice!" I said, throwing up my hands. Leo turned his face away so William couldn't see him laugh. "Maybe your friend needs to toughen up," I added, and William groaned.

"For real, Gen. Don't be a bitch."

I scoffed. He was always so protective of his best friend, convinced I was the instigator.

"Ah, leave them alone. They'll be fine," Abigail cut in. "Toodaloo! We're off to have some real fun!"

"Sure," I drew out with sarcasm, and we watched them walk away toward the green and blue neon lights.

"You don't have to babysit me," I said.

"I'm not. I don't want to go with them." He kept his voice plain and shoved his hands in his jeans.

"Okay," I responded and started walking. We stopped and bought some cotton candy to munch on while we waited in line for the ride. Time flew by as we chatted and laughed in line.

Soon we were seated in our own gondola on the wheel with sugary lips and sticky fingers.

"Gum?" I offered once seated, holding up the package.

"Are you saying my breath stinks?"

"Yes," I lied. Leo never stunk unless it was after basketball.

He laughed and nudged my shoulder with his as he took the gum, then said, "Wait. I want more cotton candy."

"You're going to get a tummy ache," I teased.

He patted his stomach. "I'm a big boy. I can handle it." He swiped the bag of candy from me. "Let's play a game."

"Okay," I said as the ride began to twirl toward the sky.

"Close your eyes."

I did.

"Now, open your mouth," he demanded, and I cocked an eye open. He had a hand in the cotton candy bag. "Close them."

I sighed and shut my eyes again, loving this more than I would let on.

"You say your favorite is pink cotton candy, but I want to see if you can tell which is which with your eyes closed."

"Oh, this will be easy," I said, sticking out my tongue. He set a cloud of sugar on my tongue. It dissolved. It was sweet, but with a somewhat sour aftertaste. It was the blue kind. "Blue. Okay, next one."

I heard him let out a breath of a laugh and then just seconds later another piece of cotton candy was on my tongue. "That's pink," I said.

"You can tell the difference?" he exclaimed, and I laughed, opening my eyes.

"They're two different flavors, Leo."

"Uh…of food coloring!" he argued.

I laughed again. "They are actual flavors."

He shook his head. "They're just sugar."

"I bet you could tell the difference," I suggested.

"Try me," he said, shutting his eyes and sticking out his tongue.

I pulled a small piece of blue first and placed it on his tongue. He closed his mouth and I tried not to watch him lick his lips, but his mouth was right there and my mouth watered.

Saving the best for last, I gave him a piece of pink cotton candy. I repeated the same action, only this time he opened his eyes to catch me watching his mouth.

Heat crept up my neck, and I looked away.

"They taste the same."

"I'm worried about your taste buds," I remarked with a smirk.

"I'm worried about yours."

I laughed, looking out at the fairgrounds and searching for something to say so the space between us wasn't filled with awkward silence.

"Scones after this?" he suggested and smiled.

"Those are overrated."

He held a fist to his chest. "So offensive."

"I want an elephant ear."

"Fine," he said, grinning. For a brief moment, his eyes landed on my lips. But before the moment could turn into anything else, he pulled out his phone and added, "Picture time!"

I propped my hands under my chin and smiled my stupidest, cheesiest smile. He raised an eyebrow and gave his best smolder. It was a dumb picture and we both laughed when we looked at it. "I'm getting this printed."

"And you better give me a copy."

"Of course." He smiled, his eyes falling from my lips to my eyes yet again. As he moved closer, I could smell the sweetness on his breath and my skin buzzed with nerves. His hand brushed against my thigh, and he drew back. "Sorry," he muttered.

I laughed. "It's okay." But that wasn't what I meant. What I meant was *I want you to*. I wanted him to touch my thigh. I wanted him to kiss my lips and hold my hand. I wanted him and I didn't want anyone in the world to know about it but us.

As we slowed near the top of the Ferris wheel, I turned to him.

"It's okay if you like McKenna," I blurted.

"I don't."

"But it's okay if you do," I said. "She's nice, I promise."

He let out a low chuckle. "I know. But I'm not interested like that."

"Okay."

"Okay."

We stared for a moment, and my mouth felt like it was going dry as he moved closer. Then he said the words I knew in my heart even without his confirmation, "I like you, Evie."

I swallowed hard and nodded. "William can't know."

"No." He shook his head, and held out his pinky. I wrapped my pinky around his and covered both our hands with my other hand, pulling it close to my chest.

We didn't have to say what we were promising. It was an unspoken oath to not tell anyone what we were confessing.

"I like you too, Leo. Like, really like you—"

He cut me off with his lips, running his hands in my hair. It was out of nowhere and yet, it was just like I dreamt it would be every night before I went to sleep. He was my brother's best friend. He infuriated me. He pushed my buttons. He made me angry. And I liked it so much. Heat warmed inside me as we kissed. Butterflies took flight. This was nothing new. We often stayed up long after William had gone to bed and talked until the sun rose. He was over at the house most days, so I got to know him better than I knew anyone. I'd come to terms with living with these feelings bursting in my chest for the rest of the days I knew him. Leo had this effect on me all the time, but never with his hands in my hair and his tongue rolling against mine. With his lips kissing me, how I felt about him was a whole new experience.

I never loved the taste of something more.

"I want to be alone with you," I whispered, cupping his face with my hands.

"We are alone." He smiled, eyes drifting over my face.

"Alone, alone." I swallowed. I hoped he understood. The way his eyes moved over my face let me know he did, but he was afraid to say it out loud.

"You're serious?"

I nodded. "Yes."

So we lied. We said I didn't feel well, and he drove me home. Abigail and William stayed with McKenna and Rachel and would hitch a ride with them later.

When we got to the house after the thirty-minute drive, I poked my head into my parents' room. They were already asleep, but woke when I opened their door. Mom glanced at the clock. "It's only ten," she said. "Curfew is at midnight."

"Yeah, I know, but I got sick on a ride," I lied without any remorse.

"Oh, Genny Bear…" Dad mumbled, still half-asleep.

"Oh, honey, there's Ginger Ale in the refrigerator if you want some," Mom added.

"I'll get some, thanks," I said.

"Want me to lay with you?" she asked, but I shook my head.

"No, it's not that serious. Just need to lay down. Love you."

"Love you too, honey."

I closed the door and shuffled down the hallway. Leo was waiting in my room. I didn't tell her he came home with me.

We waited thirty minutes to ensure my parents had fallen back asleep before he kissed me again. But this time it wasn't polite. His hands were on my waist, and I wrapped a leg around him; he gripped my thigh and I pulled at his clothes.

We made out for at least thirty minutes before I took off his shirt. I'd seen him without one before but never in this context. My gaze followed my fingers in wonder as I touched the ridges of his muscles.

"I thought we were just kissing," he said, barely a whisper.

I shook my head. I wanted to do more. I never had. In high school, nothing is a secret. Everyone finds out everything, and often with embellished details. But this, with Leo, would never get out. He wouldn't let it, and neither would I. He made me feel safe—like I could do anything I wanted as long as I was with him.

It was awkward, really, how it all happened. We stood and took off our own clothes and I laid down on the bed, arms clutching my chest. His eyes danced around the room with nerves and hesitancy but the way he rolled on the condom and

134

moved his body to situate himself between my legs screamed confidence. At least, back then I thought so.

He paused. "Are you sure?" he asked.

I ran my thumb over his bottom lip and nodded.

He held himself against me, rubbing back and forth in slow and deliberate movements. My legs clenched against his thighs and I swallowed, my nails digging into his shoulder blades.

He looked at me, his arms held my body, but his eyes held something more.

He pushed in. Slow, small movements, lighting me on fire inch by inch in the most confusing way.

I moaned and gasped at the same time, dragging my fingers down his back. It was a painful and incredible sensation woven together into one feeling.

"Leo!" I cried out, squeezing my eyes shut. Tears of pain and pleasure leaked out the corners of my eyes.

"You okay?" he breathed against my lips, his eyes studying my face.

I tried to slow my breathing but my heart pounded and my adrenaline spiked.

I nodded. "Yeah," I said. "I'm okay."

"Are you ready?" he asked with dark eyes.

"That's not it?" I was shocked.

"Not all of it."

"Oh my god…" I swallowed hard. It already hurt and burned so bad.

He laughed. A low rumble that made heat pool between my legs even more. "We can stop."

I pressed my eyes closed, willing myself to find the courage but I barely believed my body could take any more. I breathed out, steadying myself.

"No, don't stop. I'm ready."

"You don't have to be tough, Evie," he whispered, brushing his knuckles over my cheek bone.

It wasn't just the sound of his voice or the way he touched me. It was the way I loved him and the way I knew I always would.

"I'm not tough, Leo. I just want you," I breathed back.

135

He ran his fingers through my hair until his palm cradled my face. He waited a moment, eyes drinking me in, heart pounding against mine. Then he trailed a hand down my body and slipped his fingers between my legs, moving his fingers in small circles as he kissed me. Our lips melted together, devouring each other in long, sensual gulps of passion until our connection was even more slick and he slid all the way into me.

I cried out again. Louder that time and he pressed a gentle hand against my mouth. "Shh-shh," he whispered. "Does it hurt?"

I realized then that there is such thing as a stupid question. I nodded, biting my lip.

"I'm sorry. Should I—do you want me to stop?"

He looked so tortured about hurting me, and I was so confused because I was in pain but I in no way wanted to stop. I shook my head.

Sex with Leo was like being broken open in the most vulnerable way. I laid my heart and body out before him, letting him have me, consume me. This was me letting him win.

"Okay. You good?" he asked as he began moving inside me.

I nodded, stunned for words as my mind tried to adjust to the pleasure and pain.

He moved in slow, long, smooth strokes that made me gasp and moan and pitch my hips toward his. Soon we found a rhythm. Beads of sweat pooled on my neck, and heat swirled from between my legs throughout each vein in my body. I begged with my mouth, my hands, and my body for him to send me over the edge.

"Leo! Oh my—" I cried out against the palm of his hand.

A fleeting smile danced over his face as he pressed harder and faster inside of me. Then his body shook and he collapsed, breathing heavily into my shoulder.

Moments, maybe minutes passed before our breathing slowed and we spoke.

"Holy shit, Evie."

I smiled at him, euphoria still pulsing everywhere I had sensation. "Holy shit."

I was swollen and sore after, but he held my hand and we

talked about basketball and feelings until William and Abigail arrived home with Rachel and McKenna an hour later. Mom and Dad always let friends stay at our place late at night. She said she'd rather lose sleep because of a house full of teenagers than lose sleep wondering where we were.

Then we watched a movie and pretended none of it happened at all.

13

WEDNESDAY

"I'm going to take a quick shower," I say as we enter my apartment. Leo nods, slipping off his shoes by the front door, lining up my heels next to his. I restrain a smile. "Do you want to take a shower, or—?"

He bites his bottom lip and smiles, dragging his eyes over me before looking at the floor. He's uncomfortable, or at least uncertain. I realize the insinuation in my question and clear my throat.

"I meant after me." I shoot a thumb over my shoulder. "William brought his dirty clothes here a couple of weekends ago when their washer broke. They're clean now…obviously. But um, yeah." I wring my hands in front of me, cringing at my rambling.

He laughs. "Sure. I can wear William's clothes."

I nod and retreat to my bedroom, letting out a quick breath behind my door. My gaze lands on the green box next to my bed. I hurry over to it and shove it into my closet, out of sight. Walking to my bathroom to turn on the shower, I feel oddly aware of Leo's presence in my apartment. I even keep my breathing shallow as if he can hear me. I laugh at my ridiculousness, testing the stream of water with my hand. As I reach behind me to unzip my dress, I remember my fingers can't grasp the zipper. I try to reach over my shoulder, but I'm even less successful. I suck in like that will change the position of the zipper, and still can't reach it. I twist and contort and bend until I am even sweatier than I already was.

Looking at myself in the mirror, fogging up from the running shower, I contemplate ripping the dress off. Then I attempt to and barely even hear the thread rip.

Helpless, I drop my hands.

Shit. I wish Abigail were here.

I pad over to my door and open it with a reluctant swing.

"Leo!" I call, walking down the hall. "Quit snooping around, I need your help."

He strides around the corner from the kitchen, a tall glass of ice water in hand. "What's up?"

It takes me a moment to register his words because his button-up is off and his muscles fill out his undershirt more than they did when he was eighteen. Of course they do. Then my eyes land on a part of his tattoo sleeve I don't remember seeing. On the front of his bicep is a tiger with green eyes and orchid flowers woven around the side of its face.

I knew about the Bible verse on the inside of his arm, and the evergreen trees on his tricep. The mandala on his elbow bleeds into a mixture of floral and geometric designs and disappears under his shirt sleeve. The tiger always peeked out from under his shirt, but I've never seen the full tattoo in person. Only in pictures of him in his college basketball pictures or if he posted a shirtless picture on Instagram that I did my best to always scroll past. But I've certainly never noticed the flowers surrounding the tiger.

My eyes bulge for a moment. Then I blink heavily and away from his distracting body art.

"I like your tattoo," I say.

"Did you come out just to tell me that?" He smirks, a look of smug condescension on his face.

I shake my head and suppress my desire to strangle him.

"No, I just don't remember seeing it before."

"Well, thank you."

"You're welcome," I respond, standing like a stupid statue with my hands clasped in front of me.

Leo looks down at me expectantly.

"Oh! Can you unzip my dress please?" I ask, turning around.

"Sure," he says, but it sounds like a growl, rumbling over my skin and heightening my senses. He steps closer, unclasping the top of my dress and sliding the zipper down. I try not to breathe too heavy or swallow too hard.

When the zipper reaches my lower back, I turn. "Thank you."

"Wait," he says, grabbing my waist. I glance at him over my shoulder, he's studying something on my back, and he runs his knuckles over my shoulder blade. I pretend it doesn't make me shiver. "You didn't put on sunscreen."

"Oh," I chuckle uncomfortably. "Oh, well."

"Do you have any aloe?"

"I'm sure I do." I let out a huff. "I'll be right back."

Holding my dress to my chest, I hurry back into my bedroom and hop in the shower. Confusion washes over me with the suds of my body wash as I move through the motions of showering. Most moments with Leo are completely comfortable and ordinary. He's just Leo. Then other moments, he says one word with a certain tone or touches me in the most platonic way and it sends a million lightning bolts down my spine and sets the pit of my stomach ablaze.

As I rinse my loofah, letting the suds run down my chest, I stare at my razor and shaving cream perched on the white stone of the shower.

Absolutely not, I think. My emotions have been so unpredictable this week. The heat. The wedding. Leo. I need something, anything to keep me in check. And tonight I'm choosing prickly legs.

Toweling off, I pull on gray cotton shorts and a white tank top, then grab a pair of William's black basketball shorts and a gray t-shirt from the hamper in the bedroom and set them on the counter in the bathroom.

When I return to the kitchen, Leo is sitting on a barstool flipping through his phone, his ice water drained. His bored expression turns into something more affectionate as he meets my gaze.

I turn away, seemingly unbothered, but I'm not. I am very bothered. I can feel every nerve ending in my body—open, burning, waiting for something to happen.

"Uh, there's a pair of shorts and a t-shirt on the bathroom counter. And I set out an extra washcloth. Use whatever you want in the shower," I say, entering the kitchen. When I go to pull open the cupboard to grab a glass for myself, I notice he's already poured me one.

"Thanks," he says, standing.

"Thank you," I say, holding up the ice water. I've instantly relapsed into my emotional support ice water years.

He walks away, and I hear the water in the shower running a few moments later. I chug the water, refill it and chug half of the second glass.

God, I'm thirsty. And nervous. And anxious. And excited. And hot.

Literally. I'm so damn hot.

My skin has a pulse, the pinkness of the sunburn deepening now that I've showered and slathered myself in lotion.

I drink the rest of my water then grab two sparkling waters out of the refrigerator and place them on the coffee table. I turn on ESPN to watch the highlights from game two of the finals. The Warriors won. Of course.

"Do you think you could beat Stephen Curry in HORSE?" Leo asks behind me, his caramel skin dewy and water beading off the tips of his hair.

"Yes," I answer without hesitation and a mischievous smile plays across my mouth.

"So cocky." Leo laughs, flopping next to me on the couch with a bottle of aloe vera. "Even with the old lady knee?"

"Even with the old lady knee," I confirm. I glance at the bottle of green goo and then meet his eyes. "So I see you snooped through my bathroom."

"I needed to get aloe for you."

My eyes fill with playful contempt.

"And I snooped," he confesses. "But honestly, Evie, you're not that interesting, just very disorganized."

My jaw drops and I kick his thigh. "You are so nice to me."

He smiles at my sarcasm. "Seriously, not a single sex toy."

"No one keeps sex toys in the bathroom."

He laughs, heat hitting his cheeks, then he looks at me. "So I should check the bedside table?"

I grin. "Or you could mind your business."

He ignores me and flips open the lid of the aloe vera. "Turn around."

"So bossy."

"Evie." He stares pointedly.

"Fine," I relent, turning around to face the wall of windows. The sun is setting and falling fast. It's a beautiful, clear sunset. It's more pink than orange.

"Your shoulders are as pink as the door at the restaurant," he teases.

"I thought it was salmon," I tease back, twisting my wet hair and bringing it over my shoulder, baring my back for the sunburn treatment.

He snorts out a quick laugh and squirts aloe in his palm. It makes a farting noise.

"Excuse you—"

"Excuse me—"

We say at the same time.

I smile at him over my shoulder. He smiles back but there's something else in his expression—a hesitation that makes him bite his lip and me to look away.

He places his palm over my shoulders with gentle care, running his fingers under the strap of my tank top. I shiver as the gel cools my burning skin.

"Hold out your hand," he says, and I do as he squirts some in my palm. "For your chest."

"Thank you," I say, and apply the cool gel to my neck and sternum.

He refills his palm with more gel and continues application

on the other side of my back.

"Can I ask you a question?" he asks.

My heart pounds. "Yes."

"What's the point of the bridal party luncheon?"

I laugh, nerves dissipating. "The same point as the rehearsal dinner, I guess."

"And that is…?"

"To ease the nerves of a perfectionist's heart," I say, fiddling with the hem of my gray shorts.

I sense him nodding. "And I have to go?"

"Yes, unless you want Mrs. Wellington knocking down your door."

He laughs. "Well, she won't find me. I'm staying here tonight."

I jerk back. "I didn't invite you."

"Yes, you did." He stops rubbing aloe into my shoulders and turns me around.

I open my mouth to protest but close it. Every part of me wants him to stay. It's been a relief to feel something other than animosity toward him.

"Fine," I say, pressing myself off the couch. "I'm making popcorn."

"Do you have popcorn sprinkles?" he asks, leaning an elbow over the back of the couch as his eyes follow me into my kitchen.

I smile to myself. No one calls popcorn seasoning that, but I know exactly what he's talking about. The same way he knows I call shredded cheese sprinkle cheese.

"Of course," I say, placing an unpopped bag of popcorn in the microwave. "Kettle, white cheddar, or truffle salt?"

"Oh, fancy options."

"Just pick."

"Kettle."

I nod to confirm. I don't know how Leo and I do this. We constantly go from hesitation and nerves to being just how we used to be. Knowing each other like the backs of our hands.

After grabbing a white ceramic bowl from the cupboard, dumping the bag of popcorn in it, and topping it with popcorn sprinkles, I walk toward Leo on the couch and then pause.

"Open up," I tell him, and he does.

I toss a piece of popcorn in his mouth. He chomps down on it.

"Nice shot," he says.

"You know me." I wink, setting the popcorn on the coffee table.

Leo grabs a few pieces and takes one between two fingers. "Open up."

I oblige. The popcorn goes flying past my hcad.

"Leo! That was terrible."

"Hold on." He adjusts on the couch as if his shoulder position had anything to do with his terrible aim. "Let me try again."

He tosses another piece.

It hits me in the shoulder.

"You could have had that!"

"If I was squatting!"

He laughs. "Okay. Again."

He tries again. It hits my belly button.

"What the hell?" he says, looking at the popcorn like it's the problem.

I click my tongue against my teeth. "Blaming the ball, are you?"

"Shut up. I haven't done this in a while. It's hard."

"That's what she said," I tease.

His mouth twitches with amusement but he otherwise ignores me. "Open. Up," he demands.

He shoots. He… misses.

Again.

And again.

Popcorn hits my eye, hair, my hip. Everywhere but my mouth. "Seriously?"

"Do over," he says.

I roll my eyes and then open my mouth. Popcorn shoots past my head.

"Dude, at this point, I'm going to make you vacuum."

He laughs, long and loud. I smile at his laugh as it warms in

144

my belly. He holds a piece of popcorn in each hand, fully loaded. He tosses one and it hits my cheek.

"Come on!" he exclaims, grabbing a replacement piece, and standing to face me, arms outstretched with competitive passion.

"Temper, temper," I chide.

"It hit your cheek! I'd like to see some effort, Michaels."

I laugh like a giggly college girl.

He throws another piece. I duck and catch it on my tongue.

His arms shoot up and he hollers in celebration. "Yes! Score!"

My mouth drops. "Pretty sure you would have missed if I didn't duck."

"Pretty sure I made the shot." He steps closer, the second piece still in his hand.

"Pretty sure I get the assist." I cross my arms.

He's close now—a foot away—a smile on his face lingering from his laughter.

"Open up."

I restrain a smile and do as he says. He places the second piece of popcorn in my mouth. He's smiling down at me, his fingers lingering on my chin and his palm resting on my throat. My pulse is no doubt revealing all the things he makes me feel.

"Slam dunk," he whispers.

I swallow against the palm of his hand, my vision fixed on his brown eyes. Letting out a breath of a laugh, I avert my gaze and regain some composure.

"You still get an S," I say.

"If you say so." He smiles.

H-O-R-S, H-O-R.

The game is almost over now.

"Dance with me," he says, his hand running down my neck and gripping my shoulder.

I glance at the TV, a somber commercial about adopting abandoned pets is playing. "Really?"

He grins. "Yes."

I laugh, but I step into his arms, letting his hands rest on my waist and mine around his neck.

"Remember when your mom taught us how to waltz the night before prom?" he asks and a laugh bubbles out of me.

"It was the Foxtrot," I correct.

He narrows his eyes, his expression trying to remember the details. "Right. Same thing—" it's not, he knows this, but it makes me laugh again anyway. "I've been practicing."

I raise my eyebrows. "You're kidding."

"No." He straightens, placing one hand on my waist and the other clasps my hand. "Shoulders back, Evie."

I roll my eyes, even as I feel my soul being tugged back into a memory. I barely remember the steps, but it would seem Leo hasn't forgotten.

Slow-slow. Quick-quick.

It reminds me of the night we first learned these steps. We told my mom we'd never dance the Foxtrot. *You will,* she said. *Maybe not tonight, but one day you will.* We laughed so hard Dr. Pepper sprayed out of our noses and she made all three of us clean the carpet.

Slow-slow. Quick-quick. Over and over. Leo practically carries me all around my apartment, until I miss the step, stub my toe on the glass coffee table, and crash into his chest.

He hugs me tight over the shoulders and I feel the laugh rumbling out of him more than hear it.

Then slowly as our laughter subsides—the commercial long over—the silence starts to scream.

I can practically hear every question he wants to ask. All the ways he wants to rehash what happened eight years ago. I can still feel the ache in my chest that throbbed with each breath for months after the night we said it was over.

But instead of bringing it up, I lean into him, tightening my arms around his shoulders and resting my head on his chest. The sound of his heartbeat is as familiar as my own. The smell of his skin even with my body wash on it is still distinctly Leo. His large hands encase my hips, and his thumb sliding against the flesh of the bone poking out of my shorts is sending ripples of heat to my core. I feel as if this whole week is playing tricks on me, like a fever dream filled with heat, wedding bells, and memories. But I don't care. I don't want to wake up. Not yet, at least.

"Do you think about that night?" he asks.

I shrug in his arms. "Not as much as I used to." *But I still think of all the other nights.*

"Why not?"

I pause, staring out the window, pressing my lips together before I can speak. "Leo, it was so long ago."

"You never told your brother." A statement, not a question.

I shake my head.

"You tell him everything."

"So do you," I counter.

His gaze is intense, his jaw is pulsing, and agony is written on his face. I wonder if it's painful for him to look at me. I want to ask what's hurting him because it couldn't possibly be me. Ending it was his idea. Not mine. It's been eight years. We've both moved on. At least, mostly.

Just as the tears behind my eyes begin to burn, I find the courage to speak.

"Why are you doing this, Leo?" I ask. "And why this week? Is it the wedding? Are you pissed William is getting married first? Are you worried he'll find out—"

"No," he cuts me off.

"Then what?"

He bites his damn lip and buries his eyes in the carpet. I take hold of his face and make him look at me.

"What?" My eyes dart around his face searching for a clue. "It's still me. Yeah, we did something stupid as teenagers and hurt each other's feelings, but we can let it go. I *did* let it go."

His mouth twitches like he wants to smile but he doesn't. "You keep saying it was a long time ago, but it doesn't feel that long, you know? We said we would forget, move on. Act like nothing happened…"

Wrong. He said those things. Not me. I knew I'd never forget.

"But you've stayed in the back of my mind, Evie. For eight years. I haven't stopped thinking about it. I haven't stopped regretting it."

I drop my hands. "Why are you being so hard on yourself

right now?"

He presses his lips together, the intensity of his gaze blazing through me. I want to prove I'm fine, that I've forgiven him for breaking my heart. But the tension is tangible. I tilt my chin up, closer, our breaths entangled, my lips brush against his. He lets me. But only a moment before he pulls away, shooting pangs of rejection in my gut.

"Because—" he whispers just as his phone rings. We both drop our gaze to his phone on the coffee table.

He winces as the name Taylor lights up my now dimly lit living room. His fingertips hesitate, but he ultimately grabs the phone and looks at me, "Excuse me. I'm so sorry, but I have to take this," he says, taking his phone down the hallway.

I press the heels of my hands into my eyes. I know better. I didn't shave my legs for a reason. I shouldn't have invited him up. Leo and I don't know how to be alone with each other. We never have. Ferris wheel rides. Sleepovers after William had fallen asleep and we stayed up to finish the movie. At the basketball court at the park before any of our other friends got there. Late at night in my bedroom staring at the ceiling and discussing Invisible String Theory. No one ever suspected anything. At least, our friends and William didn't. But one time, Mom came into the family room while we were watching a movie with William and his girlfriend, Rachel, and said, "No blankets!" William thought she was referring to him, but she grinned at Leo and me. We quickly unraveled our fingers and tossed the blanket on the floor.

I stare desperately at the hallway as he continues his conversation.

When he returns, I pretend I was just watching basketball highlights and not trying to decipher the murmurs in the hallway.

He sits next to me. I glance at him. He looks too big and too comfortable for my couch. He looks like a man dressed like a college boy in those stupid shorts and t-shirt, hiding his real girlfriend from me so he can fuck with my head and get laid at my brother's wedding.

"Who was that?" I ask, staring at the TV.

"Someone I work with."

I glance at him. "Are you together?"

He lets out a chuckle. "No."

I nod. I don't know if I believe him.

"Does she think you are?"

He shakes his head and opens his mouth to speak but I turn to face him and say, "Sorry I tried to kiss you."

My embarrassment is written on my face. But Leo ignores it. He moves closer in one swift motion, one hand on my waist, the other gripping my thigh. The intimacy is far too comfortable and terrifying at the same time. I don't know what to think right now.

"I just wanted to see if we both remembered the dance."

I give one small, uncomfortable nod. "Then why are your hands on my thighs?"

He glances down where his hand is outstretched along my thigh, then meets my eyes. He doesn't let go; he tightens his grip. "I just...when I'm alone with you, everything comes back."

I don't argue because I agree completely. But we both seem to fear the ending we know is inevitable. The crash. The burn. His ability to run. And his inability to tell my brother how he feels about me.

"Then maybe we just shouldn't be alone," I say, defeated. I stand and toss him a blanket, avoid his expression, and walk to the hallway. "Goodnight, Leo."

14

THURSDAY

I can't tell if the smile I wake up with is because I hear the sounds of Leo vacuuming in the living room, or simply because I'm waking up with him in my apartment.

Arching my back to stretch, I then roll out of bed, not bothering to brush my teeth or my hair. I head down the hall and watch Leo vacuuming my living room. He looks up and grins, his brown eyes sparkling in the summer sun warming through the windows, pulling out the flecks of gold.

To most people, he's tall and brooding. Serious with an unexpected quip. But to me, he's adorable.

He shuts off the vacuum and returns it to the linen closet. "I cleaned up my mess.'"

"Thank you," I say, passing him into the kitchen. "Want coffee?"

"Please."

"Oat milk or almond?"

"Oat."

"Mocha or caramel?"

"Neither."

I whirl around and my jaw drops. "Who are you? The Leo I know has a sweet tooth."

"The Leo you know used to play basketball for hours and hours every day." He pats his stomach. "I'm being smart."

"You're twenty-six. Live a little," I say, splashing caramel in his cup.

He glares, then smiles as he watches me make his latte; milk is in the frother, and the espresso shot dribbles into the mug.

"Did you sleep okay?" I ask.

"I slept great."

I bite my lip and nod, focusing on the espresso.

"Evie?"

I look at him, reeling in my expression.

"We're good, right?"

I pour the frothy milk into his espresso shot, swirling the top to make an almost beautiful design. I slide him the coffee mug.

"We're good," I confirm, then lean in. "And you can tell all your girlfriends in San Francisco I won't ever try to kiss you again."

He looks almost disappointed, but I ignore it. I'm too embarrassed about last night's rejection. "You don't need to worry about Taylor."

"Fantastic. And Taylor doesn't need to worry about me," I confirm.

He opens his mouth to overexplain, but I wave him off. "Don't," I say as I pour the rest of the milk into my double shot of espresso. "It's fine. We were always a bad idea, right?"

I try to laugh but it's uncomfortable and choppy as the sound leaves my throat. It was a loaded thing to say based on Leo's expression. His jaw pulses before he sips his coffee.

I pull my mug to my lips and take a sip, staring at Leo over the rim.

"Evie…" he begins.

"No one calls me that," I interrupt.

"I do," he says. I stare at him, heart fluttering, and then set my mug down.

"I need to hurry up and get ready," I say, ignoring his

directive as I yawn and stretch.

His mouth stays open, his eyes in a trance of hesitation. Then, I see him decide to not push the subject as his eyes fall to his coffee. He takes a sip and sets it down, settling his hesitation. "I like your hair."

The little shit. "I did it just for you," I say, mussing up the bird's nest I've created in my slumber.

He lets out a breath of a smile, rotating his mug in his hand. "I need to head out and grab clothes for the luncheon."

I nod. "I need to fix my hair."

He laughs, drawing his eyes back to me. He bites his lip, then asks, "See you there?"

I smile. "I'll see you all week."

I dress in white jeans and a floral blouse with tan wedges. I regret my clothing choice about two point five seconds after I step out into the heatwave. The parking garage for my apartment feels like a sauna. I hop in my car, blasting my AC but it's struggling and takes a full five minutes before the air pushing through the vents is remotely cool.

Holy hell, this is not Western Washington. We don't do this here. Washingtonians are wimps when it comes to heat. I check the dash. It's one-oh-one. And it's only eleven.

I pull into the restaurant parking lot, located twenty minutes north of downtown, and quickly realize our event is outdoors.

"Freaking fantastic," I mutter, stepping out into Satan's asshole.

Listen, I'm happy to be here. Happy to help. Happy my brother is marrying the love of his life and he loves her. But it's swampy hot. I want to go jump in the Sound and swim with the orcas. I want to lay on my couch in the air conditioning and watch Netflix. I don't want to do another stupid wedding event with Aunt Bernie and Aunt Wilma giving the centerpieces side-eye or Lorraine rolling her eyes at Abigail's pink hair or berating someone for wearing white.

My gaze falls to my lap just as panic swims up my chest. I'm wearing white jeans. I'm screwed.

My lower back is damp by the time I enter the venue and get quickly escorted to the back patio.

It's gorgeous. The lattices are covered with wisteria in full bloom and round white tables are scattered around the patio. Each table has a bouquet of white roses and blush-colored napkins fanned to perfection at each place setting. I take in the setup and wonder why I'm here. It's just lunch and it's already decorated to the nines.

"She roped you into coming in early too," I hear muttered next to me and immediately squeeze Abigail.

"I'm so glad you're here!" I say.

"Right. But *why* are we here?" she wonders aloud, gesturing to the picturesque patio. "And why the hell don't Cora, Taite, and April have to come early?"

"I figured you knew why April isn't here." I raise my eyebrows with so much suggestion that Abigail blushes.

"I know nothing of her whereabouts," she lies, unable to restrain her smile.

"Tell me everything."

She grins wide, and speaks through her teeth, "Everything is not appropriate in front of Mrs. Wellington."

I follow her gaze over my shoulder to see Lorraine dressed in a white sleeveless dress and white sandals with the smallest of heels.

"Of course, *she* can wear white," Abigail mutters, then plasters a smile on her face as Lorraine approaches us. "Lorraine, hi!"

"Oh, the darling Michaels girls. My lifesavers," she says, arms outstretched. She pulls back and sweeps her gaze over me. Pursing her lips and raising her eyebrows, she says, "Hmmph."

Thankful that's the only remark I get about my attire, I decide to move the conversation along, leaving no room for recourse about wearing white pants to a bridal event like an idiot.

"How can we help?" I ask as a bead of sweat forms between my shoulder blades and glides down to my tailbone. I'm already so sweaty.

Lorraine hesitates and her eyes bounce off my pants again.

Her lips twist like she just licked a lemon and she clears her throat. She disapproves, but not enough to comment.

"Well, I have the napkins in the back of my car as well as the place cards," Lorraine answers, hands clasped in front of her mauve lips.

"That's it?" Abigail asks, a hint of irritation in her voice.

I shoot her a quick be-polite warning glare. "I didn't realize you were going to do assigned seating."

She pulls a manilla folder out of her oversized Louis Vuitton bag. "This is the seating chart," she beams. "Everything always runs more smoothly when seating arrangements are made ahead of time."

I nod and hold out my hand, but she doesn't hand me the folder. She hands me the keys to her Escalade in the parking lot.

"It's all in the back," she says.

"Great," I grit out through a forced smile, and drag Abigail by the elbow out to the scorching parking lot.

Abigail is visibly irritated—tight lips, shoulders pulled back, and a slight glare she can't help.

I open the back of the SUV and spot the handmade place cards in a white box.

"Is this even necessary? What the fuck?"

Abigail is almost always the unfiltered version of my thoughts.

"Well, they are pretty," I admit, admiring the light pink, shimmery paper and names written in perfect calligraphy on each.

"No. Those are fine. This," she says, gesturing to the box of white napkins folded into the shape of birds.

I snort out a laugh. "Oh, Nora's going to hate that. She said no doves."

"Well, maybe they're swans," Abigail says, lifting one out of the box.

"I don't get the bird thing for weddings, I'm sorry," I confess.

Abigail makes the folded fabric flap, the beak pecking toward my face. "Quack, quack, Gen. The task at hand is much too hard to get accomplished without our help."

I laugh and then settle myself before we reenter the back patio. "Be nice," I whisper to Abigail. Her eyes practically topple off her face.

"Ah, you're back," Lorraine says, arms outstretched like she's welcoming us to her oasis as if we weren't already here. "If you girls could put the napkins on each place setting, I'll get started on the seating chart."

It takes Abigail and me all of three and a half minutes to do the napkins. After discarding the box, we return to our leader for the next task.

"Oh, perfect," she says, handing each of us a stack of cards. "Abigail, those cards are for that table in the corner and Genevieve, yours are for the one right here."

"Great," I say, taking the stack. It's clearly the head table.

William.

Nora.

Leo.

Taite.

Terrence.

Cora.

John.

Abigail.

Marcus.

April.

Me.

Damien.

Wait. Damien? What the hell?

"Um, Lorraine, I think there's been a mistake," I say, holding the card out to her.

"What's that, dear?"

"Damien isn't coming. This should be Jake's seat."

"Oh, no, Jake can't make it. William said he got tied up at work. But Damien will be here so I figured you two might like to sit with each other." She scrunches her nose and places a hand on my shoulder.

"Oh, I'd rather not—"

She hushes me with pursed lips, placing his card next to mine. "Don't worry. I won't say anything to Nora or William, but I heard from his mother that Damien was at your apartment the other night and said things went well." She winks, then gestures to the thick, hot air. "Love is in the air. Forgiveness is beautiful."

I'm too stunned to speak. Clearly, Damien and I interpreted the other night differently.

"Ma'am," the host of the restaurant interrupts. "Guests are starting to arrive. Would you like them to come out or shall we have an impromptu cocktail hour in the bar?"

"Twenty minutes early?" she says, aghast. "Yes, please, let's direct them to the bar."

I breathe in deep through my nose and turn back to the table, plucking Damien's name off the table.

"Like hell…" I mutter and switch it with the table behind us.

"Why did you put Aunt Wilma at our table?" Abigail comes up behind me.

I cross my arms. "Because I would rather have anyone else sit at the table besides Damien."

She snorts. "Why is he coming?"

I throw up my hands. "Who knows?" I've given up on trying to understand his necessary involvement in my brother's wedding.

"Well, the doves have been planted with the place cards," she says. "Shall we grab a cold beverage?"

"I think I'll need it," I mutter. "Almost as much as I need you to tell me about April."

"Drinks first," Abigail says, dragging me to the bar.

We order glasses of white wine and politely greet Mr. Wellington and the aunts before returning to the patio.

"So…?" I ask, sipping from my glass.

Abigail grins. "She's fun."

I raise my eyebrows. "Really?"

Fun isn't a word I'd use to describe April. Smart. Put together. Nice. Not necessarily fun.

"Really," Abigail sighs through a wistful smile.

"She just seems so serious," I counter.

"Well, you don't know her like I do, now do you?"

"So things got heated last night?"

She shrugs, nonchalant, twirling her glass of wine. "We fooled around a bit." She pauses, staring at the patio like she's caught in the dream of the night before. Then she looks up at me with a bright smile. "And she's fun."

I laugh. "Well, it would seem the wedding is going to be a blast for you then."

"Oh, yes, ma'am." She clinks my glass, smiling. Then her eyes land on the restaurant doors leading out to the patio. "Oh, she's here. I'll be back."

She won't be back. I'm certain of that now that I just saw the smile on April's face when she catches eyes with my cousin. They'd actually make the perfect couple in a very opposites-attract kind of way.

"Okay, what happened last night with April and Abigail?" Nora says instead of hello.

"None of our business."

She smirks, giving me side-eye as we both watch the two interact across the room. The movements are subtle. April's hand on Abigail's arm. Abigail brushing April's hair over her shoulder. And then the prolonged eye contact and smiles. Oh, man. These two are in trouble.

I glance at Nora. "I'll tell you later."

"Tell you what?" William asks, consuming me with a big bear hug.

"Ugh, William, it is too hot to hug people like that."

Nora groans. "I know, I'm so worried about tomorrow. The Glasshouse was so hot yesterday and it's supposed to be even hotter tomorrow."

As much as I'm not looking forward to the heat and how miserable we're all going to be, I don't want her to worry.

"Everything will be fine," I say. "Oh, look Nona and Gampa are here. Gosh, look how cute Nona looks in her hat."

Dressed in baby blue and pearls with a white hat, Nona looks like she came straight from church. She spots me and William and flashes an open-mouth smile, tugging on Gampa's short-sleeve button-up. He whips around. The expression on his face is equal parts delighted and surprised—the signature grandparents seeing their grandchildren's faces.

We walk over to them, meeting them near the center of the room.

I take in Nona—she smells like Clinique perfume and chocolate chip cookies. Nostalgia and comfort wash over me.

"It's so good to see you guys. How was your flight?" I ask.

"Oh, fine, fine," Nona says, then she pushes the back of her hand on my forehead. "You all right, dear? You feel like you've just walked through fire."

I laugh because it most definitely feels like it.

"Well, it is a hundred degrees outside, Mary," Gampa says, then holds open his hands to me. "You look so grown up, Genevieve."

He has said this every time he's seen me for the last ten years.

"And William!" he adds, pulling him in for a hug. "Man of the hour!"

"Thanks, Gampa." William smiles then pulls an arm around Nora. "We're thrilled you two made it."

Nora briefly hugs our grandparents. "Truly. It means so much to William and me."

"Oh, it's our pleasure," Nona says, glancing around.

"Here, let me help you find your seats," Nora says.

"Is the wedding outside too because it is hotter than Hades—" Gampa is saying, as they walk away and I feel an arm come around me.

"Hey, darlin'," says a familiar voice.

"Hey, Dad." I pull him in for a hug.

"Do you think I have to keep my jacket on? I'm sweating bullets under here, but I don't want Lorraine to comment on me not being formal enough."

"It's one-hundred and eight degrees. No one cares what Lorraine thinks. Not even Lorraine." I nod in her direction. She's chatting with the aunts, my grandparents, and her husband while continually dabbing a napkin to her neck.

My dad laughs. "Thank God," he says, slipping off his coat.

"Here," I say, holding out my hands. "I'll put it at your seat."

"My seat?"

"There's a proper seating chart." I wink, and he rolls his eyes. It's light-hearted and not loaded. Lorraine drives us all crazy, but we also love her.

I hang his jacket on his chair and take a sip of my wine, realizing it's already too warm. As I turn to walk back inside to see if the bartender can toss a few ice cubes in it, Leo walks in.

There's swagger in his stride as he looks at me from across the room with his perfect, stupid smile. The memory of last night when I tried to kiss him floods back to me, and I blink my eyes away, looking for anyone that could possibly want to talk to me.

He starts walking toward me and the already scorching patio heats by at least twenty degrees.

"Leo, what the hell, man?" William says, coming from behind me and stepping between us. "Where have you been?"

My eyes dart between them. I have no idea what's going on.

"What's wrong?" Leo asks William, unbothered.

"I've been calling you all morning and it kept going straight to voicemail."

"My phone died."

"And you can't charge it?"

"Genevieve doesn't have an iPhone."

"What does her phone have to do with anything?" Sweet, clueless William.

"I was at Genevieve's all night," Leo answers, pulling out his phone.

William's head snaps back and he looks at me. "Why?"

My mouth is dry as the Sahara but as I open it to respond, Leo beats me to it.

"I stayed over," he says, nonchalantly. No weight. No biggie. Completely blasé.

I look at William and swallow. He simply laughs, amused by the idea.

"Stealing her AC?" he asks.

"Ha, ha," Leo chides. "Mom has AC, thank you very much. I was there for the cable. After dinner, I went over to watch the highlights. Stayed for the comfy couch."

"You can't watch the highlights on your phone?" William queries.

"Nope," Leo responds, stuffing his hands in his pockets. "Phone died."

A smile sneaks its way over my lips at Leo's snide remark.

William rolls his eyes. "Well, we have a problem."

"If it's wedding related, I don't want to know," Leo heckles.

William shoots him a quick glare, then says, "Please. It's so stupid but I promised Nora I'd get it taken care of."

Leo waits for the task to be revealed.

"The lady that made Nora's veil was supposed to hand-deliver it this morning but she couldn't make it because her dog is sick or something. Anyway, Nora won't let me go because she doesn't want me to see it before the wedding."

Leo shrugs. "That's fine. Where do I need to pick it up?"

"Vashon Island."

Leo laughs. "You're joking."

"He's not. Her name is Amalie, and she makes the most beautiful custom veils." Nora appears out of thin air and answers for William.

I nod. I've been hearing about this veil lady for months. "It's true."

"Oh, please, Leo," she pleads. "It would mean so much to me. And Genevieve can go with you."

I cough into my wine glass. "I can?"

She waves me off, still looking at Leo. "That way you don't have to go over there alone." She shrugs and looks at me. "If you want."

"I'm sure Leo will be fine," William chimes in.

Leo glances down at me and then sighs. "I'll check the ferry schedule and figure it out."

"Thanks, man. I owe you." William slaps his back, and he and Nora turn to mingle with the rest of the wedding party and relatives that have arrived.

Leo half smiles, shaking his head.

"You know, I—" but my breath cuts out when Damien walks out on the patio, muddying up the beautiful atmosphere with his presence.

"Why the fuck is he here?" Leo asks over rigid syllables.

I swallow, glancing at Leo and back at Damien. "He was invited," I say, my voice strangled.

Leo stares down at me, his phone still open to the ferry schedule in his hand. "Do you want him here?"

"Do you care if he is?" I ask, pretending I'm unperturbed as I look at him. I wish I knew what his expression meant. He seems a little angry. A little afraid. A little irritated. And at this point, I don't know if it's because of what I said or because of the fact that Damien is walking toward us and he does, in fact, care.

"I care about what you want," he says in my ear.

"When have you ever?" My voice edges toward a whisper. Damien is now in earshot.

"Get your backbone ready."

My head snaps toward Leo at his loaded statement.

"Genny!" Damien says, holding his arms out for me. "It's so good to see you!"

He's so casual, and it's completely ridiculous. I step to him, letting him kiss my cheek and squeeze my waist and hating every millisecond of it.

"What a surprise." My voice is monotone even to my own ears.

"Is it though?" Damien cocks an eyebrow at me. "And of course, you're with Leo. Good to see you."

He's dismissing him, but Leo just nods and doesn't leave.

"Genny, can we talk?" Damien asks, eyes flitting to Leo.

Leo is unmoved, standing next to me like a bodyguard and I want to wrap my arms around him and say, *please, protect me from this monster forever.*

"About what?" I ask.

Damien looks around, his chin jerking back. "I just want to talk."

I see Leo press his lips together, biting back his smile, emboldening me. "Now isn't a good time." I flash a smile dripping with sugar and manners. "Have a wonderful lunch. I'm glad you could make it."

I take hold of Leo's elbow and start walking away from

161

Damien.

"Where are we going?" Leo asks, smiling down at me.

"Anywhere," I say, relief lapping at my bones the more steps we take away from Damien. Squeezing his elbow tighter, I add, "Thank you."

A moment of stillness absorbs us. Leo holds my entire being with his eyes. I swallow the reoccurring urge to kiss him, biting my lip and looking away.

"We should get a drink," I say, distracting myself from how he makes me feel.

"Pace yourself. It's hot out."

I groan as we step inside and reach the bar. "I miss my AC."

"Me too." He smiles at me. I try not to read into it. It's just a smile, and he's just Leo. And I just tried to kiss him last night. But we didn't. He rejected me, and I'm almost certain in my jealous little bones it has something to do with someone named Taylor.

When we return to the patio with our beverages refreshed, Damien is sitting at our table. I clamp my jaw shut so hard my teeth hurt.

I storm to the table, leaving Leo to seat himself.

"I think your seat is over there, Damien," I feign politeness.

Damien's mouth turns down, his green eyes revealing nothing but obnoxious innocence as his fingertips hold up his name card, making it shimmer.

"Oh, no. Your cards must have gotten mixed up because you had Aunt Wilma sitting next to you," Lorraine says, a tender hand on Damien's shoulder.

"Ah," I say, plastering a smile on my face and looking down at Damien. "Well, thank you, Lorraine, for sorting that out. You're a lifesaver."

She scrunches her nose at me with a smile and squeezes my shoulder.

My smile drops when she turns around and I stare down at Damien, before plopping into my chair like a pouty teenager.

"You can't even sit next to me?" Damien asks in my ear.

"You aren't supposed to be here."

"You said it would be fine."

"To come to the wedding," I argue. "This is for the wedding party and family."

"I'm practically family to the Wellingtons." He raises his eyebrows, then smiles in a way I used to find ridiculously adorable. "You're kind of stuck with me."

I bite the inside of my cheeks so I don't smile, scooting my chair away from him an inch like a petulant child.

I catch eyes with Nora across the table. She smiles but it's mostly a cringe and an apology distorting her perfect face.

"Well, Cora, you look like you're about to pop," Damien says. The delivery is charming, but the message is not.

Cora's eyes send arrows of fire into Damien.

"Six more weeks," John answers, rubbing a hand on his wife's leg.

"Nice. Wish I could eat for two!" Damien says, and Terrence chuckles uncomfortably next to him.

"Damien…" I say though he's not my responsibility. I don't know why I want him to stop. Then I look at Cora's flushed cheeks, round belly, and irritated face, and think, *I'll stop him for her.*

"It's just a joke," Damien says, leaning into me.

"But it's not funny," I say quietly.

Damien gives me a look of sullen disgust and opens his mouth to berate me or tell me to be quiet or, for all I know, apologize, but he doesn't get the chance because Leo speaks.

"Jules, right?" Leo asks.

Cora tilts her head fondly. "You remembered her name. See? I knew I always liked you, Leo." She elbows her husband. "John tried to tell me you were a player in college, and I just refuse to believe it."

I cough into my wine and Leo looks at me and away quickly.

"Wrong," William declares. "He seemed like a player, but it was an image."

"A lot of things about Leo are an image," Damien mutters. I wince and shiver like a spider just crawled across my neck.

"Did you say something?" Leo asks. He's only four people away, it's not surprising he heard Damien, but I can tell he's hyper-aware of me and Damien. I hate it. But I also love it.

Damien shakes his head. "Nothing that concerns you."

Leo stares at Damien, then looks at me. His eyes darken, but his expression otherwise gives nothing away.

I give my head a slight shake when he makes eye contact with me. *Let it go.*

Our attention is pulled away as the Wellingtons rise from the table behind us, glasses in hand to toast—yet again—to the lovely couple.

"Well," Barry begins. "I promised Lorraine I'd save the good stuff for tomorrow." He holds up his glass and studies it a moment. "I wasn't sure if she meant the scotch or the toast, but I figured a good thing never goes to waste."

Lorraine smacks his arm and a rough chuckle hums through the patio.

"Now, I always wanted a son. Call it a cliché or whatever you may, but I did. I wanted a boy to play ball with in the backyard, to crack jokes with at the end of the day, to take fishing on Saturday mornings, and watch football with on Sunday afternoons. Someone I could see myself in." Barry pauses for effect and smiles across the patio at his only daughter, dressed in a white sundress and with hair curled to perfection. "Then God gave me Nora."

Everyone laughs again, all eyes on Nora.

"And it was just the most perfect reminder that God sometimes does give us exactly what we want but he delivers it in the most unexpected package."

I smile at my soon-to-be sister-in-law, happiness brimming in my eyes.

"And bonus, she's marrying someone as great as William. And let me tell you, Will, I can't wait for you to be a part of the family. Cheers!"

We raise our glasses, clinking them as far as they can reach. Leo holds my gaze when our glasses touch until I press the wine glass to my lips. Everyone else at the table digs into their meals in front of them but in these moments, I've hardly registered that there's food in front of me or people around me. Just Leo.

A hand slides over my knee making me jump and break my stare with Leo.

"I love Nora's dad," Damien whispers, his lips touching my ear.

I give a curt nod and clamp my mouth shut as I scoot away.

"Did you try the polenta, Genny, it's delicious," Damien says, holding his spoon out to me.

"I've had it before. Thank you," I say, waving off his offering. I press my napkin to my lips.

He smiles, his eyes lingering on my skin like my sunburn. I offer him an uncomfortable smile and continue to eat the food off my own plate.

"But like, not as good as the spot in Brooklyn," he adds, anticipating my reaction.

I laugh as the memory surfaces. It was the first time I went to New York with him, and I was determined to walk over the Brooklyn Bridge before our flight early the next morning. About halfway across, it began to rain. Then quickly the steady rain began to pour and we were sprinting, our soaked tennis shoes sloshing against the wet pavement. We reached the end and he wrapped me in his arms and kissed me in the rain. We went to a quaint Italian bistro a few blocks away to have a warm meal. My hair was dripping, and he wiped the smudged mascara under my eyes with his fingertips. We drank red wine and he ordered the food because he had been there before and knew all the dishes I 'must try.' I must not have paid attention to what he ordered though because when my food arrived, I shoveled the warm, creamy dish in my mouth and said, 'These are the best mashed potatoes I've ever had!' Damien laughed until he couldn't breathe.

What can I say? I had never had polenta.

"Best mashed potatoes ever," I respond to Damien, letting myself be the butt of his implied joke.

"The moment I fell in love with you," he says, his gaze staying on me.

"Excuse me," Leo says, standing and leaving the table.

I freeze, my fingertips now cold despite the heat on this patio.

"Damien, I—" I begin but am interrupted by a tap on my shoulder.

"Genny Bear, can you walk Gampa and Nona to their car?" my dad asks. "The heat's a bit much for them and they'd like to get back to their hotel."

"Oh, of course." I jump up in a hurry, the chair legs scraping against the concrete.

I escape the patio with my grandparents and cross the scorching pavement to their rental car. Nona pats my arm as she maneuvers into the vehicle. Her movements are slow and she actually uses my hand for support, reminding me my grandparents are getting older.

"Love you, Nons," I say, kissing the side of her head and then looking to the driver's seat. "Gampa, please get the lady back to her hotel safely."

"Roger that." He salutes with a chuckle.

I close the door and watch them pull out of the parking lot. When I turn back to the restaurant, I try not to groan as I see Damien.

He approaches me with determination.

"What?" My voice is clipped. Just because I laughed about a good memory does not mean I need a private moment with this man ever again.

"I need to tell you something," he says.

I gesture for him to hurry it along and tell me.

"I have a kid."

I laugh—an evil cackle into the summer swamp air. Damien with a kid is quite comical.

"That wasn't a joke," he breathes, turning away from me like he's ashamed.

"Do you know who the mother is?" I ask, incredulous.

He whips around, a mixture of confusion and comedy consumes his face. I'm unsure if he's about to laugh or scream.

"Yes…" he says slowly, a panicked yet amused smile on his face.

Then I hear myself. "I mean, I didn't…" I clear my throat, shaking my head. "Are you serious?"

He nods. "I didn't know. Not until a couple of weeks ago did I even think it was a possibility." He twists his lips. I can't tell if he's about to cry or hit something.

I swallow, carefully navigating my thoughts. I want to know everything, but I don't want to treat any of it like it's my business. We are not together—I don't care. "How far along is she?"

He rubs his jaw. "She already had him."

A tender yet angry emotion wraps around my throat. It's embarrassing to realize our entire relationship is now tainted with his infidelity.

But I fake it.

"You have a son!" I plaster a smile on my face, tears leaking out the corners of my eyes. The words escape my lips with so much forced enthusiasm that I know I sound like a fraud.

Damien freezes and lets out a breath. "I have a son," he repeats but his words are etched with disbelief.

"How old is he?" I grit my teeth because he better be five. Damien and I have only been broken up for six months. I know how pregnancy works.

"Two months."

"Fuck," I breathe. My hands fly to my head, and I pace away.

He reaches me, grabbing my hand and making me face him. "Genny, listen—"

"Don't touch me!" I whip around, ready to beat the shit out of his perfect, lying face.

I hold a hand to my mouth. I feel a million things right now ranging from pure rage to completely not giving a damn.

"Genny," he repeats, his precious green eyes are sad and tender and completely full of utter bullshit.

"Don't." My voice betrays me and trembles over the word.

"I didn't know," he says, and I scoff.

"What? You didn't know you fucked someone else while we were together?" I'm shouting in the middle of the day, melting on the hot pavement of the parking lot of heat and humiliation.

I've been so concerned about being the bitchy sister-in-law forbidding a family friend from coming to the wedding, and now I'm wondering how I've played the bigger person so long to someone that never deserved it.

"You have to believe me, Genny," he pleads.

The information moves around my mind like whiplash, and his asking me to believe his innocence makes my thoughts stand completely still. "No, I don't have to do anything right now. Who is she?"

"You don't know her," he says, and I let out a jittery, deranged laugh. "Genny, I'm telling you now because I don't want you to find out from anyone but me."

"How noble."

"Babe, it was a mistake. I wanted to forget about it but—"

"But you have a love child," I finish with disgust. "Congratulations. I'll send you a gift."

Tears fill his eyes as his gaze drops to the pavement. Empathy makes an unwelcome appearance in my heart and then I remember: we're done. Done, done. I don't love Damien. I don't want to be with Damien. I can be the bigger person, even though he just proved he doesn't deserve it. I let out a deep, exhausted breath.

"I'm sorry," I say, softening my voice. "Are you freaking out?"

"I'm freaking out." His gaze focuses on me. I can sense everything he's worried about with just a single stare.

"What was the other night about then?"

"Everything I said to you was real. I meant it. The results of the DNA were just emailed to me this morning."

"But you knew it was a probability."

He nods. Slow. Deliberate. Hesitant.

I nod in response, releasing the tension in my jaw. "So you just thought: win her over then tell her about the kid?"

"No."

"Then what?"

"How do you tell the woman you love that you might have a kid with someone you barely know?"

I wave a hand in the air. "Spare me the R&B lyrics, please."

He doesn't laugh. His entire expression is consumed with guilt and remorse but I know, deep down, he's afraid.

"Fine. You just do," I tell him. "You say the words. You say, I might have a kid with someone I barely know. And it happened while we were together, and I'm sorry, and I'm a complete jackass, and I understand if you never want to see me again. Then you admit that you didn't care if you hurt me because all you've ever cared about is yourself and your ugly art."

He should be remorseful. He should bow his head with shame. But he doesn't. Instead, he has the audacity to stare directly in my eyes and say, "I've always cared about you, Genny. I have always loved you."

"You sure? It doesn't feel like it." I cross my arms.

"We said no matter what. We said those things because we loved each other. I still love you, and I want you to remember that you once loved me too."

Sadness consumes me, but I don't cry. "None of those promises matter if you betrayed me. Love doesn't do that. Love shouldn't embarrass me."

"I never wanted to embarrass you."

"But you did." I shrug. "You have. Thank you for that."

"I'm just trying to be honest."

"Well, the truth is embarrassing, I guess." I click my tongue against my teeth. I have tried so hard to not regret being with Damien for so long. I have constantly given him the benefit of the doubt and told everyone our time together was not a waste. But now I have no defense left for him. I sigh, forcing myself to be the bigger person yet again. "Are you going to meet him?"

"Is that really a question?"

I swallow hard. "Are you excited?"

"Terrified."

"Yeah."

"Yeah," he agrees, staring down at the pavement.

And just like that, I've forgotten I'm angry. I've forgotten he didn't tell me right away. I've forgotten he's broken my heart in a million different ways. He makes me feel blind rage, but I can still wish him well and continue to move on with my life.

"Can we still be friends?" he asks, his puppy dog eyes still full of hope.

"No," I say simply and without hesitation. I turn to go inside, hoping I never have to speak to him again.

Hurrying through the restaurant, the chill of the AC cuts my skin like a thousand razor blades then immediately feels like a cool washcloth.

I lean back on the wall, breathing out and letting my sweaty, damp, and overly emotional body enjoy the cold.

"Did you need an AC break too?"

I open my eyes to Leo's voice. He's at the end of the bar, phone in hand and eyes glued to the TV behind the bar.

I nod. "And a Damien break." I almost gag saying his name.

Leo laughs, but the sound is more of *tisk*.

"I hate him a little bit."

"Me too," he says, not asking for clarification.

"Are you watching highlights?" I laugh out the question as I step closer and see ESPN playing behind the bar.

He shoots me a playful glare. He doesn't answer my question. "You gonna snitch?"

I grin and slide onto the barstool next to him.

"I'm actually going to dip out early and see if I can hit the three o'clock ferry."

"But how will you avoid Mrs. Wellington's wrath," I tease.

"Hey, I'm doing her daughter a favor."

I bite my lip and nod. He's right. She'll love him even more for making the trek to Vashon Island. I don't envy him for having to run the errand, but I'm so jealous he gets to leave. I'm hot and completely bothered by Damien. I want an hour of no pleasantries in the car. I want to be next to the water on a boat, even if it is a ferry. I want to pick up the veil and be the hero.

"Can I come?" I ask, propping my hand under my chin. He licks his lips slowly, hesitating. *Always* hesitating. "I promise I won't kiss you."

He smiles with a breath through his nose. He pushes his phone back into his pocket. "Yeah, you can always come."

15

THURSDAY

Leo agreed to drive me over to my apartment first so I could change into more weather-appropriate attire for the ferry ride. I want to peel off my sweat-soaked blouse and jeans like I want to peel the conversation with Damien from my mind. I stare in a daze as the buttons on the elevator ding one floor at a time.

"Damien cheated on me," I say without emotion. I'm not necessarily upset, but our entire relationship seems to be illegitimatized by this arduous fact. It's unreal. I feel like I need to say it out loud a few times to know it's true.

Leo turns his face toward me. "Is that new information?"

I look at him, surprised.

"He seems like a cheater," he says, shrugging.

I scoff out a small laugh. "You really can't stand him."

"Nope."

I sigh. "He has a baby," I say more to the air of the elevator as I tilt my head back and close my eyes.

I can tell Leo is struck silent. A second passes, and then the elevator lurches, and I open my eyes. He pushed the emergency stop button.

"What are you doing, Leo?" I half-laugh as I speak.

"Say that again, I don't think I heard you correctly," he demands.

"Really? Stopping the elevator?" I chastise. "You're the most dramatic person."

He waits, jaw tight.

"He has a two-month-old son and based on how math and biology work, he was cheating on me well into our three-year relationship." I tip my head against the wall of the elevator again, staring at the stainless-steel ceiling.

"Are you okay?" he asks, his voice soft and deep.

I let out a laugh. "Surprisingly, yes."

He reaches for my hand and squeezes, making me smile.

"I mean six months ago I would have been devastated. But I guess now I just…" I meet Leo's eyes and stop.

"Now what?" he asks.

"Now I just know there's more for me out there," I finish, then add, "but he's still a total dick."

Leo laughs, and I bite my lip watching his smile transform his face.

"I would love to punch him in the face," he says, laughter still in his voice.

I smirk at him, appreciating the sentiment, but it's also quite overboard. "Why do you hate him so much? I mean, besides this situation."

"I have my reasons." He steps toward me—his already close proximity being eaten up inch by inch. Jealousy and contempt fill his eyes.

"Care to elaborate?"

He swallows hard and looks away.

"Seriously? What did he have that you wanted?" I question, heart hammering.

A pause, and then, "You, Evie. He had you."

The silence that follows screams at me. It claws at my heart until my emotions and mind are racing. Every word, every comeback, every sentiment comes to a halt on the tip of my tongue. I'm not speechless because there's nothing to say. I'm speechless because there's too much. Everything I need to tell him is pushing and shoving to the front of my mind and none of it is clear or coherent.

I lick my lips to buy time, contemplating whether or not to speak or kiss him.

"Everything all right in there?" the loudspeaker announces, snapping us out of whatever moment we were creating.

"Accidental," Leo says, breaking his stare from me and pressing the button again.

The elevator doors slide open and the moment is gone, making me realize I'm too scared to get it back.

My heart pounds three times the speed of our steps down the hallway but when we reach my apartment door, I open it and manage to say, "Come on in."

The air is at least ten degrees cooler in my apartment than in the hallway.

"I feel like we're breaking out of jail," I say, diffusing my own pent-up emotions.

Leo laughs, running a hand behind his neck. It would seem the elevator will keep our secrets for now, and we'll have amnesia until we decide to remember the words we exchanged.

"Can't take any more socializing?"

"Of course not." I flash him a look over my shoulder as I toss my keys and purse on the counter and make my way toward my bedroom. "Give me a sec, I just need to throw on some shorts."

He looks away with an expression I can only interpret as shy embarrassment, like I'm already naked walking down the hallway.

I enter my room and head straight to my closet, attempting to let go of the feeling that just shot through me and what I saw flashing in his eyes. As I step into my closet, I stub my toe hard against the cardboard of that stupid green file box and fall forward into the abyss of cotton, polyester, and silk. I reach for my life and grab onto a sweater hanging on the top rod to keep me from falling, but instead of helping me stay on my feet, the rod comes crashing down with me.

Damn cheap wire closet shelves.

I land on my elbow with a loud clatter, and a sharp pain

shoots up to my shoulder. I groan loudly as I roll onto my back, my body tangling in the fallen clothes.

"Evie, you okay?" Leo hollers, his voice increasingly closer.

"I'm fine," I yell through the layers of clothing piled on top of me.

There's a snort. "You sure? You look far from it."

I groan again.

"Need help?"

I push the fabric from my face, slowly digging my face a hole to the surface until I see Leo's face looking down at me, biting back a smile. "I tripped."

"And took the whole damn closet with you."

I press my lips together. "Basically."

He lets out a low laugh, one I can tell is sitting inside his belly, and he won't unleash it unless I give him permission. But I refuse to give him the satisfaction.

He scoops a pile of clothes off of me and plops it on my bed.

"You know, we do have a ferry to catch," he says.

"You know they do run every hour," I retort, sitting up.

"They do?" He turns to me, confused.

I shrug. "I assume."

He throws a sweatshirt at me and it whips me in the face. "Thank you," I mutter with sarcasm dripping off from my words as I peel the sweatshirt off my face. He's standing over me now, examining the quarter-sized holes in the drywall. They look like bullet holes.

"I can help you fix this later, but we really should get down to the ferry."

"Yeah, it's fine. That was my winter side anyway."

"You're what?"

"My winter clothes side," I answer, standing and digging through the drawers on the opposite side, pulling out a pair of jean shorts and a white crop top from the hanger above.

"Is that a thing?"

"When you don't share a closet, it can absolutely be a thing," I say, then kick the green box out of the center of the closet from under the pile of clothes. "Damn thing made me trip," I mutter more to myself.

"What's in it?"

I smile with a breath, and the word tumbles out before I can stop it. "You."

"What?" he asks, brow furrowed.

I stand, dropping my hands on my thighs. "There's a lot of you in that box. My dad found it in the attic and wanted me to take it."

Leo's mouth forms a loose O. He pauses and then speaks. "I'm sorry? What do you mean, me? What's in there? A lock of my hair? My baby teeth? A vile of my blood?"

I laugh, picking up the box to move it out of the way. "I wish."

"You witch," he taunts, stepping closer.

"How'd you find out?" I hold a playful hand to my mouth. "Don't burn me at the stake, sir."

He stares down at me, amusement in his eyes, and his right cheek twitches. "Depending on what's in there, there are a lot of things I could think to do to you that don't include burning you at the stake."

I swallow, color draining from my face as I grip the handles of the box.

"What's in there?"

I twist away. "Nothing."

"Evie…"

"Leonardo," I say, turning to shove it further back in the closet, beneath the mound of winter sweaters and suede jackets.

Leo grabs my hand still holding the box and gently coaxes me to face him. "Let me see. Come on, let's reminisce."

"We have a ferry to catch," I argue.

"They come every hour."

I roll my eyes, sighing and somehow, releasing the box into his grasp.

He takes it to the bed and sets it next to the pile of clothes he took off of me, gently discarding the lid. I wring my hands as I watch him.

"Why are you so nervous?"

I take in a breath, realizing I'm yet to let one go. My

175

shoulders are tight, and my palms are sweaty.

He pulls out the picture of us by the fire. "You ripped it."

I nod.

"And this one too." He holds up the two pieces of the picture of us on the Ferris wheel, to read his worn handwriting. *Scones are better than elephant ears.* His lips twitch as he reads it, running a finger over the tear through the word better. Then looks at me with eyes asking why.

"You made me sad," I shrug.

His jaw pulses and his Adam's apple drops with his eyes as he continues to dig through the box. He stares four extra heartbeats at the picture of us on the porch where he's holding the basketball. I don't have to ask why.

"Leo, I don't know if you should—"

He pulls out a stack of movie tickets and gum wrappers, neatly stacking them into separate piles as he takes note of the movies seen and words written. "You saved them." A statement. Weighted. Heavy. Full of memories and regret and mistakes.

My mouth is open, my tongue is dry, and my mind is blank. Imagine the biggest crush of your entire life discovering the shrine you built for them as a teenager and picking through it piece by piece. Because that's what is happening now, only it's a million times worse than I ever imagined.

Without words or the courage to pretend I don't care, I take my shorts and shirt into my bathroom and close the door behind me. I peel my sweaty clothes off of me and slip into the cool fabric of my jean shorts and cotton crop top.

"Evie," Leo says through the door.

"Almost done," I say, now aware my voice is trembling. I look at my reflection and the skin around my eyes is blotchy like I'm about to cry. I splash water on my cheeks then dab lotion on my sunburned shoulders and pull on my t-shirt.

"Evie, we need to talk."

I ignore him, spritzing my hair with dry shampoo and running my fingers through it. I dab a little concealer under my eyes and put on extra deodorant, already feeling a million times better. At least, physically.

Swinging open the door, I nearly slam into Leo's solid chest.

He's bracing the doorway, with his mouth open like he's about to say something.

"You ready?" I ask, ducking under his arm.

He grabs my elbow, swinging me around to face him. "I had no idea."

I snort. "Every grown woman once had a boyfriend box. Don't feel so special." I wince at my word choice. He was never my *boyfriend*.

He presses his lips together not at all taking my insults and jabs as bait. "I meant something to you," he says, following me down the hall.

I slip on my sandals and check my purse for my wallet and keys. "My keys are still on the counter," I mutter, grabbing them and putting them in my purse in a hurry.

"Evie."

The air in my lungs releases with a long, slow blow. "You meant something to me," I confirm, meeting his eyes. "But it was a long time ago. Can we go now, please?"

He slips a hand in his pocket, tilting his head just so. I hold his gaze not giving in to him trying to convince me to confess to anything.

Finally, he nods, and we ride the elevator down to the street, slip in his car, and drive for thirty minutes in almost silence. The air is full of discomfort and hesitation. How do we say any of this now when it shouldn't even matter anymore?

His fingers twitch and his eyes dart slightly. He's contemplating how to put me down easy. I know it. He's trying to remind me that what we did was a mistake. One that he's apologized for over and over.

When he drives his car onto the ferry, he places the car in park and I reach for the door handle for a quick escape. His hand lands on my arm, holding me in place.

I turn to face him with a helpless expression. "What?" I ask, but my eyes say, *let it go, please, I beg you*.

He pulls out his wallet and removes what looks like a piece of paper from the leather pocket. As he unfolds it, I see exactly what it is: his copy of the photo of us on the Ferris wheel. Only his isn't torn. It's bent and creased and the color has faded, but it's us, together, with smiles plastered on our faces and our biggest fight still ahead of us.

He drops the photo on my lap and says, "You meant something to me too. You always have."

16
THURSDAY

I stare at him.
I swallow.
I nod.
I blink.
Each simple gesture and action feels like it's taking a million years to complete. I hold the worn picture in my hands, wondering why he kept it all these years and knowing the exact answer at the same time.

"Good," I say finally. "I should mean something to you."

The statement is loaded, and the memory starts to feel suffocating as it replays in my mind, so I put the picture on the console and I escape the car and make my way upstairs to the deck of the ferry boat. It took Leo way too long to say it, and it infuriates me that I'm still so happy to hear it.

Leaning my elbows against the railing with the warm air whipping past my face feels like I'm on a tropical island and not in the Pacific Northwest during a heatwave.

You meant something to me too. I replay his voice in my head over and over, knowing his footsteps are the ones approaching me from behind.

"I fucked it all up, didn't I?" his voice says behind me. I don't have to turn to look to know his hands are in his pockets, his sunglasses clinging to his button-up, his jaw twitching, and his perfect light brown skin glowing in the heat of the sun.

"It takes two," I say, unable to look at him. I know if I turn around and meet his perfect eyes with his angry jaw and overwhelming presence, I will fall all the way apart. I will turn into a seventeen-year-old again and I'll remember the heartbreak of that night. It's been easier to ignore it and keep every feeling zipped up and tucked away in the recesses of my adolescent heart.

My eyes fall closed as he leans up against the railing next to me. The ferry ride is twenty-two minutes. I have twenty-two minutes to keep it together before we're off the boat and distracted enough by the world around us that we forget this conversation.

I glance at him and immediately cut my eyes back to the navy water before me sparkling in the sun, because I know that look. It's forceful. It's tender. It's the look that reminds me he always knew me best. I clamp my jaw shut and swallow hard.

"Never have I ever been as honest with someone as I am with you."

I scoff.

"What? You don't think that's true?"

I keep my gaze glued on the water. "No, it is painfully true. You have cut me to pieces with your honesty."

"I was young—"

"I didn't ask for an excuse."

"It's just a reason—"

"Same thing!" I bite back as I continue interrupting with a stubborn refusal to meet his eyes.

"You're still angry." A statement. Not a question.

"Angry isn't the word I'd use." I wince at my confession.

My words hang in the thick, humid air and I want to snatch them back up and swallow them whole.

"G, look at me," he whispers, then even more softly, "Evie."

I stare at his hands draped over the railing like a disobedient child. I hate his stupid hands. I hate how his veins stick out. I hate how his ring finger is slightly crooked from when he jammed it his senior year in high school during the championship game when he beat Tyler Howard to the rebound. I hate that I was the one getting him ice that night when he slept over and William was telling him to suck it up. I hate that I remember how we used to hold our hands together palm to palm to see how small mine were next to his because it was a lame excuse to touch each other. I hate how soft they are. I hate how I used to hold them under covers so no one would see. I hate that we're the reason my mom implemented the 'no blanket' rule.

"Evie…" he repeats, his voice soft and low as he covers my hands with one of his.

My forehead crumples and I squeeze my eyes shut.

"It's just me," he says.

I give a small nod. It is just him. Just Leo. But that's the problem.

I open my eyes and meet his stare. His eyes are intense, his mouth soft, jaw sharp. I know his face. It's so familiar that I know what he's thinking. But feeling? Never. I could never determine exactly what emotions were running through him. He was a million contradictions for so many years until that night he told me he wouldn't miss me when he was gone, and my entire teenage heart shattered in an instant.

I narrow my eyes and purse my lips. I want to scream *why now? Why this week?* But I know if I do, the guards standing watch over my heart will surrender without stepping foot into battle. Leo does that to me, and I know this, so I clamp my mouth shut and continue to glare at him.

"You look like you want to strangle me," he says with a breath of a laugh.

"No," I say, continuing to stare him down. "I want to make you run lines. Then make you start over because you didn't touch the line with your fingers like the cheater you are."

He smirks. "I'm not a cheater."

"You cut corners."

He laughs. "Really?"

"Really. And then when you're done running lines, I want to make you do a five-minute wall sit." I am carelessly deflecting.

He raises his eyes. "Impossible."

"God, boys are such babies. A five-minute wall sit is not impossible."

The right side of his mouth twists into a smile as he starts to lean back to no doubt check out the curve of my backside. I stop him abruptly with a hand on his arm.

"So inappropriate," I say, and he raises his eyebrows and then laughs.

Then I do too, and I hate it. I hate that I can't help but laugh in his presence. I hate that we joke and talk and goof off. I hate that we're fine—completely fine—until we're not. We are absolutely not fine.

As our laughter fades, I realize my hand is still on his arm and I peel it away with an uncomfortable jerk. He watches me pull away, then finally he speaks.

"I want to make things right between us. It's long past time."

I shake my head. "It doesn't matter anymore."

"It should matter." He steps closer, his presence slicing through my guard and unearthing my animosity.

"Fine!" I nearly shout. "You want to know how I felt? What that all did to me?" He nods, and I continue, hair whipping in my face from the wind. "You made me feel cheap. You made me feel like a conquest—a bet that you won. You…" I swallow so hard it hurts. "You broke my heart."

"That was the last thing I wanted to do," he says, reaching out to me. I can feel everything inside me crumbling.

"Yeah, well, sometimes the last thing you want is all you get. Sometimes it's all that's left," I say, relieved to finally be honest with him. "And I knew I'd just have to get over it. You're William's best friend. You aren't going anywhere. So I moved on. I've ignored it. I've tried to hate you. I've told myself I'm over you…repeatedly." I pause, hesitant to say my next words. "Until you show up and I realize I'm not."

Leo tilts his head thoughtfully, and says, "I want to make it up to you."

"How does Taylor feel about that?" I cut in because I refuse to be that person.

He freezes, a glimpse of hesitation flashes in his eyes. "Taylor has nothing to do with us."

"You know that makes you sound like a real jackass."

He presses his lips together in frustration, chewing on the side of his cheek. "I work with Taylor."

"And you take calls from her in the middle of the night?" I question, but I sound jealous and insecure.

"She lives in Hawaii—it wasn't even late her time. You know what—" He shakes his head and laces his fingers over his head, anger at his fingertips.

"You look like you want to strangle me," I say, watching him closely.

He drops his hands and turns to face me, his shoulders relaxing as a laugh escapes him. "No. I just want to make you run lines."

I can't help it. I smile. I laugh. Then I shove him like I'm a stupid teenager with a crush on my brother's best friend. He catches my arms mid-shove and pulls me closer to him, messing up my hair and squeezing my shoulders.

"You're infuriating," he says.

"You're impossible."

With my ear still pressed against his chest, I feel him still and hear him swallow hard. "You don't need to worry about Taylor."

"I wasn't," I lie.

"Please stop arguing," he says, turning down and tilting my face to his, forcing me to look into his eyes. "She is not my girlfriend. She never was. We work together. There are a lot of stupid things I have done and probably will still do but cheating is not one of them."

I nod, pressing my lips together. He's going to say something and whatever it is will knock me unsteady. I can sense my heart unraveling before he even opens his mouth to continue.

"I want you to know I know better now. I wouldn't say

183

what I said to you back then, now," he says, reaching for my hand and intertwining my fingers with his.

I let him and I know exactly why: we both have been starving for each other. We've spent eight years a few states and a whole world apart. We've muttered apologies and made small talk when we've had to. But all that's ever done is create tension and now we're both about to combust.

"What if now is too late?" My eyes begin to well because it's true. Too much time has passed without an apology for us to sweep it all under the rug.

And we both know it as we stare at each other, both too stubborn to admit it out loud. He doesn't look away and I don't either, even though every bone in my body is telling me I need to or I'm going to melt right here on this boat. He chews on his bottom lip, stepping closer. I reach up and pull his lip from his teeth.

"Stop doing that," I whisper.

"Don't tell me what to do." He's still moving closer. Just a foot away.

"Someone needs to make sure you behave."

Inches away. Leonardo Bishop is inches from my face.

Then breaths. He bends down slowly. I can practically taste his lips. The memories. The tears of our last kiss.

A horn blares through the hot, humid air letting us know we're about to dock on Vashon Island.

I close my eyes and turn my face. His lips fall on my forehead and his arms around my shoulders, pulling me deeply against his chest.

"This is a bad idea," I whisper, no matter how much his arms and heart feel like home.

"We were always my favorite bad idea."

17
THURSDAY

"What do you mean no one is answering?" Nora asks over the phone.

I clear my throat. "I don't know how else to word that."

Leo snorts out a small laugh.

"Look, let me call her and see what's going on. You're sure you're at the right house? 1777 *Bank* Road. It's right off the main strip. You know the downtown spot with all the restaurants?"

I glance at the white house with black numbers reading 1777 and then glance at the street sign. Bank Road. "Yep," I say. "Want to give me her number? I can call her."

She groans. "No, allow me. I'll call you back."

The line cuts out quickly and I can tell by the tone of her voice that Nora has all but had it when it comes to wedding stuff.

"She mad?"

"Frustrated," I correct.

"Do you like making excuses for her?"

"No, I prefer to recognize that her feelings are valid." I look

185

up and down the street, lined with evergreen trees and old houses. Vashon has its own exquisite charm. It's kind of like its own universe in the middle of the Puget Sound. It's only a ferry ride away, and yet I sometimes feel like I've traveled back in time when I'm here. Not in a bad way, but in an old, small town, quaint kind of way.

Vashon is a town where you still know all your neighbors and wave hello to strangers on the sidewalk. You can tell the difference between a daytime visitor and a new resident. And if you've just moved onto the island, I'm sure you're met with fresh pastries and a handmade soy candle to welcome you to the town.

I sigh, taking in the salty air and beautiful quaintness of the town my mom loved.

"You thinking of your mom?" Leo asks.

I unleash the full version of the smile that was touching my lips. "Always."

He smiles gently and nods, hands in his pockets, brow glistening in the heat. "So what's the plan? Do we break in?"

I laugh. "You wish, pretty boy."

He lets loose an unbridled smile that makes my stomach flip. "Then what?"

I plop down on the stoop of the old house and pat the place next to me on the black step. "She's going to call the lady. I'm sure she's close—we're on an island. She can't be far."

Leo sits down next to me, elbows on his knees, and I lean back on my hands, taking in the sight of him and the strong scent of the lavender and green hydrangeas blooming next to the porch.

"Can we call a truce?" I ask, cutting through the quiet summer air.

He turns to me with a puzzled expression.

"This whole make up for lost time, rehash the past, and try to apologize better gig? Can we just not this week?" I clarify in the worst way. "Because I already feel so emotional with the wedding and thinking of my mom, I just…I just need to not talk about what happened."

"Are you upset about what happened with Damien?" he

asks.

I'm surprised at how little this has to do with Damien. "No, Damien is a side show. I don't care."

Leo smiles a little and asks, "But you care about me?"

"Can we not?" I huff.

Leo licks his lips and nods slowly. "Okay, but only if you promise that we will."

"Leo—"

"We need to talk about it. All of it, Evie." He stares at me with a pointed expression making all my objections dry up in an instant.

I open my mouth to protest one last time but my phone cuts through my thoughts.

"Hey, Nora."

"You're going to kill me," she says.

"Why? Are you calling the wedding off?" I smile mischievously, and Leo bends down to listen in on the call.

"Yes, and I'm eloping with William in Mexico and only you and Leo are invited." She laughs again—a delirious, hopeless sound.

"What happened?"

"Amalie—the lady that made the veil—isn't on the island…"

I sit upright, ready to head back to the dock. "So, should we meet her somewhere on the mainland—?"

"…But the veil is on the island."

Break in, Leo mouths, pointing at the side window, and I laugh.

"What's so funny?" Nora asks.

I swat Leo's shoulder. "Nothing—just Leo. So what should we do?"

"Amalie said she'll be there in two and a half hours…*hopefully.* Could you guys wait?"

"I guess," I say with a reluctant swallow, my armpits heavily perspiring.

"I'm so sorry," Nora whines. "This is just the worst. I feel so disorganized."

"It's fine. We'll go grab something from the bakery and then come back," I reason, though this is entirely inconvenient and way too hot to be meandering about a town I rarely visit since my mom died.

After saying goodbye, I get off the phone with Nora and turn to Leo with an apology-stricken face.

"Amalie is getting a one-star review on Etsy," he deadpans.

A laugh escapes me. "Shut up." But I don't disagree. "Want to go to the bakery?"

"Do they have AC?"

"They must," I say as I stand, and Leo follows me down the road until we turn along the main strip in downtown Vashon.

When we reach the bakery, my sweaty palms grab the door handle and swing the door open, letting the cold air-conditioned air from the inside cut against my skin in the best way.

We groan simultaneously. "Gah, it's so cold in here."

"It feels amazing!" Leo exclaims spinning in a childish yet giant circle.

"Welcome in! I'm Willy. What can I get you?" the man behind the counter asks. He's wearing an apron over the top of a Hawaiian shirt which does not at all fit the quaint, old-timey-ness of the restaurant. The checkout counter is paneled with old cupcake tins. The floors are rustic, wide, wooden planks with deep knotting. The glass dessert case is nearly empty as dinner time approaches and closing time nears.

I step to the glass and peer inside. There are four chocolate croissants left. Two apple turnovers. One peanut butter bliss bar. Three giant crinkle cookies. Three sugar cookies. And only one slice of cookies and cream mousse cake with caramel sauce. The rest of the trays hold nothing but crumbs.

"I want one of everything," Leo says.

I laugh. Willy smirks and eyes us both.

"No, seriously. Why not?"

I pat his tummy, which is much too chiseled to be referred to as a tummy. "Because you asked for sugar-free coffee this morning, remember?"

Leo chuckles. "Yeah, but look!" he holds his hands out toward the glass case like Vanna White after a contestant bought a vowel.

"Fine," I say, crossing my arms and nudging him with my shoulder with a side smile. I look at Willy. "One of each please."

He nods. "You bet," he says, slipping on plastic gloves and opening the case. "You two staying cool today?"

"Absolutely not," I laugh. So does Willy.

"We've been running around for her brother's wedding tomorrow, and we have not stopped sweating," Leo adds.

"This is the coolest we've been since this morning at my apartment," I add, watching Willy take the peanut butter bar out of the case.

Willy chuckles. "Well, I'll bet your brother is thankful to not be out in this heat."

"True."

"The wedding on the island?" Willy asks.

"No, it's at the Chihuly Garden and Glass in downtown Seattle."

Willy draws back. "What brought you over here?"

"The wedding veil," Leo and I answer in unison.

Willy chuckles. "Amalie Santini?"

I tilt my head. "How'd you know?"

"Amalie is known for her custom veils," he says, setting our box of treats on the counter. "And her bed and breakfast."

"That was a bed and breakfast?" I ask, not remembering any signage that indicated such.

He nods. "One of the few remaining ones. But the only one with Ms. Amalie's eggs benedict. If you ever get the chance, you should stay there. Ask for the orchid room. It's best for couples." He winks.

"Oh, Willy, we're not..." I let out a sharp uncomfortable cough-laugh.

"We're just friends," Leo says, his voice smooth. Completely unperturbed.

Willy draws back, arms crossed over his potbelly, and smiles. "Could have fooled me."

"We've known each other since we were kids," I overexplain as if it matters.

"I can see that," Willy says, and I want to say, *See what? How can you tell? We've been in here for five minutes.* "Any coffee or cocktails before I ring you up?"

"Anything cold," I answer.

He pulls two large bottles of water out of the refrigerator and two cans of white wine. Yes, cans.

He plunks them inside the brown paper bag with the baking company emblem printed on it and says, "On the house."

The luxury.

"Thanks, Willy," Leo says like they're good ol' friends.

"I'd offer to let you stay in the AC for longer, but I have to close up and get home to the misses. But I tell you what—if you head down to the water, the sea breeze will fool you into believing it isn't as hot as it is outside. Plus, no one will bother you for drinking."

"Ah," my eyebrows shoot up and I smile as I take our bag of goodies. "Well, thank you for that tidbit of information."

Leo tilts his chin down, trying not to laugh at my awkwardness.

"Have a good one!" Leo hollers with a quick wave, holding the door open for me.

Once we step out into the sauna that is the air of June, the cool, dampness of my crop top immediately sticks to the sweat beading on my lower back. When we get his rental car, it feels like we might suffocate or melt—both options are plausible—and it takes a solid five minutes before the AC actually kicks in. Just in time for us to park at KVI Beach. The beach is still pretty busy, but it's beautiful. And as the sweltering one-hundred and ten-degree heat cools to a balmy ninety-nine, people will start heading out to make sure their homes have not melted completely.

"I like Willy," Leo says as we hop out of his car after we arrive.

"You like everyone that feeds you."

"Not true. You've never fed me, and I like you."

I pretend it doesn't make me want to smile. "I made you popcorn."

"Ah, yes. Decadent," he teases.

"With popcorn sprinkles."

He laughs and holds up his hands. "Fine. You feed me. You

win."

"Does—" I begin and then stop.

"Does what?"

I open my mouth, hesitating, then fix my eyes on the ground. "Nothing."

He dips his head to my level, but we keep walking. "Just say it."

"No."

"Why not? Was it embarrassing? A middle of the night confession?" He stops me just before we reach the boardwalk leading to the pebbled beach of the Sound. "Did you actually kill William's goldfish in middle school? Because I've long suspected it was you."

"What? No!" I laugh, stepping onto the pebbled beach. My sandals shift under my feet, and I stumble, grabbing onto Leo's stupid muscular arm. He laughs his stupid, perfect laugh. "You think of the most random things," I say, righting myself and finding a good spot near the water to sit.

"It's been on my mind for the last fifteen years." He grins down at me as I sit on the rocks in front of a long piece of driftwood and sit against it. "Admit it: you forgot to feed Jupiter the goldfish when Will and I were at that basketball tournament, and she died the morning we got home."

My mouth drops. "I would never forget to feed Jupiter. I cannot believe what you're insinuating!"

"Fine, I'll believe you but only if you tell me what you were going to say." He pauses and waits.

"I don't remember." Because for a split second I don't. But as I stare at his face, patiently waiting for me to be honest, I remember the thought that crossed my mind. It's stupid really. Immature. I shrug. "Fine. I was just wondering if Taylor feeds you."

I cringe. That sounded more sexually kinky than I wanted it to. Never mind immature, needy, and desperate. I look away from him and fix my eyes on the pebbles below my feet, then the water glistening in front of us with a steamboat gliding through the water. Anything but the restrained smile on Leo's face.

I give him a sidelong glance expecting to see a taunting and victorious expression, but I don't. Leo's face is completely placid as his gaze roams over my face.

"What? I know…it's stupid. I meant it as a joke but it didn't come out that way—"

"You're jealous."

I swallow, turning away. "I am not."

An amused and satisfied smile lights up his face. "It's okay if you are. But I want you to know that whomever you've created Taylor to be in your mind is not correct." He shakes his head, pulling something out of the pastry bag. "Like, I guarantee it's way off."

I shrug and nod. A juvenile response to my feelings because Leo nailed it. I'm jealous. Stupidly jealous. And I have no right.

Even when I think of all the ways we loved each other. All the ways we hurt each other. All the ways life could have been different now. I still know I have no claim on him.

"I'm not with anyone, Evie. I'm single," he answers my unspoken question.

"Okay." I try to keep my voice steady, but the word comes out meek and small, only telling him how much I care.

"Here, try this," he says, changing the subject with sweets and holding out a black plastic fork covered with the cookies and cream cake.

I take a bite.

"Oh my god," I moan, licking my lips. "That's so good."

He stabs the cake again and takes another bite. "I know, right?"

I take the fork from him and grab another bite. He smiles at me.

"Blind taste test?"

I lick the caramel from my lips. "How? I know what we ordered."

"Humor me," he says.

"I've spent a good portion of my life humoring you."

"What's a few more minutes?"

I reel in my grin, close my eyes, and open my mouth—a willing participant just like when we were teenagers.

Something touches my tongue quickly. It's sweet, salty, and most definitely is Leo's finger.

"Ugh! What the hell, Leo?" I shriek, jerking my head back, and he laughs.

"Sorry, I wasn't ready and your tongue was right there."

I open my eyes to glare at him, but he shoves his clumsy hand over my eyes. I fall back onto the pebbles holding on to his forearm for dear life. "Don't open your eyes!" he scolds.

I laugh, trying to squeeze my eyes shut but my curiosity is trying to force them open.

"Calm down," he laughs. "You ready?"

"Yes." My shoulders drop as I hear the pop of a can.

"Open your mouth."

"Oh, so now you want me to—"

"Just do it. It's going to be cold."

I jerk back as cold metal touches my bottom lip. Leo curls his hand around the back of my neck and shushes me softly. "Trust me," he whispers. Then a small amount of cold, tart liquid pours into my mouth.

I swallow it down and lick my lips, realizing where this came from. "The canned wine!"

"You're so smart!" he teases, sarcasm dripping from his voice.

I cock one eye open. "Can I open my eyes now?"

His hand smacks my forehead as he tries to cover my eyes. "No!"

"Ow, Leo! I figured it out. It's canned wine."

"But Willy gave us two different kinds. Rosé and sauvignon blanc. I want you to tell me which one you like better."

I smile despite myself and open my arrogant mouth to receive another taste. I know rosé like I know pink cotton candy. It's my favorite.

The cold metal touches my lips and the wine pours in. This one is more tart with hints of citrus.

"Which one do you like better?" he asks.

I contemplate a moment. "Let me try the first one again?"

He pours the first wine into my mouth. It's good, I mean for canned wine. But the taste is more floral.

"Okay, the other one now."

I sense his smile behind the hand he's holding up to my eyes. "You trying to get drunk?"

"Yes," I joke, slurping the wine off the lip of the can. I play with the liquid in my mouth for a moment. "That one is rosé. I like that one better."

"I know you do, and no, it's not."

I open my eyes. "Wait. What do you mean?"

"You picked sauvignon blanc. You always say you like rosé more than sauvignon blanc, but you don't, not really."

I throw up my hands. "It's canned wine, Leo."

"It's facts, Evie," he mimics. "You always order rosé and then barely touch it but if someone pours you a glass of sauvignon blanc, you ask for a second glass."

I cross my arms and peer at him. "What's your point?"

I look down as he hands me the can of sauvignon blanc. I swipe it from him reluctantly and take a long drink, then give him the can to drink from, and he does with a small, satisfied twitch of a smile.

"The point is I pay attention. And I know you, more than you think I do. I never stopped knowing you even when I said I would," he says, placing a hand on my knee. "Also, that means we're tied again. H-O-R-S, H-O-R-S."

"Oh, you really think you're going to take this one, don't you?"

"Want to make a bet?" he asks.

I shift closer. "Always."

"Whoever loses has to take the other out to dinner."

"Thrilling."

He squints at me. "Would you rather the loser go streaking through Pike Place?"

"It'd be slightly unoriginal but it'd be a fun sight," I tease, dragging my eyes up and down his body.

"Hey, now, I'm not losing. That'd be your ass flying by and making the fish throwers drop the fish."

I throw my head back as a laugh escapes my throat. "They never drop the fish!"

"They've never had Genevieve Michaels's fine ass to distract them."

I shake my head, pressing my lips together. He's teasing, I know he is. But it still makes my cheeks warm, and a fire ignites in my chest burning down my center. My mind spirals as my feelings grow out of control around him. I've wanted for so long to let it all go. Move on. But everything about us together is so easy...yet excruciatingly, irrevocably painful.

"Hey," he says, tilting my chin to face him. "Don't look so sad."

I force a smile as my hand finds his. Staring down at our hands, I wonder how someone can be so familiar and unrecognizable all at the same time. He'll always be the Leo I knew—a distant memory, a treasured childhood frenemy—but I wonder if somehow, I can let him be someone I know right now.

I let out a soft sigh, licking my lips as my mind falls back on my search for words. My palms start sweating and a drop of perspiration rolls down my back. I can't think in this heat. Everything I want to say seems fuzzy and incoherent. My heart drums in my ears and I press my eyes closed trying to collect myself. I don't though. Instead, my nerves get the best of me, and I hop up.

"Let's swim," I declare, slipping off my sandals.

"Excuse me?" Leo questions, his eyes sweeping over my body.

"I'm hot. I've had half a can of wine." I waggle my eyebrows like an idiot, then continue. "Plus, I can't stop sweating. It's one hundred degrees outside. The veil isn't ready. Let's swim."

Leo stands next to me. "You're serious."

"Yes, I'm serious."

His fingers hesitate over the buttons on his shirt as his eyes watch me with curious intent.

"I dare you, Leo," I say with a glare.

He lets out a small laugh and licks his lips, shaking his head as he begins to unbutton his shirt. "I never said no to a dare."

My gaze catches his, and we freeze with the memories. I swallow, breaking away from his consuming stare. "Great, let's go, pretty boy."

He tosses his shirt on top of my bag and unhooks his belt in one swift motion. It cracks like a whip as it leaves the last loop. A vice made of liquid heat traps my insides and I clear my throat, dropping my gaze like I'm not allowed to look. Not like it's something I've never seen. I don't have to look at Leo to know he's smiling at me victoriously. He knows he's far too good-looking. Needs to watch his sugar intake, my ass. His arm muscles are thick curves wrapped in his tattoos, and I could probably grate cheese on his abs...or lick off maple syrup. Really, both options are possible.

"Race ya!" he says with a playful grin.

"You're on." I smile back, letting the sea breeze whip through my hair and setting up my posture to take off. "On your mark. Get set. G—"

Like the cheater he is, Leo takes off before 'go,' but I saw it coming and eat at his heels. Not one to lose, I reach out and grasp at whatever I can get my hands on. My fingers curl into his shorts and give them a yank but he's too strong, pulling me out to the edge of the water no matter how much I dig my heels in the sand.

"Hey, that's cheating," he laughs, still dragging me like a rag doll.

"Oh, *this* is cheating? Listen to yourself, Leonardo," I tease, letting go quickly, making him stumble forward and crash into the shallow water.

I laugh, victorious, as I continue to run out in the water. The cool, small waves ripple and splash against my shins, then my thighs until I'm waist deep and I fall back into the water with my eyes closed, letting the cold, saltwater wash over my senses. The coolness of the water soothes my sunburned shoulders under my cropped t-shirt. I don't realize how hot I am until the water hits my skin to cool me off. It's rare for the frigid water of the Puget Sound to feel comforting, but today, it's perfect. My smile is wide, and I let out a euphoric sigh, opening my eyes to see Leo wading toward me.

What once was a playful and victorious grin is now a nervous and shy smile.

"Feels good, doesn't it?" I ask, luring him out of his nerves.

He chews his lip and his eyes glint as he lowers his body into the water and swims toward me. His nerves quickly settle into something more confident.

I lick my lips as he approaches. Both of us are crouching in the water, face to face, with our knees bumping each other's and our arms wading around us. Our fingers touch, and I swallow my heart as it leaps into my throat. I move closer, wanting to feel his slick body under the water more than I want to run from it. Leo smiles over at me, eyes drifting over my face.

"That's HORSE. I win," he says.

I cackle. "No, you didn't."

"My feet hit the water first."

"Because you cheated!"

"Semantics." He rolls his eyes, moving closer. His Adam's apple bobs, making me want to wrap my hands around his neck.

"One, you're impossible. And two, that's not the correct use of that word."

He shrugs, a smile pulling at one side of his mouth.

I shake my head. "I'm getting you a dictionary for your birthday."

He chuckles, sinking so low, the water drifts over his mouth. My gaze falls toward his mouth, and his lips twitch in a small smile letting me know he noticed. Leo has always been at arm's length even when he's been in my actual arms. He's always been two seconds too late, a kiss too soon, a heartbreak in the wings. Untouchable. Impossible.

And everything I ever wanted.

A pained expression passes over his face, and I know the same thoughts are spiraling through his mind. We're either going to be smart enough to ignore it. Or stupid enough to fall back into it.

I clear my throat. "Anyway, you can't win with a false start."

His expression changes and his eyes tell me he's enamored with me. I can tell he's fighting his feelings right before my eyes. "All's fair in love and war," he says.

I toss my head back and laugh. "This isn't war, and this isn't I—"

But he cuts me off, pulling me to him by the nape of my neck and our lips crash together.

I gasp, but I don't object. I relax into his arms as he kisses me with enough passion to make my head spin.

It all happens too fast and so slowly at the same time. One moment, I'm trying to win an argument, and the next, Leo's hands are cradling my face, and his body is pressed up against mine, and I'm realizing I'm always going to fall. I'm always going to be at his mercy. I wrap my legs around his waist and his fingers dance in my wet hair as his tongue parts my lips. My body pulses with fire. Lava pours through my veins and down my center as his hands run down my back and curve over my hips, holding me in place. I hold his face in my hands and drink him in. The heat of summer radiates off his skin as one hand covers the width of my back and the other grips my thigh. A small groan escapes the back of his throat, making me squeeze my legs tighter around his waist.

We kiss for a long minute that's over too soon.

Leo pulls back, his lips brushing against mine and his thumbs pressing deep into the flesh of my hip bones. "God, I have missed you for too long."

My heart aches and my eyes fill with tears. "But you said you wouldn't."

18
THURSDAY

"You told me you wouldn't miss me," I say.

He nips at my jaw. "I know."

"You told me we were a mistake," I continue.

He presses his lips against my collarbone. "I know."

"That we'd never work."

He draws back. "I fucking know." His tone hitches with anger, but I don't want to stop this confession. "But I messed up. I have regretted the words I said to you every day since they left my mouth. You are my biggest regret. I was a stupid teenager that was freaked out because I just slept with my best friend's little sister."

I nod, pressing my lips together before speaking. "Is that all I was? Your best friend's little sister?"

Leo's eyes search my face, rubbing his thumb over my cheekbone as he shakes his head. "I'm sorry," he whispers, kissing me again and pulling me tighter against him. "I've hated that version of myself every day since that night."

His apology brushes the skin on my jaw, and he kisses my neck. My body responds, and I wrap my fingers around his neck, then run a hand down his bare chest, feeling the warmth of his skin against mine. I grip him tighter between my legs, knowing how much it hurt to let him go the first time. How much I've hated keeping this secret from people I love. How stupid that the secret was always us.

I kiss him again.

"I've hated that version of you too," I confess, breathless and tugging his hair and taking his bottom lip with my teeth. "Did you end up missing me?"

"More than I thought I could miss someone." His words escape his mouth, and the ache in my chest eases. "Did you miss me?" he asks.

"No," I answer, shaking my head as his brow creases. "I just thought about you all the time."

He smiles and slowly raises an eyebrow as his hands cradle my face. "Good thoughts?"

"No," I laugh out. "A lot of those thoughts included murdering you and making it look like an accident."

His laugh is a deep rumble that tickles my skin as he glides a hand down my chest and around my waist.

"Can I change the narrative?" he asks, his voice low and smooth over the skin of my jaw. His hand slows as it curves over my hip, and he hooks his thumb on the waistband of my jean shorts. "I want to make it up to you. Let me," he whispers against my ear, and a chill rises over my flesh.

The calm, salty water rises over our shoulders, and only now do I notice the stillness of the evening. I stare at him with an expression I know only reveals a portion of the fear and hopelessness I feel at this idea. But I don't care. In this moment, I'm brave enough to drown in the impossibility of us.

My eyes move from his eyes to his mouth to his heart and back to his eyes. I nod and open my mouth to speak when my phone rings from the shore. Our eyes snap into focus, and our hands freeze.

And it's a good thing too because there are still a few families on the beach that no doubt saw us partaking in this romantic make-out session in the water.

Fantastic.

I swallow, turning back to Leo. I don't want this moment to end, but I know it has to. "That's probably William or Nora."

He nods. "Probably."

My face involuntarily moves closer to his. "I should call them back."

He nods again, his face drifting even closer to mine as he grips my waist. "Probably should."

"Yeah," I say, and then my lips are sealed on his. I pull back, my eyes catching the sun starting to go down, jerking me out of Leo's spell. "Oh shit. It's getting late. We should go. We have to catch a ferry."

Leo's eyes widen as he remembers too, and he grabs my hand pulling me through the water until we're running like baby deer over the pebbles to our pile of things. We laugh and shriek as the pebbled beach injures the bottoms of our bare feet. We fall to the ground laughing. I land in between Leo's legs, and he wraps his arms around me.

"So much for calling a truce." He smirks, and I roll my eyes. "You feel good," he whispers in my ear as I fumble with my phone to call William back.

I smile at Leo over my shoulder.

"You smell good too," he adds, and I let out a laugh.

"I'm soaking wet. I don't smell like anything," I say, trying to dry my fingers in the air so I can unlock my phone.

He laughs, a low rumble in my ear sending goosebumps over my skin. "You smell like sunshine."

"Sunshine doesn't have a smell," I say, holding the phone to my ear after dialing William.

"Yeah, but if it did, it'd be you."

Heat spreads over my body. And then I hear my brother answer, stopping the feeling in its tracks.

"Hi," I say when William answers, still in Leo's arms.

"Are you running? Why are you out of breath?" William says on the other line.

Leo overhears and snorts out a laugh, his forehead landing on my shoulder.

"Nope, just dying of heat exhaustion while we wait for your fiancée's veil to be ready," I say, steadying my voice as much as possible.

"Sorry," William mutters. "The lady just called Nora, she said she's back on the island and she apologized profusely for the inconvenience." He emphasizes the last word like this has been a hindrance for him and not Leo and me. I withhold an eye roll of irritation. Leo doesn't.

"Well, great. We'll head over and meet you guys at the hotel."

I say goodbye and hang up, meeting Leo's gaze. I'm still between his legs, cradled in his arms, staring at his perfect face with the sun setting and my head spinning.

"Ready?" I ask, but my voice squeaks because I've never been able to control my nerves after I kiss Leo.

He throws on his shirt and helps me up. We collect our half-empty cans of wine and picked over pastries in the brown bag and head straight for his car. I pick nervously at my fingers in front of me as the panic sets in.

I can't believe we just made out in the water like a couple of high schoolers sneaking behind my brother's back. That was so stupid. And irresponsible. A kiss is just a kiss unless it reopens wounds that never really healed in the first place. *Why are we like this?*

"Because we never finished the game we started all those years ago," Leo answers, and I stop completely, realizing my last sentence was spoken aloud.

Leo turns to face me, just a few feet from his car. "Look, I won't do it again if you don't want me to. But I'm not going to apologize for wanting to kiss you every time I see you."

I hesitate to speak, my heart overcoming every other sense of logic. "But we're a bad idea. Right? We shouldn't do this." I sound like I'm trying to convince myself, not Leo.

He shakes his head slowly, taking two swift steps toward me.

"You said that. You said—"

"I said you were always my favorite bad idea," he says, holding my face in his hands.

My brow creases. "I don't know if that makes me feel better."

He laughs. "We're complicated, but not impossible."

I nod, but I don't know if I believe him. We really do have a lot to talk about. A lot to rehash. A lot of reasons to remember why we're a bad idea that won't end well.

Because the past isn't past. It never is. It's a part of him. It's a part of me. It's a part of us. And it will always be our story, no matter how terrible it ends.

I curl into his arms, resting my head on his chest, wishing I could memorize his heartbeat. "Let's just get that stupid veil."

We arrive at Amalie's with damp clothes and wet hair. She opens her front door with a quizzical look that evaporates into a laugh.

"That hot, huh?"

I let out a timid laugh. "Yep. We are just here to pick up Nora Wellington's veil."

Amalie is not at all who I expected. She's wearing a multi-colored caftan with at least seven bangle bracelets on each wrist. Her hair is a long, dusty brown with streaks of gray swooped into a French braid. Her brown eyes are framed with thick-rimmed glasses and her smile is warm and inviting. She shuffles to the side and lets us in. "Can I get you a towel?"

"No, thank you—"

"Yes, please," Leo says at the same time.

Amalie smiles and motions for us to follow her down the long floral wallpapered hallway. The floors are deep cherrywood and the molding is exquisite, framing the top and bottom of the wall and wrapping around the curved staircase that leads to the second floor. The air is cool and smells like clean linen. It's actually quite adorable. I could totally see this as a bed and breakfast.

"Well, I really do appreciate you two waiting. My apologies for getting the pick-up date mixed up. Normally brides don't cut it so close to the wedding date." Amalie huffs out a laugh, handing us each a plush white towel.

"Oh, no worries." I wave her off, pressing the towel against the damp skin on my neck. "We'll just be grabbing it and then taking a ferry back over to the mainland."

She freezes. A flash of surprise and then worry dances over her face. "Oh dear," she says, and I glance at Leo.

"'Oh dear' what?" he asks.

She winces as she smiles. "The last ferry already ran."

My mouth drops. Leo explodes into laughter, running a hand down his face.

"That's a joke, right?" I ask.

"I'm afraid not," she answers, wringing her hands. "Nora said you two knew that." I gape at her. "She did, she said not to worry, her friends will figure it out."

I look at Leo, *Can you believe this?*

He hasn't stopped laughing. "That's so Nora."

I squint at him because I don't understand how that's so Nora, but I don't care to ask right now. "When is the next one?"

"Seven a.m. sharp," Amalie answers with a nod.

I glance at my watch. It's eight o'clock. We spent far more time at the beach than I thought. I turn to Leo. "What do we do? Sleep in your car?"

He shrugs, shaking his head like he's given up hope. "I guess."

Amalie looks between us. "Oh, nonsense. You can stay here. I don't have guests coming until tomorrow afternoon. The orchid room just needs a few towels, and it would be suitable."

My manners want to object but what else are we going to do?

"Thank you, Amalie, you're a lifesaver."

She smiles and meets my eyes. "Chin up, honey. He looks harmless." She winks at me, and I laugh uncomfortably, not realizing how upset my face must have been.

"Truly, Amalie. Thank you. What do I owe you?" Leo asks.

She waves a hand and shuffles up the stairs, beckoning us to follow. "A good review on Etsy."

Leo laughs.

She pauses, a hand on the railing, and turns to face Leo, eyebrows raised. "That wasn't a joke."

"Yeah, Leo. Reviews are important," I add.

He laughs and shakes his head. "We will leave you the

shiniest five-star review for this. I promise."

She winks at him. "Robes are in the closet. You can wear those while I wash your wet clothes if you like."

"Oh, I don't mind doing it—"

She holds up a hand. "No one runs the washer but me. House rules." She smiles. "There's a laundromat bag in the closet too. Put your wet clothes in there and set it outside the door. I promise I won't disturb you two." She winks again, and I withhold a laugh as my cheeks burn with humiliation. "Breakfast is usually at eight-thirty but seeing you two need to get ready for a wedding tomorrow, how's eight sound?"

I breathe out relief and stress. "Fantastic."

She nods, opening the room and handing Leo the old brass key. "Enjoy."

We enter the orchid room and it is exactly what a picturesque bed and breakfast should be. Muted orchid wallpaper, hand-painted in shades of white, cream, and taupe. Board-and-batten climbs three-quarters of the way up each wall. Two club chairs sit by the bay window with a small wooden table between them stacked with books and several orchids in white pots. A plush, king-sized bed sits in the center of the far wall, draped in white bedding and surrounded by a cream-tufted headboard. Nerves flutter in my heart because I know what happens when Leo and I are alone together, and I don't feel at all prepared.

"I know what you're thinking," he says, his voice low and deep behind me. I turn my head in his direction. "How does she keep all those orchids alive?"

I laugh, feeling so thankful for how stupidly perfect he is. He throws a robe at me. It hits me in the face.

"You change first."

19

THURSDAY

"Nora sucks," I say, tossing my almost dead phone on the bed and lying back on the pillows. My hair is still damp from the shower and smells like expensive shampoo.

Leo emerges from the bathroom with a laugh, skin dewy and wrapped in a white robe. We look like a couple of honeymooners.

This bed and breakfast feels almost spa-like. The bathroom is stocked to the brim with toiletries, including salon-brand shampoo, toothpaste, and disposable razors—thank God for that because I really needed to shave before the wedding.

"Are you speaking ill of your sister-in-law?" he gapes at me, stuffing his clothes in the laundromat bag and setting it outside the room.

I peer at him out of the corner of my eye, not changing my position. "Yes."

He laughs, shuts the door, takes three quick strides, and jumps on the bed. He crashes next to me, making me flop and laugh, and I want to shove him off the bed.

"She knew we'd get stuck."

Leo lays on his belly, cradling the pillow under his head. He half-shrugs.

"That's Nora," he says, at the exact same time my mind thinks, *that's so unlike her.*

I prop myself on my elbows. "Why do you not like her?"

"I like her. It's not that I don't. I just think she has a selfish streak and sometimes it's exhausting. Will would bend over backward for her. Making phone calls and arrangements last minute because she didn't have her shit together."

I twist my mouth. "It's her wedding."

"So? That doesn't mean the world turns for her."

I snort.

"Listen. I get weddings are all about the bride and the ceremony and tradition, but you can still be a decent human and not purposely get the best man and maid of honor stranded on an island the night before the wedding."

"I'm not the maid of honor."

"Semantics." He rolls his eyes.

"Again, wrong use."

His face hardens, and he props himself up to stare me down. "I swear you argue just to be heard."

"I think you just get mad when I'm right." I flash wry smile.

"Oh my god." He buries his face in the pillow groaning, then pops his head back up. "By the way, I'm not sleeping on the floor."

I grin. "Not so chivalrous anymore."

"I am not even going to pretend. I slept on your lumpy-ass couch last night, and my twin bed from high school the night before, and if I'm going to show you up on the dance floor tomorrow night, my bad back needs to sleep on a good mattress."

"Such an old man," I taunt, shaking my head.

"Says the lady with the bum knee."

I giggle, flopping back on the pillows.

"Can I ask you something?"

"Maybe." I smirk at him.

"Do you miss playing basketball?"

A breath escapes me as I smile. "Always. You?"

He pauses, hesitating with a simple question. But I feel like I know the answer. Leo has always been so talented on the court and I know when his plans in the NBA fell through, that he'd want to find another way to play.

"I was thinking of going overseas," he says finally.

My eyebrows raise, though his answer is only mildly surprising. "I thought you liked your job in San Fran."

"I do. But I only have a few more years where I actually could play, you know?"

I nod. "What country?"

"France."

"*Oui?*" I smile at him.

"*Oui.*" His eyes drift over my face like he's searching for my permission.

San Francisco feels far enough away. France is an impossible distance, further reminding me why this will never happen. It will never work.

"Is that really happening?" I ask.

"It's a real possibility. I'm just waiting to hear back." He pauses then adds, "Taylor is my agent. We *work* together."

I nod, my mind racing as I try not to laugh at myself. "Why didn't you just say that?"

He shrugs. "I don't like talking about it since it's still not one hundred percent happening."

I understand. Without the contract signed, it still can feel like an idea and not an actuality.

"Would you visit me?" he asks, snapping me out of my thoughts.

I let out a small laugh. "Do I have to?"

He throws a pillow at me, and I laugh again. I sit up, pushing back on the plush headboard. His eyes fall to the six-inch scar on my knee.

"What would we tell William?" I ask.

"That you're thinking of playing overseas too."

"With my old lady knee?"

"And my bad back," he reasons, reaching out and running his fingers over my scar.

I lose myself in what I'm really asking, wishing he'd just

answer. But he doesn't. Not right away at least. He just stares at my knee, gingerly running fingers up and down the length of my scar.

"Does your scar bug you?" he asks, looking up at me with curious concern.

"Not anymore. It used to tingle but that went away four years ago."

He nods, his gaze fixed on the scar on my leg. "You must have gone through a lot after it happened."

I nod. I did. One surgery, a year of physical therapy, and losing so much of how my body used to perform and function. When it happened, I remember hearing it pop inside my brain before I felt the stab of pain. As soon as I collapsed on the court, I knew. I knew what was wrong, and I knew what it meant for me and basketball. I sobbed as soon as the team trainers wheeled me to the locker room.

His fingers stop in their tracks, and he slowly grips my calf and raises my knee to his lips, kissing the raised flesh softly. "Sorry I wasn't there."

My throat catches and I swallow hard. "Don't be silly, you were in the middle of your second college season."

He nods slowly, biting his bottom lip. His eyes take in my tanned legs poking out of the oversized white robe.

"I got your flowers though," I say, my voice strangled. He looks up and smiles, his eyes seem to get stuck in a memory. "And the pack of gum," I add. My voice wobbles and I don't want to cry so I stare out at the window—the night sky barely dark outside.

"That was stupid." He scoffs out a laugh, his cheeks flushing.

"It wasn't. That was our thing," I add, reaching out and running my hand over his head, feeling his hair under my fingers.

It was our thing. Passing small one-sentence notes on gum wrappers. We'd eat the gum and write something to each other on the wrapper then carefully fold it back up so it looked like an actual piece. Then we'd pass them back and forth. When I hurt my knee in college, Leo sent flowers to the hospital. Then when

I got back to the dorm, there was a manilla envelope in my mailbox with a pack of gum in it. Only there wasn't gum, just wrappers. Each one with a note that made me happy, sad, and angry all at the same time.

You are a badass.

Basketball will miss you.

I hate this for you.

Heal up, Evie.

I bet I could beat you in HORSE now.

It was like an apology without the actual words. And the problem with that is when the words of an apology aren't said out loud, when actual remorse isn't shown, the apology really just turns into a truce.

So that's what I took it as. And I never reached out after, but I kept the whole pack of gum. It is still stashed in my bedside table next to my lip balm and hand lotion.

I collected so many gum wrappers over the years before that. I didn't keep all of them, just the important ones.

I gave you goosebumps.

I like your haircut.

Meet me at the park.

Don't look at me like that.

I like you.

I'm sorry.

We had so much to apologize for. Young love is reckless—when you're stupid enough to let the feelings grow, but unreasonable enough to tear it all apart.

"I didn't mean it," he says, cutting into my thoughts.

For a moment, I think he's referring to the gum wrappers and then I realize he means what happened that night back in high school. My fingertips freeze in his hair.

"I think you did," I say, my voice barely a whisper. Realization and my pessimism hit me as quickly as the memories. "And I think you've spent the last eight years trying to find something—anything—that compares to what we had, and you haven't found it."

He winces, glancing up at me.

"Have you?" I press.

"Have you?" he counters, propping himself over my legs.

I swallow. Not wanting to give him the satisfaction of an answer he must already know. I shake my head. "Of course not."

Leo runs his hand from under my knee and slides it up my thigh and under the robe. I draw in a short breath.

His hand stops just before my hip, and he looks up at me, moving to his knees so he's hovering over me. There isn't an ounce of doubt in his expression as his eyes search my face. The distance between us is agonizing, and the closer he moves toward me, the more painful the space becomes.

"I want to kiss you again," he says, his lips just inches from mine.

"I want to do a lot more than kiss you," I say, wrapping my hand around his neck and letting him fall into me. His lips immediately part, and I slide my tongue across his bottom lip, savoring the minty taste of his mouth. I arch my back toward his body, and he runs his hand along the curve of my back and down to my ass. He squeezes and the moan in the back of his throat lights off fireworks in the pit of my stomach.

Our lips don't part as he pulls back, taking me with him to end of the bed. He slips his legs off the bottom of the bed until he's standing. With just a look, he beckons me even closer, and I slide to meet him at the edge of the bed.

"You have no idea how much I've missed you," he whispers, tucking my hair behind my ear.

"No, I do."

A half-smile touches his mouth as he runs a finger up my thigh. "Always arguing."

I smile back. "Always picking a fight."

He pauses for a half-second, then grips the front of my robe and pulls me to his mouth, silencing any argument with his kiss. I slide my hands under his robe and run my hands over his hard chest and abdomen, running my fingers lower until he stops me by taking hold of my wrists and placing them on either side of me so I'm seated before him, leaning back on my hands. Heat follows his hands as he slides them from my wrists up my arms to my neck, bringing his mouth to just inches from my ear.

"The things I want to do to you…" His whisper sends chills down my legs and fire straight to my core. He smiles, rubbing his nose against mine. "I gave you goosebumps."

I don't argue. I just bite my lip and smile, letting him do whatever he wants to me.

He tugs on the sash tightened around my waist, pulling it open. Running his fingers over the edge of the robe from my neck to my waist, he eases the fabric off me one side at a time. It falls to my sides and he presses his hand against my chest, letting it travel down between my breasts to my stomach. His eyes follow his hands like heat from the sun. He cups each of my breasts, squeezing lightly and then pinching my nipples until I throw my head back with a moan.

"That noise, Evie," he practically groans, pulling the robe off my shoulders, and I slip my arms out. "It makes me feel crazy."

A euphoric breath escapes my lips. "Good. That's how you make me feel every single second I'm around you."

He lets out a low laugh but doesn't speak. I sit before him completely bare and not feeling an ounce of self-consciousness or fear. More than anything, I want to feel more exposed. More naked. More vulnerable. I want to feel more of Leo. I want to touch and taste and feel every part of him.

I reach for his robe as he kisses me everywhere—my neck, my jaw, my chest. His hands roam down my body until he slips his fingers down between my legs, rubbing in gentle circles, almost immediately making my legs tremble and my hands shake.

"Holy shit, Evie. You're so fucking wet," he breathes, sliding a finger inside me.

My body pulses with a shudder as I throw my head back, feeling my hair tickle the small of my back.

"I want to taste you," he says. Every part of my beating body wants him to. I want his face buried between my legs as I scream out his name. I want his fingers to dig into my hips, leaving bruises for tomorrow. I want all those things, but I need him first.

"After I get to taste you," I say, pulling his robe open.

I gape at him, running my fingers down his stomach until he's in my hands. I glance up at him through my lashes. He's staring at me with hooded eyes and his jaw pulses with anticipation. I let a smile slide over my lips before I take him in my mouth.

His fingers rake through my hair and his breathing is sharp, growing faster. Heat pools between my legs and burns hotter with every breath and moan of my name.

I almost have him, but he twists my hair in his hand and pulls me away. I can tell he's restraining himself, saving it all for me. Desire clouds his vision as I stare up at him from my knees.

"My turn," he says, pulling me up and pushing me back on the bed.

I'm practically a ticking time bomb ready to detonate, so when he goes down on me, I can barely keep any composure. With the first touch of his tongue, my back arches, my body writhes, and he keeps me still with strong hands on my hips until he slips two fingers inside me. It only takes three slow strokes before I shatter.

When I cry out, gripping the sheets and squeezing my legs around him, he lifts his head with a mischievous smile.

"I need you," I breathe, pulling him to me. "Now, Leo."

He bites my jaw and runs his mouth down my neck before finding his wallet on the window table and pulling out two condoms. I watch him roll one on, and my mind explodes in disbelief. We're doing this. It's nothing we haven't done before. But right now, this night, it means a million things.

I'm sorry.

I didn't mean it.

Let's try again.

It's still me and you.

He climbs over my body, taking both my wrists and pinning them over my head. He stares into my eyes, then down between us as he pushes inside of me.

It's more than pressure. It's more than heat. It's more than ripples of desire. It's a symphony of passion and apologies and both of us promising with our bodies that we'll never hurt each other again.

Afterward, we lay intertwined as two long-lost lovers do.

"Move to France with me," he whispers, resting his head on my stomach and rubbing his fingertips in small circles on my thighs.

I let out a soft laugh. The idea of moving to France makes this whole night feel even more like a dream.

"I'm serious."

"No, you're not," I counter.

"Quit arguing," he says, tilting his head to look at me.

"I only argue when I'm right."

He bites my hip, and I squeal.

"Hey!" I laugh. "Don't leave marks!"

"Your dress will cover it," he sneers with a sly smile. "Plus, I don't want to hide you anymore."

"HA! Anymore. You act like we've been doing this for the last eight years." I rake my fingers through his thick hair, searching his eyes for the truth.

Leo pulls me down the mattress by my waist so I'm face to face with him. "I have thought about you for the last eight years."

I study his face, partially believing, partially waiting for the world we've created the last couple of hours in this bed and breakfast to crash. My heart and my mind are leaning toward the latter no matter how sincere his eyes look.

"Not every day."

He furrows his brow. "What?"

"You haven't thought of me every day for the last eight years. There's no way." I shrug. "Because if you did, you wouldn't just now be saying something."

"You were with Damien for three of the eight," he tries to reason.

"And what? Basketball was too important the other five?"

"Evie…" he says like he's trying to charm me, convince me he's right. I'm sure he does it with all the ladies. But I refuse to give him a pass.

"I'm not saying you can't admit that you wondered. Because

I wondered about you all the time. But not every day. I didn't miss you every day. I didn't want you back every day. I didn't even check your Instagram or ask William about you for long periods of time. I had a lot of days, months—years even—that were really good. And it's okay if you did too." He listens intently with soft and searching eyes. I run a hand over his cheek. "I wanted you to be happy…even if it was without me."

He pauses like he doesn't know what to say. Then his lips twitch and a smirk appears. "You didn't want me to rot in hell?"

"Oh, I did! Much of the time I did." I laugh, not realizing tears are escaping my eyes. He wipes them away. It's a pattern of his. "But I want you to know I've been okay too. And I'm okay if you're okay."

"That's fair." He nods, reluctant to agree. "But every time I have seen you, I always felt like someone just dropped me out in the middle of the ocean, leaving me to drown. And all I could do was see the water all around me. You've always done that to me. You unsettle me. I can't think straight. I say the wrong thing, do the wrong thing, when you're the only one that's ever been right for me."

I let out a thoughtful hum. I know the feeling. Even still…

"But you wouldn't even talk to me, Leo. And if you did, it was like it was painful. Like you hated every second you had to say words to me—"

"I did," he says, propping himself on his elbows and cradling my ribcage with his hands. "I've always hated it. I'm good at a lot of things, but apologizing is not one of them. I didn't know how to speak to you without apologizing, and I never knew how to get the words out."

I nod. "Until this week."

"Until this week."

I continue to nod, pushing myself on my hands, pulling my robe on, and tightening the sash. Leo watches me, but I don't see it, I sense it, avoiding his eyes at all costs.

"So this whole week was just an apology?" I ask, picking at my fresh manicure in my lap.

He shakes his head. "No, this whole week I've just somehow been selfish enough to not let another moment slip away with regrets, and reckless enough to convince you to do the same."

He sits up next to me, the Egyptian cotton draped over his lap.

"It should have always been like this," he says, hands on mine, his face just inches away. "And you know it."

I raise my gaze to meet the intensity of his. "And whose fault is it that it's not?"

"Mine."

I stare at him, completely skeptical.

"You don't believe me."

I scoff out a laugh. "You're saying all the right things, and it just doesn't feel like it makes sense. I feel like now that your friends are settling down and getting their 'happily ever afters,' you're realizing yours might have come and gone when you were just eighteen."

He winces, biting his bottom lip and nodding. "Maybe that's part of it. But maybe there's a bigger part of me that never stopped loving you, and out of all the mistakes I've made in my life, hurting you is the only one I really want to undo."

My eyes drift over his face. I believe him. I hate it, but I do.

"But you know what you said to me, Leo. I don't even think you fully understand how hard it was for me to hear it. And not just because it came out of nowhere and not only because you left right after. It hurt the most because it was you, Leo. We picked on each other and pretended to hate each other for years, but when you walked away that night, I remember thinking, he actually does hate me. I don't think you get what that did to me."

His expression drops and his gaze lands on my stomach. He runs a ginger hand over it and a pained expression passes over his face. "Just tell me," he says, looking back at me. "Tell me what it did to you."

Back Then

PICTURE 3: BASKETBALL

"Want to play again?" I asked, dribbling the ball between my legs. The air of May was mild and the driveway was still wet from the morning's spring shower.

"Nope."

I squinted at him. Leo was never this short with me without an audience.

"You sure?"

"Yep."

"You got me to H-O-R-S…" I continued to badger him, but he cut me off.

"No. I'm over it. I'm going home," he said. He sat on the porch steps to tie his shoe, his brow was twisted and his eyes were dark and fuming. Leo wears his emotions on every inch of his skin. He never could figure out how to hide it.

I walked toward him, leaning down and placing my hands on his knees. "Fine. We can play to PIG." I flashed him a smile. I thought I was being cute. I thought I was being sexy. I thought I was letting him know the ball was in his court and I was savoring these few minutes alone with him, practically begging him to kiss me.

He glanced at me, his gaze locked with mine in complete understanding, but his jaw was tight and defensive like I was telling him I lit his house on fire.

He knocked my hands off his knees as he slid to the side, and I stumbled forward, landing on the porch steps with a clumsy thud.

"Dude, what's your problem?" I asked, embarrassment causing my neck to flush.

Things hadn't been weird since we had sex. In my mind, they were actually good. We still played basketball the same. We still talked. We still picked on each other and from the outside, nothing had changed. Only he had started pulling me behind the tree at the park and kiss me when no one was watching. Or slip notes in my room when I wasn't home. But the last few days he had been weird. And now, he was completely pissed, heightening my nerves for what I was about to say.

"You can't be so obvious, Evie," he said through his teeth, his vision fixed on the driveway and not me.

"I wasn't," I argued. "No one is out here. You know I wouldn't do anything in front of…anyone."

I hesitated with the last word because as close as I was to Abigail and the basketball team, no one ever suspected Leo had a secret relationship with me or that he took my virginity after the Spring Fair. No one. I made sure of it. I was still Virgin Genevieve to all who knew me.

Leo always knew me best and he was the only person I wanted to talk to.

"Thanks for the picture, by the way," I said, hoping this would help him admit we were still anything but this awkward interaction. As promised he had the picture of us printed and he left it under my pillow while I was out of the house last week. On the back he wrote, "Scones are better than elephant ears."

"You're wrong though. Elephant ears are way better," I teased.

He didn't react. He didn't even flinch. His mood was worsening by the second and I started replaying the last few days in my head wondering if I had done something wrong.

It didn't matter though, I needed to say this, so I took a deep breath.

"Hey, I need to tell you something..." I began, fidgeting with the basketball. As pissed as he was, I had to tell him as soon as I could. I couldn't bear the secret alone. "But like, super private."

I watched him swallow hard. He averted his eyes like he was annoyed with me. "Yeah, fine."

"Can I meet you at the park tonight?" I asked, and he shot a look at me. "Will can't know," I added.

He thought for a moment, jaw pulsing. "Yeah, I think I need to talk to you too."

When he said the words, my heart dropped to the concrete, and that gross, heavy feeling you only get when you know someone is going to break up with you sat in my gut.

A horn beeping from the car pulling into the driveway dried up everything I almost said right then.

"Hey, you two! Where's William?" Mom asked after she pulled into the driveway.

"Bathroom," we answered in unison.

"Gotcha," she said, slinging her purse over her shoulder.

"Were they able to fix your phone, Ms. Clara?" Leo asked. I took note of his change in temperament.

She groaned. "No, I had to get a new one. Which is irritating but the camera is great!" Mom was already swiping through her new smartphone, then she held it up to us. "Say 'cheese!'"

I turned so Leo and I were back to back with a tough guy expression and crossed my arms over the ball in front of me. I didn't know what Leo's expression was, but Mom laughed.

"You two are adorable!" she smiled as she looked at the photo on her phone screen. "I swear, I should have done that thing where I took your guys' picture in the same place every year." She tucked her phone away. "Ah, well. I'll send it to you."

Leo let out a tisk of laugh, and I pressed my lips together. My mom loved Leo, and she often had this way of coupling us together whether or not William was around.

"You staying for dinner, Leo?" Her question was unusually

enthusiastic. As a matter of fact, every interaction was over-the-top. Panic shot through my veins, and I wondered if she did hear us three weeks ago. Or worse, if she saw what I buried in the bottom of the trash can.

But it couldn't be that. If she saw that, she'd be fuming or in tears at the very least.

"No, I'm going to be with my mom tonight," he answered.

"Understandable." She nodded.

"I should get going."

He stood to leave, and I said, "Rematch tomorrow?"

He froze and looked at me slowly over his shoulder. "Yep."

He was being colder than usual—even for Leo—so I ran after him when Mom went inside.

"What's going on, Leo?" I asked when I caught up to him halfway to his house, pulling on his arm. I swore I'd never be that girl running after a boy, but something was wrong, and I needed to know what.

He shook me off, his steps falling harder and faster on the road. "Don't worry about it."

"Don't do that. It's annoying," I said, catching my breath.

"Leave it, Evie!" he yelled.

"Temper, temper. You know you should really learn to communicate, Leo, instead of being all weird and sh—"

He stopped cold and glared at me, shutting me right up. "Dad left."

"Where'd he go?" I asked, confused.

"Fucking left. Like, left left. Gone. I came home three days ago to my parents saying they're getting a divorce and Dad was moving out."

My heart sunk to my stomach like rocks. "Leo, I'm so sorry, I didn't—"

"Nope, you didn't know."

"Does William know yet?"

"Not yet."

"You should tell him, Leo."

"I'll tell him when I want to tell him," he bit back. I could practically hear his teeth grinding as he glared at the sky—mad at the world and seemingly angry at me. "But I'm pissed, and

I'm allowed to be pissed, so leave it alone." He scrubbed a hand down his face, and I was certain he was near tears.

I threw up my hands. "Fine. I'll leave it alone." I tried to gather my thoughts, but I wasn't sure how to articulate that I still needed to tell him something. Despite the nerves and panic swarming in my gut like a kicked beehive, I told him, "But I'm here for you. You know that, right?"

A slow deliberate nod was his only response. Then his chin started shaking, and I immediately saw the boy in him I met eight years ago. Sadness pulsed at my skin and I reached out, fisting his sweatshirt and pulling him to me. Long, painful sobs escaped his chest as I wrapped him in my embrace, his tears landing in my hair.

"I'm sorry, Leo. I didn't—I'm so sorry." Life already doesn't make sense when you're eighteen. It gets even more confusing when your parents are getting a divorce, and the family you thought you had implodes.

"I hate them!" he yelled with an exhausted sob of frustration.

"I hate them if you hate them," I said. I didn't though and I knew deep down he didn't either. Leo loved both of his parents. But I also know that's why the divorce hit so hard.

It was in that moment, standing there under the streetlight, that I realized I was also crying, and I pulled back. Leo saw the streams rolling down my face and reached out to wipe them with his thumbs. There was a tenderness and an understanding in his eyes when he looked at me. My heart saw his heart at that moment, then he dipped his head down and kissed me. It was soft and he only lingered for a few seconds. He pulled back with a pained expression, and I couldn't tell if it hurt to kiss me or hurt to stop. Then he cupped his hands around my face and kissed me again, harder this time and with more passion. It tasted like salty tears.

"Eleven tonight?" he asked, pulling back.

Recollection and apprehension pinched at my gut.

I nodded. "If you want to."

A sadness filled his eyes, his expression growing even more somber. "Yeah," he said, his gaze dropping to the street. "Yeah, we need to."

I stood with my back against the tree, staring at the empty basketball court. It was the same tree he kissed me behind four days ago. A day before his dad left. A day before I knew.

"I have to make this quick." Leo's voice made me jerk around.

I nodded. "You feeling any better?"

He shot me a look. Clearly not.

"Sorry, that was dumb. I just…don't always know what to say."

His jaw pulsed.

I hesitated, trying to muster up the courage to speak. "I just…" I blew out through my lips.

"Can I go first?" he interrupted.

I nodded, relieved. What I needed to tell him didn't feel real yet, and I knew if I said the words out loud, it would become real and destroy our futures.

"We can't do this anymore," he said, his words far too simple to be confusing.

"What do you mean?"

"Me and you…messing around. It ends now."

I stepped closer, my heart rocketing in my chest. "Are you breaking up with me?"

He let out a sharp, condescending laugh. "We're not together. We never were."

I blinked in response. Leo was always a little mean, but this felt evil. I didn't even recognize him.

"Okay…" I whispered because I was stunned. I didn't know what to say. I ran my fingers through my hair, my eyes buried in the grass below my feet, too shocked to speak and too sad to understand why. "Right. I should've never assumed we were." My throat tightened and my voice shook, but I managed to get the words out. "So this afternoon, the kiss didn't mean anything?"

"No." He answered so quickly it felt like he slapped me. I could feel the heat of his words on my cheek.

"I don't know why you're doing this." A whisper was all my teenage heart could manage.

"You don't get it, Evie," he snapped, and I jerked back. "You don't think. You're impulsive. You say whatever you're thinking, whenever you want, and you do whatever you want without worrying about the consequences! Will can never know about us. He can't..." he shook his head. "My family already fell apart. I'm not going to lose my best friend over you. You aren't worth it."

I recoiled at his anger as he spit vile words at me, my hands landing on my belly like he punched me in the gut. "What are you talking about?"

"Us, Evie! I'm talking about us!' He threw a hand out and the draft it created made me jerk back. "Me. You. It's all been a stupid mistake."

"Leo, I'm sorry—I thought you wanted to—"

"You thought I wanted to?" He stepped closer with each word. His forehead was so bunched up and his jaw so tight, I barely recognized him in the moonlight. "Wanted to?" He scoffed with disgust. "Whatever gave you that impression?"

I blanched, my heart sinking deeper in my gut as my mind raced back to that night. Did I ask him if he wanted to? Or had I just assumed? He kissed me, but I asked to leave. I took off his shirt. I wanted more. The entire night flashed before my eyes on loop, and I felt so stupid.

"I thought you liked me," I said, my voice as small as a mouse. "You said it."

"Liked you?" he spit. "Evie, I can't stand you."

My chin trembled as I shook my head. I couldn't tell if he was forcing the words out or restraining himself from being even harsher. There is no feeling of foolishness like wanting someone that doesn't want you back.

"We're done," he said. "This shouldn't have happened, and it will never, ever happen again."

I didn't even nod. He took three steps away, then turned to face me with an expression I couldn't read. "Graduation is in two weeks, and I'm gone at my grandparents' house for the summer while Mom figures everything out, then I'm off to college, so…" He paused to swallow, and I wondered if it was because he was spitting out words he didn't mean, and swallowing all the words he actually wanted to say. "I'm gone next week and I'm not coming back, so just forget about me."

"That's what you want?"

"That's what I want."

The sadness in my gut evaporated and was replaced with burning rage as he walked away.

"Liar," I said, my voice trembling.

"What?" he asked, stopping his footsteps.

"Fucking liar!" I stalked toward him, throwing my arms up and pointing an angry finger at him. He caught my forearms in the air, his touch practically burning my skin.

"Stop, Evie."

"No! No, you can't say that and just fucking leave!"

"Let it go, Evie! We fucked up. We made a mistake! It never should have happened! Move on. You won't even miss me."

I swallowed, dragging my fist down his chest. I turned my tear-streaked face up to meet his brown eyes and pulsing jaw. "But will you miss me?"

His jaw clenched, a twitch really. His eyes fell to the grass. He pushed me away gently, taking a small step back.

"Will you?" I repeated, my chin trembling and chest quaking with a fear I've never known.

Say it. Say it. Call this what it is, I begged him with my eyes, but my seventeen-year-old self was too chicken to say it out loud first.

His Adam's apple dropped. "No."

"Look at me!" I yelled, moving closer and taking his face in my hands. "Look at me. If you mean it. Look at me when you say that."

He shook his head, clenching his fists at his side.

"You can't, can you? Because you know you'll miss me. You know this wasn't a mistake. You know—"

"It was!" he yelled, silencing me. He let out a shuddered breath. "I won't miss you, Genevieve."

His words pinned me into place like knives on a cutting board. Harsh, clipped, and angry—leaving no room for interpretation. But his eyes said something else.

"You don't mean it," I stumbled through the words with heaving sobs.

"Evie, stop," he begged, holding my arms, his voice close to cracking. "We have to—it has to stop." His eyes dropped and bounced off the ground. He was looking at me but not really. His eyes were glazed like he was lost in his head, his logic obstructing him from feeling his emotions. "Don't text me. Don't call me."

I shook my head. "You don't mean it. Please, you can't mean it."

He didn't speak. He just took another step back. And another. Then another. Each one like bullets in my chest.

Then he turned and walked back to his house, while I stood there frozen in the street with his baby growing next to my broken heart, not knowing if any words would ever make him stay.

20

THURSDAY

"You know earlier at the beach when you said you've always known me?" I ask, staring at the ceiling.

He nods in my peripheral.

"It was never that you didn't know me, Leo. It was that you hurt me." I shrug. "You were mean, Leo. You were so mean to me. You broke my heart. And it's taken a really long time to put it back together, but I'm okay. I don't want you to worry about what happened because it won't do either of us any good."

"I was terrible to you. I wish I could go back and change every word I said. I had to muster up so much courage to break up with you that night, and I was so mad about the whole situation that it came out all wrong." He swallows hard. "I was a scared and angry kid that took it out on you. I would never say those things to you now."

"Leo…that night," I sit up, glancing at him but afraid to make complete eye contact. He looks like he's waiting for me to tell me all the ways he destroyed me. But what I'm about to say might also destroy him. "I was pregnant."

The last word comes out with a hundred shaking syllables.

His head jerks back, his mind racing behind his brown irises. "You were? We used a condom…"

I nod, my eyes immediately swelling. The shame and regret prevent me from meeting his eyes. "I know, but I got pregnant anyway. I think we were just too young and naïve to know the condom broke… I'm sorry I didn't tell you."

"Why didn't you?" He doesn't seem angry. He seems confused.

My gaze shifts from my hands to his face. "You mean right after you got done telling me you couldn't stand me and I was a huge mistake?"

I drop the statement in his lap, and he doesn't respond right away so I continue.

"A couple of weeks after that night, I started bleeding and lost the baby… It doesn't…" I shrug, words sticking like sap to the roof of my mouth. "There was never really a baby anyway so…"

His mouth has gone slack, his cheeks have lost color, and his eyes wander the room while he absorbs the information. I should have told him. I would have eventually.

My mom thought I had a stomach bug. I could only eat peanut butter toast and thew up every other day, and fell asleep by eight every night. I googled clinics and researched when I was supposed to go to the doctor. I didn't ignore the pregnancy, but I avoided telling anyone. Then one day I woke up feeling better on almost all accounts until my abdomen started cramping and I started to bleed.

I was devastated and relieved all at once.

I knew I had a miscarriage, and I know it was for the best. I was only seventeen. But it didn't make it any less traumatic especially since no one knew.

Leo was the only one I wanted to tell anyway, but he was gone all summer, and then off to college to be a superstar. I channeled all my hurt and anger into my senior year, graduating with a 4.0 GPA and my best season to date, landing a partial scholarship to play for Gonzaga.

All's well that ends well.

After a few more moments of letting him process, I can't

not fill the awkward silence with more words.

"Look, I get it," I say, and his eyes snap to me. "I was wrong not to tell you. But I was so scared. We were so young. And I was so into you. When I saw that I was pregnant, I remember thinking, 'It's fine, Leo will know what to do,'" my voice trembles and I clear my throat. "But you were already done with me, and I realized I should have known better. And honestly, it was too big and too terrifying for a teenager to handle anyway. I should have never expected you to know what to do. Then you left for your grandparents', and you never called, never texted, never apologized, and I thought, maybe it was all in my head." I shrug, glancing away before our eyes lock again. "I thought it was never real for you like it was for me."

Leo is so quiet that all I can hear is the scream of the air-conditioning blasting through the vents.

"Can you say something? Because I'm really embarrassed I'm telling you all of this," I say.

"I feel like whatever I say won't be enough."

I nod out of reflex, but I don't understand what he means.

Enough what? Enough to make it right? Enough to express how mad he is at me for not telling him? Enough expletives to send me into a dumpster fire and burn to death?

"Okay," I murmur, swinging my legs over the bed to retreat to the bathroom. He clearly needs a minute, and I need to splash water on my face.

Just as I'm about to stand, he grabs my elbow and pulls me back against his bare chest, arms encasing me.

"I'm sorry you were alone," he says, his voice soft and low against my ear.

I relax into him, the dam inside me breaking and the tension and regret that's been wrapped around my spine for eight years melt into his arms. I cry for the scared girl I was. And I cry for what I thought Leo and I would be.

Choking on a sob, I squeeze my eyes shut and shake my head. "I'm fine. I promise. I'm oka—"

He pulls tighter. "I swear to God, Evie, if you tell me you're okay and everything is fine, and it's not a big deal, I will snap you in half."

"Always choosing violence." I laugh through my tears, turning to face him. "But I am okay. I wasn't then. But I am now." I force a smile that is both genuine and a guise. I'm certain some of this emotion is simply from keeping this bottled inside me for eight years. I brush my knuckles over his cheekbone. "I promise."

He takes my face in his hands. "I'm so sorry I wasn't there for you the way I should have been. I was so selfish. I only cared about what was going on with me."

"Your parents getting a divorce is a big deal." I reason and press my mouth into a closed-lipped smile, shrugging. "I forgave you a long time ago."

"Did you though?" He fixes his skeptical eyes on me.

"No," I confess without hesitation, and we laugh together.

He swipes his thumb over a tear that just ran down my face. He kisses the wet spot on my cheek. Then again. And again. A trail of apologetic kisses land in succession on my face. "Will you forgive me now?"

I nod, and he unleashes his full smile, raking his fingers in my hair and drawing me to him. His kiss ignites something I shoved inside me a long time ago. Something that was harboring a little resentment. Something that tried to move on. Something that tried to put on a brave face. Something that's reminding me right now that I'm still in love with Leonardo Bishop.

"I love you, Evie. Do you know that?" he asks. I've always wondered if he loved me then, but I never heard him say it out loud. I never imagined he could love me now. "I have always loved you. Not in any other way I have ever experienced. I love you in a can't-sleep, you-drive-me-crazy, can't-stop-thinking-about-you, I-wonder-what-she's-doing-now kind of way."

His words heat my skin, warming my heart, but instead of returning the sentiment, I ask, "Then why were you gone so long? You've avoided me for years."

He slides his thumb over my bottom lip, and whispers, "Maybe because being away from you was the only way I could pretend I didn't love you."

My lips twitch and I almost smile. "You're so stubborn."

His eyes drift from my mouth to my eyes and his forehead

falls to mine.

We stay like that for a long moment. Not kissing. Just holding each other. Sitting in the feeling of free falling into a love we never fell all the way out of.

I want to tell him I love him, but the words stay trapped on my tongue.

"I've been so mad at you," I confess finally.

Leo's gaze searches my face and I know he hears the desperation in my voice. I know he knows I'm holding back, keeping my cards close to my chest. His hands slowly trail down my neck and under my robe. Everything inside me tugs and pinches and pulls. He grips my waist and trails kisses down my neck.

I can feel him hard against my leg, and I hike a knee onto the bed next to him and push him back. I grab another condom from the bedside table, open it, and roll it on. He grabs my wrist and moans my name as my hand glides down with the latex. My blood heats and my body pulses as I straddle him, sinking down and letting him fill me. Holding his jaw with one hand, I brush a soft kiss over his mouth then sit upright, moving my hips in long, slow circles.

Every touch is intentional. Every ache is met with pressure. Every desire is met with a promise. Leo's hands roam my skin, fingers sinking into my flesh and his eyes intent on absorbing the entire moment.

"I'm taking you to France," he breathes, still watching me.

A laugh escapes my chest and he squeezes my waist tighter, helping me move on top of him.

"I'm not playing this time. I'm keeping you forever." His words are a playful breath of affection, but they land straight in my heart and sink into my doubts.

I freeze for a half-second, staring down at his dark eyes. They're smoldering. Searing into my skin with familiarity and comfort and love. Even still, fear creeps up my spine.

"But we're a bad idea."

He sits up, cradling my back. His face is just inches from mine and he stares deep into my eyes. "You're my favorite bad idea."

A slow smile spreads over my lips as he eases me away from the ledge of self-destruction and doubt and back into a world of uninhibited bliss.

He flips me over on my back, palming the back of my knee as he moves deeper inside me. He pulls almost all the way out and then pushes back in hard with a moment's pause. Then again, slowly picking up speed until I can't distinguish the difference between pleasure and pain. He leans down and kisses me, swallowing my moans and taking pleasure in my own satisfaction.

"You feel so good," he moans into my mouth and I whimper. He runs his hand up my neck and slips two fingers into my mouth. I suck, wetting them, and he pulls them out before sliding them between my legs and moving in slow circles.

I take his lip between my teeth and pull as an electric current ripples through my body, and my eyes fall closed getting lost in the feeling.

"Open your eyes." The hum of his deep voice wakes up even more of my exploding nerves. I obey, staring directly at him. "I want you to look at me when you come."

I smile at him. With my voice low, I practically beg him, "And I want you to make me come."

He bites his lip, and his eyebrows draw together in a way that tells me he knows he's about to make my toes curl and my fingertips tingle. He's looking at me as if making me feel this way is the easiest and best thing he's ever done, and he moves inside me like he's discovering me for the first and maybe only time. Hard and slow, tilting me just right so he hits the spot that makes me blind with pleasure. I arch my back so hard, it's almost like there's no gravity between me and the sheets—just a sheer force of desire keeping me afloat at the hands of Leo as he thrusts into me. I rake my fingernails down his back, slowly being driven to the edge one heartbeat and movement at a time.

"Don't leave marks," he taunts in a low whisper. I smile, knowing he's mocking my earlier words.

"Your suit will cover it," I pant, lifting my hips to meet him.

Leo flashes a slow and seductive smile before biting my collarbone and kissing my neck, intensifying the ache building inside me.

He grips my legs and runs up my thighs, his fingers digging into my flesh as he quickens his pace. Pleasure explodes inside me, making me levitate as I cry out, nails running down his back. I feel everything all at once—a deep pulsing, a burning, a savage tear of lust rolling down my core.

He smiles down at me through hooded eyes. A smile of satisfaction hints at his swollen lips, as he waits, letting me catch my breath before we continue.

He watches every movement and every facial expression I make, learning my body all over again.

Words are scarce as we move with each other, but a symphony of breaths and moans fill the air until we're both overwhelmed with our senses and crash completely with each other once again.

I fall back on the bed. Our breaths both catch in the night and sweat glistens over our sunkissed bodies.

"Holy shit, Evie."

I turn and smile over at him, intertwining my fingers with his. "Holy shit," I agree, still reeling. "Are we really doing this or is this just for tonight?"

Leo leans over me, meeting my mouth with his and kissing me softly. "We've always been an always kind of thing."

I smile against his lips. "You sure?"

"One hundred percent."

My heart leaps, and I believe him. My teeth sink into my bottom lip, and I try to restrain a smile.

We lay there for several minutes before a thought hits me— one of the main reasons we fell apart. "Which one of us is going to tell my brother?"

He kisses my nose and rests his forehead on mine. "Whoever loses HORSE."

Another laugh ripples out of me. I never want to stop this game. I want to play with Leo forever. I want to run wild with him. I want to dance and sing and scream through every moment of the rest of our life together, no matter what anyone else thinks.

It's always been Leo. Even when it wasn't. We loved each

other then. We didn't know it. But we do now.
And now is all we have left.

21

WEDDING DAY
FRIDAY

I wake up with my leg curled over Leo's waist and my face smashed against his chest.

The heat of the week is searing our skin, making us both hot to the touch. My sunburn has turned a nice shade of pinkish tan and Leo's skin has darkened, especially on his forearms. I wrap my fingers around his arm and I slide my hand all the way up his tattoo, passing the trees and the mandala and landing on the tiger on his bicep.

I trace the flowers with my index finger as his eyelids flutter awake.

His eyes find me immediately and a giant smile spreads over his lips. "Good morning."

"Morning," I say, gripping his bicep and squeezing.

He pulls me tight against him. "Mmmph. You feel good."

"You feel better," I say, curling into his warm skin.

"Can we stay here?" he whispers into my hair then kisses the top of my head.

"I have never wanted to do something more." I look up at him and smile. He lowers his lips to mine, kissing me softly. I feel him harden under my leg and smile through the kiss.

He notices.

"It's the morning," he reasons with a playful smile.

"Oh, yeah, that's the only reason?"

He nods then laughs, scrubbing a hand down his face. I sit up and straddle him, pressing myself against him for a brief second before hopping off him and skipping to the bathroom. "I need to brush my teeth and we need to shower. We've got a wedding to look presentable for." I pause and raise my eyebrows over my shoulder just before I disappear into the bathroom, "Oh, and breakfast is in forty minutes."

I try to focus on cleaning my teeth and ignore the fact that I had sex with Leo twice last night, and now he is naked in the bed of a bed and breakfast we're staying at together because we're stranded on an island the day of my brother's wedding.

What even is life at this point?

I giggle to myself.

"What's so funny?" Leo asks, coming up behind me completely naked.

I jump and hit my cheek with the toothbrush.

"Whoa, easy, Evie," he says, reaching out and cradling my face while wiping the toothpaste off my cheek.

I spit in the sink as he puts toothpaste on his toothbrush. "Nothing," I mutter, then cup water into my mouth with my hand and spit again, looking at him through the mirror as he turns on the shower while brushing his teeth. "I was just thinking how crazy it is that we're here. I feel like we're a world away from real life…"

My voice trails as I get a full view of him. I can't stop gawking at him. It's unfair, really, how attractive he is from head to toe. I kind of wish he did put on a few pounds after college. I kind of wish his muscles softened, and he developed adult acne or something—anything—so that I wouldn't be swallowing my heartbeat and wanting to jump his bones while he brushes his teeth.

He spits in the sink and takes a long drink from the faucet.

Everything about him is dizzying right now; the edges of my vision are fuzzy as if I'm in the middle of a dream. Leo's always been my most frustrating and impossible dream.

My gaze wanders over him while he slips into the shower.

"You coming in?" he asks from under the stream of water. He runs his hands over his head and water sprays me from the open shower door.

I step onto the stone tiles of the shower floor and shut the glass door behind me. The water streams from the top of his head, down his neck, and over his torso. A fantasy of me drinking it off his skin dances across my mind. Then I remember he's actually in front of me, and this isn't a dream or a fantasy. It should feel serendipitous, but it almost feels orchestrated—as if the master plan always resulted in him being with me.

A laugh escapes me. He opens his eyes and peers at me as water drops over his lashes. "Really? You're laughing at me?"

"Sorry, you just hog the water like you hog the ball," I tease, though I know I'm deflecting from my feelings.

He reaches out and pulls me to him so we're both standing under the shower head, and then he kisses me. Long and wet with his hands in my hair. The water pours down on us, making it feel almost like drowning. The kind of drowning that feels like a surrender. The kind of drowning that you beg for.

His hands caress my bare back and I reach between us and take his erection in my hand. "Is it still the morning?" I ask in between kisses.

He smiles against my mouth. "It's still the morning," he confirms, kissing me again. "I'm out of condoms," he murmurs against my mouth.

"I've been on birth control since I was eighteen," I answer, because after what happened of course I have been. He pulls back, his gaze dancing all over my face with a question. "And I haven't been with anyone in months. I'm clean."

The right side of his mouth curls into a small grin. "Me too."

With that, I take his jaw in one hand, trusting him and kissing him hard as I move the other hand in long, slow strokes along his length. His throat makes a low rumble as I pull slowly on his bottom lip with my teeth.

He takes my wet hair in one hand and pulls, tilting my head back, not breaking his expression as he gazes down at me with hooded eyes.

"Where have you been?" he whispers. A rhetorical question we both know the answer to. But when he says it, it feels more like, what the hell have we been doing without each other?

"Waiting for you to apologize for being an asshole," I answer, nipping at his jaw and running my tongue down his neck. A breathy groan escapes him, and he draws back. He holds up a finger between us and makes a quick circle, demanding I turn around.

My fingertips shake as I press them against the tiles even before he touches me. I wait for the pressure, but it doesn't come. Instead, he moves my hair gently off my back, exposing my neck. He rubs a thumb over my neck and then follows it with a kiss. Soft yet sensual. His thumb continues sliding down each vertebra and is followed immediately by his lips until he kisses my tailbone. Everything inside me is pulling tight and aching for his touch.

"I need to feel you now, Leo," I breathe.

A low rumble of his laugh echoes in the shower then his teeth sink into the meaty flesh between my ass and hip. A sound of surprise pushes past my lips but is immediately met with a moan, wishing he'd do it again.

"Be patient. I like taking my time with you," he says, running his hands over my slick skin and down the back of my thighs. "Turn around."

His demand creates a heartbeat in my core, but I do what I'm told, leaning back against the shower wall. He pulls my leg over his shoulder and I whimper as he goes down on me. My body is trembling with anticipation. The slow build to my climax is as maddening as it is invigorating. All my senses are screaming.

Then finally, when I'm almost there—breathing heavy and pleading for him to finish me—he stands with his knees slightly bent. Spinning me around, and he pushes inside me. I attempt to grip the smooth tile, and he pins my arms above my head by the wrists. My tiptoes scrape the surface of the shower floor, making me feel like I'm suspended in the air with each thrust. There's nothing to hold onto. It's like I'm floating into oblivion until the tingles hit my nerve endings and course through me to my center. Leo presses one palm against the shower wall and wraps the other around my waist, holding me tight against his chest until we come down together one breath at a time.

"You're too much," he says.

I let out a sleepy laugh and tilt my head back on his shoulder. "We need to get ready."

"Do we have to go to the wedding?"

I laugh again in response as I grab a washcloth and squirt body wash on it and lather up Leo's skin. I clean every inch of him and when I'm done, my hand lingers on his tattoo sleeve.

"Why did you ask Nora what my favorite flower is?" I ask, washing the suds off the orchids on his arm.

"Because I thought it was peonies." He shrugs. "Terrence was asking who did my tattoo when we were golfing, and William made an offhand comment that orchids are your favorite flower." I look up at him and am met with something burning in his eyes. "And I said, no, her favorite flower is a peony. William was adamant. So I texted Nora."

I look at the tattoo, realizing how similar his orchids are to the ones on my hip.

"That's weird," I say finally.

"That I used to know your favorite flower?"

"No, that William knew." I let out a laugh. "What brother knows his sister's favorite flower?"

He chuckles. "Well, to be fair, you do have a giant tattoo of orchids and lilies," he says, running his thumb along the tattoo from my ribcage over my hipbone to my thigh.

"I am a walking billboard."

"That's what tattoos are for, right?" He smiles, dripping body wash on another washcloth and taking his turn cleaning me.

I nod. "Why'd you get orchids?"

"I just liked how they looked with the tiger," he answers,

running the sudsy washcloth down my core.

I laugh. "No hidden meaning?"

"Nope. Sometimes people just get tattoos because they want to, Evie," he teases, and I laugh because I know. I get asked what mine means all the time. Even if there's a meaning, not everyone needs to know.

"Even the tiger?" I ask because I still want to know about his.

His hand freezes over my shoulder, then he pulls the washcloth off and wrings it out.

"Let's do your hair," he says instead, shifting me under the water and getting my hair completely wet. His brow is furrowed. I know he's thinking about something, wondering if he should tell me. But I'm not going to pry anything out of him.

When I step out of the water, he starts shampooing my hair, moving the pads of his fingertips against my scalp in diligent circles until I'm certain this dream has turned into me waking up in a hair salon getting a scalp massage.

Once I'm fully lathered, he guides me back under the stream, running his fingers through my hair and rinsing out the shampoo.

"The tiger," he begins hesitantly, "is from your birth year."

I laugh.

"I'm serious."

I open my eyes and step out of the water. "What—" I stare in a complete daze, but he turns me around and applies conditioner to my long, wet blonde strands. "You got a tattoo for me?" I ask, stunned.

When he spins me around again, he's smiling wide. "No, weirdo. I just like tigers," he says, and then shoves me under the water.

"Leo!" I shriek, laughing with water spilling down my face. "You're impossible!"

My eyes are shut as the water continues to pour down but his mouth finds mine.

"No," he whispers against my mouth. "I've just loved you a really long time."

22

WEDDING DAY
FRIDAY

Leo brings our clothes to the bathroom while I blow-dry my hair in a complete state of bliss.

"Amalie is the best," Leo says smelling our clothes. "I have never smelled better clothes. Here. Take a whiff."

He throws my crop top at me, and it lands in my almost dry hair.

"Oh my god. It smells like sunshine," I tease with a mischievous smile.

Leo's nostrils flare as he withholds his smile and immediately tries to put me in a head lock. I ward him off with my blow dryer. He yells with a dramatic, "Ah, my eyes!" shielding his face with his hands.

"You'll never win with me, Leo." I laugh, returning the blow dryer to my roots. "But the clothes do smell good."

He steps closer to me like he wants to invade all of my space. His hand wraps around my neck gently and he kisses me. "Hurry up. We have breakfast to eat."

"And a ferry to catch," I add, shutting off the blow dryer and wrapping the cord around it.

"Okay, but eggs benedict, Evie." He splays his hands in front of him. One holding his button-up and the other his pair of khaki shorts.

"Your best friend's wedding, Leonardo," I counter.

He glares with a smirk and throws my shorts at me; they hit me in the face. He makes me want to tackle him and pin him to the bed in all the best and worst ways.

After we dress and make our way downstairs, I realize my phone battery is completely drained. I didn't bring a charger with us to Vashon and Leo has a stupid iPhone so he couldn't share his.

"Can you text William and—"

"Already did," Leo answers, cutting me off.

"And Nora, please. She isn't with William."

Leo smiles. Small. Slight. And completely scrumptious. I don't know what beast he woke up inside me, but I want to bite the smile off his face and ravage him in the linen closet, licking him from head to—

"Good morning, you two! Breakfast is in the rose room." Amalie's voice cuts through my naughty thoughts, and I blush because certainly she's a saint and heard them.

"Amalie, thank you so much for your hospitality. The room was fantastic." Leo grins, and I try not to laugh because apparently I am not a real adult yet, and all I can think of is all the ways the room was fantastic and zero of those reasons have to do with the room or the hospitality.

Even though the pillows were divine.

"Well, the eggs benedict will be out shortly," Amalie says with a sweet smile, guiding us down the hall to the rose room.

And that it is. Pink rose wallpaper from floor to ceiling and two round dining tables cloaked in a blush pink tablecloth, surrounded by two stuffed cream chairs. Baby's breath and a single white rose sit in a vase in the center.

"Can I get either of you a lavender honey latte or fresh-squeezed orange juice?"

"A latte would be great," I answer.

"Same, please," Leo adds.

Amalie shuffles to the kitchen as we sit down. I stare out the front window at the azaleas, wondering what it'd be like to run a bed and breakfast and also how Leo and I will exist together outside of this place.

Just as I swallow my nerves and muster up the courage to speak, I feel Leo's large hand slide over my knee.

"We'll figure it out," he whispers.

I look up at him and nod.

"We have a lot to discuss," he adds.

I chew my lip, nodding again.

"But not today, okay? Today let's have fun. Let's be us. We'll tell William some other time."

I twist my lips, a smile tempting me. "Scared of William now?"

"Never," he scoffs, crossing his arms. He pauses, contemplating his own response then leans forward. "A little, but—"

I silence him with my hand cupping his cheek. "Not today." I offer a reassuring smile. "Today we're just going to have fun."

His smile matches mine, and he leans in and kisses me. Everything about the kiss feels completely right. Normal, even.

But when Amalie drops off the eggs benedict a moment later, her mouth twitches in a downward smile. We told her yesterday we weren't together. Now she just saw him kiss me like this is an average Friday morning.

"Enjoy," she adds, eyebrows raised.

Leo says thank you, and I bury my eyes in the English muffin and hollandaise sauce.

We eat through fits of giggles, and kiss between sips of coffee. His hand constantly finds my knee and my fingers continually find his hand. It's the best breakfast I have ever had. I smile to myself as I slurp down the last bit of my lavender honey latte.

Leo watches me, an elbow on the table while gingerly running his thumb over his bottom lip.

"What?" I ask with a breath of a laugh.

He opens his mouth to speak but he breathes out a laugh

instead, his gaze falling to the empty coffee mugs between us before landing back on me. He takes my hand in his.

"Uh-oh. Are you about to get weird? Freak out again?" I question, half-teasing, half-afraid.

"No," he laughs.

"You sure?" I press.

"Shh, Evie, just let me talk."

I press my lips together, eyebrows arched, as I let him speak.

He holds my hands in both of his. I can feel the nerves pulsing on his fingertips as he chews on his bottom lip. He's nervous. I have a ridiculous flash of thinking he's about to propose, and I snort but disguise it with a laugh.

He studies my face. His familiar eyes dance all over my skin with my favorite expression. But there's a hint of something else too.

"I meant everything I've said to you this week, Evie," he begins. "I want to do this for real. But there is something we should talk about."

I swallow the English muffin in my mouth.

"I'm going to be living far away…"

I nod. I know this, but my attention is quickly diverted to Amalie waltzing into the room.

"And the veil!" She's holding a blush pink box with a strand of cream satin ribbon draped over it. She sets it in front of us. "Shall we take a looksie?"

I smile and nod, dazed by the interruption as she opens the box to reveal the beloved veil.

I gasp. "Oh my goodness, Amalie!" I stand, delicately pulling the veil out of the box.

"Do you like it?" she asks, hands clasped next to her smile.

"It is exquisite!" I breathe. The perfect shade of off-white. Mid-length and lined with lace. There are pearls hand sewn throughout the veil. I rub my thumb over one and my eyes sting with tears. I look at Amalie. "My mother loved pearls."

She squeezes my shoulders, her eyes glistening. "So I've heard."

I nod and sniff, placing the veil in the box and wipe my cheeks. "Oh my goodness. I can't get my tears on this." I let out an emotional laugh.

Amalie nods, placing the lid on the box. "Nora made sure to incorporate pearls for your mother."

"She's a good one, huh?" I say and feel Leo's presence next to me. He wraps his hand around my waist and I lean on his shoulder.

"She will be a lovely sister-in-law," Amalie agrees.

"I wish Mom could be here," I add, chin trembling. I sigh, exhausted, overwhelmed, and emotional. "How the hell am I going to get through a toast without crying?"

"Easy!" Amalie says playfully. "Think of gas prices."

I laugh.

"Now that makes me want to cry," Leo adds, shaking his head.

"Fine," Amalie says, tying off the ribbon into the perfect bow. "Then think of how much you love them. Because even if the speech comes out with tears, everyone won't need to hear how much you love them. They'll see it."

It's stupid, but I hug her. Then Leo hugs us both and we laugh. A silly moment now permanently seared into my mind.

By the time we head out with only the clothes on our backs from yesterday, the veil, a dead cell phone, and my purse, a sense of dread punches me in the stomach.

And apparently, it shows on my face.

"What's wrong?" Leo asks.

I shrug. "Nothing," I say. *I just don't want this to end.* But I don't say that last part out loud. I should. We need to think this all the way through. But today is about William and Nora, not the impossibility of us.

We get in the rental car, the veil safely buckled in the backseat.

"Evie, about what I was going to say in there—"

"Can we not?" I ask, turning in the passenger seat. "Not because I don't want to hear about it. Not because I don't think we need to talk about… everything. We do. I know that. But I am an embarrassing ball of emotions right now, and I can't do any big conversations. I know San Francisco is far."

"So is France."

I jerk back like the words flicked me in the nose. Last night hearing about France felt like a dream—a simple thought that danced through my mind. France seemed like something way down the road—the long haul, the future, the endgame. I realize now that he says it, I am all those things to Leo too.

"So is France," I agree, nodding. "But let's just be us today, okay? We'll worry about the rest later. And no telling anyone about last night." I hold out my pinky. "Or this morning."

He smiles and wraps his around mine then brings my hand to his lips and kisses my knuckles, sealing the promise.

Leo puts the car in gear, and we drive to the ferry dock. I hold his hand, and he presses his lips to my knuckles, trailing kisses to my wrist. We watch the sun as it glistens on the water as the ferry pushes away from the island. Wrapped in his arms, I feel safe and secure. I feel closer to happy than I have since Mom died.

I realize Leo is my endgame too. He always has been.

But when the horn blares and the ferry docks back in Seattle, I'm worried we are about to step foot back into real life and let everything we uncovered last night fall to waste.

23

WEDDING DAY
FRIDAY

After the ferry ride back to West Seattle, we stop by Leo's mom's house to get his tux. She lives just outside of downtown in the same duplex she purchased after Leo's dad left in high school. I've never been here, but it feels familiar as we pull up. His mom always overdid it with flowers at the old house and her front porch space here is no different. I always say Leo is a whole memory. But so is his mom.

Clay pots painted in every shade of the rainbow are overflowing with begonias, petunias, and gardenias and litter the walkway leading up to the front door of her little grey duplex.

"Should I just get ready here?" Leo asks as I follow him to the door.

I glance at my watch. "I have my makeup appointment in an hour, and I still need to grab my dress from my apartment." I cringe, wondering if I'm being inconvenient.

He nods. "Okay, that's fine. I'll just grab the tux and my shaving kit."

"You're going to shave?"

He half-shrugs, half-nods.

I step closer, grabbing his jaw. "But I like you a little scruffy."

His lips turn up as he peers down at me, two breaths away from a kiss. "But how would Nora feel about that for the pictures?"

I laugh, my hand sliding down to his chest, and his grip tightens around my waist. We pause for a half moment before he pushes me up against the side of his mom's house, his hands encasing my ribcage and his thumbs gently rubbing my sides. His gaze drifts from my eyes to my lips as he slowly moves in. My breath catches on his just as the door squeaks open and a white Pomeranian flies out, yelping and jumping on Leo's legs.

"Is that Genevieve?" his mom exclaims.

"Hi, Ms. Louisa," I say, stepping out of the position Leo has me in and giving her a hug at the front door.

She smells like fresh-baked cinnamon rolls and vanilla bean lotion—exactly how I remember her. And I realize how much I've missed her.

"It's been so long, honey," she says, still squeezing me and rocking from side to side.

"I know. I've missed you," I mutter, her black curls sticking to my lip balm.

She pulls back, taking me by the shoulders and examining me. "Always the sweetest, best girl for my boy."

She shoots Leo a look and then winks at me.

"Oh—" I open my mouth to protest, but she cuts me off.

"Secret is safe with me." She winks again but this time at Leo. "I've been waiting for you two to happen again."

I whip around, my mouth dropped in Leo's direction.

What? He mouths.

Again? I mouth, and he grins then scrunches his nose.

"Come in," Louisa says, missing the interaction. "Chakra!" she yells at the dog, who hops up the steps and disappears past Louisa's ankles into the house.

I follow, chin down, wondering what Leo's mother knows about us.

Just before I make it through the front door, Leo grips the waist of my jean shorts and pulls me back to him. My back hits his chest with a *hmmph*. He wraps an arm over my chest and leans down to my ear.

"She always knew," he whispers.

"Knew what?" I whisper back.

"Everything."

I look up at him, vision zeroing in on his placid expression. I always knew Leo was close to his mom. When his dad moved away, their bond became even tighter. But I didn't know she knew about anything that ever happened between us. My cheeks grow hot as the reality of this knowledge seeps in.

"So, I imagine the two of you had a fun little adventure on Vashon last night," Louisa says, cutting into my thoughts.

"It was… unexpected," Leo says.

I close my eyes, and try to suppress my embarrassment.

"Can I get you two anything before you head to the hotel?" she asks.

"No, thank you. We ate earlier. Now it's just a race for time." I glance at my watch as if I actually care about my makeup appointment. "Going to be a busy day."

She nods with a smile, tossing Chakra a small dog treat. "Little William is getting married. I can hardly believe it."

"It's exciting," I agree. "You'll be there, right?"

"With my dancing shoes."

"Good. It will be a fun night."

"Wedding of the decade," Leo adds coming up behind me with the suit hung over his shoulder. He kisses my cheek.

I gape at him, the color draining from my face.

Louisa giggles and takes a sip of coffee. "Leo has had it bad for you since he was twelve, Genevieve. You don't need to act surprised. He used to come home from hanging out at your house and talk endlessly about how much you drove him crazy, mostly because you beat him at everything—HORSE, free throw contests, Yahtzee. Then one day he told me how funny you are." She smiles into her coffee and takes a sip. "I knew he was a goner after that."

I let out a breath of a laugh. "You're quite intuitive. No one else knew."

"Oh, your mom did." She laughs, eyes falling into a memory. "God rest her soul. But she knew."

My heart tightens and I try to smile, but it's impossible because I want her here so badly that I could cry. Ever since she died, she's been this missing piece of my heart, hollow and desperate for her to return. But over time, I've gotten used to the condition of my heart—the pain never completely dull, but tolerable at least. Except when something big happens. My college graduation. My first job. My first apartment. My first promotion. My breakup with Damien. William and Nora's wedding.

It's like the events of my life are magnifying the fact that she's gone, and no matter how hard I pray or scream at the sky, she won't ever come back.

Leo, sensing my vulnerability, runs his hand down my back and holds on to me.

"I wish she could be here for you and your brother," Louisa adds, stepping closer and giving me a tight squeeze. She pulls away and wipes my wet cheeks with a soft smile. I didn't realize any tears fell. "Now, I didn't mean to go and make you cry."

I wipe my cheeks and force a smile. "It's okay."

Louisa smiles at me fondly and says, "You two better get going. I don't want you to be late."

Leo kisses the side of her forehead. "Bye, Ma."

I let out a breath in the car as I swipe the seatbelt over my chest.

Leo smiles over the console at me.

"She knew," I state, staring at him.

"She knew," he confirms.

"Like, that we slept together?"

"Yeah."

My jaw drops. "Stop it. Do you tell your mother about all your sexual encounters?" My hands fly to my mouth. "Did you tell her about last night?"

Leo chuckles. "Relax. She knows nothing about last night. But she caught us about to kiss on her front porch so I'm assuming she put two and two together. She's not stupid."

"Why did you tell her about…" I clear my throat, "…high school?"

Leo looks over his shoulder as he pulls his rental out of the driveway, then glances at me as he puts the car in drive. "She sensed a change in my behavior. And obviously, that was for a lot of reasons. She and Dad were fighting a lot—it was right before he moved out. Then one day she asked if I had sex, and the rest tumbled out." He shrugs. "I didn't give her details, but her mother's intuition knew I had my first time, and I told her it was you."

I'm stunned, my mind dazed on the other side of this memory. Then mortification washes over me like a bucket of ice water. "Did she tell my mom?"

Leo releases a nervous chuckle. "God, I hope not."

I slap my hands to my forehead and drag them down my face, feeling the burning blush on my cheeks. "Mom never said anything if she did," I say, staring out the window. "Wait. I was your first?"

He half-smiles and bites his bottom lip. "You didn't know?"

"You were Leonardo Bishop! You dated everybody! The locker room was full of talk about Leo and how many points you scored at the game or how good you looked during the games." I laugh to myself. "Girls would literally squeak on the bleachers when you took off your warm-ups before the game started. I hated it."

He laughs, but it's small and embarrassed. His eyes stay on the road.

I grin at him, feeling stupidly proud of myself. "I took your virginity."

He laughs again, harder this time. "I'm aware."

"And I'm never giving it back," I tease, and he glares at me, mischief in his eyes.

I smile in response and lean back in my seat, tilting my head back against the headrest. We have so much to talk about. But instead of saying those words out loud, I say, "I've missed you."

Leo takes my hand in his, kissing the back of it then turning it over and nibbling on my wrist, making me smile. "I've missed you. Even when I said I wouldn't, I knew I would."

24

WEDDING DAY
FRIDAY

"Where *the hell* have you been?" Abigail says through clenched teeth as she exits the hotel room to the hallway. "Your ex is causing so much drama…"

I glance behind me and offer Leo a timid smile. At first, I think she's talking about Leo, and my stomach somersaults but when I look at Leo, he seems hyper-focused and irritated, and I realize the ex in which she's speaking.

"Damien? What do you mean?" I ask.

"William found out about the *baby*," Abigail practically seethes, tightening her grip on my arm. "Why didn't you tell me? It's no wonder you disappeared after he told you. Are you okay?"

I laugh, realizing how it must have looked at the luncheon yesterday. Me storming off to an island after I found out my ex cheated while we were together and has a love child, but oddly… "I'm fine," I say.

She raises her eyebrows.

"What? It's not my baby…"

Leo lets out a breath of a laugh and presses his lips together when Abigail looks at him.

"You!" She says the word like a threat, and he laughs again.

"I'm going to go find Will's room," he says, ignoring Abigail's searing stare as he dips down and kisses me on the cheek, then disappears down the hall.

"Really?" she asks, despondence written on her face.

"I know. I'll fill you in about Leo, I just—"

"I don't give a fuck about Leo right now, Gen." She crosses her arms, her jaw is tight. "Are you sure you're okay?"

I shrug, remembering how white-hot rage burned my blood yesterday at lunch. I should be devastated that Damien has a kid. I should be devastated that he cheated and lied to me for years. But I'm not.

"I guess," I say. "Look, Damien and I broke up six months ago. And yeah, it makes me angry knowing how he treated me and having to find out this way, but… I didn't want to get back together, and now I just feel really lucky we ended when we did."

She tilts her head. "So why did you leave me here all morning with a crazy fucking bride and her even crazier fucking mother? *And* an ex-boyfriend that is trying to be the main character in someone else's wedding."

"Is he really here?" I ask.

"He said he still wants to come tonight and Will is pissed."

I snort out a laugh. "None of that feels like our problem, does it?"

Abigail draws back, arms crossed and studies me with suspicion. "You had sex."

My cheeks heat and I suppress a smile as we step over the threshold into the presidential suite, ignoring her observation entirely.

"But also, let me warn you about the annoyance level in here…"

"Why? Did Lorraine comment on your hair again?" I ask.

"I wish she would…" Abigail says, shaking her head.

"Your hair looks beautiful," I say, withholding a laugh as I gesture to her bent blonde and pink waves and side part clipped on one side. It's elegant, and classic, with a touch of Abigail's bright personality.

Abigail blows out air. "Can we start drinking?"

A laugh escapes my chest. "Yes. It is a wedding."

She swipes champagne off the counter as we pass farther into the hotel room.

It's a mess.

Dresses are hung and laid out on the couches and the king-sized bed, and makeup stations in each corner for the bridesmaids. I say a quick hello to the other bridesmaids as I walk through the bedroom to the master bathroom to find Nora in a white silk robe—the one I had embroidered for her that says Mrs. Michaels on the back in blush pink thread—getting her hair curled. Her eyes are closed like she's praying, and her skin is dewy and flawless.

"I have the veil," I say, holding out the box to her.

She opens her eyes and her mouth drops, realizing I'm here and so is her precious veil. "Oh, Genevieve!" She stands, immediately getting yanked back down in her chair because her head is attached to the curling iron wrapped around her hair. She smiles up at me. "You're a lifesaver."

I shrug and smile, setting the box on her lap like an offering because I don't have the audacity to say the stunt she pulled with me and Leo on Vashon was rude and inconsiderate, while also hands-down being one of the best nights of my life.

I've decided to let it slide.

"How was Vashon?" she asks nonchalantly.

I smile. "Fine."

She raises her eyebrows, opening the box and examining the veil inside. Her eyes well. "Your mother loved pearls." Her gaze turns to me, her smile bright. She reaches her hand out to me, and I take it, squeezing tightly.

Emotion suffocates my neck and I nod. "She loved pearls."

Abigail throws a wad of tissue in both our faces. "All right, all right. No crying yet."

Nora and I laugh, wiping the few tears that have fallen. Today will be a day full of emotion, but the crying can come later.

"Not right now when we need to get our faces picture ready. No one wants swollen eyes in the pictures that will hang on the walls for decades to come," Abigail says, pouring two glasses of champagne. She diligently adds a drop of orange juice. "*Hopefully,*" she adds, handing us each a glass.

I take a long gulp before Abigail grabs my arm, pulling me tight against her. Her mouth is just inches from my ear. "I want all the fucking details. And by 'fucking details,' I mean *fucking* details."

I laugh and half-choke on my champagne.

"What did you just say to each other?" Nora asks, glancing between us.

"Nothing." I try to remain casual, but my cheeks are on fire.

Nora grins, hidden knowledge buried in her lips. "I probably know."

"What? I—" I begin, but I'm quickly cut off by Lorraine.

"The caterers said they will not change Aunt Bernadette's meal at the reception!" Lorraine enters the room with a huff, hands on her hips and exasperation biting at her nerves.

"It'll be fine," Nora says.

"But how? She accidentally chose steak, but she is now a pescatarian and needs the salmon." Lorraine stares at herself in the mirror, fidgeting with her hair and then dabbing tissue against her damp forehead.

Abigail and I exchange a look and sip our champagne. Abigail gets shuffled into her make-up chair by her make-up artist.

"What did you order, Genevieve?" she asks.

I swallow the champagne in my mouth. "Salmon."

"Would you be willing to switch plates? We'll be discreet. No one would even know."

"Except Genevieve, Mom." I glance at Nora as she speaks. Her eyes are closed but I can see the frustration in her body. "She ordered the salmon."

"Right, and Aunt Bernadette—"

"Can eat beforehand if it's that big of a deal."

"Nora. You are being so inconsiderate. And quite frankly so

rude to your aunt who traveled all the way from Philadelphia to see you marry William."

I retreat into myself as I watch this interaction, wanting no part of it while also wanting it to deescalate quickly.

"It's fine. I'll eat steak—" I begin, taking a seat in the chair next to her.

"No." Nora stands. "No, Genevieve will eat what she ordered and so will Aunt Bernadette."

"But Nora—"

"Mom, please!" Nora says, exasperated. "With the utmost respect. No one cares what she forgot to order. Leave it alone. She ordered wrong. She will survive on steak and mashed potatoes. I'm more concerned about how hot it will be anyway so please, drink some water, sit next to the AC, and I beg of you, don't give me a single update until after the wedding. At this point, I do not care. I just want to get married and run away to Tahiti."

I freeze, too scared to even breathe as my eyes dart between Nora and her mother.

I see Ms. Lorraine gulp, and I withhold a laugh.

"Well, Nora. I'm just—this is not how you..." Lorraine begins to stammer, her voice breathless and her brow sweating. The room fills with an awkward quiet. Each makeup artist keeps their eyes fixed on the faces in front of them. My makeup artist takes a cool cleansing wipe to my face and presses her lips together in such a tight line, that the skin surrounding her lips turns white. I side-glance at Abigail, and she's drowning her witty comeback in champagne.

I kind of feel bad for Lorraine, but I'm mostly proud of Nora.

Lorraine searches the room for someone to side with her but our eyes avoiding hers is all the answer she needs before she stomps her foot and turns out of the room. The door to the suite slams shut moments later.

"Didn't know you had it in you, Nora," Abigail says, and April pokes her half-curled head in the room.

"What the hell happened?"

Nora's cheeks are red, and her eyes are closed. "Nothing

that will matter tomorrow."

I smile at her. "I love that."

She shrugs. "Your dad said that to me."

My eyes snap in her direction. "He what?"

"He said to me and William that the most important thing to remember all day today is that if it isn't something that will matter tomorrow, then it doesn't matter."

My chest warms and I smile. "That's perfect."

"Your mom told him to tell you and William on your wedding day," she adds with a glance over at me.

"Oh." My chin snaps back, and I try to avoid grinding my teeth. It's sweet, really. And I'm happy mom passed on so many nuggets of wisdom to share with me and my brother after she passed, but coming out of Nora's mouth when I'm nowhere near a day like today for myself feels like a smack on the cheek.

Someone pinches my elbow, and I glance over as Abigail refills my champagne and offers a sympathetic glance. I wonder if Nora realizes she spoiled it for me. I also wonder if it will even matter in the long run. I smile at Abigail, thankful she understands.

My mind falls back on the last couple of days with Leo as my makeup artist begins working her magic. It swims in the memory of his hands all over my body. His kisses on my lips. The words he whispered in my ear. And no matter how vivid the memories are, they feel like a dream, and I can't help but wonder: did it really happen the way I remember, or is my mind playing tricks on me?

Once my hair is curled to perfection, and my false eyelashes are secured on my wing-tipped eyeliner, I head to William's hotel room. Not for Leo. But for my brother. I want to see him one last time before he ties the knot.

"You can back out now. You don't have to marry into that… family," I tease William as I hoist myself onto the countertop while he adjusts his bowtie in the mirror, making him laugh.

"You love Nora," he says.

"I do," I nod. "But you are dealing with an impossible

mother-in-law so Godspeed, brother."

He twists his lips and shoots me a glare. "I'd do anything for Nora."

"I know, and that's why I know this is going to work," I say, smiling. "Hey, what was the gift she got you?"

William pulls up his pantleg to reveal dress socks with basketballs on them, and I laugh. They're so ugly. It's perfect.

"She's letting you wear those?"

He nods. "And she got them for all the groomsmen."

I love this so much. As prim and proper as Nora and her family can be, she knows how to let William be himself.

"And!" he adds, leaving the bathroom area and returning with a light gray shoebox. He flips open the lid. "Air Force 1s for all the groomsmen and me for the reception."

My jaw drops at how generous the gift is, though I know Nora paid for all our hair and makeup and bought everyone silk pajamas with our names embroidered on the backs. I didn't get to wear mine for obvious reasons.

"I'm jealous, I want a pair," I say.

He nods along to my statement and closes the box. "It's a big day." He lets out a deep breath.

I smile fondly at my brother and nod. "It is."

"Are you proud of me?"

"Like mom would be," I answer through the emotions twisting in my chest.

"Thanks, Gen." He rests a hand on mine, hesitating with his next words. "Mom wrote me a letter."

Chills trail down my arms and goosebumps rise on my skin. It's like I can feel her in the room. "She did?"

He smiles, his eyes lost in the ground in front of him. "She did. My 'Wedding Day' letter. Dad brought it to me last night."

My chin shakes, and tears spring to my eyes and I wonder what the point of wearing makeup today was. "What did it say?"

He laughs a little, and I backpedal.

"You don't have to tell me if you don't want. That's a special thing you can have that only you and Mom know," I add.

He nods, agreeing. "It was good, Gen. Sometimes I'm scared I've forgotten what her voice sounds like, but then—and

I know it sounds crazy—it was like I could hear her saying each and every word." He swipes under his eyes and laughs.

I smile knowing exactly what that kind of happy-sad feels like.

"Dad gave it to me and said, 'Mom knew I could never find the words, so she wrote them down for me.'"

My heart twists and bursts as I laugh even though I'm still crying a bit. I miss her so bad.

"She wrote one for you too. Don't worry," he adds.

"Of course she did," I say, smiling and suddenly wanting to take this vulnerable moment and tell him about Leo. "Hey, can I tell you somethi—"

But my confession is cut short as the groomsmen shuffle into the suite. They're loud and arguing. At first, it seems friendly—a group of grown men that had a few drinks but then there's a clatter, making William and I spring to our feet and exit the bedroom.

"What the fuck?" William asks at the sight of Terrence holding Damien by the collar up against the wall.

"Jesu—"

"How many times do we have to tell you to get the fuck out of here!" Terrence yells, and I'm quite embarrassed for him. Both of them.

"Oh my god." I roll my eyes and let out a sigh because this is ridiculous. "Terrence, let him go."

"No, I'm sick of his shit! William and Nora said he can't come after what he did to you, and he doesn't know how to take no for an answer."

"No, he doesn't," I agree.

"All right. Damien. Get out," William says, stepping forward like a proper gentleman. "Then, after you leave, remember you may not show your face at the wedding."

"William…"

"No. Fuck off," William says. "I'm not putting my sister through seeing your face ever again."

My mouth drops open. I'm equal parts surprised and proud of my brother. Then Damien looks at me with his sad, puppy-dog eyes. His hair is perfectly disheveled; an entire story is written in his eyes.

"Genny…" he whispers, his voice low like it's only us.

"Damien, I've tried to be nice—"

William steps between us. "And a lot of this has been my fault, but I am so sick of how entitled you are when it comes to my sister. You blew your shot, dude. Lorraine really wants you at the wedding, so I've been cordial," he pauses as he steps closer to Damien, "But I swear to God, if you even attempt to call her, it will be the last fucking time your fingers work."

I snort. "William, relax."

He steps back, buttoning the sleeves of his dress shirt. "I swear, Gen, you are never going to date a 'so-called' friend again."

I ignore him. There is way too much testosterone and nerves in this room. I need to return to the bridal party suite, unclip the curls in my hair and put my dress on.

"What's going on?"

His voice rumbles all over my body, and a smile spreads over my face. I turn to see him standing just in front of the hotel room door as it clicks closed. He almost smiles but stops, and I see his tongue glide along his teeth, then his gaze flits to Damien behind me. His eyes darken.

"Damien was just leaving," I cut in before anyone says anything else.

Leo drops his gaze to me. "He was?"

I nod, force a smile, and beg my arms not to wrap themselves around him.

"You good?" Leo asks.

I nod.

"That how you doing your hair?" he asks, and I know he's being a dick on purpose to diffuse the situation. And most likely to keep what happened between us under wraps.

I scoff out a laugh. "Fuck off, Leo."

"Can you two please fucking get along?" William says, exasperated.

"He started it," I say, and William shoots daggers at me with his eyes.

"Gen, don't pick a fight with my best man. Please. I swear,

all my dreams would come true if you two just got along for more than five minutes." William pinches the bridge of his nose and throws back the whiskey. His frustration with us is palpable, and I feel terrible for putting on this charade and lying to William.

I swallow hard, hoping my blush cools off. I sneak a sidelong glance at Leo. He's chewing on his bottom lip, withholding a smile. *God, I love him.* The thought flashes so quickly over my mind that I clear my throat, stumbling backward. I realize I'm not ready to tell William. I want to. But he's about to have a stress-induced aneurism. He's also about to get married, and he has no idea his little sister has been in love off and on with his best man for fifteen years.

"Damien, let's go," I say, grabbing his arm. His eyes dart around the room. He looks bamboozled, confused, and stupid drunk even though I know he's not. He's simply an entitled prick.

Just as the hotel room door swings shut, I glance at Leo. His jaw is tight and his gaze is on my hand that's holding Damien's arm.

He hates this guy and I know it. I even understand it.

But my job right now is to keep my brother happy. I can't comfort Leo right now. Even though it's all I want to do.

"What the hell is going on, Genny?" Damien asks as I steer him toward the elevator.

I punch the down button and cross my arms, glaring at him. "Well, my brother is getting married and you keep managing to piss everyone off because apparently for the three years we were together, you couldn't manage to keep your dick in your pants."

He clicks his tongue on his teeth, annoyed with little old me. Typical. "No, I mean with Leo."

I choke, scoff, and laugh all at once. "What?"

"You fucked him."

He says the statement as an accusation. The stream of imperfections in our relationship pours into my mind until all I see is red and how absolutely none of this is his business.

"We broke up six months ago, Damien."

"Do you fuck all your brother's friends?"

My chin snaps back. The hardest lashes sting the most when they have a lick of truth to them.

I laugh to recover as anger steam rolls inside my ribcage. "You aren't his friend, Damien. You don't count." I don't even care that I just confirmed his suspicions. The thing about guys like Damien is they don't know how to let go, even when the person they've been holding on to wants to burn them alive.

Damien steps toward me, and this short elevator ride feels more like a torture chamber than a ten-floor descent. "He'll never love you like me."

I roll my eyes until they land on him. His sad eyes, the perfect swoop of his hair. His perfectly tanned skinned. His hands that held mine, and his heart that supposedly loved me for years.

"You're right."

"I told you—" he breathes, stepping closer to wrap his arms around me.

But I stop him.

"He won't ever love me like you did, because he actually knows me. He actually wants to love *me*." I shake my head. "You wanted me to check a box. You wanted me to mold my life to yours. You wanted me to be what you wanted, without ever just wanting me for who I am. And you certainly didn't love me enough to be faithful."

Damien's eyes soften with tears as the elevator dings, and the doors glide open. He steps out into the lobby, but I don't follow.

"Let us go, Damien. Go be a good dad," I say, my voice soft. "Because whatever you're doing here only makes you look like a jackass."

His jaw drops and the doors close. I hope it's the last time I ever see his face.

I lean back against the mirrored elevator wall, thinking of how I need to change into my dress, unclip my curls, and tell Leo he's it for me.

He always has been.

25

WEDDING DAY
FRIDAY

It's hard to describe the feeling coursing through me when I see Leo walk out of the holding room at the museum. I watch him follow Terrence to where the rest of us are standing, waiting for the procession. I soak him in from head to toe as he adjusts his cufflinks. His polished wing tips. His perfectly tailored suit. The white rose attached to the collar of his jacket. He, as always, looks like he just walked out of a magazine. But this time, instead of feeling a burning animosity in my chest, my heart flutters. It's almost like I'm floating, and my mind wanders and spirals, wondering if this last week was a dream.

But then he looks at me and a smile cuts across his features and his eyes glint in the evening light pouring through the glass ceiling.

Hi, he mouths and a flush sweeps up my neck.

Hi, I mouth back.

We stay in line, pairing off the way we did for the rehearsal just two days ago.

"You look nice, Genevieve," Terrence says, offering me his arm.

I take it, smiling, and blink away from Leo as Taite takes Leo's arm in front of me. "Thank you. You look nice too."

Even though the AC is blasting, my hands are sweaty, and I know once the doors open, we'll feel the heat of the sun piercing through the glass ceiling.

God, I miss the coolness of the hotel.

"Sorry my hands are sweaty," I mutter to Terrence.

He leans in and says, "Don't worry. I will be standing in a puddle after this ceremony."

I let out a long laugh, then cover my mouth with my sweaty palm.

Leo's eyes flash over his shoulder and his lip snarls slightly.

I snort out another, smaller laugh, and Leo shakes his head.

It's an adorable dose of jealousy.

I open my mouth to say something—wanting to pull him close to me so I can whisper words for only him to know. But the music grows louder as the doors open and the wedding begins.

We emerge down the aisle through the sea of familiar faces. Family. Friends. Random relatives. A history of two people written on the faces of every guest. William is standing at the end of the aisle with the officiant. He's pressing his thumb against his wrist, a nervous habit he's always had. He used to do it during presentations in school, when he was introduced to virtually anyone's parents, and that one time he was interviewed for the local paper for the championship game.

My lips spread into a genuine smile, and I nod at him. His eyes glisten, but he smiles and nods back.

When Terrence and I part at the end of the aisle and stand in our respective places, I try my best to fix my eyes on the rest of the wedding party coming down the aisle. Cora and John. April and Jake. Abigail and Marcus.

But I can feel his eyes on me. His gaze is warmer than the heat wave penetrating the glass museum. I tilt my chin so we're face-to-face.

You're beautiful, he mouths, and I bite my lip to contain my grin. My heart wants to leap out of my chest and I want to throw myself in his arms. Instead, I clear my throat and look toward the end of the aisle as Nora stands in her princess-like wedding dress, holding onto her father's arm.

She is radiant, elegant, and staring at my brother like he's the only man in the room. She loves him. I know she does. And after her father gives her away and she takes William's hand in front of me, I'm convinced she's going to love him forever.

Finally, after many long minutes of the sun trying to melt us through the glass, the vows are said and rings are exchanged. The officiant says, "I now pronounce you: husband and wife. William, you may kiss your bride."

William moves a step closer, taking the delicate veil in his fingers and moving it away from Nora's face. Her smile is radiant, and her eyes are on the love of her life.

When they kiss, the wedding party erupts in cheers and applause. They turn to face their guests, arms raised and smiles uncontainable.

And my heart bursts with uninhibited, uncontrollable happiness as my brother marries his person.

We file down the aisle and escape to the holding room where Nora and William take turns signing their marriage license. Thank Jesus, the AC is working here. I can feel the sweat dripping down my tailbone.

Leo is William's witness, and as he's signing, Nora turns to me with another pen in hand.

"Will you be my witness?"

I glance at the pen in her hand and then meet her eyes with a smile. "Absolutely."

The cheers and commotion continue behind me as I fall behind Leo to sign the document.

"Time for shots!" Terrence hollers, pulling out individual bottles of cinnamon whiskey and passing them around. Leo takes mine and patiently waits for me to dot the last "i" in my signature.

As I cap the pen, Leo's hand slides on my back and he leans

into my ear.

"You are killing me in that dress," he whispers, handing me the shot of whiskey and pretending he didn't just say those words in my ear. I hope my face is playing it as cool as he is.

"Everybody ready?" Terrence asks, holding his up in the air. Everyone does the same. "To William and Nora taking the plunge!"

The whiskey goes down easy and finishes with a smooth blend of sweet and spicy. When I lick my lips, it's hard not to notice Leo's gaze fall. It's even harder to not feel his entire presence in the air next to me. The heat of his skin, the strength in his body, the memory of everything he's ever done to me. I'm trying my best to stay composed and normal and breathe easily without blushing, but it's practically painful to do when all I want is to run to him, jump inside his arms, and tell the whole world I am in love with him.

But I don't.

Our time will come, and I'm realizing how long I'm willing to wait.

Back Then

PICTURE 4: THANKSGIVING

"What did William do this time?" I asked, staring at my parents on the blue couch across from William and me.

Mom forced a smile. Dad didn't. He just stared at the carpet; his eyes drooped and his mouth sagged into a frown.

William and I looked at each other, silently asking the other what was going on with sibling telepathy, and both coming up blank.

"There is no easy way to tell you two this…" Dad began, but his voice was clogged, and he choked on what I knew was a cry. He didn't let it go. He pressed his lips into a straight line while his chin shook and he white-knuckled his wife's hand.

Mom was more poised, shoulders back, gently rubbing the back of Dad's hand with her thumb. "I have cancer."

"No, you don't," William said, disbelief apparent in his tone.

Dad wiped his eyes with his thumb and index finger. Mom offered a sympathetic smile.

"I do," she said, her voice soft like she was going to tell us a bedtime story.

I shook my head. I didn't know what to say. There was a

quake in my chest. My sternum was acting as a dam, brittle and unstable but trying its damnedest to hold back the flood of emotion teetering inside me.

"What kind?" William asked. He was rubbing his knees and fidgeting so much as if the news made him buzz with energy. I was the opposite. I had gone completely still, ice running through my veins.

"Colon."

"Fuck," I muttered.

"Language," Mom said but her lips twitched. Whether it was to cry or laugh, I still don't know.

"Sorry," I said.

She took a breath. "I don't want you to worry. Right now I feel mostly okay. But we want you to know before you go back to school."

That was the moment the tears came and I sobbed, hunched over like a little kid that fell off her bike and needed her mom to comfort her. I went straight to her lap. I held her. She held me back. I cried in her shoulder, and she rubbed my hair.

"But I still need you," I cried.

She hushed me and rocked me back and forth. "I'm not gone, sweet girl. I'm right here. I'll always be right here."

My brother put his head on her other shoulder and cried too, but his sobs were softer. Dad rubbed our backs with shaky hands, but he didn't speak much that night. This was his worst fear. We held out hope, we really did. But that night, we fell apart together as a family, so that the next day we could carry on together, too.

It was the Monday of Thanksgiving break, and I already didn't want to do anything but hold my mom and love the cancer out of her. I didn't want to go back to school. I didn't feel like anything mattered.

Later that night, I thought of all the friends I wanted to tell. For a fleeting moment, Leo crossed my mind, and I was so embarrassed with myself. But I was also determined to have a real conversation with him for the first time in four years. I knew I'd see him at Terrence's house the next night. I could tell him then.

But I didn't. I ended up seeing him kissing Sophia Hanson and decided to drink tequila until I forgot my own name.

Two hours later, I was puking in the rhododendron bushes in the front yard. Leo caught me through the window and rushed out to hold my hair back while I was doubled over. I continued to wretch until my stomach was empty. Then I stood straighter, wiped my mouth with the back of my hand, and tried to look less drunk, which always has the opposite effect. He asked if I was okay and I slapped his hands away and told him to fuck off.

Abigail got me in her car to take me home. When I made eye contact with Leo through the passenger side window of her car, there was tender regret in his eyes and I wish I didn't notice it. I closed my eyes as my brain spun, and I prayed I'd forget his face… or better yet, I prayed I'd forget the whole week.

Three days later, I had mostly recovered from the party, and I was trying my best to muster up some enthusiasm for the holiday. On Thanksgiving there are two types of families: the ones that drink mimosas and watch the parade, and the ones that run 5ks.

My family happened to be the kind that did both.

The Bishops didn't always come to our house for Thanksgiving, but after Leo's dad moved to California, Mom always gave Louisa an open invitation. This year, I didn't even remember they were coming after hearing the news about Mom's cancer until Leo rang the doorbell at 7:30 a.m.

"What are you doing here?" I asked, wearing a bright orange running shirt and knee-high socks with turkeys on them. He was wearing a turkey hat.

Drawing back with a look of contempt, he said, "What do you think? Beating you at the Turkey Trot." Then he shoved my shoulder.

"Right, right," I muttered, unbothered.

"Puffin' for the stuffin'," he added with an embellished grin.

"Fantastic," I said, tight-lipped and annoyed.

"Ready?" William asked in his matching socks as he slipped

passed me through the door.

I nodded.

"All right, let's go, kids," Dad said, flipping his key ring around his fingers.

"Is Ms. Clara coming?" Leo asked, and my throat constricted so tight I thought I couldn't breathe.

"Not this year," Dad told him, and we all got in the car.

I didn't know why William hadn't already told him. But at some point, during the race he did. I know because Leo didn't trip me halfway or cut me off at the finish line. He rubbed the top of my head and said, "good job." I shot him a suspicious glare.

"It's going to be okay, Evie," he said when I didn't respond.

Tears filled my eyes and my gaze locked on his. "Please don't call me that."

His expression, his posture—everything about him—froze. Then finally he nodded and said, "Right."

I didn't talk to him much the entire day. I attached myself to Mom and Louisa like a leach. I helped baste the turkey and set the table. It wasn't until we were dishing up dessert that Leo really crossed my mind. Mom was taking candid pictures of everyone while we cut the pies and dished them up on paper plates with autumn leaves printed on them. I had just plopped a piece of apple pie and pumpkin pie on my plate and covered it in whipped cream.

I went overboard until the whipped topping resembled Mt. Rainier, and William made a comment. I snorted. Then Dad asked, "Leo, where is your girlfriend tonight? I thought she would have stopped by."

I gritted my teeth. I knew exactly where Sophia was, and I hated that I knew. She was with her family that didn't like Leo. A bitter side of me understood, I didn't like him at that moment either.

"Leo doesn't have a girlfriend!" My mom laughed and scoffed simultaneously. The abrasiveness of her certainty made me jerk with laughter and one of my pieces of pie toppled over my plate, landing on the pie dish. I picked it up and plopped it back on my plate, laughing harder than I had all day.

Mom snapped a picture, but I never asked to look at it. I never got to see Leo behind me, restraining a smile.

I was so determined to stop caring about him, I didn't even talk to him when he stopped me in the hallway later that night to say, "Sorry about your mom." I simply gave him a tight-lipped nod and he asked if I wanted to talk about it. I did. But I was stubborn and so angry at him, remembering how he ripped me to shreds when I told him the same thing when his parents divorced.

I knew he cared. I just knew if I continued to care about him, I'd get my heart broken just like before. Looking back, maybe I should have just talked to him. Maybe I should have called it even. Maybe I should have told him how I really felt. Maybe I should have gone outside to play HORSE until it was too cold to feel our fingers. Maybe we would have kissed in the moonlight. Maybe we would have apologized for being young and stupid and naïve. But we didn't do those things.

"I don't know why you and Leo are so mean to each other," Mom said later when we were watching *Miracle On 34th Street*.

"We've never liked each other," I answered, staring at the television.

She giggled. "That is the biggest lie you've ever told."

I didn't answer her.

"You two will work it out."

I remained expressionless. "Work out what?"

She patted my hand and smiled. "Whatever it is you aren't telling me. One day, you'll work it out."

I swallowed hard but I didn't continue the subject. I leaned my head on her shoulder and said, "I love you, Mom. I can't imagine life without you."

"I'm not going anywhere. And even if I do, I want you to know I'll always, always be with you." Her voice was steady but as she kissed my head, her tears soaked my hair.

26

WEDDING DAY
FRIDAY

We re-enter the now-reception room and do our stupid but also incredibly fun and fitting bridal party dance, before taking our seats at the bridal banquet table to stuff our faces with dinner. After the plates are cleared, the DJ announces it's time for champagne and toasts.

I white-knuckle the index cards in my hand as I wait for my turn.

Taite goes first. She tells a funny story about Nora in elementary school that is both heartwarming and unexpected. The crowd chuckles, and she offers congratulations and raises her glass in a toast.

I take a small sip. A bead of sweat slides from the back of my neck and down my spine until I feel it disperse into the plunging fabric on the back of my dress. The DJ announces the Best Man, Leonardo Bishop, is next.

My heart rotates in my chest and I swallow my nerves, doing my best to mimic composure. Leo leans over the table as he pushes his chair back to stand. In the process, he sneaks a look and a perfect smile at me.

I restrain mine, wanting to tackle him and kiss him all over his pretty, perfect face. He stands, taking the mic from Taite.

He shifts the mic from one hand to the other, his gaze dropping to the black tablecloth in front of him and then glancing at my brother. They exchange an expression that seems to read, *I'm about to go there.*

Then Leo looks at his mom, sitting at the table to the right of us and she smiles wide, already clutching tissues to her chest.

Leo takes in a quick breath, clears his throat, and begins.

"My mom once told me real love isn't the kind of love that feels good all the time. Sometimes it's the kind of love that challenges you. It bends and breaks and molds you. It forces you to grow when nothing in you wants to. It's the kind of love that pulls you out of trenches and dances with you on mountain tops. It's the kind of love with blisters and scars." Leo pauses and looks directly at me. "It's the kind of love that loses the fight and apologizes. The kind of love that feels so good, it hurts because it forces you to grow."

Emotion swirls in my chest, and we hold the stare for another few pounding heartbeats. I want to smack him for making me cry before I have to give my toast. But I can't look away no matter how much he makes my heart bleed.

"She said that is the kind of love worth protecting," he continues, looking out at the guests and then back at William and Nora with a wide smile. "I think my Mom was right and I'm so happy my best friend has found it in Nora. Congrats, my friend. I wish you both a lifetime of happiness!"

He raises his glass. There are more cheers and applause. But I can't see anything because my eyes are blurry with tears. I blink twice and wipe the large teardrops off my cheeks.

I hear the DJ say my name and I stand, looking down at the notecards in my sweaty hand. The ink has spread due to the perspiration in my palms and dread washes over me. I knew I should have typed it on my phone.

Mild panic rolls over me, but I'm almost immediately snapped out of it as Leo rests a hand on my back and hands me the mic. His long fingers entangle with mine as I take hold of the mic and stare back at Leo. He's giving me a *you-got-this* look, but the cards in my hand would say otherwise.

"Your speech was supposed to be funny," I whisper.

He leans, smiling, and whispers, "Just remember what Amalie said."

I jerk toward him and whisper, "To think about gas prices?"

He laughs. Then covers his mouth, composing himself. He's so damn cute. His reaction makes me smile and forget that everything I planned to say is now a smudge of black ink in my hand.

I set down the cards.

"Well…" I begin with a breath. "I had a beautiful speech prepared for the two of you, I swear, but it would seem that it's so hot in here I sweat through the ink and ruined my perfect bullet points." The guests laugh and I chuckle lightly. "But it doesn't matter what I planned to say. Because it won't matter tomorrow." I smile, tears rising in my eyes as I look directly at Nora. I notice William squeeze her shoulder. "And the only thing that will matter tomorrow is how much everyone in this room loves you both and will support you as you start your life together. Mom would be so proud of you, William." I nod at him, his eyes wet with fresh tears. "And that you two are husband and wife—entering the beginning of forever and holding on to the love of your entire life. Cheers!" I exclaim, releasing my nervous chest with a breath before I take a sip of champagne.

The toasts continue with Nora's parents but I barely pay attention because I can only feel the energy between Leo and me. It's buzzing and charged, and I swear if we don't touch each other soon, this whole steaming reception room is going to combust and the only way it won't is if I ignore him. So I do my best to do just that for all the first dances.

I keep my gaze fixed on the dance floor glowing in the evening sun, while the blown glass casts every hue of the rainbow over my brother and Nora in a kaleidoscope of color.

I love this part of the reception: the first dance.

Because isn't that what life is? A dance. Sometimes we know

the steps. Sometimes we look ridiculous. Sometimes it's hard. And sometimes it's as easy as falling in love.

When the song ends and the music starts up again, the DJ turns it up a bit, indicating the serious part of the reception is coming to a close. Drinks are refilled, bellies are full, and everyone is itching to dance.

But there's only one thing I want to do.

"Nice shoes," I say, coming up beside Leo as he rolls up the sleeves of his button-up, revealing the bottom of his tattoo sleeve.

"Thank you," he replies, dipping his head just enough to make me think he's going to kiss me.

I jerk back.

"You okay?" He reaches out a timid yet strong hand toward me.

I let out a small laugh. "No, I just…" I turn my head away. That was a stupid thought. He wouldn't kiss me here.

"Do you want me to kiss you right now?" he asks, dipping his head and giving me a smug smile.

Yes. But I don't say it. I do my best to imitate his smile. "No, I'd like you to take a shot with me."

"Shot for shot?" he queries with a half-smile.

I let out a quick groan of disgust. "Absolutely not."

He laughs. "Tequila?"

"Never."

He laughs again as he follows me toward the bar. "Why don't you drink tequila anymore?"

I splay my hands on the bar and order a shot of whiskey and a shot of tequila with tajin around the rim, then roll my head in his direction.

"Ahh, you look lovely, Genevieve!" a woman with brown curly hair says, squeezing my arm.

I thank her and her companion says, "Such a beautiful wedding."

"It is," I agree. They take their drinks and head to their table.

"Who was that?"

I shrug. "A relative of Nora's maybe?"

274

He rolls his eyes. "Answer my question."

"I just did."

"No, why don't you like tequila?"

I nod. "Ah, Thanksgiving break junior year of college," I say as if that's a sufficient answer.

The bartender slides the shots toward us, and Leo slips a twenty in the tip jar, raising his eyebrows at me.

"And?"

Embarrassment turns in my stomach. "You don't remember?"

He tilts his head, my humiliation burning brighter in my gut.

"Oh, come on, Leo."

A smile grows on his lip as he watches me. I can't tell if he's messing with me or not.

I hold up my glass with a smirk.

"Cheers," he says, meeting his glass with mine. I throw back the brown liquor, knowing I'll need it to tell this story.

"Terrence Flynn's party."

His mouth turns down and he shakes his head, drawing a blank.

I twist my lips, not believing him for a second. "Leo, you held my hair while I puked over the Flynn's bushes."

He frowns and shrugs. I have a feeling he's letting me get away with this embarrassing moment. Either that, or he's making me confess to it so he can have a good laugh.

I clear my throat before I speak. "It's stupid. I just drank too much tequila."

His jaw twitches and I know it's because he's remembered something. He grabs my wrist and stops me. "Tell me."

"I just did."

"That's not the story."

It's not. But it is. That is the story. I'm just not telling him why. My jaw is set and my eyebrows knit together. I catch a glance from William as he holds a glass of champagne. Nora is draped on his arm and they're talking to another couple of friends from work, who look like they may be heading out.

Be nice, he mouths, glaring at me.

I throw up my hands. *I am!* I mouth back.

275

My brother is in for a real treat when he realizes I'm in love with the guy he's been begging me to be nice to since we were kids.

"Ahhh, congratulations on your new sister!" a woman with a slicked-back bun and large gold earrings squeals, pulling me out of my conversation with Leo and into her arms. It takes me a moment to register who she is. Then it hits me: William's co-worker. She was at the shower, but I still don't remember her name. "Your speech was phenomenal."

"Oh, thanks," I say, a sheepish response to her mildly drunken compliment as she walks away.

"And who was that?" Leo murmurs in my ear.

"I don't remember her name."

He laughs. "Weddings are terrible."

"They are not. They're romantic."

"They're ostentatious."

"They're tradition."

He laughs.

I place a hand on my hip. "Why is that so funny?"

"So because of tradition, you have to invite a bunch of people you don't know to watch you make one of the most important decisions of your life."

I don't disagree. I had very similar thoughts about bridal showers just days ago. But this is Nora and William's wedding, and they can invite whomever they want.

"You agree," he says.

"I didn't say that."

"You're smiling."

"Doesn't mean I agree."

"Always arguing."

"Always picking a fight."

He steps closer, absorbing the oxygen between us.

"You're infuriating," he says.

I smile wider, biting my lip to contain the tingles he sends through my body.

"Why are you smiling like that?" he asks, though his smile is begging to be unleashed. I can tell by how the corners of his mouth twitch.

"I'm happy." I look up at him and I see the rush of every emotion I'm feeling pour through his eyes.

He leans down to my ear. "I want to kiss you so bad right now."

My heart flutters, but I stay composed as the DJ calls the newlyweds to the dance floor.

"Can't," I respond. "The money dance has just commenced, and I have some dollar bills to shove down Nora's dress." I take two backward steps away from him, still smiling. "Plus, I don't think it'd be fair to steal the attention away from Mrs. Nora *Michaels.*"

He shakes his head and smiles, not breaking his gaze away from my eyes until finally I turn around and cut in while Nora was dancing with our cousin, Jeffrey.

I soon get replaced by Cora. Then John. Then Ms. Louisa. Then Gampa. Then Mr. Wellington. Then several people that look vaguely familiar, but I don't remember. I laugh out loud when Leo cuts in between my dad and William, and they immediately start dancing the Foxtrot. Their friendship is adorable, and my heart swells as I remember for the second time this week how our mom taught all three of us how to do it the night before prom in our living room. I think of the laughter and the Dr. Pepper spraying from our noses. I think of the stubbed toes and carpet cleaner. I think of how much I love that Leo wanted to practice with me just two nights ago in my apartment.

We'll never dance the fox trot, Mom, I remember saying all those years ago.

You will, she had said. *Maybe not tomorrow, but you will.*

Tears wet my lashes as the memory so vividly plays like a home movie in my mind. Then, just as I'm about to step away to compose myself, Leo steps back, taking a wad of cash out of his pocket and making it rain over the precious couple. Everyone roars with laughter, and my tears disappear.

My mom would have loved this moment.

"I wish you were here, Mom," I whisper.

A familiar arm rests on my shoulders. "Me too, Bear. Me too," Dad says.

I'm so glad he didn't say something like, she is here. Because I want her physically here. I want to smell her hair and feel the weight of her arms as she hugs me. I want her laugh to ring in my ears and to watch her outdance me underneath the strobe lights.

People mean well when they say, *she is here*, or *she'll always be with you*. Even Mom did before she died. But it's really just an insensitive bandage on a wound that will never heal completely. I lean on Dad's shoulder, wordless, feeling happy and heartbroken all at the same time.

The song ends and the money is collected, and the DJ puts something more upbeat on. It doesn't take long for the dance floor to fill up with tuxedos and gowns, and for everyone to be a little sweaty from dancing, not just the sauna the heatwave has created.

Four songs later, I'm flushed and in need of some water.

"Another round?" I hear Leo's voice behind me.

"After a glass of water," I answer, handing him a cup too.

"Party pooper." He half-pouts.

"It was one hundred and ten degrees today and we are in a glass oven."

"The sun is going down. It's cooling off."

Always picking a damn fight. I cross my arms, letting my cup of water dangle in one hand. "You know I often dream of strangling you."

"I thought you just wanted to make me run lines," he says.

My cheeks ache from trying not to laugh. He grins and downs the water in three gulps then makes that annoying 'ahh' sound people make when they've just chugged something but he's oddly attractive when he does it.

"Shots now?" he asks.

"I hate you." I finish the rest of my water.

He holds his hand in a sweeping, gentlemanly gesture. "Genevieve Ann Michaels, you have never, ever hated me."

I take his hand. "Oh, but I've wanted to."

"Look at you two getting along!" William slings his arms around our shoulders, dampness immediately seeping into my arms.

"Gross, William, you're sweaty!" I shriek, smacking him lightly.

"We're all fucking sweaty!" William exclaims, the edges of his words would indicate he's getting pretty toasted. "Are we having another round?"

"We are," Leo confirms, then turns to the bartender. "Two tequila, one whiskey."

"Thank you." I offer a smug smile, and Leo scrunches his nose at me.

When the bartender slides over the glasses, we raise them for a toast. "To William!" I say.

But just before the glasses touch our lips, William stops us. "No, no, no. To my two best friends!" Then we throw them back.

I smile at my brother, half-drunk and full-on happy.

"I mean it, Gen. You and this guy are my very best friends." His arms are around our necks, pulling us in for a group hug while he pours out his heart. "Don't tell Nora."

I snort, and Leo dips his head in a smile.

William shouts *love you* as he walks away. Leo and I linger back from the disco ball and dance floor.

I look at Leo, and he tucks a loose strand of hair behind my ear in a quick, undetectable movement so no one notices but me.

"What happened at the party?" he asks.

"What party?" I feign confusion. I know what he's talking about.

"When you drank so much tequila, you gave it up for life."

I breathe out. "Well, if you really must have me refresh your memory, Mom was just diagnosed with cancer and had told William and me when we got home from college for break. She insisted we go to the party even though all I wanted to do was curl into her side and soak up as much time with her as I could. It was—" I stop to take a breath. "It was our last Thanksgiving together. We didn't know it then but a part of me wondered."

Leo nods, intent on listening.

"Anyway, I had this *life-is-short* moment and was going to seize the opportunity to talk to you and clear the air or…" I don't know how to finish the sentence because, at the time, so many imaginary things crossed my mind and none of them came true. "But when I spotted you, you were very… occupied."

I look up at Leo. He's chewing his bottom lip, his eyes twisted in a memory. He nods. "I was still with Sophia."

I draw in a sharp, painful breath. "I always knew you dated—of course you did. I did too. But seeing you kiss someone else made me want to throw up, so I drank tequila until I did."

His hand is on my lower back, an apology written in his fingertips.

"It's okay. It's stupid. Actually seeing you with someone felt like a nightmare, so I turned the night into one. I got wasted. Puked in front of the house and yelled at you in front of everyone."

"Evie, I didn't know you saw me kiss Sophia. I would have never if I knew you were standing there—" His expression is apologetic. I grab his chin.

"All's well that ends well, right?"

He smiles. "Can I make it up to you?"

My arms burn to wrap themselves around him, kiss his face, and hear his heart beating against mine.

"You already are," I answer. He grips the back of my dress where his hand rests and my insides pinch together. I smack his hand away but I smile. "I have a dance floor to return to, Leonardo. My favorite wedding song is on, and I'm pretty sure Gampa and Nona have had enough champagne to dance with me."

"*Wobble* is your favorite wedding song?" he questions. A slow smile spreads over his lips as he follows me.

"It is not a fun wedding reception until it plays."

"You don't even do the dance right," he accuses me with a mocking smirk and I throw my hand to my offended heart.

"That's disrespectful," I respond, glaring at him and trying not to smile. "I just need to find your mom to lead the steps."

He rolls his eyes. "Fine. Time for me to find Aunt Wilma to dance."

I laugh. "You're going to make Aunt Bernadette so jealous."

He brushes my elbow with his fingertips. "That was my plan all along."

I shoot him a lighthearted glare, and Leo disappears in the crowd. I spot Nona and Gampa swaying side to side, clapping to the offbeat with elated smiles on their faces. Their cheeks are flushed just enough to let me know they've enjoyed the bottomless champagne tonight.

"All right, Gampa, you ready?" I ask, with outstretched hands to them both. "Nona?"

"I've been waiting for you all night!" Gampa says, twirling me around like he used to on Christmas morning. Nona dances beside us. We find Ms. Louisa right away and she is leading the pack of wedding guests through the steps.

This is the part of a wedding everybody loves: when the rituals are all over, the heels come off, and everyone can finally let loose.

Somewhere between three and five songs later, I'm desperate for Leo. I feel like a jealous schoolgirl as we all dance and laugh and sing. He's taking turns dancing with his mom, Nona, and the Philadelphia aunts. I even saw him spin Cora in a few circles. He's adorable, so perfect in my mind, but right now I want him to be only mine.

At least for a moment.

I catch eyes with Leo as he does the sprinkler with Aunt Wilma, and raise an eyebrow at him, then I make a bee-line for the hallway. The bathrooms are at the end of the hall and I'm sure guests will start moseying their way down here to relieve their bladders, but I don't care.

I walk to a small alcove that leads to the janitorial closet but provides enough of a hiding place for me and Leo. I hear him behind me. Sense him, really. The atoms in my body are now distinctly aware of him at all times.

His hand finds my hip first and he spins me around, pressing me against the wall and sliding a hand down my neck. The thrum of my heart heats my skin, and I open my mouth to speak but he silences me with his lips, kissing me like we haven't seen each other in years when really, it's only been minutes.

"We're going to get caught," he mumbles against my mouth,

and I laugh. "I'm serious, Evie."

"I don't feel like caring anymore, Leo," I whisper, still kissing him and raking my fingers down his back. His skin is warm beneath his button-up, and I'm hungry to feel it against my bare skin.

Just as he grips the side of my dress and I slide my knee up to his hip, we hear someone clear their throat and pull away from each other immediately. My eyes snap to the origin of the noise and land on Abigail. She's grinning a stupidly smug smile with her arms crossed as she taps her toe on the hardwood floors.

"Hi," I squeak, my voice like a mouse, even though I'm relieved it isn't anyone else. Abigail already has a very clear idea of what Leo and I got into last night.

Leo lets out a low rumble of a laugh.

"I love this situation. Really, I do. But can we not screw each other in the hallway. There are children present." Her tone is sarcastic, her smile not leaving her face. "And by children, I mean your brother."

I press my eyes closed, and Leo takes a step back. Nothing like mentioning William to cool us down.

"Are you going to tell him?" Abigail asks, hand on her hip.

"Not today," we reply in unison.

Abigail cackles. "Then quit sucking face."

"Who's sucking face?"

My eyes widen as I see Cora emerge from the bathroom, wobbling only slightly to accommodate her swollen belly.

"Oh. My. Gosh," she says, a look of pure shock and elation on her face.

"What's wrong?" John comes up behind her with Terrence, and I'm sweating even more.

Leo looks at me. I don't meet his gaze, but I sense it.

"Nothing!" Cora squeals. "Oh, Nora is going to be so happy!"

Terrence's gaze, which has been studiously switching between me and Leo, jerks to Cora. "She will?" He's confused. I'm confused. We're all a little confused.

"Oh yes, Nora was Team Leo from the get-go!" Cora

chirps.

"No, she wasn't," I argue.

"She was!"

Leo and I zero in on her. She flushes.

"Secretly. I heard her say it to William though, and he was… yikes. He said Leo would never because Genevieve is not his type," she laughs, then emphasizes a little too loudly, "At all!"

John places a gentle hand on her shoulder. "Are you serious?"

"Well, it's not like that," I breathe out, trying to diffuse all these stupid eyes on us. "I've just had a lot to drink and…"

My voice trails because I don't want to explain this and I would like very much if the attention centered on us dissipated so everyone can go back to celebrating William and Nora. I look at Leo.

"And it was nothing," he says, definitive. "A small kiss. Abigail is making a big deal about nothing."

She throws her hands up. "I'm not the one squealing."

Cora snorts and rolls her eyes. "Oh but this could be—"

I shake my head. "Cora, please don't—"

"Maybe just not tonight," John adds, making eye contact with Leo.

"Oh my gosh, you are all acting like William is some big scary man and he is not," Cora says.

I let out a breath of a laugh, and Leo's phone rings. His entire demeanor changes. His shoulders cinch back, his backbone straightens a bit more, and his fingers grip the phone tighter as his eyes register the name.

He glances at me with a mixture of hope and worry in his eyes. "Excuse me."

I watch him escape out the doors at the end of the hall, then turn to everyone else.

"Shall we dance?"

We all make our way back to the dance floor and a few songs later, I realize Leo hasn't returned so I set off on a hunt to find him.

I walk outside into the warm summer air. The sun is down, the Space Needle is lit up in the distance, and the party inside is at its peak. My heart flutters with giddy nerves when I spot Leo sitting on a bench right away. But as I step closer, the skip in my step falters. There's a stunned expression covering his face as he stares down at his phone like the most unexpected scenario just shot through it.

"Is everything okay?" I ask, walking toward him with timid steps.

It's clear by the way he startles that he didn't hear me approach. There's elation in his eyes that immediately switches to concern when he looks at me. For a moment, he just stares, expressionless with hints of excitement and shock around the edges.

"I need to tell you something."

"You keep saying that," I say as I nod, heart hammering in my ear. I will myself to calm down but I don't know how and I have no idea what it is he's about to say. He turns and stands to face me and his expression morphs into a smile.

"France is happening."

The words hit me before the meaning of them does. The squint in my eyes morphs into a smile I can't contain. "France is happening!" I repeat his words, but with more enthusiasm.

He takes my face in his hands and kisses me hard on the mouth.

"Wha—how—when?" the questions stumble out of my mouth, making no sense yet making perfect sense to Leo.

"Taylor just called… I—" he lets out a shout of celebration, scooping me into his arms and twirling around. I squeal and giggle, holding him tighter, and remembering how stupid I was to assume Taylor was anyone else to him.

"I'm so proud of you," I say, holding his face in my hands. My heart sinks as I realize how much I'm going to miss him when he's gone. But he'd be gone anyway. Home for him is San Francisco, not here. A million thoughts and plans tumble through my mind, but I disguise all of them with a question. "When do you go?"

"Tuesday."

I blink and he sets me down. It's so soon, it takes me a whole five seconds to process the words. So much so I must have misunderstood.

"I'm sorry. Tuesday?"

"Tuesday," he confirms.

I cross my arms and raise my eyebrows, guarding my heart and punctuating my disappointment. "For how long?"

"Two years."

I nod slowly. "You said it like it was just a possibility."

He tucks my hair behind my ear. "It was just a possibility until my agent called to confirm the details of the contract."

"They didn't want another day to pass without you knowing," I say, realizing the hour.

He grins. "It's tomorrow in France."

"Wow, you get to go live in the future." My tone is coy, but my heart is hammering with selfish disappointment.

"It's my last chance." He smiles wider, and I remember the boy in him. The one who dreamed of moments like these when I kicked his ass in HORSE.

I nod slowly, forcing a smile. I have no say, no claim, no stake in the war and yet… I'm so terribly sad.

But I smile wide enough that my cheeks hurt.

He draws in a breath, but he doesn't let it go. I worry he can see the mask I've placed on my face, and I worry even more that he doesn't like it. He reaches out with his hands and drops them immediately as he sees me cross mine tighter across my midsection. His eyes search my face as if I have the answer he needs. But it's nonsense really. I've never been his answer. I've never been his main focus. I was always on the side.

"I still want you to come," he says.

I scoff out a laugh, burying my eyes in the pavement so he doesn't see the hesitation in my expression.

"I mean it." He leans down, forcing me to look at him.

"I just don't know—" I begin, then smile as I meet his eyes. He's perfect. He's everything to me. All my doubts evaporate in his eyes. "We'll figure it out."

He bites his lip and smiles. "Promise?"

"Pinky swear," I confirm, and he kisses me again. My face is in his hands and I'm lost in the kiss. Completely lost in the life we could have but don't. The world is spinning. My lips tingle and all I want to do is stay here in his arms, until I hear...

"What. The. Fuck?"

I part from him and whip around to see William standing just past the threshold. His sleeves rolled up, bowtie gone, and cheeks warm from dancing and celebratory drinks.

"Hey, Will," Leo says, his calm demeanor returning.

William zeroes his vision on us, his eyes darting between Leo and me. He looks so confused. Clueless and oblivious to what I know half the wedding party realized earlier. Nora bounces out of the door, landing on William's back with a petite squeal.

"I knew it. I knew it. *I knew it*!" she shrieks, elation pulsing in her tone. She didn't know it. But then she adds, "Aww, look at how cute, Willy!"

William looks at her. "What do you mean? This isn't cute."

"Oh, look at them. This is perfect." She grins, clapping her hands at her mouth.

Leo ignores them both and steps toward my brother. "I'm headed to France!" He annunciates the last word as he claps William's hand and brings him in for a hug.

"For real?" William shouts, half-laughing and slapping Leo on the back. He must have known about the possibility.

I look at Nora in her wedding gown. She's smiling and staring at me with her nose scrunched and hands clasped by her mouth. She looks like an evil villain that just mated with a stork delivering babies.

"Nora..." I roll my eyes.

Oh my goossssh, she mouths, and I stifle a laugh.

She takes my hands and pulls me to her until we're forehead to forehead. "This is the best!"

"Not tonight." I zero my eyes on her new husband—my brother—celebrating Leo's contract in France. They are talking names and positions and stats and, of course, his departure date.

I swallow hard as the word "Tuesday" leaves Leo's mouth again. His gaze lands on me when he says it, and I force a smile.

"But wait..." William shakes his head as a look of disgust sits on his face. "Why the hell did you kiss Genevieve?"

Leo's mouth drops but I can tell there's a smile buried in

there.

I don't want to do this. Not here and not now when I'm entirely unsure of what this means for us, and if there's even an 'us' to contend with.

I step forward.

"Leo was just messing around," I say, waving a hand. "I caught him when he got the call." I raise my eyebrows at Leo, rocking back on my heels. "Congratulations, Leo. Seriously."

"Last call!" Terrence shouts from the back door. The muffled sound of *The Electric Slide* echoes through the glass.

"Well, we better get in there. Wouldn't want to miss *The Electric Slide*," I huff with a laugh.

"Oh, please, *The Electric Slide* is for our parents," Nora laughs, linking my arm and we start to make our way back inside.

"That was not a messing around kiss—" I hear William say behind me, and I press my eyes closed, not faltering my steps. "That was—it—like—" He stammers when he's upset. "What the hell?"

I sneak a glance at Leo over my shoulder. He's calm. Excited. A smile consumes his features.

I keep walking. I don't need to defend the kiss. For all I know, it could have been a kiss goodbye.

Leo starts to say something to William, but I don't hear it because Nora whispers, "He'll calm down." Then she squeals. "I'm so glad my plan worked!"

My head snaps in her direction. "Your what?"

She grins. "Amalie was super helpful orchestrating it with me."

"The veil lady was in on it?"

Nora throws her head back and laughs as we keep walking through the doors to the museum. "Yes! She makes custom veils. She was totally down to customize a love story. One-bed tropes always work."

I pause. "But Nora, how did you—"

"Know?" she finishes for me. "I saw how Leo looked at you. I heard how you two bickered. William always thought you two hated each other. I knew better. Your eyes don't lie, and neither do Leo's."

I gape at her, and she laughs again.

"I just couldn't figure out how to get you two alone because I knew—or I hoped that if you did, all the feelings would come out. But honestly, I almost thought you wouldn't need the bed and breakfast since he kept walking you home."

Now I laugh. "He really almost ruined your scheme."

"The nerve!" she teases as we enter the reception room.

"And all the comments about Terrence and setting me up with someone at the wedding?"

"Something had to light a fire under Leo," she says then leans in and raises an eyebrow. "I mean, but I did technically set you up with someone at the wedding."

I shake my head and absorb her scheming. "Wait. So you knew about high school?" I ask. The music grows louder as we get closer to the dance floor.

She blanches. "High school?"

I bite back a smile and avert my eyes.

"Genevieve Michaels!" she scolds with a shriek and a laugh. I offer no more information. "You two were always meant to be."

I shrug into a smile. I don't disagree, but everything still feels uncertain. Like we just threw rose petals in the air, and we have no idea if they'll land in front of us or get blown away in the wind.

27

WEDDING DAY
FRIDAY

We don't throw rice. Or rose petals. Or blow bubbles. We light sparklers and cheer, dancing and lining the entry to the museum as Nora and William walk to their town car on the street. They'll wind up at the hotel tonight, leave for Tahiti in two days, and step into the world of marriage.

Leo comes up behind me as my sparkler burns out, wrapping his hands around my waist and whispering in my ear, "My room or yours?"

I glance across the aisle. Abigail, whom I was going to share a room with, has her hands in April's hair and their lips are three breaths away. I look at Leo. "Yours."

We Uber to the hotel with half the wedding party arriving at the same time. The hoopla and inebriation of the event mean no one cares Leo and I are hand-in-hand as we make our way up to his room.

Everyone trots to either the hotel bar or their rooms, high on love and celebration.

Leo and I head straight for the elevator. We ride up several floors with a group of women that get off a few floors before ours. As soon as they exit and the elevator doors close, Leo grabs my face and presses me against the mirrored wall of the elevator, kissing me like it's the last thing he'll ever do. My body buzzes with need, and I slide my hands down his chest, feeling his heart pounding beneath his clothes. His hands move around my waist and down to my thigh and I wrap a leg around him as he begins to guide his hand through the slit of my dress.

Then the elevator dings and we both groan simultaneously.

We hurry to his room, and the hotel door slams shut. I stare at Leo, chewing softly on my lip, sure of what I want in this moment but unsure of what happens tomorrow.

He reaches out, touching my lip and pulling it away from my teeth.

"I get why you hate it," he says.

"You do?" I ask, wondering if he can see all of the thoughts churning in my mind. High school. Vashon. France. Seattle. Him. Me.

Us.

He doesn't answer. He kisses me, lips crashing against mine. "Please stop worrying," he says through each part and return of our lips.

I pull back and stare at him. "There is a lot to worry about though," I say, then kiss him again

He runs his fingers through my hair until they run down my neck, then down, down, down until they reach my waist. "Evie."

"What?" I stare up at him.

"I have loved you forever," he whispers, kissing just below my ear.

I tilt my head back to allow him better access, and ask, "But will you love me half a world away?"

He draws back, knowing exactly what I'm saying but answering without words. He laces his fingers in my hair and I roll my head back as he takes my mouth, consuming me. Loving me. Reminding me of everything I've missed for the last eight years and have only gotten back for the last twenty-four hours.

He pulls me deeper into the room, laying me on the bed as

his hands wander up my inner thigh until they reach the spot that makes me throw my head back and tear the buttons on his shirt. His mouth is on me—my neck, my chest—as I rip the shirt off him and undo his pants in enough of a hurry that I break the zipper.

He laughs. I groan.

He stands to discard the remnants of his clothes and I watch him, soaking in every inch of him, knowing he's moving to France in four days.

I reach for the zipper on my back, and he stops me. "Keep it on. You've been driving me crazy in that dress all night."

I rest my hands on the bed behind me as he reaches under the dress, slipping my panties down my thighs and discarding them on the floor.

"Leo…" I begin, but I'm lost as to what I need to say beyond that.

"Evie," he whispers.

I sink my teeth in my bottom lip until he kisses me, covering my body with his. He hikes up my dress and enters me slowly. I gasp and pull at his flesh as I kiss his lips and say his name again.

"I love you," he whispers.

I love you too. But I don't say it out loud. I'm afraid to. He's gone in four days. Half-a-world-away gone. So I just let him love me, pushing away all of my questions and forcing myself to forget all the ways this won't work.

It's passionate tonight. Hungry. There are a million goodbyes and I-don't-know's with each movement between us, but we don't speak them aloud. We just let our bodies ache and burn and crave until we're both standing at the top, holding onto each other while we crash down to the sheets.

After, we lay on the bed staring up at the ceiling. I run my fingers along his abdomen dreaming of a life I don't know how to create.

"Hold on," he says, reaching over to the bedside table and pulling the faded photo of us from his wallet. He unfolds it slowly and holds it up in front of us as we continue to lie on the plush pillows. "Look at these kids."

"Who would've thought?" I ask with a smirk.

"Not me!" he says, and I laugh. He traces a finger over my face in the photo. "I was so scared that night."

"Why?" I shift to look at him.

"You were just... so beautiful. And it hurt not to tell you. Then when you didn't want to go on the ride, I was so relieved, like, 'peace out, I'm with Evie for the night.'" He smiles, lost in the memory. "And I was hoping I could be smooth, but with you, I always fumbled my words and felt unsure—like at any moment you could lash out and tell the world I tried to get with you and you refused."

I laugh. "Well, I think I initiated the night."

He kisses the top of my head. "And my wildest dreams came true."

I take the photo from his fingers and stare at it a moment before setting it down and asking, "What day of the week do I remind you of."

"Sunday," he answers quickly, running his fingertips down my spine.

"Why? Because I'm easy?" I laugh. He does too, the sound a low rumble before he straightens his smile.

"Seriously. You're a Sunday," he says. I nudge him and roll my eyes, but he keeps talking. "Some people say Sunday is the beginning of the week and some people say it's the end." He squints at the wall in the distance and looks back down at me. "That's you. The beginning and the end. You always have been." He pauses again. "At least to me."

I swallow the affection in my throat, disguising it with sarcasm. "Aw, you're such a softy," I tease, but I mean it.

He smiles his perfect smile. "No one else in the world would say that about me."

Then he stops me and kisses me deep and long before pulling back, but not completely. Just enough that his lips are still brushing against mine. I smile against his mouth, and say, "I'm glad I get to be the one to say it."

He lets out a low chuckle as he pulls back.

"What about me?"

"What?" I ask.

"What day of the week am I?"

"Oh!" I say, realization striking me. Then I laugh as if I'm nervously unsure, but I'm not. I know exactly what day of the week he is. "Thursday," I answer.

He draws his square chin back—a mixture of surprise and disgust on his features. "That's offensive."

"It's not," I argue. "I love Thursdays. The week is practically over, but the weekend hasn't even started yet, so there's still so much to look forward to." I can see his mind spinning, and a line forms between his brows as he stares at the ceiling. "You know that fluttery feeling you get right before a rollercoaster drops?"

He nods, eyes inquisitive.

"Or when you're about to leave for vacation or have fun plans for the weekend?" I continue to ask and he nods again. "Thursdays are full of anticipation and plans and dreams."

He smiles, looking down at me, his teeth just barely catching his bottom lip.

"To me, that's you."

He pulls me in for a kiss, and I'm quite certain I could melt in his arms.

"What if I don't go to France on Tuesday?" he asks, gently swiping his thumb across my jaw.

"Why wouldn't you go?"

He shrugs. "What if I stay here?"

"For...ever?" I ask, but I know that's exactly what he's saying. I don't want him to say this. I don't want him to let his dreams fall away because of me. I want him to have both. I want him to have it all. I refuse to let the last five days change all the plans he has for his future. I have no idea how this will work, but I don't want his last chance to play basketball professionally to be missed because he fell back in love with me.

He nods.

"No, you're going to France, you lunatic." I laugh out the words, and he grabs my jaw.

"What if you come with me?"

"I have a job."

He nods again, expectantly. He knew I'd say that. But the expression in his eyes is so worried that it startles me. "I feel like

I just got you back."

"I feel like you're too worried you're going to lose me again."

"Am I?" he asks, propping himself over me. He is scared to lose me, I can tell. I'm scared to lose him too.

I shake my head, but it only makes me seem uncertain.

"Say what you're thinking," he says.

I hesitate. "It's just…France is far."

He nods. "The distance scares you."

I nod. How can it not? Damien was only a five-hour flight away a third of the year and managed to make a whole baby with another woman. I know Leo isn't Damien, but I'm incapable of not drawing a comparison. Long distance is a strain on every relationship.

"When you talked about France last night, it seemed like a dream. Not a plan. It felt like it didn't matter what you did with your life because this didn't feel real yet."

"Does it feel real now?" he asks.

I meet his eyes, nodding.

"You're the only thing that has ever felt real," he says, taking my hand in his and kissing my fingers. "And I know the distance scares you and I know this week came out of nowhere, but I'm not getting on a plane without knowing we're doing this."

I let out a quick laugh. "Are you forcing me into a relationship?"

"Yes, quit arguing," he snaps back, a smile tugging at the edge of his lips.

I grin. "Quit picking fights."

He sweeps his hand over my cheek and tangles his fingers in my hair. "I only ever want to fight with you. I only ever want you. Even with the world between us, you're it for me."

I search his face for doubt and come up short. My lips twitch to smile.

"You're still scared."

His statement bruises the mask I'm trying to wear for him because truth be told, I am scared. I see this ending terribly in about fifty different ways.

Instead, I say, "No, I just hate the idea of missing you. And

I hate the idea of this ending badly…again. We don't have to do this. It's only been a week."

His eyes glint in the low light of the hotel room and he nods once. "Evie, I respect you. I only want the best for you, even if we figure out that's not me. So no matter what becomes of us, that won't change. I promise you."

It's almost as if each word is hanging in the air before I let them enter my mind. I try to rearrange his statement, find the holes. But I choose to let the words rest in mind.

"We'll figure it out, Leo," I say, then kiss his knuckles. "And if we don't, we could just try hating each other again."

Leo sweeps a hand in my hair and cradles my body in his arms. "It would be easier to stop breathing than it would be to hate you."

28

SATURDAY

I couldn't sleep after 5 a.m. I tossed and turned while Leo slept soundly next to me. I snuck out of the hotel room and wound up back home at my dad's.

The sound of the basketball bouncing off the driveway wraps its waves around my chest. It's suffocating and nostalgic, but I've always felt at home standing on this driveway with a basketball in my hand.

Last night Leo said all the right things. And it all feels like it will be okay. But the reality is, he's leaving for France in three days. And I want him to. I want him to live out his last chance. I want the little boy that fell in love with basketball to play his heart out until the world tells him he's too old. But I also know France is half a world away.

I glance at my watch. It's only 8 a.m. which means it's 5 p.m. in France. Leo's day would be ending as I'm clocking in. I'd be falling asleep as he'd be waking up. If I'm honest, time is all I've thought of since last night.

"Coffee or Gatorade?" my dad says from the front porch, holding two steaming mugs in his hands.

I grin. "You're up. Sorry, did I wake you?"

"Internal clocks don't care about a late-night wedding." My dad laughs, walking toward me and holding out the coffee to me. I take it from him and let the hot liquid scald the top of my mouth. "Did you have fun last night?"

I nod and lick my lips. "It was a beautiful wedding."

He takes a sip of coffee, glancing at the sky. "The weather cooled off a bit this morning."

"I wish it did a bit yesterday but, oh well, we survived." I laugh, but it's shaky and forced.

Dad sets his mug down on the porch steps. "One-on-one?"

I smile and set my coffee on the step next to his. "You're on, old man."

He laughs, and I dribble the ball twice. "Check."

The ball hits his chest, and he bounce-passes it back. I guard the ball, trying to cut to the left but Dad's defense has always been his strength. He towers over me, and I know I'll never get over him. I try to get under but he's quick and knows each of my moves before I even do it. Probably because he taught me. Night after night, growing up it was me, William, and much of the time, Leo. It didn't matter if we had practice already that day. It didn't matter if it was one hundred degrees in the summer or pouring icy rain in the winter. We played and played and played.

I fake left and pull back to shoot. Dad jumps and his fingertips graze the ball, but it still shoots through the net with a satisfying swish.

"You still never miss," he laughs, dribbling toward the end of the driveway.

"Rarely." I flash a cocky smile because I know I am a good shot.

"Check." He tosses the ball at me and I throw it back.

We continue to play. First to ten. Then first to twenty. Then thirty. Until we are sweaty and Dad wins by two.

He frolics around the driveway laughing, arms soaring like he's never beat me before. He always beats me. Well, almost always. And I've always loved that about him. The better I got, the harder he went on me. It built character in me, taught me how to lose, and humbled me after every time I beat Leo in HORSE.

"Good game," I say, bumping elbows with my dad.

He nods with a smile and a grunt as he lowers himself onto the steps of our childhood home. His brow glistens and sweat soaks the front of his gray t-shirt on his chest.

I lower myself next to him, my heart still accelerating.

"You seem sad," he manages, though he hasn't caught his breath yet.

I push out a small chuckle. "I just lost to my sixty-year-old dad."

"I'm fifty-six!" He laughs and socks me on the shoulder. As his laughter settles, so does the sinking in my stomach. "What's up, Genny Bear?"

I want to tell him, but I can't. The emotion wraps around my throat and my eyes well up. I wipe the snot drizzling out of my nose with the back of my hand.

"You're sad about Leo leaving." A statement. A million things my dad must know to get to this conclusion. A million things I've never told him.

"How'd you know he was leaving?" I ask.

"He's been trying to go overseas for a while. He told me about tryouts not too long ago. I knew the call was coming soon, so he told me last night before everyone left."

I smile. I love that Leo went to go find my dad and tell him. I love that they're close. I love that he's getting one more chance to play. But Leo leaving in three days reminds me that if something seems too good to be true, it probably is.

"I feel so selfish," I manage through my emotions.

He nods and lets the moment linger, validating my feelings with silence. "Leo loves you."

When he says it, I think he means like a brother loves a sister, but then he tilts my chin to face him and adds, "Truly loves you. He always has."

I laugh through a cry and wipe my eyes. "Is this one of those parental intuition things that you and Louisa have?"

Dad laughs. "No, I heard it straight from the horse's mouth."

I snap my chin back. "What?"

"Leo told me he was in love with you years ago. And he was so nervous—bouncing his foot and rubbing his palms against his jeans," Dad chuckles. "And before he came back into town this week, he asked me if it'd be okay if he told you." He continues to laugh. I don't; I'm stunned. So much of this week still feels like an unintentional accident, and maybe some of it was. But on top of Nora orchestrating the bed and breakfast debacle, it is now clear Leo had the intention of letting me know his feelings.

"Why?"

Dad shrugs. "Weddings stir up a lot of feelings in folks, I suppose. But how he feels about you has never changed. Not for years at least." He lets out a huff of a laugh and his eyes get lost in a memory.

I think of all the coffee visits they must have had over the years. All the words they must have exchanged, secrets they must have confessed.

"I think the feeling was always there, but he couldn't identify it because you two met so young. Then when Mom died, all he wanted was to be there for you, but he didn't know how because you acted like you hated him."

"I did hate him," I laugh out.

Dad smiles. "You didn't though."

I'm struck silent. He's right. I didn't. My head falls as I pick at my nails in my lap.

"Then you started with Damien, and he took a giant step back. That broke his heart."

"It did not."

Dad's head bobs. "Oh, it did."

"Well, Leo certainly didn't come running when Damien and I broke up six months ago." It's easier to argue than it is to agree.

"Yeah, well that would have been tacky," Dad counters. "You have to give people a little space after a breakup, otherwise you look like a vulture."

I laugh and the thought of seeing Leo with Sophia crosses my mind. When they broke up, I made no attempt to reach out to him. Apparently, I lost all my nerve along with my tolerance for tequila that night.

"Leo never wanted to ruin your happiness and always questioned whether or not it could actually be him." I raise my eyebrows at him and he shrugs. "He never said so much, but I could see it in his face. He hated Damien. It turns out he was right about him." Dad winces. There's no doubt he's heard about Damien's baby.

"You two went deep over coffee," I laugh to disguise the unrest in my gut.

"It was a lot of years of coffee to get him to open up about you, but I'm not stupid. That boy looks at you how I looked at your mom."

My chin shakes, and I can't see his face because tears cloud my vision.

"Don't cry, Genny Bear," he says, wrapping his arm around me. "France isn't that far."

"It feels that far," I whisper. "It is literally half a world away, Dad."

"The world doesn't matter if you're in love," he reasons.

Am I in love though? I think I am but is it real? Or is it the wedding and reminiscing and the need to finish what we never did?

"Distance is impossible though. Damien only traveled to New York and San Francisco, and we were always hanging on by a thread. Not to mention, he asked me to quit my life to travel the world with him. He even had a baby with some random person and is off to meet his firstborn son he created when he was whispering *I-love-you*'s to me over the phone. And that could happen with Leo. I know it. He's already asked me to go to France." I let out a quick and heavy sigh. "Like, Boeing isn't even in France!"

Dad laughs as if my current employment status matters. I know it sounds dumb to care about my corporate job, but I do. I love my life. My apartment. My independence. My work.

Even if my heart knows I love Leo more.

"Can't I be logical about this for one minute?" I ask.

Dad releases me from his embrace and contemplates a

moment.

"You can. But if you're always logical, you'll never get to be in love. The thing is…" he says, stretching his legs in front of him. "Love should make you question your whole life. Not because that person is trying to change you, but because they've turned your world upside down in the best way."

"I don't want to change my life for anyone."

He offers a gentle smile. "You don't have to. But real love should make you consider it."

I nod, staying quiet and Dad pulls me back into a hug.

"William is going to be mad, isn't he?" I mutter into his shirt.

"Who cares? It's your life."

His words come out with a small laugh and are laced with joy. And at this moment, I realize how much I've cared about what others think. What they'll say. How I'll make them feel. When all I really should do is be honest with my own heart.

"Stay for breakfast?" Dad asks.

"Can we have artery-clogging grilled cheese?" I sniffle and wipe my cheeks.

"Made the right way," he confirms, and I smile.

We go inside and I sit at the wooden table filled with memories and love. When I take a bite of my grilled cheese, I remember how much it tastes like home.

Then I immediately think of Leo.

Because he *feels* exactly like home.

29

SATURDAY

After going to my apartment to shower, I return to the hotel to see Leo. The elevator climbs each floor slowly until it pings on the eighteenth floor. I expect my heart to flutter and twist and pound nervously with each step I take, but oddly enough, the closer I get to Leo's door, the calmer I feel.

When he opens the door, he stares down at me with his stupid, perfect, arrogant smile. He's not surprised I came back.

"Do you have to leave on Tuesday?" I ask.

He smiles wider and takes my wrist dragging me into his room. The door swings shut behind us and he presses me against the wall. His hands are in my hair, on my neck. His lips ravage me. He's not gentle at all. He's deliberately devouring me, speaking to me through his kisses instead of with his words.

"I…already…miss…you," I say through each kiss.

"I'm not gone yet," he whispers against my mouth.

"But you will be."

He pauses and pulls back.

"I don't even want you to go back to San Francisco." I stare up at him, noting the longing and uncertainty in his eyes. "And I swore I'd never do long distance with anyone again."

He steps back, stuffing his hands in his joggers, nodding in understanding and disappointment covering his features. "You're asking me not to go?"

"No," I breathe out. "No, I want you to go. I want you to enjoy every moment you can in Europe. I want you to be the starting point guard. And I want you to finally get more than four threes in a game… for once. And I want your coach to make you run lines because you're too arrogant and cocky when you do." He laughs, and I continue. "And I want you to have a fan club of French women waiting for you at the end of the game."

He drags a hand down his face and laughs. "You don't want that."

"I don't. It sounds terrible. But I have to figure out how to be okay with it, right? It's inevitable." I shrug and let out a shaky laugh. He doesn't respond. He just watches me as I stumble over my words. "So, I've been thinking and running all the scenarios through my mind since last night. At first, I thought, it's fine, this was just a week-long thing, a chapter we needed to finish. Then I thought we could try, and it'd fall apart because long distance never works." His jaw tightens as he looks down at me. "Then I thought it's too soon to worry about any of it and I just need to let you go. We'll remain friends and maybe after life settles and you come back, we can figure it out. Or not because maybe you'll find someone new, and I could be fine with that."

His Adam's apple bobs and his eyes droop. He doesn't respond.

"But I wouldn't be fine. I could pretend to be for the rest of my life, and it wouldn't be a total disaster—I've done it before. But I wouldn't be fine," I continue, fingertips shaking as I brush them against his cheek and stare into his eyes. "Leo, I can barely look at you when you're in the room without feeling like everything else has disappeared. I can't breathe. I can't think. You are an impossible feeling I've never been able to describe. Until now. I love you, Leo. I've loved you since before I knew what it meant. You made me feel things I was too young to even explain. And then I loved you even when I wanted to stop. It's never gone away. Not completely. Even when you hurt me. Even when I was angry at you. The same feeling has never left me once. So you win, Leo. I get an E. That's HORSE. You win." I throw up my hands. "I don't know what this will look like, but I don't want to spend another eight years wondering what life could be. I don't want another day without you being mine."

He clears his throat, absorbing my words. He laid it out for me last night. Now it's my turn.

I step toward him and take his face in my hands. "The thing is, Leo, circumstances, life, and the world are always going to stand in the way. There might always be something trying to drive us apart. But I don't care anymore. Because at the end of the day, I'm going to dream of you. And in the morning, I'm going to wake up and think of you. I'm going to miss you. I'm going to want you. And no matter who comes next, I will always, always wonder what if. I don't want it to be perfect. I just want it to be you."

His hands tighten around my waist as he leans down to kiss me. "It's always been you. You know that," he whispers, just inches from my lips.

I nod. "I think it always was supposed to be me and you together. It was you first. I want it to be you all the time."

He laughs and kisses me again.

"Is that too much? Too soon?" I ask, realizing I implied forever after we've been hooking up again for two days.

"I've been patiently waiting for you to admit you don't hate me. Forever couldn't come soon enough," he says, lifting me and I wrap my legs around his waist.

"What if we never pretended we hated each other?" I mumble into his neck.

"Then it wouldn't be our story," he answers.

I nod slowly, breathing in his scent.

"Sometimes the things worth keeping are the things you had to fight to get back," he says, tossing me gently on the bed. My hair splays out across the sheets, and I bounce as he hovers over me. He brushes his nose against mine, sending chills down my spine. "I like our story. It's bruised and a little jagged but so are we. It's distinctly us. I wouldn't want any other story to tell than ours."

"So we're telling people then?" I ask as my hands grip the front of his shirt.

"I've been dying to," he answers then kisses me.

"This is going to be hard though," I whisper.

"That's what she said."

I roll my eyes as I laugh, then say, "I'm serious. You're leaving, Leo. I'm going to miss you." I stare deep into his eyes. He has to understand. He has to see the impossibility of the distance, especially for a new relationship.

"I'm not losing you again. I'll stay if that's what you need."

I shake my head. "No, that's stupid. I want you to go and play. I just want us to be realistic about our future."

He stays in his thoughts for a moment. "You're it for me, Evie. I'll figure it out for the both of us if I have to. I'm not losing you."

I nod as he kisses me again, trusting his words as we fall slowly into each other, taking our time to pull away each layer of clothing that separates us until we are skin to skin. Heart to heart. Falling desperately into a love we always had but always resisted.

30

SATURDAY

William sits across the table from us at Von's—one last hurrah before he and Nora fly off to Tahiti and before Leo leaves for San Francisco tomorrow. William's hands are in fists and his eyebrows are twisted as if he's in physical pain. I'm certain being honest and upfront was a terrible idea.

"This is—" he leans back, digging his fingers in his hair like he wants to rip it out. He groans, his eyes flitting around the bar because he certainly won't look at me or Leo. Abigail snorts out a laugh and keeps eating hot wings.

"Happy honeymoon!" I sing timidly, grimacing. William glares at me.

"William, honey—" Nora says as she rests her diamond-cloaked hand on her new husband's arm.

William's gaze shoots to Nora's like bullets. I can't tell if he's pissed or just completely weirded out.

Nora raises her eyebrows, exchanging some sort of telepathic message through her eyes, smoothing out William's forehead. He says something back to her with his eyes.

Leo curls a reassuring hand over my knee that calms my

nerves, even though I'm not quite sure what I'm afraid of. William won't disown either of us. He can't. He loves us too much. We're his best friends—he said those words just last night.

"This is…" William flares his nostrils while he comes up with the right words, "…fucking weird."

"Oh God—" Abigail grunts, dropping a naked bone on her plate at the same time Nora swats his shoulder and says, "Oh stop. This is amazing!"

I press my lips into a tight line, withholding a laugh and glancing at Leo. He appears completely calm, but his cheek twitches and I know he's about to smile his perfect smile in three, two—

There it is.

"Don't fucking smile like that when we're talking about my sister. It's nasty. And you guys can't stand each other!" William argues what he thought was a plain fact about us with anger on the edges of his voice but then he starts laughing. Because he's not angry. Not really. He's probably more upset he had no idea. And also, "This is just weird." I nod a little as he groans out a sigh.

He leans back, then forward, fidgeting like the chair he's sitting in is made up of his best friend and sister's relationship, and he can't settle down and accept the idea of it. "This has been happening for years?" he asks, finally meeting our eyes.

"No—" I say at the same time Leo says, "Yes."

My head snaps in his direction, and he smiles down at me with a shrug.

"Well, kind of…" I begin.

Abigail choke-coughs and takes a long drink of ice water, waving us all off so we continue.

Leo rests his elbows on the table and leans forward. "Genevieve and I have always been into each other."

"Lies." William points a finger at him. "You two fought all the time."

"Well, yeah, because he's annoying," I say, and Nora laughs into her hand.

Leo squints down at me, withholding a smile. "We were

good at pretending," he says to William.

"But also," I feel the need to add, "No, we haven't talked much in years, not after our big fight in high school. But this week, we got to talking and—"

William nods with enough vigor and eyes bulging that I stop talking. His uncomfortable gaze skirts over the glasses on the table. A part of me feels like he's being childish, but that's just it: the child in him is freaking out because his best friend since he was twelve is telling him he's dating his younger sister.

"I don't know, you guys." William scratches his jaw like he's allergic to the conversation.

I open my mouth to respond, but Abigail pipes in first. "Oh for fuck's sake, Will. You're being ridiculous."

He glares at Abigail, and she points at Leo and me.

"You are being handed your favorite person as a brother-in-law and acting like they want to sneeze in your mouth."

"Gross," Nora says, making a face.

"They are not getting *married*, Abigail. They're just dating!" William says.

Abigail throws a hand in the air. "Whatever. At least you're finally admitting they're together."

William's face freezes with his mouth open in absolute shock… or maybe terror. Nora is laughing into her hands and I'm at a loss. I grip Leo's thigh under the table and he covers my hand with his.

"What happens if you break up?" William asks, leaning over the table, and staring directly at Leo. A protective wave washes over my brother's face.

There's a pause, and I realize maybe none of us have enough faith in Leo and me to say it won't happen.

"I know you're worried about your sister getting hurt again but I promise you, if we don't work out, I'm the one that's going to be hurting," Leo says, and William stiffens with a slight roll of his eyes. "I won't hurt her again, because I know what if feels like to lose her."

I gaze up at Leo.

"And then you can go back to reminding her to be nice to me," he adds.

William's jaw tightens and I can tell it's because he's clamping his teeth down on a laugh.

"William, I love you," I say. "But none of this is up to you, so you need to not be weird about it."

William stays quiet again, his eyes slightly narrowing on us.

"Let's go talk," Leo says, breaking the silence and nodding at the doors to the restaurant.

"Seriously?" William says, keeping his voice even with an air of irritation.

"Yeah. Let's just go." He stands, and William follows.

Once they're out the front doors, I down half my Diet Coke.

"What do you think they're talking about?" I ask, my gaze locked on the doors of the restaurant as I wring my hands together and pick at my wedding manicure.

"You, you idiot," Abigail huffs with a laugh.

I groan. "This was dumb. Why did we just throw it on him when you guys are about to leave for Tahiti?" I shake my head and finish my beer.

"Relax. Will is just protective of you," Nora says. "And after Damien, I think he's just on high alert. But he trusts Leo, and even more than Leo, he trusts you."

I meet her gaze and nod. "But what if we don't work? We're full of butterflies and hope right now but he leaves for France on Tuesday. *Tuesday!*" I run my palms over my forehead. "This isn't going to work again, and it is going to break William's heart." I'm chewing so hard on my lip I'm convinced I'm about to draw blood.

Nora grabs my hand across the table. "William's heart is fine." She pauses. "And France isn't that far."

I scoff out a laugh. "Yes. It. Is."

She shrugs and Abigail smiles over at me. "He waited eight years for you, Gen. He isn't going to just throw it away because you don't live close to each other."

I swallow hard, nodding. I'm trying to agree. I'm trying not to be the cynic in my own love story, but my stomach turns to rocks when I think of him leaving.

I've missed him for eight years. What's two more? I know I'm trying to convince myself and I'm terrified of the devil on my shoulder taunting our end before it even happens… again.

William and Leo return to the bar and for a moment, it feels like the night has been rewound. That is until William points at me and says, "No kissing in front of me."

Nora rolls her eyes, and I just look at him. My big brother. One of my favorite humans in the world. My shrug says sorry, and he presses his lips together and he shrugs too.

Life is weird when you fall in love with your brother's best friend.

"So…" I clear my throat and shift on my feet next to the security line at the airport. "This is goodbye."

Leo winces. "Don't be weird."

"I'm not," I scoff.

"You are." He steps closer to me.

"Am not."

"Always arguing." His lips pull into a slight smile, letting me know he's more amused than upset.

I sigh. "Always picking a fight."

He sweeps a hand through my hair, tucking my blonde locks behind my ear. "I love you. Goodbyes don't exist between us anymore."

My chest quakes a little when he says this. "I'm going to miss you so much."

"You've missed me for eight years, right?" he half-smiles.

"What's two more?" I add, my voice shaking.

He shakes his head with an almost irritated smile. "You're coming to visit me—"

"Oh, I am?"

"And I'm coming home on the off-season," he adds. "You'll never be rid of me. The distance is temporary, okay?" he reassures me, and I nod. "We can do this."

I let out a small laugh but his lips find mine before I can respond or object, and he kisses me like no one is watching. The heat of his lips. The comfort in his arms. The feel. The touch. The taste. I hold onto it, never wanting it to go away and certainly not wanting it to fly to San Francisco to pack a suitcase to go to France.

"I miss you already," I whisper against his lips.

"But I love you more than I miss you. And that's how I know we'll be fine."

31

MONDAY AGAIN

The sentiment was perfect. But even still, I cried all day on my couch, taping back together the pictures of us from the green file box and rereading the stupid notes he sent me on gum wrappers.

And now, as I drum my fingers on my desk, staring blankly at the computer screen on my desk at work, I wonder what the next two years are going to look like.

"You look exhausted again," my team leader, Cassandra says, leaning up against my desk with a box of donuts from the shop down the street.

I love her but I also don't want to talk about it. I laugh anyway, realizing she said these exact words to me one week ago. "I am."

"Even after a week off?" she asks, though her tone and the wink she just gave me would indicate she's joking.

"Weddings are freaking exhausting," I say, tilting my head back on my office chair and closing my eyes.

"I know. Trust me. I've done it three times myself, and I guarantee you, your brother and his wife are sleeping on a

312

beach, too tired to even have sex."

I let out a quick laugh and scrunch my nose.

She laughs and waves a hand in the air. "But what I really want to know is why you seem sad?"

"I'm not," I assure her.

"You are." She sits on my desk and opens the box of donuts, offering me one. I take a maple bar.

"I am," I confess with a shrug. "A little bit."

She raises her eyebrows and takes a bite of her donut, encouraging me to speak. The entire story of me and Leo tumbles out.

By the end of my telling, she's licking chocolate icing off her fingers and restraining her smile.

"What?" I ask, helplessly picking at my maple bar.

"I'm just wondering why you haven't bought a ticket to France yet."

"Because... I have a job. I have a life. I—" I pause, searching for words and feeling frustrated everyone thinks this is no big deal. "I can't just go to France!"

Cassandra clears her throat and wipes her fingers on a napkin. "You have not taken a vacation day—with the exception of your brother's wedding—since that asshole dragged you to New York. And even then, you only took two days. *Two.*"

I laugh and cringe a little, realizing she's right. "Wow. I'm a loser."

Cassandra shakes her head softly and smiles at me like a mother consoling a child. "You don't do anything for you."

"Yeah, but would going to France be for me, or would it be for Leo?" I ask.

Cassandra smiles. "What does your heart tell you?"

Realization washes over me quickly, releasing my fears and hesitation. She's right. I need to do what I want. For once.

I tap my fingers against the keyboard, contemplating, then look at her. "You'll approve the time off?"

She flashes a wry smile. "Yes, I'm a sucker for a fun love story."

I laugh and click on my browser. "You dare me?" I ask,

typing in Lyon, France as my destination in the search bar.

Tickets are over two grand, making all the excitement and butterflies turn into rocks sinking in the pit of my stomach. "I can't afford this."

"Yes, you can," Cassandra says, and I shoot her a glare.

"Are you giving me a raise too?"

She tosses her head back and lets out a long and loud laugh. But before she responds, my phone rings. The name "Harborview Hospital" lights up my phone screen, and the sinking feeling in my gut grows heavier as I answer and hear the woman on the other line say, "Is this the daughter of Philip Michaels?"

32

TUESDAY AGAIN

"It wasn't a heart attack," Dad says, arms crossed in the passenger seat of my car.

"Yes, it was," I argue.

"It was mild. I didn't even need a stent," he huffs.

"You had coronary angioplasty," I argue, my grip tightening on the steering wheel. "It's still a big deal."

"I feel fine. They only made me stay at the hospital for one night and didn't even need to put me under for the procedure." He laughs, but I find none of this funny.

Dad was golfing with his friend when he collapsed and was rushed to the hospital. The doctor said the combination of the heat, the stress of the wedding, and a lifetime of artery-clogging grilled cheese sandwiches made for a perfect storm for a heart attack.

They performed coronary angioplasty while he was conscious, but sedated, and now he's convinced he is invincible.

"Well, before I came to pick you up from the hospital, I went grocery shopping—"

He groans.

"Stop being dramatic, Dad. You need to overhaul your diet," I say, pulling into the driveway and placing the car in park. "I got some really good stuff."

He opens his door and mutters, "Won't be grilled cheese made the right way though."

I smirk. "Actually, there is this new kind of cheese alternative—"

"Genny Bear! No. I am not doing fake cheese."

He starts to get out of the car but I stop him. "Hold on, let me help you."

I exit the car and jog around to his side and open his door, offering my arms for support.

"I'm not broken," he argues.

"You had a heart attack."

He takes my arms and stands out of the car. The grunt that escapes his lips reminds me he is putting up a front—trying to make me believe he's tough as nails but I know he's sore and his body is exhausted.

As we make our way up the porch to the front door one slow step at a time, he mutters, "I'm not eating some pasty vegan cheese. I'd rather have another heart attack."

"You're going to try it," I say as the yellow door swings open. We step inside. It smells exactly like my childhood and the feeling of home washes over me and settles in my gut.

"Like hell, Genny Bear. I love you but I don't love fake food. It's probably made of chemicals and paper."

I snort out a laugh at this. "It's made of chickpeas."

"What's made out of chickpeas?"

I jump at the sound of his voice as he pokes his head around the kitchen wall, holding a bottle of seasoning in each hand.

My jaw drops. "Leo! What are you doing here?"

"Here to help me out and save me from your salad-shooter cheese, I'm sure. Leo, tell my daughter I can't eat fake cheese."

Leo smirks at my dad and then looks at me. "He can't eat fake cheese."

"Traitor." I flare my nostrils, then step toward him. "You are supposed to be on a plane to France right now. You texted me this morning. I told you 'safe flight.'"

"Yeah, I flew here instead. I had an emergency," he answers plainly as he hugs my dad. "You feeling better, Coach?"

Dad nods. "Never better."

I roll my eyes at the lie, crossing my arms as I wait for an explanation from Leo, but just as he opens his mouth, Dad speaks up from the kitchen.

"What are you doing in here?"

Leo grins, then rubs the back of his neck. "Removing all the spices with salt and alphabetizing what's left."

"Of course you are," I say, trying not to smile.

"You two are the worst," Dad says with no ounce of humor in his voice. "I love salt."

"So do heart attacks." I smile at him gently, and sadness overcomes his expression. "Now, let's get you in your bed so you can rest. I will bring you the best salt-free meal you've ever had."

After getting Dad comfortable in his room, television remote in hand, I head back down to the kitchen. Leo is shooting salty spice containers into the garbage can across the kitchen like it's a basketball hoop. He makes one and misses the second.

"You suck," I tease with a smile, leaning the small of my back against the counter.

He drops his head with a boyish grin. "I bought some salt-free spice mixes at the store. He still needs to have good food, right?"

My throat is choked up, but I nod.

"Sorry I didn't get here sooner," he says, swooping me into his arms.

I bury my face in his chest. "I'm surprised you came at all."

Pulling back, he says, "Why? Of course I'd come."

"Leo, you need to be in France. The team is expecting you."

"Right. And I told them the situation and they're giving me a little extra time. France can wait."

I turn away, helpless and exhausted from the last twenty-four hours as I pull out the whole grain bread to make Dad a turkey sandwich. "He's going to be fine. I got this."

317

"Yeah, and who's got you?"

The question slams into my chest and trembles into my bones.

"I'm okay—"

"I swear to God, Evie, if you tell me you're okay and everything is fine and it's not a big deal, I am going to snap you in half."

"Always choosing violence," I say, opening the refrigerator and gathering the fixings for the sandwich.

He starts to smile then stops. "You can't water these things down because it's easier to pretend everything is fine."

He's calling me out in such a gentle yet specific way. I want to argue, but I know he's right. "Did your therapist teach you that too?"

"Yes," he answers, and I stare at him as I slap a slice of vegan cheese on my dad's sandwich. Leo's gaze follows the cheese then lands on my face. "He's not going to eat that."

"He won't know the difference," I reason, adding low-sodium turkey lunchmeat.

"He'll figure it out."

I pause, my gaze searing into his skin. "Are you going to snitch?"

Leo's lips twitch to smile. "You look like you want to strangle me."

A laugh breaks free from my chest. "No, I want to make you run lines," I say, piling on spring mix and the second slice of bread and brushing the crumbs off my hands. "Then I want you to get on a plane and go play basketball in France."

"I will," he answers, then adds. "Next week."

"Good." I meet his eyes with a complacent stare and cross my arms.

"Now get over here," he says, pointing to the floor in front of him. When I don't comply, he reaches out and grabs my t-shirt, pulling me against him until I'm in his arms again. "I love you, Evie. Your family is my family, so I'm always going to show up. I'm always going to be here for you."

I shift my head so I'm looking up at him. He's staring down at me with an expression I've only ever seen on Leo's face.

Love, admiration, passion, loyalty. When Leo looks at me, I feel like the center of the universe. Each emotion draws me in and surrounds me until all I feel is safe.

Even still, I burst into tears.

"I hate you for coming," I cry with a laugh.

"Liar," he says with a smile, cradling my face in his hands.

"But I do. Because now we have to say goodbye again and I don't want to. I don't know how many goodbyes my heart can take, Leo. I don't—"

He cuts me off with his lips on mine. His fingertips comb through my hair and his mouth moves with mine until I forget why I'm sad. Leo pulls back, wiping the streams of gratitude running down my face with his thumb.

"With us, it's never goodbye, Evie." He kisses my forehead three times, punctuating the next three words. "Never. Ever. Goodbye."

EPILOGUE
6 MONTHS LATER

"Leo, I haven't talked to you in three days. What do you mean you're tired and have to go?" My blood boils as I yell at him over the phone.

"You know how crazy the season has been, Evie. I was in Spain last week. Germany the week before that. I'm exhausted," he argues. His voice isn't hiding any of his exhaustion, and I ignore the lap of guilt in my gut.

"We've been on the phone for five minutes," I say with a breath then glance at my phone as it reads four minutes and fifty seconds. "Like what's the point of having an international phone plan if you don't even want to talk to me."

"I do!" he shouts. "All I said was that I'm tired and will call you tomorrow."

"When?"

"Before practice."

"You have practice at ten your time."

"Yeah, so it will be midnight your time. Just like it is now for me."

I can practically feel the frustration coming off his voice.

The time difference is killing us.

"Fine," I say, and there's a pause. I don't know if the call dropped, if it's the weird delay from international calls, or if he's trying to collect his thoughts.

"Evie…" he says finally, his tone softening to appease my anger. Anger I know stems from how much I miss him. God, I miss him so damn much. Every single day.

After my dad had the heart attack, Leo stayed the whole week. We made meals and watched movies with my dad. He ran to refill prescriptions and I made vegan grilled cheese sandwiches that weren't half-bad. He even fixed the winter side of my closet that I broke in my apartment. Then when Sunday rolled around, Leo picked William and Nora up from the airport, only for him to have to turn around and head back to the airport for his own flight.

It was a terrible goodbye, and I cried my eyes out, not knowing when I would be able to see him again.

William and I tried to rotate shifts with Dad but I tended to take the majority of them and have only been able to visit France once. It was a short and expensive five-day trip, but I was able to see him in between his games in Spain and Monaco. I didn't get to see him play, but I was able to ease the ache I feel every day without him.

I haven't been able to make it over since and he can't disrupt his season, so we've been juggling phone calls and video chats for months.

"Leo, this is so hard, especially with the holidays coming up," I whisper, my voice shaking.

"Evie, I hate to be this guy, but I'm the one in a different country without my family for Christmas next week." His voice is sad, and guilt bites at my gut.

"You have a game on Christmas Eve," I reason. "It's not like you won't be busy."

"Yeah, I have a game, but I won't have you," he argues, his words pound on my chest. "That's hard on me too."

"I know but I haven't been able to touch you in months. I haven't been able to kiss you—"

"But at least we've talked. Evie, we've gone years without

even speaking," he interjects.

"Yeah, but talking is almost worse. When we didn't talk, I didn't think about you every day. Every second. And now, you're all I think about. I can't…" I pause and exhale.

"Don't do this, Evie."

"Do what?" I snap.

"Panic and run."

"I'm not the one who does that."

The line goes quiet, and I know it isn't because of a delay. I wipe a silent tear from my cheek.

I hear him breathe out over the line. "You knew what this was going to be. You told me to go to France."

"I know," I say, my voice so small. I know I'm being selfish.

"Do you remember when we were at Von's when I first got to Seattle for your brother's wedding?" he asks.

"Yeah."

"You said dreams are stupid without a plan," he says, and I try to find the memory of my words but they barely register. "When you said that I didn't disagree, but it was only half right. Dreams are stupid without a passion. And that goes beyond basketball and careers, Evie."

I'm quiet, listening.

"I'm talking about you."

I sniff, still staying quiet.

"Look, I get it. This sucks. I miss you every day. It kills me that you don't get to see me play and I hate that it's been months since my skin has touched yours. But this is temporary, right? We said that. You and I are forever. We said that too."

My teeth sink into my bottom lip. He's right but it doesn't make this any easier.

"I don't know how to make this better," I say finally.

"Give me three months and I'm coming home."

When he says the words, it hits me how badly I need to see him and how desperately I can't wait another moment.

"This is so hard, Leo."

"I never said it wasn't, but you know I can't come to the states right now."

I swallow hard. "You know I can't leave my dad."

"I talked to your dad last week, Evie."

I scoff, knowing what he's implying. "He's not fine. I know he told you he was, but he forgets to take his blood pressure medication and he had real cheese in his refrigerator yesterday, I saw it—"

"Evie."

I click my tongue against the roof of my mouth.

"I know you're scared. I know you don't want to lose him, and I know he is the only parent you have left. Believe me. I get it. But you can't stop living your life out of fear of losing your parents."

My throat hitches for a moment then I say, "But I've already lost one, Leo."

"I know," he whispers. There's sadness in his voice. A sadness I know is partly mine to own.

"I'm struggling."

"I know that too."

"No, Leo. Like really struggling with the idea of... us."

The line is so quiet that I know he's stunned. After several painful moments, he asks, "What do you want to do?"

I want France to be closer. I want Leo closer. I want life to be less complicated when an ocean and two countries stand between us.

"I want to miss you less," I answer.

He's quiet, and I wish I could see his expression.

"I want that too," he says finally.

I nod, knowing he can't see it. We say I love you, but it feels hollow as I hear it. For a moment, I'm terrified for us. But then I remember when he told me, *I love you more than I'm going to miss you.*

Reality strikes me as his words ring in my ears over and over. So I do what I should have done months ago.

I buy a plane ticket.

Dating someone on the other side of the world is hard, but, if I'm honest, dating an athlete is hard regardless of where they live. Their bodies and minds are pushed to the limit. Their schedule is grueling, and basketball players, in particular, don't usually get the holidays off.

I didn't want to be without Leo for Christmas. But more than that, I didn't want Leo to be alone for Christmas.

Two-thousand dollars, a single packed suitcase, and eighteen hours of travel later, I land in Lyon, France with Google Translate open on my phone at all times, knowing the lessons I've been taking on an app will not suffice.

I manage customs and the airport fine, but when I hail a taxi, mild panic rises in my chest. Solo international travel is for the brave of heart and I have learned I am not.

"*Boscolo Lyon Hotel s'il vous plait,*" I say with a clipped American accent as the driver slides back into the driver's seat. *Boscolo Lyon hotel please.*

"*Oui,*" he nods, throwing the car into drive, and I breathe out a sigh of relief. I'm almost there. "*Combien de temps allez-vous rester?*"

I pause, furrowing my brow. "*Peux-tu dire ça plus lentement?*" *Can you say that slower?* I practiced this line for weeks, along with a few others I knew I would need to say. French is hard.

He flashes me a knowing smile in the rearview and repeats the line slowly.

I catch the words "time" and "stay," realizing he's asking how long I'm staying. "*Deux semaines,*" I answer, *two weeks.*

"Ahh," he smiles and nods. "*C'est une belle période à visiter.*" *It is a beautiful time to be here.*

"*Oui.*" I smile, shifting my gaze out of the window and watching the French street lightly dusted in snow as we drive. There is something so special about France, and Lyon in particular has its own unique charm. The cobbled stone streets are narrow and the buildings are lit up with Christmas lights.

We pass the *Bistrot de Lyon,* and I watch a couple dressed in warm winter coats and scarves enter the red doors. I imagine the smell of croissants and café au lait breezing past me.

France during Christmastime was a wonderful idea, even if getting here terrified me.

When we pull up to my hotel, the exterior is remarkable. The cream stone with ornate molding around each window is highlighted by warm up-lighting, and the golden revolving door looks like a carousal. I pay and thank my driver, then step into my hotel like I'm stepping into a dream.

I check my watch. The game is in one hour, and it will last close to three. He'll have to shower and do press and then I will be waiting for him like one of his French fans.

I sneak into my seat at the brand-new arena wearing a black and gold LDLC Asvel hoodie. I know Leo won't see me because he zones out when he plays. At least he finally mastered focus. So much so that it would seem the basketball court is his own universe when he's on it.

His team is as good as their stats imply, and I can tell he and the other guard, Mathias Martín, play well together despite the many arguments they've had in the locker room that he's told me about. Leo has a phenomenal game and when his fourth three-pointer swoops through the net, I almost jump out of my seat screaming and rush the court and congratulate him.

LDLC Asvel beats Barcelona, 93-75.

An hour after the game, I'm still waiting outside the player entrance wearing my hoodie and wrapped in a puffer parka and beanie with gloved hands. My heart hammers and my hands start shaking as the door opens and players start walking out. People are speaking English, French, Spanish, and Chinese, and I'm struck by how incredible this experience is. Just a bunch of kids from all over the world that grew up loving the same sport and get to play together. It's unreal and I feel incredibly selfish that I'm just now here to experience it; I should have visited months ago.

My nerves heighten with the more players that pass by me. Finally, I see him.

He doesn't see me. His eyes are on his phone, his earbuds are in, and he's wearing an LDLC Asvel puffer coat with joggers and clean white Jordans. He's smiling at his phone and I ignore the buzz in my back pocket because I know he's texting me about the game.

"Hey, Leonardo Bishop," I call, grabbing his attention.

325

"Where are you staying tonight?"

He freezes, glancing around before zeroing in on me. His dark eyes widen as they meet mine. He even glances behind him, like he's wondering where the camera is. It takes him an entire ten seconds before he reaches me, cradling my face in his hands and kissing me.

"Are you insane?" he asks, barely pulling away.

I nod into his lips. "A little bit."

He laughs against my lips and kisses me again. It's crazy how two weeks with someone I used to know changed my whole life.

"Were you expecting a French woman begging for your affections?" I ask, wrapping my fingers around his neck.

"It wouldn't be unusual," he teases, and I refrain from letting jealousy rise in my gut.

I kiss him again then say, "I've missed you."

He cradles my cold cheek with his warm hand. "You know I've missed you."

"I'm sorry it took me so long to get here," I say, gripping the fabric of his coat and staring up at him.

He lets out a breath through a smile. "I'm just happy you're here."

I smile at him. "Twenty-four points. Eleven assists. Fifteen rebounds. Another triple-double for you," I say, smiling at him proudly. "Also, you didn't even let Lorenzo sneak pass you once with his pump fake."

Leo laughs. "I watched his feet," he says, grinning wide.

I nod and laugh, remembering us as a couple of kids, in love with basketball and each other. *"Je suis fier de toi."* *I'm proud of you.*

"Impressionnant, mon amour," he responds. *Impressive, my love.*

I stare at him, my eyes full of love and admiration for someone I've known for almost my whole life and have fallen more in love with each day. "You're my dream. You know that, right?"

He kisses me once and nods.

"I want you forever," I add.

"You have me," he breathes, swiping a gentle thumb over my bottom lip.

"I am never letting you go. Because I've tried, and I can't imagine a world where I'm not with you. Even if you are a world away, you need to know you belong to me." I draw in a shaky breath, my emotions getting the better of me. "We're going to make this work."

He pauses as he studies my face. "I never had any doubt. Evie, you changed everything for me. Even when I'm here, all I think about is you," he says. He tucks his fingertips in my hair, and we both can't contain our smiles. "Come on," he whispers against my skin. "We're in France, and this is our first Christmas together-*together*."

"*Joyeux Noël, mon amour,*" I say. *Merry Christmas, my love.*

"*Je veux tous tes noëls,*" he says, and I squint as if narrowing my vision will help me hear better and translate the words faster. "*Et je veux tous tes étés.*"

It takes me a second for all the words to register. *I want all of your Christmases. And I want all of your summers.* I smile, cupping my gloved hand over his cheek just as it begins to snow.

"*Je te veux juste,*" he adds. *I just want you.*

I groan into his mouth and kiss him. "Your French is getting too good, *monsieur.*"

He unleashes his perfectly irritating and disarming smile.

It's this moment that confirms what I hoped for: the first love of my life is also going to be my last.

The Letter From My Mama
2 YEARS LATER

Genevieve,

My dear sweet girl. Today is your wedding day. You found him, didn't you? Or rather, you stopped fighting what found you a long time ago.

Your dad told me to write a different letter. "Just in case," he said. Maybe that letter is somewhere. I don't know. I haven't written it yet. Maybe it exists with mothballs and file boxes in the attic, but I don't think you'll read it. You won't need it anyway, because I'm convinced, as I always have been since you were a teenager, that you are going to marry Leo.

Dad thought I was crazy, and said me and Louisa needed to stop scheming. I can't say I blame him, but here's what I do know: you light a fire under Leo that only the woman meant for him can. And more than that, he looks at you with a tenderness only a husband does his wife.

I never wanted to push you two together growing up but, God, did I ever pray you two would finally find each other. Completely at least. I remember thinking when you two were teenagers, that they're doing something behind my back—holding hands under blankets, kissing behind the old oak tree at the park. I was probably right, but you never told me. And that's okay. I get it. Talking to your mom about that kind of stuff can be weird.

But then, something switched. Your playful animosity morphed into this thick, sappy hatred and I desperately wanted to know what really happened.

You never told me though. And I let it go. Even at this last Thanksgiving. I kept wondering when you would leave my side to go hang out with Leo and challenge him to a game of HORSE. But you never did. And I never got the answers I wanted because I never asked. I'm sorry I didn't, but I have faith it will still work out.

Because here's what I do know: Leo is turning into such a good man. He is sweet and kind and I know he loves you very much. Even more than that, I know you love him, Genevieve. I see it in your eyes. I've heard it in your words.

You two fight like crazy, but it doesn't make me think you two aren't meant for each other. Because the fighting never stops. Fight for him. Fight for you. Fight for each other. For your family. For the life you want.

Don't go down without a fight, my sweet girl. The best things—the things worth holding onto until you breathe your last, are the things you have to guard and protect while you annihilate the hurt, the distractions, and the pain.

So fight well, Gen. Fight well. Because in this world, no matter the circumstance, you don't get to stop fighting.

But love him too. Be good to him. And let him know if he is not being good to you.

And as you put on your pearls and curl your hair today, please remember I love you. I wish more than anything in the world I could hear you say, "I do." As you walk down the aisle—though it probably isn't an aisle. It's probably a vineyard or a mountain top or the middle of an old-growth forest or a warm sandy beach. But no matter where you marry the love of your life, as you walk down the aisle, remember: if it won't matter tomorrow, it doesn't matter.

Have the most beautiful wedding day, my child. I miss you. I am wherever you are even if that feels like an obnoxious cliché you wish you didn't have to hear. I won't leave you. I am where you need me. I love you with every breath I have ever breathed.

Happy wedding day.

Love always,
Mom

I fold the letter and slip it back into my bag, then glance at my hair curled to perfection in the mirror. The pearls drape around my collar bone and the ivory lace of my dress dances on my skin. I step out onto the patio and take my dad's arm as we step into the dewy grass of the field in the countryside of Lyon, France. Rolling hills tower in the distance, and Leo is standing in the warm, golden hues of the setting sun waiting for me.

ACKNOWLEDGEMENTS

When I first started writing *You First*, it was supposed to be a short story, but these characters had other plans. I always say my books come directly from the mouths of the characters and when I started writing Leo and Genevieve, they would not stop talking. I was writing and writing and writing, not getting close to the end of what they had to say and realized I had written half a novel. So I kept going and it was an absolute joy to get to know them.

And now, here they are, out in the world and it's time for me to let them go.

Publishing a book is both like a birth and a funeral. I've labored through writing, editing, reformatting, proofing, and allowing these characters to take up crazy amounts of my brain space for the last year, and now I finally get to introduce them to the world. But I'm also saying goodbye. Once I publish a book, it's as if the characters have left my world of imagination and get to enter yours, and these two are really hard for me to say goodbye to. I've enjoyed writing Leo and Genevieve so much and I'm thrilled to have them a part of my book family.

I could not continue to write without the loving support of my husband, Darren. He's always appreciated my imagination and has never let my dreams die even when the logic in me said it was time to let it go. I'm so thankful for you and I love you so much. Also, shout out for catching that misspelling of someone's name. Professor Popeski would be so proud.

My kids are always a huge part of why I do what I do. My reasons to wake up and my reasons to work hard. My three little heartbeats running around reminding me why life is meaningful and filled with whimsy, joy, and humor. Thank you, Emmie, Maci, and Isaiah. Mama loves you big time.

To my early readers, Riley, Amy, Trisha, Alejandra, Cristina, Kelsey, and Patrick. Thank you for letting me send my work to you when it is the most vulnerable, and for being honest with how I can improve the story. I appreciate each and every one of you.

My editor, Annie. Sometimes I send you manuscripts and know what you are going to say about certain things, and then I cackle into the midnight air while I read your comments. I appreciate you approaching editing with the rawness of real life.

Jamie McGillen, my fabulous proofer. I always let out a breath I very much know I'm holding after you run your eyes over my books. I appreciate your eye for my grammatical errors and pesky missing two-letter words.

To my cover designer, Erika. For those that don't know, I have held one hundred percent creative control over all of my books, including covers. That is, until this one. I had a vision I could not create on my own and the incredibly talented Erika Plum took my 87 messages and created the cover for this book. Bless you, your patience, and your talent, Erika! Thank you! (PS—cover designers do not get enough credit.)

And last, but never least, my readers. I wonder if there is ever going to be a time where it doesn't blow my mind that you picked up this book and read it. As a reader myself, I know what the world of books looks like. There are thousands upon thousands of books to choose from, and millions of reasons to pick one up, and somehow, this one landed in your hands and I am forever grateful and indebted to you.

XO,

Caitlin

ABOUT THE AUTHOR

Caitlin Moss is the author of six novels. She lives in the Pacific Northwest with her husband, three children, and Goldendoodle. She loves connecting with her readers on social media.

**For more visit
caitlinmossauthor.com.**

caitlinmossauthor

caitlinmosswrites

caitlinmossauthor

CaitlinRMoss

Made in United States
Troutdale, OR
10/27/2023